THE RAPTURE OF THE NERDS

COMING SOON FROM CORY DOCTOROW AND TITAN BOOKS

PIRATE CINEMA
(June 2013)

HOMELAND
(September 2013)

THE

CORY

RAPTURE

DOCTOROW

OF THE

CHARLES

NERDS

STROSS

TITAN BOOKS

THE RAPTURE OF THE NERDS
Print edition ISBN: 9781781167441
E-book edition ISBN: 9781781167458

Published by Titan Books
A division of Titan Publishing Group Ltd
144 Southwark Street, London SE1 0UP

First edition: April 2013
1 3 5 7 9 10 8 6 4 2

A CIP catalogue record for this title is available from the British Library.

Printed and bound in Great Britain by CPI Group Ltd.

Did you enjoy this book? We love to hear from our readers.
Please email us at readerfeedback@titanemail.com or write to us at
Reader Feedback at the above address.

To receive advance information, news, competitions, and exclusive offers online, please sign up for the Titan newsletter on our website: www.titanbooks.com

CORY

For Alice. I renew my vow not to fork any
new instances without your permission.

CHARLES

For Feorag. Just because!

JURY SERVICE

Huw awakens, dazed and confused.

This is by no means unusual, but for once Huw's head hurts more than his bladder. He's lying head down, on his back, in a bathtub. He scrabbles for a handhold and pulls himself upright. A tub is a terrible place to spend a night. Or a morning, come to think of it—as he blinks, he sees that it's midafternoon, and the light slanting in through a high window limns the strange bathroom's treacly Victorian fixtures with a roseate glow.

That was quite a party. He vaguely remembers the gathering dawn, its red light staining the wall outside the kitchen window as he discussed environmental politics with a tall shaven-headed woman with a blue forelock and a black leather minidress straight out of the twentieth century. (He has an equally vague memory of her defending a hard-core transhumanist line: Score nil–nil to both sides.) This room wasn't a bathroom when he went to sleep in it: Bits of the bidet are still crawling into position, and there's a strong smell of VOCs in the air.

His head hurts.

Leaning over the sink, Huw twiddles the taps until they begin to dribble cold water. He splashes his face and runs his hand through his thinning hair, glances up at the mirror, and yells, *"Shit!"*

There's a spindly black biohazard trefoil tattooed on his forehead. It wasn't there when he went to sleep, either.

Behind him, the door opens. "Having a good morning?" asks Sandra Lal, whose mutable attic this must therefore be. She's playing with a small sledgehammer, tossing it into the air and catching it like a baton-twirler. Her grotesquely muscled forearm has veins that bulge with hyperpressured blood and hormones.

"I wish," he says. Sandra's parties tend to be wild. "Am I too late for the dead dog?"

"You're never too late." Sandra smiles. "Coffee's in the kitchen, which is on the ground floor today. Bonnie gave me a subscription to House of the Week and today's my new edition—don't worry if you can't remember where everything is, just remember the entrance is at ground level, okay?"

"Coffee," Huw says. His head is pounding, but so is his bladder. "Um. Can I have a minute?"

"Yes, but I'd like my spare restroom back afterwards. It's going to be en suite, but first I've got to knock out the wall through into the bedroom." She hefts her sledgehammer suggestively.

Huw slumps down on the toilet as Sandra shuts the door behind her and bounces off to roust out any other leftover revelers. He shivers as he relieves himself: Trapped in a mutating bathroom by a transgendered atheist Pakistani role-playing critic. *Why do I keep ending up in these situations?* he wonders as the toilet gives him a scented wash and blow-dry: When it offers him a pubic trim, he hastily retrieves his kilt and goes in search of coffee.

Sandra's new kitchen is frighteningly modern—a white room job that looks empty at first, sterile as an operating theater, but that *oozes* when you glance away, extruding worktops and food processors and fresh cutlery. If you slip, there'll be a chair waiting to catch your buttocks on the way down. There are no separate appliances here, just tons of smart matter. Last night it looked charmingly gas-fired and Victorian, but now Huw can see it as it truly is, and he doesn't like what he can see. He feels queasy, wondering if he ate anything it had manufactured. But relief is at hand. At the far end of the room there's a traditional-looking dumb worktop with a battered old-fashioned electric *cafetière* sitting on it. And some joe who looks strangely familiar is sitting there reading a newssheet.

Huw nods at him. "Uh, where are the mugs?" he asks.

The guy stares at Huw's forehead for an uncomfortable moment, then gestures at something foggy that's stacked behind the pot. "Over there," he says.

"Uh, right." The mugs turn out to be glassy aerogel cups with walls a centimeter thick, light as frozen cigar smoke and utterly untouched by human artistry and sweat. There's no sign of the two earthenware mugs he made Sandra for her birthday: bloody typical. He takes the jug and pours, hand shaking. He's got the sweats: *What the hell did I drink?* he wonders as he takes a sip.

He glances at his companion, who is evidently another survivor of the party: a medium-height joe, metabolism pegged somewhere in his mid-thirties, bald, with the unnaturally stringy build that comes from overusing a calorie-restriction implant. No piercings, no scars, tattoos, or neomorphisms—apart from his figure—which might be natural. That plus his black leather bodysuit means he could be a fellow naturalist. But this is Sandra's house, and she has distressingly techie tastes.

"Is that today's?" he asks, glancing at the paper, which is lovingly printed on wood pulp using hot lead type by the historic reenactors down the other end of the valley.

"It could be." The fellow puts it down and grins oddly. "Had a good lie-in?"

"I woke up in the bathroom," Huw says. "Where's the milk—?"

"Have some freshly squeezed cow juice." He shoves something that resembles a bowl of blue ice cubes at Huw. Huw pokes at one dubiously, then dunks it in his mug.

"This stuff *is* organic, isn't it?"

"Only the best polymer-stabilized emulsions for Sandra," the joe says sardonically. "Of course it's organic—nothing but carbon, hydrogen, nitrogen, oxygen, and a bit of phosphorous and sulfur." Huw can tell when he's being wound up: he takes a sip, despite the provocation. "Of course, you could say the same about your kilt," adds the stranger.

"Ah." Huw puts the mug down, unsure where the conversation's leading. There's something disturbing about the joe: A sense of déjà vu nagging at the edges of his mind, as if—

"You don't remember me, do you?"

"Alcohol has this effect on me at times," Huw says in a grateful rush. "I've got an awful memory—"

"The name's Bonnie," says the man. "You spent most of the early hours trying to cop a feel by convincing me that Nietzsche was responsible for global cooling." Huw stares at him and feels something in his head do an uneasy flip-flop: Yes, the resemblance is clear, this *is* the woman he was talking to last night.

"'S amazing what a good bathroom can do by way of gender reassignment surgery these days, you know?" the bald guy—Bonnie?—continues. Then he winks at Huw with what Huw realizes, to his horror, is either lascivious intent or broad and filthy-minded humor. "How's your hangover? Are you up to picking things up where we left off?"

"Aaaugh," says Huw as the full force of the postparty cultural hangover hits him between the eyes, right beneath the biohazard trefoil, and the coffee hits his stomach. "Need fresh air *now*…"

Huw makes sure to wake up in his own bed the next morning. It's ancient and creaky, the springs bowed to conform to his anatomy, and he wove the blankets himself on the treadle-powered loom in the back parlor that Mum and Dad left him when they ascended, several decades before. (Huw is older than he looks, thanks to an unasked-for inheritance of chromosomal hackery, and has for the most part become set in his ways: incurious and curmudgeonly. He has his reasons.) His alarm clock is a sundial sketched on the whitewashed wall opposite in bold lines of charcoal, slightly smudged; his lifestyle a work of *wabi* in motion.

He yawns and sits up, pauses for a moment to get his bearings, then ventures down the comfortably unchanging stairs to retrieve his post. There is no email. He doesn't even have electricity in the house—not since he ripped the wiring out and plastered over the wounds in the walls. The dusty tiles in his vintage late-nineteenth-century terraced home are cold beneath his bare feet. A draft leaks around the ill-fitting outer door, raising gooseflesh on his bare legs as he picks up the dumb paper.

Two-thirds of the mail is spam, which goes straight onto the compost-before-reading pile, but there's also a genuine letter, complete with a hand-drawn bar code—what they used to call a *stamp*—on the envelope. Someone took the trouble to communicate with him personally, putting dumb matter in motion to make a point. How quaint, how formal! Huw approves.

He rips the envelope open with a cracked fingernail. He reads: *Your application for international triage jury service has been provisionally accepted. To activate your application, present this card in person to…*

He carries the notice through into the kitchen, puts it on the table so he can keep an eye on it as he eats. He barely notices the morning chill as he fiddles with the ancient Raeburn, loading kindling and peat and striking a fire to heat the Turkish coffeepot and warm his frying pan. Today is Huw's big day. He's been looking forward to this day for months.

Soon, he'll get to say what he thinks about some item of new technology—and they'll have to listen to him.

Welcome to the fractured future, the first century following the singularity.

Earth has a population of roughly a billion hominids. For the most part, they are happy with their lot, living in a preserve at the bottom of a gravity well. Those who are unhappy have emigrated, joining one or another of the swarming densethinker clades that fog the inner solar system with a dust of molecular machinery so thick that it obscures the sun. Except for the solitary lighthouse beam that perpetually tracks the Earth in its orbit, the system from outside resembles a spherical fogbank radiating in the infrared spectrum; a matryoshka brain, nested Dyson spheres built from the dismantled bones of moons and planets.

The splintery metaconsciousness of the solar system has largely sworn off its pre-posthuman cousins dirtside, but its minds sometimes wander nostalgiawise. When that happens, it casually spams Earth's RF spectrum with plans for cataclysmically disruptive technologies that emulsify whole industries, cultures, and spiritual systems.

A sane species would ignore these get-evolved-quick schemes, but there's always *someone* who'll take a bite from the forbidden fruit. There's always someone who unaccountably carries the let's-lick-the-frozen-fence-post gene. There's always a fucking geek who'll do it because it's a historical goddamned technical fucking imperative.

Whether the enlightened, occulting smartcloud sends out its missives as pranks, poison, or care packages is up for debate. Asking it to explain its motives is about as productive as negotiating with an ant colony to get it to abandon your kitchen. Whatever the motive, humanity would be much better off if the cloud would evolve into something uninterested in communicating with meatpeople—or at least smart enough to let well alone.

But until that happy day, there's the tech jury service: defending the Earth from the scum of the post-singularity patent office.

After breakfast, Huw dresses and locks the front door carefully behind himself and tells his bicycle—his one truly indispensable piece of advanced technology—to unbolt itself from the rusting red drainpipe that stains the brick side of his house with green moss. He pedals uncertainly to the end of the road, then eases out into traffic, sneering as the omnipresent web of surveillance routes the peoplemovers around him.

Safe cycling is one of the modern conveniences that irritate him most. Also: polite youngsters with plastic smiles; overemotional machines; and geeks who think they understand technology. Geeks, the old aristocracy. He'll show them, one of these days. Huw wobbles along the side of the main road and pulls in beside the door of the Second Revolutionary Libyan consulate.

"Sayyid Jones? I am pleased to meet you." The young man behind the desk has a plastic smile and is far too polite for Huw's taste: Huw grunts assent and sits down in the indicated seat. "Your application has been forwarded to us and, ah? If you would be pleased to travel to our beautiful country, I can assure you of just one week's jury service."

Huw nods again.

The polite man fidgets with the air of someone trying to come up with an inoffensive way of saying something potentially rather rude. "I'm pleased to inform you that our ancient land is quite tolerant of other cultures' customs. I can assure you that whatever ISO-standard containment suit you choose to bring with you will be respected by our people."

Huw boggles. "What huh?"

"Your, that is, your—" The smiler leans across his desk and points at Huw's trefoil-marked forehead. The finger he points with meets resistance. A plastic sheet has hermetically sealed Huw's side of the room off from the rest of the consulate. It is so fantastically transparent that Huw doesn't even notice it until the smiler's finger puckers a singularity in its vertical run, causing it to scatter light at funny angles and warp the solid and sensible wood-paneled walls behind the desk into Escheroid impossibilities.

"Ah," Huw says. "Ah. No, you see, it's a joke of some sort. Not an official warning."

"I'm very glad to hear it, Sayyid Jones! You will, of course, have documents attesting to that before you clear our immigration?"

"Right," Huw says. "Of course." *Fucking Sandra.* Whether or not she is directly responsible for the tat is beside the point: It happened on her premises. Damn it, he has errands to run before he catches the flight! Tracking her down and getting her to remove the thing will take too long.

"Then we will see you soon." The smiler reaches into a desk drawer and pulls out a small tarnished metal teapot, which he shoves gradually through the barrier. The membrane puckers around it and suddenly the teapot is sitting on Huw's side of the desk, wearing an iridescent soap bubble of pinched-off nanohazard containment. "Peace be with you."

"And you," says Huw, rising. The interview is obviously at an end. He picks up the teapot and follows the blinkenlights to the exit from the consulate, studiously avoiding the blurred patches of air where other visitors are screened from one another by the utility fog. "What now?" he asks the teapot.

"*Blrrrt*. Greetings, Tech Juror Jones. I am a guidance iffrit from the Magical Libyan Jamahiriya Renaissance. Show me to representatives of the Permanent Revolutionary Command Councils and I will be honored to intercede for you. Polish me and I will install translation leeches in your Broca's area, then assist you in memorizing the Koran and hadith. Release me and I will grant your deepest wish!"

"Um, I don't think so." Huw scratches his head. *Fucking Sandra,* he thinks darkly; then he packs the artifact into his pannier and pedals heavily away toward the pottery. It's going to be a long working day—almost five hours—before he can sort this mess out, but at least the wet squishy sensation of clay under his fingernails will help calm the roiling indignation he feels at his violation by a random GM party prankster.

Two days later, Huw's waiting with his bicycle and a large backpack on a soccer field in a valley outside Monmouth. It has rained overnight, and the field is muddy. A couple of large crows sit on the rusting goalpost, watching him with sidelong curiosity. There are one or two other people slouching around the departure area dispiritedly. Airports just haven't been the same since the end of the Jet Age.

Huw tries to scratch the side of his nose, irritably. *Fucking Sandra,* he thinks yet again as he pokes at the opaque spidergoat silk of his biohazard burka. After work yesterday he went round to remonstrate with her, but her house has turned into a size 2,000 Timberland hiking boot, and the doorknob in the heel said Sandra is wintering in Fukushima this year. He can tell a brush-off when he hears one. A net search would probably turn her up, but he isn't prepared to expose himself to any more viruses this week. One is more than enough—especially in light of the fact that the matching trefoil brand on his shoulder glows in the dark.

A low rumble rattles the goalpost and disturbs the crows as a cloud shadow slides across the pitch. Huw looks up, and up, and up—his eyes can't quite take in what he's seeing. *That's got to be more than a kilometer long!* he realizes. The engine note rises as the huge catamaran airship jinks and wobbles sideways toward the far end of the pitch and engages its station-keeping motors, then begins to unreel an elevator car the size of a shipping container.

"Attention, passengers now waiting for flight FL-052 to North Africa and stations in the Levant, please prepare for boarding. This means you."

Huw nearly jumps out of his skin as one of the customs crows lands heavily on his shoulder: "You listening, mate?"

"Yes, yes, I'm listening." Huw shrugs and tries to keep one eye on the big bird. "Over there, huh?"

"Boarding will commence through lift *BZZT GURGLE* four in five minutes. Even-numbered passengers first." The crow flaps heavily toward the huge, rusting shipping container as it lands in the muddy field with a clang. "All aboard!" it caws raucously.

Huw wheels his bike toward the steel box then pauses as a door opens and a couple of confused-looking Australian backpackers stumble out, leading their telltale kangaroo-familiars. "Boarding now!" adds the crow.

He waits while the other three passengers step aboard, then gingerly rolls his bike inside and leans against the guardrail spot-glued to the wall. "Haul away lively, there!" someone yells above, and there's a creak of ropes as the cargo container lurches into the air. Even before it's clear of the goalposts, the huge airship has cut the station-keepers and is spooling up to its impressive fiftyknot cruising speed. Huw looks down at the town and the medieval castle unrolling beneath him and takes a deep breath. He can tell this is going to be a long trip.

His nose is itching again.

Air travel is so slow, you'd almost always be faster going by train. But the Gibraltar bridge is shut for repair this week, and the Orient Express lacks appeal: last time Huw caught a TGV through the Carpathians, he was propositioned incessantly by a feral privatized blood bank that seemed to have a thing for Welsh T helper lymphocytes. At least this tramp floater with its cargo of Christmas trees and chameleon paint is going to give Huw and his fellow passengers a shortcut around the Mediterranean, even if the common room smells of stale marijuana smoke and the other passengers are all dubious cheapskate hitchers and netburn cases who want to ship their meatbodies around instead of doing the decent (and sanitary) thing and using telepresence instead.

Huw isn't dubious; he's just on jury service, which requires your physical in-the-flesh presence to prevent identity spoofing by imported weakly godlike AIs and suchlike. But judging from the way the other passengers are avoiding him, he *looks* dubious: it's probably the biohazard burka and the many layers of anti-nanophage underwear he's trussed up in inside it. *There has got to be a better way of fighting runaway technology,* he tells himself on the second morning as he prepares to go get some breakfast.

Breakfast requires numerous compromises. And it's not just a matter of accepting that, when he's traveling, natural organic wholefoods are rare enough that he'll have to subsist on synthetic slop. Most of the airship's crew are uplifted gibbons, and during their years of plying the skyways over North Africa and parts east, they've picked up enough Islam that it's murder getting the mess deck food processors to barf up a realistic bacon sandwich. Huw has his mouth-lock extended and is picking morosely at a scrambled egg and something that claims to be tempeh with his fork when someone bounces into the seat beside him, reaches into the folds of his burka, and tears off a bite of the sandwich.

The stranger is a disreputable backpacker in wash-n-wear tropical-weight everything, the smart-wicking, dirt-shedding, rip-stopping leisure suit uniform of the globe-slogging hostel-denizens who write long, rambling HOWTOs online describing their adventures living in Mumbai or Manhattan or some other blasted corner of the world for six months on just five dollars. This one clearly thinks himself quite the merry traveler, eyes a-twinkle, crow's-feet etched by a thousand foreign sunsets, dimples you could lose a fifty-dollar coin in.

"'Ello!" he says around a mouthful of Huw's sandwich. "You look interesting. Let's have a conversation!"

"You don't look interesting to me," Huw says, plunking the rest of his food in the backpacker's lap. "Let's not."

"Oh, come on," the backpacker says. "My name's Adrian, and I've loads of interesting anecdotes about my adventures abroad, including some rather racy ones involving lovely foreign ladies. I'm very entertaining, honest! Give me a try, why don't you?"

"I really don't think so," Huw says. "You'd best get back into your seat—the monkeys don't like a disorderly cabin. Besides, I'm infectious."

"Monkeys! You think I'm worried about monkeys? Brother, I once spent a month in a Tasmanian work camp for public drunkenness—imagine, an *Australian* judge locking an *Englishman* up for drunkenness! There were some hard men in that camp, let me tell you. The indigenes had the black market liquor racket all sewn up, but the Maori prisoners were starting up their own thing, and here's me, a poor, gormless backpacker in the middle of it all, dodging homemade shivs and poison arrows. Went a week without eating after it got out that the Maoris were smearing shit in the cook pots to poison the indigenes. Biowar, that's what it was! By the end of that week, I was hallucinating angels and chewing scrub grass I found on work details, while the prisoners I was chained to shat themselves bloody and collapsed. I caught a ballistic out of there an hour after I'd served my sentence, got shot right to East Timor, where I gorged myself on gado-gado and rijsttafel and got food poisoning anyway and spent the night in the crapper, throwing up chunks of me lungs. So don't you go telling me about monkeys!" Adrian breaks off his quasi-racist monologue and chows down on the rest of Huw's lunch.

Fuck you too, Huw manages to restrain himself from saying. Instead: "Yes, that's all very disgusting. I'm going to have a bit of a nap now, all right? Don't wait up."

"Oh, don't be a weak sister!" says Adrian. "You won't last five minutes in Libya with an attitude like that. Never been to Libya, have you?"

"No," Huw says, pointedly bunching up a fold of burka into a pillow and turning his head away.

"You'll love it. Nothing like a taste of real, down-home socialism after dirty old London. People's this and Popular that and Magical Democratic the other, everyone off on the latest plebiscite, holding caucuses in the cafés. It's fantastic! The girls too—fantastic, fantastic. Just talk a little politics with them and they'll bend your ear until you think you're going to fall asleep, and then they'll try to bang the bourgeois out of you. In twos and threes, if you're recalcitrant enough. I've had some *fantastic* nights in Libya. I can barely wait to touch down."

"Adrian, can I tell you something, in all honesty?"

"Sure, mate, sure!"

"You're a jackass. And if you don't get the fuck back to your own seat, I'm going to tell the monkeys you're threatening to blow up the airship and they'll strap you into a restraint chute and push you overboard."

Adrian rears up, an expression of offended hauteur plastered all over his wrinkled mug. "You're a bloody card, you are!"

Huw gathers up his burka, stands, climbs over Adrian, and moves to the back of the cabin. He selects an empty row, slides in, and stretches out. A moment later, Adrian comes up and grabs his toe, then wiggles it.

"All right, then, we'll talk later. Have a nice nap. Thanks for the sarnie!"

It takes three days for the tramp freighter to bumble its way to Tripoli. It gingerly climbs to its maximum pressure height to skirt the wild and beautiful (but radioactive and deadly) Normandy coastline, then heads southeast, to drop a cargo of incognito Glaswegian gangsters on the outskirts of Marseilles. Then it crosses the Mediterranean coast, and spends a whole twenty-two hours doodling in broad circles around Corsica. Huw tries to amuse himself during this latter interlude by keeping an eye open for smugglers with micro-UAVs, but even this pathetic attempt at distraction falls flat when, after eight hours, a rigging monkey scampers into the forward passenger lounge and delivers a fifty-minute harangue about workers' solidarity and the black gang's right to strike in flight, justifying it in language eerily familiar to anyone who—like Huw—has spent days heroically probing the boundaries of suicidal boredom by studying the proceedings of the Third Communist International.

Having exhausted his entire stash of antique dead-tree books two days into a projected two-week expedition, and having found his fellow passengers to consist of lunatics and jackasses, Huw succumbs to the inevitable. He glues his burka to a support truss in the cargo fold, dials the eye slit to opaque, swallows a mug of valerian-laced decaf espresso, and estivates like a lungfish in the dry season.

His first warning that the airship has arrived comes when he awakens in a sticky sweat. *Is the house on fire?* he wonders muzzily. It feels like someone has opened an oven door and stuck his feet in it, and the sensation is climbing his chest. There's an anxious moment; then he gets his eye slit working again, and is promptly inundated with visual spam, most of it offensively and noxiously playing to the assumed orientalist stereotypes of visiting Westerners.

Hello! Welcome, effendi! The Thousand Nights and One Night Hotel welcomes careful Westerners! We take euros, dollars, yen, and hash (subject to assay)! For a good night out, visit Ali's American Diner! Hamburgers 100 percent halal goat here! Need travel insurance and ignorant of sharia banking regulations? Let the al-Jammu Traveler's Assistance put your mind to rest with our—

Old habits learned before his rejectionist lifestyle became a habit spring fitfully back to life. Huw hesitantly posts a bid for adbuster proxy services, picks the cheapest on offer, then waits for his visual field to clear. After a minute or two he can see again, except for a persistent and annoying green star in the corner of his left eye. Finally, he struggles to unglue himself and looks about.

The passenger lounge is almost empty, a door gaping open in one side. Huw wheels his bicycle over and hops down onto the dusty concrete apron of the former airport. It's already over forty degrees in the shade, but once he gets out of the shadow of the blimp, his burka's solar-powered air-conditioning should sort that out. The question is, where to go next? He rummages crossly in the pannier until he finds the battered teapot. "Hey, you. Iffrit! Whatever you call yourself. Which way to the courtroom?"

A cartoon djinni pops into transparent life above the pot's nozzle and winks at him. "Peace be unto you, O Esteemed Madam Tech Juror Jones Huw! If you will but bear with me for a moment—" The Iffrit fizzles as it hunts for a parasitic network to colonize. "—I believe you will first wish to enter the terminal buildings and present yourself to the People's Revolutionary Airport Command and Cleaning Council, to process your entry visa. Then they will direct you to a hotel where you will be accommodated in boundless paradisaical luxury at the expense of the grateful Magical Libyan Jamahiriya Renaissance! (Or at least in a good VR facsimile of paradise.)"

"Uh-huh." Huw looks about. The airport is a deserted dump—literally deserted, for the anti-desertification defenses of the twentieth century, and the genetically engineered succulents frantically planted during the first decades of the twenty-first, have faded. The Libyan national obsession with virtual landscaping (not to mention emigration to Italy) has led to the return of the sand dunes, and the death of the gas-guzzling airline industry has left the airport with the maintenance budget of a rural cross-country bus stop. Broken windows gape emptily from rusting tin huts; a once-outstanding airport terminal building basks in the heat like a torpid lizard, doors open to the breeze. Even the snack vendors seem to have closed up shop.

It takes Huw half an hour to find the People's NeoRevolutionary Airport Command and Cleaning Council, an old woman who has her booted feet propped up on a battered wooden desk in the lobby beneath the International Youth Hostelling sign, snoring softly through her open mouth.

"Excuse me, but are you the government?" Huw asks, talking through his teapot translator. "I have come from Wales to serve on a technology jury. Can you direct me to the public transport terminus?"

"I wouldn't bother if I were you," someone says from behind him, making Huw jump so high, he almost punches a hole in the yellowing ceiling tiles. "She's moonlighting, driving a PacRim investment bank's security bots on the night shift. See all the bandwidth she's hogging?"

"Um, no, as a matter of fact, I don't," Huw says. "I stick to the visible spectrum."

The interloper is probably female and from somewhere in Northern Europe, judging by the way she's smeared zinc ointment across her entire observable epidermis. Chilly fog spills from her cuffs at wrist and ankle and there's the whine of a Peltier cooler pushed to the limit coming from her bum-bag. About all Huw can see of her is her eyes and an electric blue ponytail erupting from the back of her anti-melanoma hood.

"Isn't it a bit rude to snoop on someone else's dreams?" he adds.

"Yes." The interloper shrugs, then grins alarmingly at him. "It's what I do for a living." She offers him a hand, and before he can stop himself he's shaking it politely. "I'm Dagbjört. Dr. Dagbjört."

"Dagbjört, uh—"

"I specialize in musical dream therapy. And I'm here on a tech jury gig too. Perhaps we'll get a chance to work on the same case?"

At that moment the People's Second Revolutionary Airport Command and Cleaning Council coughs, spasms painfully, sits up, and looks around querulously. *I'm not working! Honest!* She exclaims through the medium of Huw's teapot translator. Then, getting a grip: "Oh, you're tourists. Can I help you?"

Her manner is so abrupt and rude that Huw feels right at home. "Yes, yes," he says. "We're jurors and we need to get to a hotel. Where's the light rail terminal or bus stand?"

"Are no buses. Today is Friday, can't you read?"

"Friday—"

"Yes, but how are we to our hotel to ride?" asks Dr. Dagbjört, sounding puzzled.

"Why don't you walk?" The Council asks with gloomy satisfaction, "Haven't you got legs? Didn't Allah, the merciful, bless you with a full complement of limbs?"

"But it's—" Huw consults his wrist-map and again does a double take. "—twelve kilometers! And it's forty-three degrees in the shade!"

"It's Friday," the old woman repeats placidly. "Nothing works on Fridays. It's in the Koran. Also, union regs."

"So why are you working for a Burmese banking cartel as a security bot supervisor?" Dagbjört asks.

"That's—!" The Council glares at her. "That's none of your business!"

"Burma isn't an Islamic country," Huw says, seeing which direction Dagbjört is heading in. *Maybe Dagbjört's not a fucknozzle after all,* although he has his doubts about anyone who has anything to do with dream therapy, much less *musical* dream therapy—unless she's in it only for purely pragmatic reasons, such as the money. "Do you suppose they might be dealing with their demographic deficit by importing out-of-time-zone *Gastarbeiters* from Islamic countries who want to work on the day of rest?"

"What an astonishing thought!" snarks Dagbjört. "That must be illegal, mustn't it?"

Huw decides to play good cop/bad cop with her: "And I'm sure the union will have something to say about moonlighting—"

"Stop! Stop!" The People's Second Revolutionary Airport Command and Cleaning Council puts her hands up in the air. "I have a nephew, he has a car! Perhaps he can give you a ride on his way to mosque? I'm sure he must be going there in only half an hour, and I'm sure your hotel will turn out to be on his way."

The car, when it arrives, is a gigantic early-twenty-first-century Mercedes hybrid with tinted windows and air-conditioning and plastic seats that have cracked and split in the dry desert heat. A brilliantly detailed green and silver miniature temple conceals a packet of tissues on the rear parcel shelf and the dash is plastered with green and gold stickers bearing edifying quotations from the hadith. The Council's nephew looks too young to bear the weight of his huge black mustache, let alone to be directing this Teutonic behemoth's autopilot, but at least he's awake and moving in the noonday furnace heat.

"Hotel Marriott," Dagbjört says. *"Vite-schnell-pronto! Jale, jale!"*

The Mercedes crawls along the highway like a dung beetle on the lowest step of a pyramid. As they head toward the outskirts of the mostly closed city of Tripoli, Huw feels the gigantic and oppressive weight of advertising bearing down on his proxy filters. When New Libya got serious about consumerism they went overboard on superficial glitz and cheesy sloganizing. The deluge of CoolTown webffiti they're driving through is full of the usual SinoIndian global mass-produced crap, seasoned with insanely dense technobabble and a bizarrely Arabized version of discreet Victorian traders' notices. Once they drive under the threshold of the gigantic tinted geodesic dome that hovers above the city, lifted on its own column of hot air, Huw finally gets it: He's not in Wales anymore.

The Council's nephew narrates a shouted, heavily accented travelogue as they lurch through the traffic, but most of it is lost in the roar of the air conditioner and the whine of the motors. What little Huw can make out seems to be pitches for local businesses—cafés, hash bars, amusement parlors. Dr. Dagbjört and Huw sit awkwardly at opposite sides of the Merc's rear bench, conversation an impossibility at the current decibel level.

Dr. Dagbjört fishes in her old-fashioned bum-bag and produces a stylus and a scrap of scribable material, scribbles a moment, and passes it over: DINNER PLANS?

Huw shakes his head. Dinner—*ugh*. He's gamy and crusty with dried sweat under his burka and can't imagine eating, but he supposes he'd better put some fuel in the boiler before he sleeps.

Dagbjört scrolls her message off the material, then scribbles again: I KNOW A PLACE. LOBBY@18H?

Huw nods, suppressing a wince. Dagbjört smiles at him, looking impossibly healthy and scrubbed underneath her zinc armor.

The Marriott is not a Marriott; it's a Second Revolutionary Progress Hostel. (There are real hotels elsewhere in Tripoli, but they all charge real hotel bills, and what's left of the government is trying to run the tech jury service on the cheap.) Huw's djinni delivers a little canned rantlet about Western imperialist monopolization of trademarks, and explains that this is the People's Marriott, where the depredations of servile labor have been eliminated in favor of automated conveniences, the maintenance and disposition of which are managed by a Residents' Committee, and primly admonishes him for being twenty minutes late to his first Committee meeting, which is to run for another two hours and forty minutes. It is, in short, a youth hostel by any other name.

"Can't I just go to my room and have a wash?" Huw asks. "I'm filthy."

"Ah! One thousand pardons, madam! Would that our world was a perfect one and the needs of the flesh could come before the commonweal! It is, however, a requirement of residence at the People's Marriott. You need to attend and be assigned a maintenance detail, and be trained in the chores you are to perform. The common room is wonderfully comfortable, though, and your fellow committee members will be delighted to make you most very welcome indeed!"

"Crap," Huw says.

"Yes," the djinni says, "of course. You'll find a WC to your left after you pass through the main doors."

Huw stalks through both sets of automatic doors, which judder and groan. The lobby is a grandiose atrium with grimy spun diamond panes fifteen meters above his head through which streams gray light that feeds a riotous garden of root vegetables and tired-looking soy. His vision clouds over; then a double row of shaky blinkenlights appears before him, strobing the way to the common room. He heaves a put-upon sigh and shambles along their path.

The common room is hostel-chic, filled with sagging sofas, a sad and splintery gamesurface, and a collection of random down-at-heel international travelers clutching teapots and scrawling desultorily on a virtual whiteboard. The collaborative space is cluttered with torn-off sheets of whiteboard covering every surface like textual dandruff. Doc Dagbjört has beaten him here, and she is already in the center of the group, animatedly negotiating for the lightest detail possible.

"Huw!" she calls as he plants himself in the most remote sofa, which coughs up a cloud of dust and stale farts smelling of the world's variegated cuisines.

He lifts one hand weakly and waves. The other committee members are sizing him up without even the barest pretense at fellowship. Huw recognizes the feral calculation in their eyes:

he has a feeling he's about to get the shittiest job in the place. *Mitigate the risk,* he thinks.

"Hi, there, I'm Huw. I'm here on jury duty, so I'm not going to be available during the days. I'm also a little, uh, toxic at the moment, so I'll need to stay away from anything health-related. Something in the early evening, not involving food or waste systems would be ideal, really. What fits the bill?" He waits a moment while the teapots chatter translations from all over the room. Huw hears Arabic, Farsi, Hindi, Spanish, French, English, and American.

Various whiteboards are reshuffled from around the room, and finally a heroically ugly ancient Frenchman who looks like an albino chimp squeaks some dependencies across the various boards with a stylus. He coughs out a rapid and hostile stream of French, which the teapot presently translates. "You'll be on comms patrol. There's a transceiver every three meters. You take spare parts around to each of them, reboot them, watch the Power-On Self-Test, and swap out any dead parts. Even numbered floors tonight, odd floors tomorrow, guest rooms the day after." He tosses a whiteboard at Huw, and it snaps to centimeters from his nose, acrawl with floorplans and schematics for broadband relay transceivers.

"Well, that's done," Huw says. "Thanks."

Dagbjört laughs. "You're not even close to done. That's your *tentative assignment*—you need to get checked out on every job, in case you're reassigned due to illness or misadventure, or the total quality management monitor thinks you're not pulling your weight."

"You're kidding," he says, rolling his eyes.

"I am not. My assignment is training new committee members. Now, come and sit next to me—the Second Revolutionary Training and Skills-Assessment subcommittee is convening next, and they want to interview all the new arrivals."

Huw zones out during the endless subcommittee meetings that last into early evening, then suffers himself to be dragged to the hotel refectory by Doc Dagbjört and a dusky Romanian Lothario from the Cordon Bleu Catering Committee who casts pointed and ugly looks at him until he slouches away from his baklava and dispiritedly climbs the unfinished concrete utility stairway to sublevel 1, where his toil is to begin. He spends the next four hours trudging around the endless sublevels of the hotel—bare concrete corridors optimized for robotic, not human, access—hunting buggy transceivers. By the time he gets to his room, he's exhausted, footsore, and sticky.

Huw's room is surprisingly posh for what is basically an overfurnished concrete shoe box, but he's too tired to appreciate the facilities. He looks at the oversized sleepsurface and sees the maintenance regimen for its control and feedback mechanism. He spins around slowly in the spa-sized loo and all he can think about is the poxy little bots that patrol the plumbing and polish the tile. The media center is a dismal reminder of his responsibility to patrol the endless miles of empty corridor, rebooting little silver mushrooms and watching their blinkenlights for telltale reds. Back when it was a *real* hotel, the Marriott employed one member of staff per two guest rooms: these days, just staying here is a full-time job.

He fills the pool-sized tub with steaming lavender and eucalyptus-scented water, then climbs in, burka and all. The djinni's lamp perches on the tub's edge, periodically getting soaked in the oversloshes as he shifts his weight, watching the folds of cloth bulge and flutter as its osmotic layers convect gentle streams of water over his many nooks and crannies.

"Esteemed sir," the djinni says, its voice echoing off the painted tile.

"Figured that one out, huh?" Huw says. "No more madam?"

"My infinite pardons," it says. "I have received your jury assignment. You are to report to Fifth People's Technology Court at 800h tomorrow. You will be supplied with a delicious breakfast of fruits and semolina, and a cold lunch of local delicacies. You should be well rested and prepared for a deliberation of at least four days."

"Sure thing," Huw says, dunking his head and letting the water rush into his ears. Normally the news of his assignment would fill him with joy—it's what he's come all this way for—but right now he just feels trapped, his will to live fading. He resurfaces and shakes his head, unintentionally spattering the walls with water that's slightly gray. Dismal realization dawns: *That's another half hour's cleaning.* "How far is it to the courthouse?"

"A mere two kilometers. The walk through the colorful and ancient Tripoli shopping mall and souk is both bracing and elevating. You will arrive in a most pleasant and serene state of mind."

Huw kicks at the drain control, and the tub gurgles itself empty, reminding him of the great water-reclamation facilities in the subbasement. He stands and the burka steams for a moment as every drop of moisture is instantly expelled by its self-wringing nanoweave. "Pleasant and serene. Yeah, right." He climbs tiredly out of the tub and slouches toward the bedroom. "What time is it?"

"It is two fifteen, esteemed sir," says the djinni. "Would sir care for a sleeping draft?"

"Sir would care for a real hotel," Huw grunts, momentarily flashing back to the hotels of his childhood, during his parents' peripatetic wandering from conference to symposium. He lies down on the wide white rectangle that occupies the center of the bedroom. He doesn't hear the djinni's reply: he's asleep as soon as his head touches the pillow.

A noise like cats fucking in a trash can drags Huw awake most promptly at zero-dark o'clock. "What's *that?*" he yells.

The djinni doesn't answer: it's prostrate on the bedside table as if hiding from an invisible overhead ax blade. The noise gets louder, if anything, then modulates into chickens drowning in their own blood, with a side order of Van Halen guitar riffs. "Make it stop!" shouts Huw, stuffing his fingers in his ears.

The noise dies to a distant wail. A minute later it stops and the djinni flickers upright. "My apologies, esteemed sir," it says dejectedly. "I did not with the room sound system mixer volume control interface correctly. That was the most blessed Imam

Anwar Mohammed calling the faithful to prayer, or it would have been if not for the feedback. The blessed Imam is a devotee of the antique Deutsche industrial school of backing tracks and—"

Huw rolls over and grabs the teapot. "Djinni."

"Yes, O Esteemed Sirrah?"

Huw pauses. "You keep calling me that," he says slowly. "Do you realize just how rude that is?"

"Eep! Rude? You appear to be squeezing—"

"Listen." Huw is breathing heavily. He sits up and looks out the window at the sleeping city. Somewhere, 150 gigameters beyond the horizon, the sun might be thinking about the faint possibility of rising. "I am a patient man. But. If you keep provoking me like this—"

"—Like what?"

"This hostel. The fucking alarm clock. Talking down to me. Repeatedly insulting my intelligence—"

"—I'm not insulting!—"

"Shut *up*." Huw blows out a deep breath. "Unless you want me to give you a guided tour of the hotel waste compactor and heavy metal reclamation subsystem. From the inside."

"Ulp." The djinni shuts up.

"That's better. Now. Breakfast. I have a heavy day ahead and I'm half starved from the sandwiches on that fucking airship. I want, let's see... fried eggs. Bacon rashers. Pork sausages. Toast with butter on it, piles of butter. Don't argue, I've had a gray market LDL anticholesterol hack. Oh yeah. Black pudding, hash browns, baked beans, and deep-fried bread. Tell your little friends in the canteen to have it waiting for me. There is no 'or else' for you to grasp at, you horrible little robot. You're going to do this my way or you're not going to do very much at all, *ever again*."

Huw stands up and stretches. His bicycle notices: it unlocks and stretches too, folding itself into shopping mall mode. Memory metal frames and pedal-powered microgenerators are some of the few benefits of high technology, in Huw's opinion— along with the ability to eat seven different flavors of grease for breakfast and not die of a heart attack before lunchtime.

"Got that?"

"I told them, but they say these Turkish food processors, they don't like working with non-halal—"

The djinni shuts up at Huw's snarl. Huw picks up the teapot, hangs it from his bike's handlebars, and pedals off down the hotel corridor with blood in his eye.

I wonder what my chances are of getting a hanging judge?

After breakfast, Huw rides to the end of the hotel's drive and hangs a left, following the djinni's directions, pedals two more blocks, turns right, and runs straight into a wall of humanity.

It's a good, old-fashioned throng. From his vantage point atop the saddle, it seems to writhe like an explosion in a wardrobe department: a mass of variegated robes, business attire, and exotic imported street fashions from all over, individuals lost in the teem. He studies it for a moment longer, and sees that for all its density it's moving rather quickly, though with little regard for personal space. He dismounts the bike and it extrudes its kickstand. Planting his hands on his hips, he belches up a *haram* gust of bacon grease and ponders. He can always lock up the bike and proceed afoot, but nothing handy presents itself for locking. The djinni is manifesting a glowing countdown timer, ticking away the seconds before he will be late at court.

Just then, the crowd shits out a person, who makes a beeline for him.

"Hello, Adrian," Huw says once the backpacker is within shouting distance—about sixty centimeters, given the din of footfalls and conversations. Huw is somehow unsurprised to see the backpacker again, clad in his travelwear and a rakish stubble, eyes red as a baboon's ass from a night's hashtaking.

"Well, fancy meeting *you* here!" says Adrian. "Out for a bit of a ride?"

"No, actually," replies Huw. "On my way somewhere, and running late. Are there any bike lanes here? I need to get past this mob..."

The backpacker snorts. "Sure, if you ride to Tunisia. Yer bike's not going to do you much good here. And don't think about locking it up, mate, or it'll be nationalized by the Popular Low-Impact Transit Committee before you've gone three steps."

"Shit," grunts Huw. He gestures at the bike and it deflates and compacts itself into a carry-case. He hefts it—the fucking thing weighs a ton.

"Yup," Adrian agrees. "Nice to have if you want to go on a tour of the ruins or get somewhere at three A.M.—not much good in town, though. Want to sell it to me? I met a pair of sisters last night who're going to take me off to the countryside for a couple days of indoctrination and heavy petting. I'd love to have some personal transport."

"Fuck," says Huw. He's had the bike for seven years; it's an old friend, jealously guarded. "How about I rent it to you?"

Adrian grins and produces a smokesaver from one of the many snap-pockets on his chest. A nugget of hash smolders inside the plastic tube, a barely visible coal in the thick smoke. He puts his mouth over the end and slurps down the smoke, holds it for a thoughtful moment, then expels it over Adrian's head. "Lovely. I'll return it in two days, three tops. Where're you staying?"

"The fucking Marriott."

"Wouldn't wish it on my worst enemy. Here, will half a kilo chiseled off the side of this be enough?" He hands Huw a foil-wrapped brick of Assassin-brand hash the size of a paving stone. "The rest'll be my deposit. The sisters're into hashishim-revival. Quite versatile minds, they have."

Huw is already copping a light buzz from the sidestream Adrian's blowing his way. This much hash would likely put him in a three-day incontinence coma. But someone might want it, he supposes. "I can work with that. Five hundred grams, and you can have the rest back in return for the bike. Four days' time, at the Marriott, all right?"

Adrian works his head from side to side. "Sure, mate. Works for me."

"Okay. Just bloody look after it. That bike has sentimental value, we've come a long way together." Huw whispers into the bike's handlebars and hands it to Adrian. It interfaces with his PAN, accepts him as its new erstwhile owner, and unfolds.

Adrian saddles up, waves once, and pedals off for points rural and lecherous.

Huw holds the djinni's lamp up and hisses at it. "Right," he says. "Get me to the court on time."

"With the utmost of pleasures, sirrah," it begins. Huw gives it a sharp shake. "All right," it says aggrievedly, "let me teach you to say, 'Out of my bloody way,' and we'll be off."

Huw doesn't know quite what to expect from the Fifth People's Technology Court. A yurt? Sandstone? A horrible modernist-brutalist white-sheathed space-age pile?

As it turns out, like much of the newer local architecture it's an inflatable building, an outsized bounce-house made of metallic fabric and aerogel and compressed air. The whole thing could be deflated and carted elsewhere on a flatbed truck in a morning, or simply attached to a dirigible and lifted to a new spot. (A great safety-yellow gasket the size of a manhole cover sprouts from one side, hooked into power, bandwidth, sewage and water.) It's shaped like a casino owner's idea of the Parthenon, cartoonish columns and squishy frescoes depicting mankind's dominance over technology. Huw bounds up the rubbery steps and through the six-meter doors. A fourteen-year-old boy with a glued-on mustache confronts him as he passes into the lobby.

"Pizzpot," grunts the kid, hefting a curare-blower in Huw's direction. Huw skids to a stop on the yielding floor.

"Pardon?"

"Pizzpot," repeats the boy. He's wearing some kind of uniform, yellow semi-disposable coveralls tailored like a potato sack and all abristle with insignia. It looks like the kind of thing that Biohazard Containment Cops pass out when they quarantine a borough because it's dissolving into brightly colored machine parts.

"The People's Second Revolutionary Technology Court Guardsman wishes to see your passport, sirrah," his djinni explains. "Court will be in session in fifteen seconds."

Huw rolls up his sleeve and presses his forearm against the grimy passport reader the guardsman has pulled from his waistband. "Show me the way." A faint glowing trail appears in front of Huw, snaking down the hall and up to a battered-looking door.

Huw stumbles up to the door and leans on it. It opens easily, sucking him through with a gust of dusty air, and he staggers into a brightly lit green room with a row of benches stretching round three walls. The center of the room is dominated by two boxes; a strangely menacing black cube a meter on a side, and a lectern, behind which hunches a somewhat moth-eaten vulture in a black robe.

Faces and a brace of self-propelled cameras turn to watch Huw as he stumbles to a halt. "You're late," squawks the vulture—on second thoughts, Huw realizes she's not an uplifted avian, but a human being, wizened and twisted by age, her face dominated by a great hatchet of a nose. She's obviously one of the sadsacks on whom the anti-aging gene hacks worked only halfway: otherwise, she could be one of his contemporaries.

"Terribly sorry," Huw says. "Won't happen again."

"Better not." The judge harrumphs consumptively. "Dammit, I deserve some respect! Horrible children."

As the judge rants on about punctuality and the behavior of the dutiful and obedient juror (which, Huw is led to believe, has always been deplorable but has been in terminal decline ever since the abolition of capital punishment for contempt of court back in the eighteenth century), he takes stock of his fellow inmates. For the first time he has reason to be glad of his biohazard burka—and its ability to completely obscure his snarl of anger—because he knows at least half of them. The bastard pseudo-random-number generators at the Magical Libyan Jamahiriya Renaissance's embassy must be on the blink, because besides Doc Dagbjört—whom he half expected—the jury service has summoned none other than *Sandra Lal,* and an ominously familiar guy with a blue forelock, *and* the irritating perpetually drunk centenarian from next door but one. There are a couple of native Libyans, but it looks as if the perennially booming Tripolitanian economy has turned jury service evasion into a national sport. Hence the need to import guest jurors from Wales.

Fuck me, all I need is that turd Adrian to make it a clean sweep, thinks Huw. *This must be some kind of setup.* An awful thought occurs to him: *Or a* reality show. *Jesus Buddha humping the corpse of Oliver Cromwell, say it's not so?* He collapses on a bench in a rustle of static-charged fabric and with a sense of dread waits for proceedings to begin.

The Vulture stands up and hunches over the lectern. All the cameras abruptly pan to focus on her. "Listen up!" she says, in a forty-a-day voice that sounds like she's overdue for another pair of lungs, "*I* am Dr. Rosa Giuliani—that's doctor of law, not doctor of medicine—and I have volunteered my services for the next two weeks to chair this court, or focus group, or theater or whatever. *You* are the jury, or potential consumers, or performing animals. Procedurally, the MLJ have given me total autonomy as long as I conduct this hearing in strict accordance within the bounds of international law as laid down by the Hague Tribunal on Transhuman Manifestations and Magic. Some of you may not fully comprehend what this means. What it means is that you are here to decide whether a reasonable person would consider it safe to unleash Exhibit A on the world. If Exhibit A turns out to be a weapon of planetary destruction, you will probably die. If Exhibit A turns out to be a widget that brings everlasting happiness to the whole of humanity, you will probably get to benefit from it. But the price of getting it wrong is very high indeed. So I will enforce *extreme* measures against any fractional halfwit who tries to smuggle a sample out of this room. I will also nail to the wall the hide of anyone who talks about Exhibit A outside this room, because there are hardware superweapons and there are software superweapons, and we don't know what Exhibit A is yet. For all we know, it's a piece of hardware that looks like a portable shower cubicle but turns out to install borgware in the brain of anyone stupid enough to use it. So—"

Giuliani subsides in a fit of racking coughs. She gathers herself.

"We follow a set procedure. A statement is delivered by the damnfool script kiddies who downloaded the memeplex from the metasphere and who are applying for custodial rights to it. This will describe the prior background to their actions. Second, a preliminary activation of the device may be conducted in a closed environment. Thirdly, you rabble get to talk about it.

Fourthly, you split into two teams: advocates and prosecution. Your task is to convince the members of the other team to join you. Finally, you deliver your majority verdict to me and I check it for procedural compliance. Then if I'm lucky, I get to hang someone. Are there any questions?"

Doc Dagbjört is already waving a hand in the air, eager to please. The judge turns a black gaze on her that reminds Huw of historical documentaries about the Ayatollah Khomeini. Dagbjört refuses to wilt.

"What," says Giuliani, "*is* it?"

"About this Exhibit? Is it the box, in? And if so, how secure the containment is? I would hate for your worries to depart the abstract and concretize themselves, as it were."

"Huh." The judge stalks out from behind her lectern and kicks the box, hard. Going by the resulting noise, she's wearing steel toe-caps. Huw whimpers faintly, envisaging imminent post-singularity gray goop catalyzed nano-annihilation, beyond any hope of resurrection. But the only terrible consequence is that the judge smiles, horribly. "It's safe," she says. "This box is a waste containment vessel left over from the second French fast breeder program."

This announcement brings an appreciative nod from a couple of members of the audience. (The *second* French fast breeder program was nothing to do with nuclear reactors and everything to do with breeding disaster-mitigation replicators to mop up the eight giga-Curies of plutonium that the first program scattered all over Normandy.) Even Huw is forced to admit that the alien memeplex is probably safe behind the Maginot line of nanotech containment widgets lining a hyperdiamond-reinforced tungsten carbide safe.

"So when do we get to see it?" asks Huw.

Judge Giuliani turns her vicious gaze on him. "Right *now!*" She snarls and thumps her fist on the lectern. The lights dim, and a multimedia presentation wobbles and firms up on top of her lectern. "Listen up! Let the following testimony entered under oath on placeholder-goes-here be entered in the court record under this-case-number. Go ahead, play, damn you."

The scene is much as Huw would have imagined it: A couple of pudgy nocturnal hackers holed up in a messy bedroom floored in discarded ready meal packs, the air hazy with programmable utility foglets. They're building a homebrew radio telescope array by reprogramming their smart wallpaper. They work quietly, exchanging occasional cryptic suggestions about how to improve their rig's resolving power and gain. About the only thing that surprises Huw is that they're both three years old—foreheads swollen before their time with premature brain bridges. A discarded pile of wooden alphabet blocks lies in one corner of the room. A forlorn teddy bear lies on the top bunk with its back to the camera viewpoint.

"Ooh, aren't they *cute?*" says Sandra. "The one on the left is *just like* my younger brother before his ickle widdle accident!"

"Silence in court, damn your eyes! What do you think this is, an adoption hearing? Behold, Abdul and Karim Bey. Their father is a waiter and their mother is a member of the presidential guard." (Brief clips of a waiter and a woman in green battle dress carrying an implausibly complicated gun drift to either side of the nursery scene.) "Their parents love them, which is why they paid for the very best prenatal brainbox upgrades. With entirely predictable results if you ask me, but as you can see, they didn't..."

Abdul and Karim are pounding away at their tower of rather goopy-looking foglets—like all artifacts exposed to small children, they have begun to turn gray and crinkly at the corners—but now they are receiving a signal, loud and clear. They're short on juice, but Karim has the bright idea of eviscerating Teddy and plugging his methanol-powered fuel cell into the tots' telescope. It briefly extrudes a maser, blats a signal up through the thin roof of their inflatable commodity housing, and collapses in exhaustion.

The hackers have only five minutes or so to wait—in which time Abdul speed-reads through *War and Peace* in the original Russian while Karim rolls on his back, making googling noises as he tries to grab his feet—for they have apparently found the weakly godlike AIs of the metasphere in a receptive mood. As the bitstream comes in, Abdul whacks his twin brother upside the head with a purple velour giraffe. Karim responds by irritably uploading a correctly formatted patent application with the godvomit as an attachment.

"I hate smart-aleck kids," mumbles the bald guy with the blue forelock, sitting across the room. The judge pretends to ignore him.

"These two miscreants are below the contractual age of consent," Huw says, "so how come their application is being accepted?"

"Here in the MLJ, as you should well know, seeing you're staying here and there was a copy of the Lonely Planet guide in your room," the judge croaks, "ever since the People kicked out the last of the dictators, your civil rights are a function of your ability to demand them. Which is a bit annoying, because Karim demanded the vote six months ago, while Abdul is a second lieutenant in the People's Cyberspace Defense Agency and a dab hand at creating new meme viruses. In fact, there's some question over whether we shouldn't be dragging him up in front of a court-martial instead."

Judge Giuliani seems to have forgotten to snarl; her delivery is becoming almost civilized as the presentation from the subpoenaed crib-cam fast-forwards to the terrible two's attempt to instantiate the bitstream in atoms, using a ripped teddy bear as a containment vessel.

"Ah, here it is. Observe: The artifact is extremely flexible, but not so flexible that it can gestate in a psuedoliving toy. Abdul's own notes speculate that gestation may be supported in medium-sized dogs, goats, and camels." Over the lectern, the display zooms in on the teddy bear's swollen gut. The bear is jerking spasmodically and twitching like a Tourettic children's TV host, giggling and stuttering nonsensical self-worth affirmations. The gut distends farther and the affirmations become more disjointed, and then a long, sharp blade pokes through the pseudoflesh and flame-retardant fur analogue. "There are indications that the artifact floods its host organism with endorphins at metamorphosis-time," says the judge. The rent in the bear's belly widens, and out climbs a shimmering *thing*.

It takes Huw a moment to understand what he's seeing. The artifact is a tall, metallic stalk, at first coiled like a cobra, but gradually roused to full erectness. Its glistening tip dips down toward the bear. "See how it sutures the exit wound?" the judge says, a breath of admiration in her rough voice. "So tidy. Jurors, take note, this is a *considerate* artifact." Indeed, the bear's fur has been closed with such cunning that it's almost impossible to see the exit wound. However, something has gone horribly awry inside it, as it is now shaking harder than ever, shivering off its limbs and then its fur. Finally its flesh starts breaking away like the sections of a tangerine.

The artifact stands erect again, bounces experimentally a couple times, then *collapses* in a way that Huw can't make any sense of. He's not alone, either. The jurors let out a collective uncomprehending bleat. "Look closely, Jurors!" the judge says, and the scene loops back on itself a couple times in slomo, from multiple angles, then again in wireframe. It makes Huw's mind hurt. The artifact's stalk bulges in some places, contracts in others, all the whole slipping through and around itself. His potmaker's eye tries to no avail to understand what's happening to the topology and volume.

"Fucking lovely," Sanda Lal says. She's always had a thing about trompe l'oeil solids: "Nicest Klein bottle I've ever seen."

A Klein bottle. Of course. Take a Möbius strip and extrude it one more dimension out and you get a vessel with only two sides, the inside and outside a single continuous plane. Glassblower shit. *Fucking show-offs.*

The young brothers are on hands and knees before the artifact now, staring in slack-jawed concentration, drool slipping between their patchworks of baby teeth and down their chins. The cam zooms in on the artifact, and it begins to fluoresce and pulse, as through digesting a radioactive hamster. The peristaltic throbbing gives it motion, and it begins to work its way toward the hamper in the corner of the room. It inches across the floor, trailed by the crawling brothers, then knocks over the hamper and begins to burrow through the spilled, reeking linens.

"It's scat-tropic," Doc Dagbjört says.

"Yes," the judge says. "And scat-powered. Karim notes that its waste products are a kind of silt, similar to diatomaceous earth and equally effective as a roach and beetle powder. It also excretes water and trace elements."

"A fractional-dimensional parasitic turd-gobbler from outer space?" Huw says. "Have I got that right?"

"That's right, ma'am," says the blue-forelocked joe. "And it's pretty too. I'd gestate one, if only to eliminate the need for a bloody toilet. Quite a boon to your average WHO-standard pit latrine too, I imagine."

"Of course *you'd* gestate one," Huw says. "Nothing to you if your body is dissolved into toxic tapioca. I imagine you're just about ready to join the cloud anyroad."

Sandra casts him a poisonous glare. "Fuck you, and the goat you rode into town on," she said. "Who the hell *are* you, anyway?"

"Judge?" Doc Dagbjört says, desperately trying to avoid a mass execution, "my co-juror raises an interesting point. What evidence do we have to support Adbul's assertion that the artifact can safely gestate in mammals or, more specifically, primates?"

The judge grunts irritably. "Only simulations, of course," she says. "Are you volunteering?"

Doc Dagbjört sits back hastily. "Just asking!"

"Are you all seated comfortably?" Giuliani asks. "Then I

shall continue." She whacks her gavel on the lectern and the presentation rolls boringly on. "Here's what happened next." It's a dizzying fast-forward montage: The space monster digests the twins' nappy hamper then chows down on their bedding while Abdul—or maybe it's Karim—hastily jury-rigs an EMP gun out of animatronic toys and an air force surplus radar set. The twins back into a corner and wait, wide-eyed, as the *thing* sprouts a pink exoskeleton lined with throbbing veins, rabbit ears, and a set of six baby elephant legs with blue toenails. It squats in the middle of their room, hooting and pinging as it digests the pile of alphabet blocks. Karim—or maybe it's Abdul—improvises a blue goo attack using the roomful of utility fog, but the ad hoc nanoweaponry just slimes off the space monster like so much detergent.

"At this point, the manifestation estivated," announces the judge.

"Duh, wassatmean?" asks one of the other jurors, one whom Huw doesn't know—possibly a nationalist from the Neander valley.

"It went to sleep," explains Doc Dagbjört. "Isn't that right, Judge?"

"Damn straight." The judge whacks her gavel again. "But if I get any more lip out of you, sunshine, I'll have you flogged 'till the ivory shows. This is *my* trial. Clear?"

Dagbjört opens her mouth, closes it, then nods.

"Well," says Judge Giuliani, "that's that, then. The thing seems to have fallen deeply asleep. Just in case it wakes up, the MLJ Neighborhood Sanitation Committee have packed it into a Class Four nanohazard containment vessel—which I'm standing on right now—and shipped it over here. We're going to try a directed revival after lunch, *with* full precautions. Then I'll have a think about it, you damned meddling baboons can rubberstamp my verdict, and we'll wrap up in time for tea. Do it my way and you can all go home three days early: rock the boat and I'll have you broken on the wheel. Court will now adjourn. Make sure you're all back here in three hours' time—or else. *And...* cut!"

In case the message is insufficiently clear, the bench Huw is perched on humps up into an uncomfortable ridge, forcing him to stand. The Vulture storms out of the courtroom in a flurry of black robes, leaving a pool of affronted jurors milling around a lectern containing a sleeping puddle of reified godvomit.

"All right, everyone," says Doc Dagbjört, clapping her hands together. "How about we go and find the refectory in this place? I could murder some meze!"

Huw slouches off toward the entrance in a black mood, the teapot clanking at his hip. This isn't going quite the way he'd imagined, and he'll be damned before he'll share a refectory table with that sanctimonious Swedish Girl Scout, much less Sandra and her gender-bending (and disturbingly attractive) friend. Someone is quite clearly doing this in order to get under his skin, and he is deeply pissed off. On the other hand, it's a long time since breakfast—and there must be somewhere that serves a decent goat curry in Tripoli.

Mustn't there?

It is insanely hot on the sidewalk outside the court, hot and crowded and dusty, and even with his biohazard burka pumping away heat as fast as it can, Huw is sweating. His skin itches everywhere, but especially on the shoulder, where he can feel his skin crawling every time he thinks about the glowing trefoil tattoo.

The court is located in a district full of bleached white shells, buildings thrown up by massively overengineered mollusks. Unable to breathe without oxygen supplies, having erected a habitable structure, they die in order to provide a delicious moving-in feast for the residents. It's cheap favela architecture, but durable and far better than the tent cities of a previous century; snail cities have power, recycling services, bandwidth, and a weird kind of hobbit-ish charm. Some of the bigger shells have been turned into storefronts by various cottage professionals, and Huw is drawn toward one of them by the mouthwatering smell of roasting meat.

There are elaborate cast-iron tables outside the shellfront, and cast-iron chairs, and—luxury of luxuries—a parasol over each. There are people inside the shell, but the outside tables are deserted. Huw wilts into the nearest space and puts his teapot down on the table. "You," he grunts. "Universal translator for anyone who comes my way. I expect service with a smile. *Capisce?*"

"Your wish is my command," pipes his djinni.

A teenaged girl in a black *salwar kameez,* white face paint, and far too much eye shadow and silver spider-jewelry saunters over, looking for all the world like a refugee from a goth club in Bradford. "Yeah? Whatcher want, granny?"

"It's mister," Huw says. "You the waitress?"

"Yeah," she answers in English, staring at him idly. Her earrings stare too—synthetic eyeballs dangling from desiccated optic nerves. "You trans?"

"No, I'm a biohazard. What's on the lunch menu?"

"We've got a choice of any cloned meat shawarma you fancy: goat, mutton, ox tongue, or Rumsfeld. With salad, olives, cheese, falafels, coffee or Coke. Pretty much anything. Say, are you *really* a biohazard?"

"Listen," Huw says, "I'm not wearing this fucking sack because I *enjoy* it. Your Ministry of Barbarian Affairs insisted—"

"Why don't you take it off then?" she asks. "If they call you on it, just pay."

"Pay—"

"What's wrong with you? You one of those dumb Westerners who doesn't get baksheesh?" She looks unimpressed.

Huw stifles a facepalm. *I should have known…* "Thanks. Just get me the goat shawarma and falafels. They're cloned, you say?"

She looks evasive. "Cloned-ish."

"Vatmeat?" Huw's stomach turns.

"You're not a racist, are you? Nothing wrong with being vatted."

Huw pictures a pulsating lump of flesh and hoses, recalls that the top-selling album of all time was recorded by such a being, and resigns himself to eating vatmeat rather than getting into a religious argument. "I'll take the goat. And, uh, a Diet Coke."

"Okay." She turns and beams his order to the kitchen, then wanders over to the bar and begins to pour a tall drink.

Huw takes a deep breath. Then he pinches the seal node on his burka and gives it a hard yank. As gestures of defiance go, it's small but profound; he feels suddenly claustrophobic, and can't stop until he's tugged the whole thing off, up and over his head, and yanked down the overalls that make up its bottom half, and stomped them all into the gray dust under his boots.

The air is dry, and smells *real*. Huw finally begins to relax. The waitress strolls over bearing a large glass, loaded with Coke and ice cubes. As she gets close, her nose wrinkles. "You need a bath, Mr. Biohazard Man."

"Yeah. Well. You tell the Ministry." Huw takes the drink, relishes a long swallow, unencumbered by multiple layers of smart antiviral polymer defenses. He can feel the air on his face, the sunlight on his skin. He puts the glass down. *Wonder how long I'll take to work up a suntan?* he thinks, and glances at his wrist. He freezes.

There's a biohazard trefoil on the back of his hand.

Huw stands up, feeling dizzy. "There a toilet here?" he asks.

"Sure." The waitress points him round the back. "Take your time."

The bathroom is a small nautiloid annex, but inside it's as chilly and modern as Sandra Lal's. Huw locks the door and yanks his tee and sweatpants off. He turns anxiously to check his back in the mirror over the sink—but the trefoil on his shoulder has gone.

It's on the back of his hand. And it itches.

"Shit," he says quietly and with feeling.

Back at the table, Huw bolts his food down then rises, leaving an uncharacteristic tip. He picks up the bundle of dusty black biohazard fabric and strolls past the shops. One of them is bound to be a black market nanohacker. His hands are shaking. He isn't sure which prospect is worse: finding he's got a big medical bill ahead, or trying to live in ignorance.

"Teapot," he whispers.

"Yes, sir?" "Where's the nearest body shop? Doesn't have to be fully legal under WIPO-compliant treaty terms, just legal enough."

"*Bzzt*. It is regrettably not possible for this humble unit to guide you in the commission of felonies, O Noble Sirrah—"

Shake. "There is legal and there is *legal*," Huw says. "I don't give a shit about complying with all the braindead treaties the Moral Majority rammed through WIPO in the wake of the Hard Rapture. I just want somewhere that the local police won't arrest me for frequenting if I pay the usual. Whatever the usual happens to be around here. Can you do that? Or would you like to tell me where the nearest heavy metal reclamation plant is?"

"Eeek! Turn left! Left, I say! Yes, ahead of you! Please, do me no injury, sirrah!"

Huw walks up to a featureless roc's egg and taps on it. "Anyone at home?" he asks.

A door dilates in the shell, emitting a purple-tinged light. "Enter," says a distinctly robotic voice.

Inside the shell, Huw finds himself in a room dominated by something that looks like a dentist's chair as reinvented on behalf of the Spanish Inquisition by H. R. Giger. Standing beside it—

"Does your sister work at the diner along the road?" he asks.

"No, she's my daughter." The woman—who looks young enough to be the waitress's twin, but wears medical white and doesn't have any body piercings that blink at him—looks distinctly unimpressed. "And she's got an attitude problem. She's a goth, you know. Thinks it's so rebellious." She sniffs. "Did she send you here?"

Huw holds up his arm. "I'm here because of this," he says, dodging the question.

"Aha." She peers at his trefoil. "Do you know what it is?"

"No, that's why I'm here."

"Very well. If you take a seat and give me your debit token, I'll try to find out for you."

"Will there be any trouble?" Huw asks, lying back on the couch and trying not to focus on the mandibles descending toward him.

"I don't know—yet." She fusses and potters and mumbles to herself. "All right, then," she says at length. "It's in beta, whatever it is."

"Oh yes?" Huw says, in a way that he hopes sounds intelligent.

"Certainly. That's the watermark—it's compliant with the INEE's RFC 4253.11 on debug-mode self-replicating organisms. Whatever host medium it finds itself in, it advertises its presence by means of the trefoil."

"And—?" Huw says.

"And that means that either the person who made it is conscientious, or is working with an RFC-compliant SDK."

"I see," Huw says. He supposes that this is probably interesting to people in the biz, but he has no idea what it means. It's an alien culture. He prefers concrete stuff he can get his hands on. None of these suspicious self-modifying abstractions that suddenly make you sprout antlers.

The hacker mutters to herself some more. "Well," she says, and

"Hmmm," and "Oh," until Huw feels like bursting. "Right, then."

Huw waits. And waits. His whole fucking life seems to consist of conversations like this. He's read some hilariously naïve accounts of life in the soi-disant "Information Age" about "Future Shock," all those dim ancestors trying to make sense of their rapidly changing world. They fretted about the "singularity"—the point at which human history goes nonlinear and unpredictable and the world ceases to have any rhyme or reason. Future shock indeed—try living in the fucking singularity, and having your world inverted six times before breakfast.

"Well, that's it. I can do it in vitro or in situ, up to you."

"Do it?"

"Accelerate it. What, you think I'm going to *decompile* this thing? That code is so obfuscated, it may as well be cuneiform for all the sense I can make of it. No, there's only one way to find out what it does: accelerate its life cycle and see what happens. I can do it in your body—that's best, it's already halfway there—or I can do it in glass. Your choice."

"Glass!" Huw says, his heart racing at the vision of an unlicensed tech colony cutting out of his guts, like the thing in the courtroom.

The hacker sighs a put-upon exhalation. "Fine," she says. Let's get you cloned, then." Before he can jerk free, the instrument bush hovering over him has scraped a layer of skin from his forearm and drawn a few milliliters of blood from the back of his hand, leaving behind an anesthetized patch of numb skin that spreads over his knuckles and down to his fingertips. Across the room, a tabletop diamond-walled chamber fogs and hums. The mandibles recede and Huw sits up. A ventilation system kicks in, clearing the fog from the chamber, and there Huw sees his cloned hand taking shape, starting as a fetal fin, sundering into fingers, bones lengthening, protofingernails forming. "That'll take a couple hours to ripen," the hacker says. "Then I'll implant it and we'll see what happens. Come back this time tomorrow, I'll show you what turns up." She rubs her thumbs against her forefingers.

Huw sticks his hand out to touch hers and interface their PANs so he can transfer a payment to her, but she shies back. "I don't think so," she says. "You're infectious, remember?"

"Well, how shall I pay you, then?" he says.

"Over there," she says, gesturing at a meatpuppet in the corner, a wrinkled naked neuter body with no head, just a welter of ramified tubules joined to a bare medulla that flops out of the neck stump like an alien nosegay. Huw shakes the currency zombie's clammy hand and interfaces with its PAN, transfers a wad of baksheesh to it, and steps back, wiping his hand on the seat of his track pants afterwards.

"This time tomorrow, right?" the hacker says.

"See you then," Huw says.

Back at the courthouse, the People's Second Revolutionary Technology Court Guardsman doesn't even blink as Huw unrolls the multiple thicknesses of burka he'd wrapped around his telltale hand—which is starting to itch like it's acrawl with subcutaneous fire ants—and forearm.

As he steps into the gloomy courtroom, he thinks that he's

alone: but after that moment he detects movement and slurping sounds from the shadows behind one of the benches. A familiar head with a blue forelock rears back, face a rictus of agonized enjoyment. Huw makes out a female head suctioned to the joe's chest, teeth fastened to his nipple. *Christ,* Huw thinks, *he and Sandra are having a snog in the fucking courtroom. The Vulture's going to string them up by their pubes and skull-fuck them with her gavel.*

Then the head turns, worrying at the nipple in a way that looks painful (though it appears to be doing wonders for the joe) and Huw sees that it isn't Sandra Lal masticating that tit; it's Doc Dagbjört. He feels a sear of jealousy jetting from his asshole to his shoulder blades, though whom he is jealous of he cannot exactly say. He clears his throat.

The lovebirds spring apart and stand. Doc Dagbjört's shirt is hiked up around her armpits and before she gets it pulled back down, Huw is treated to a stunning display of her chestular appendages, which are rather spectacular in a showy, fantastically perfect way. The joe is more casual, stretches and yawns and pulls his own sweaty leather shirt down. Then he does a double take as he recognizes Huw.

"You!" he says. "The hell are you doing here?"

"You know him?" Dagbjört asks. She's blushing a rather lovely and fierce Viking red.

Huw partially unrolls his burka from his arm and dangles it in front of his face. "So do you, Doc," he says.

"The transvestite?" she says.

"I'm not trans," Huw says. He rewraps the burka around his

arm, which is throbbing with itch and needles of alternating ice and fire. "Just got a nasty little itch and took a while to figure out who to bribe." He glares at the guy with the blue forelock, Bonnie the party animal. "You wouldn't happen to know anything about it, would you?"

"Who, me?" Bonnie frowns right back at him. "What did you think you were doing barging in here, anyway?"

Huw crosses his arms defensively. "In case you hadn't noticed, this is a courtroom and the Vulture's going to be back in about—"

The door bangs open behind him and he turns round. "Where *is* everybody?" croaks the black-clad judge. "Dammit, I expect punctuality in my courtroom!"

Judge Giuliani crosses to her box and stands behind it, tapping her toe on the floor and glowering furiously at the doorway as, one by one, the delinquent jurors filter in. Her stare is lost on Sandra, who sees Huw as she opens the door and nearly jumps out of her skin. Huw smiles at her sweetly and she edges around the far side of the room and sits down as far away from him as possible. So while the Vulture is busy tearing a strip off the Neanderthal, he gets up, walks over, and sits down next to her.

"Hello, Sandra," he says warmly. "How's it going?"

Sandra leans away from him, looking afraid. "Where did you get *that*?" she asks, eyeing his biohazard-wrapped wrist.

"I thought you and me, we could talk about it." Huw smiles. It's not a friendly expression. "I picked it up at your place a week or so back?"

"Listen, I have *no idea* what this is about, but I don't like it! I don't hang out with people who do that sort of thing, least not without warning. Are you sure you weren't jarked by a stranger on your way over?"

"Silence in court!" says Giuliani, waving her gavel at Sandra, who cowers, trying to get as far away as possible from both the judge and Huw. Huw crosses his arms, annoyed. *Is she telling the truth?*

"You pukes had better listen up right now! We are about to begin the most dangerous part of the proceedings! Are those of you who believe in physical resurrection all backed up to off-site storage? And are the rest of you all up to date on your life insurance policies? Because if not, you're too fucking late, haa haa! It is time to *open the box!*"

"Oh *shit*." Huw hastily begins to untangle his burka, in the hope that its advanced biocontainment layers will help if the monster that hatched from the scatotrophic Klein bottle from outer space turns out to be unfriendly. His wrist itches hotly in sympathy, then mercifully stops.

Giuliani twirls her hammer round and presses a button; it turns into something like a cross between a pocket chain saw and a whittling knife. "Now, I am about to open the containment," she says, standing over the ominous black cube with a raised knife. "With any luck, it's just sleeping. If it isn't, well, all I can say is it damn well better behave itself in *my* courtroom."

She leans forward and slaps one hand on a side of the box. Something heavy goes *clunk* inside it. A hand goes up from the far side of the jury box. "What is it *now?*" says the Vulture.

"Please, Judge, can I go to the bathroom?" Bonnie is waving an anxious hand in the air.

"Oh fuck off, then," snarls the judge. "Five minutes! Or you'll be sorry!"

She yanks at the lid of the biohazard containment and Bonnie takes off, scampering behind the benches as if his arse is on fire—or maybe he's just afraid that it will be, in a few seconds.

The box deconstructs itself into a pile of bubbling pink slime, to reveal the space monster the brothers Bey downloaded. It squats, curled up, in a nest of shredded teddy bears; two of its six legs are wrapped over what ought to be its snout, and it is making a faint whistling noise that it takes Huw a few seconds to recognize as snoring.

"Behold, the stinking pile of godvomit!" says the Vulture. She stands over it, arms akimbo, Swiss Army chain saw at the ready, looking almost pleased with herself. "Exhibit A: asleep. It's been this way for the past eighteen days, ever since the Bey twins created it. Any questions?"

A susurrus of conversation sweeps the jury benches. "That's funny," Huw says, "my arm doesn't itch anymore."

"Shut up about your arm already!" Sandra says. "Look!" She points at the box, just as the space monster emits a deep grunting sigh and rolls over on its side, snuffling sleepily.

"Six limbs, bilateral symmetry, exoskeleton. Has anyone tried deconstructing its proteome yet?" asks Doc Dagbjört, looking rather more cheerful than the situation warrants.

"From inside the containment? No." The Vulture looks thoughtful. "But from traces of carapace scraped off the walls of the Bey residence nursery, we have obtained a partial genotype. Tell your guidebooks or familiars or whatever to download

Exhibit B for you. As you can see, the genome of the said item is chimeric and shows signs of crude tampering, but it's largely derived from *Drosophila, Mus musculus,* and a twenty-first-century situationist artist or politician called Sarah Palin. Large chunks of its genome appear to be wholly artificial, though, written entirely in Arabic, and there's an aqueous-phase Turing machine partially derived from octopus ribosomes to interpret them. It looks as if something has been trying to use the sharia code as a platform for implementing a legal virtual machine. We're not sure why, unless it's an obscure joke."

"Does the metasphere have a sense of humor?" Huw says. He clears his throat—the dust must be getting to him, because it feels as if he's developing a ticklish cough.

"If it didn't, my life would be a lot simpler," the Vulture says. A door at the back of the courtroom bangs, Bonnie coming back from the toilet. Huw notes with a spike of erotic shock that Bonnie is female again, a forelocked vision of heroin-chic skin and bones. "As it is, it makes it hard to tell a piece of sculpture from a practical joke, a new type of washing machine, or an alien superweapon."

"Urk." Huw subsides into a fit of coughing; it doesn't help his throat.

"Can we wake it up?" Doc Dagbjört asks. "If I play it some music, perhaps it can the dream awaken from?"

Oh shit, musical dream therapy, Huw realizes with a sinking feeling. *So* that's *why she's on this panel.*

"That is a possibility," the Vulture concedes. She prods the sleeping space monster with a steel-toe-capped boot, but it just snores louder and burrows deeper into its nest of disemboweled toys. "I prefer electroshock, myself."

"Shit." Sandra says. Huw glances sideways at her, sees her cowering away from him. "Shit!"

"What is it?" he asks.

"Your—" She stops, and rummages in her fanny pack. After pulling out a mirror, she passes it to him. "Throat."

At the other end of the bench, Doc Dagbjört is explaining the healing properties of ambient postindustrial music to an interested judge and a couple of less skeptical jurors. Huw holds up the hand mirror and points it at his throat.

Huw stares at the mirror nearly cross-eyed and focuses on his stubbly Adam's apple. It has been completely covered with a familiar biohazard trefoil, surrounded by ranked miniature trefoils, each of them fractally ringed with smaller duplicates, and so on, into hairy infinitude that no doubt extends down to mitochondrial detail.

Huw clutches his hands to his throat and feels it buzzing, vibrating, just as Dagbjört lets fly with an eerie ululation. She sings the quasi-melody rather well, noodling around from a ghostly, bluesy I-IV-V progression to something pentatonic that sounds like the wind whistling over the blasted steppes of some distant Eastern land and then into something Celtic and complicated.

The buzzing under his sweating fingertips heightens. The godvomit is vibrating too, beginning a bobbing sinuous cobra dance, and it begins to sing too, a low droning *ommmmmm* that resonates in Huw's bones, in Huw's throat, in Huw's mind.

His tongue stirs in his mouth and he feels a great, preverbal welling from his larynx. He feels a burst of Tourettic obscenities tickling at his lips like a sneeze, and he moves his hands from his throat and claps them over his mouth, but it's too late: he's singing too.

If you can call it singing. He's giving voice to *two* wordless melodies simultaneously, meshing in artful discord with each other and the joint song of the Kleinmonster and Dagbjört. One voice is basso profundo, the other a Tiny Tim falsetto, and the Kleinmonster is turning its attention on him—he can *hear* it thinking joyful thoughts to itself. His skin crawls with creeping horror as his voice box secedes from his autonomic nervous system, and he flees the courtroom, pursued by the mystified stares of his co-jurors and the glare of the Vulture.

He stumbles for the loo, struggling to keep the alien song inside his chest, lips clamped tightly shut. He has a titanic, painful, rock-hard erection, and he thinks wildly of autoerotic asphyxiators who blow their loads in ecstatic writhing as their oxygen-starved brains stage endorphin-fueled fireworks displays on the backs of their eyelids. He is certain he is dying. He falls to his knees on the rubber tiles of the lav's floor and begins to retch and weep.

He feels a tentative hand caressing his shoulder and he turns his head. Through a haze of tears, he recognizes Bonnie, her eyes smoldering with barely controlled lust. "You're so fucking *transhuman*," s/he says, and clamps her mouth to his, ramming her tongue in almost to his gag reflex. She pins him to the yielding tiles and straddles him, grinding her/his crotch against his.

It's enough to shock him out of despair and into anger. He pushes hard against her bony xylophone chest and spits. "You are *sick*," he says, rolling away. The song is dying now, just a buzz of harmonics that pick at his pulse. "God!"

Bonnie smirks at him and does a cat stretch on the tile before climbing to her feet. She shakes herself and tosses her fringe and gives him another smirk. "Really? I could have sworn you wanted it," she says, and leaves him alone.

Huw pulls himself to his feet and staggers for the door, his throat no longer itching, but *wriggling*. He pushes weakly against the door and steps out into the corridor, where he confronts the entire court, which has apparently adjourned to follow him. The Vulture's fists are fiercely planted on her hips.

"You're infected," the Vulture says. Her voice is ominously calm. "That's unfortunate. We've got a nanocontainment box for you until we sort it out. We'll pull an alternate juror from the pool." Sandra, Bonnie, Dagbjört, the caveman, and the centenarian are all staring at him like he's a sideshow curiosity. "Come along now, the guardsmen will take you to your box." The guardsmen are a pair of hulking golems, stony-faced and brutal-looking. They advance on him with a thunderous tread, brandishing manacles like B-movie Inquisitors.

Huw's mind blanks with fear and rage. *Bastards!* he tries to scream, and what comes out is an eerie howl that makes the jurors wince and probably terrifies every dog within a ten-kilometer radius. He feints toward them, then spins on his heel and dashes for the front doors. Curare darts spang off the rubber walls and rebound around him, but none hit him. He leaps off the courtroom steps and runs headlong into the humanswarm, plowing into its midst.

He runs without any particular direction, but his feet take him back to the hacker's egg-shaped clinic of their own accord. He turns his head and scans the crowd for jurors or officers of the court. Seeing none, he thumps the egg until the door irises open, then dives through it.

The hacker is laid out on her table, encased in the instrument bush. Her fingers and toes work its tendrils in response to unknowable feedback from its goggles and earphones. Huw coughs in three-part harmony, and she gives her fingers a decisive waggle that causes the bush to contract into a fist near the ceiling.

She looks at him, takes in Huw's watermarked throat and two-part snoring drone. "Right," she says. "Looks like you're about done, then." The teapot at his belt translates efficiently, giving her a thick Brummie accent for no reason Huw understands.

"What the fuck is this shit?" Huw says, over his drone.

"No need for that sort of language," she says primly. She gets up off her table and gestures toward it. "Up you go."

Reluctantly, Huw climbs up, then watches the bush descend on him and encase him in a quintillion smart gossamer fingers.

"I uploaded your opportunistic code to a mailing list," explains the hacker. "It was a big hit with the Euros—lucky for you it's their waking hours, or it could have been another twelve hours before we heard back. You've solved quite a little mystery, you know.

"The betaware you're infected with has been floating around the North Sea for about a month now, but it has failed to land a single successful somatic infection—until now. Lots of carriers but no afflicted. Best guess at its origin is a cometary mass extruded from the cloud that burned away protecting its payload.

66

"So it was quite the mystery until I pasted your genome into a followup. Then it was obvious—it's looking for specific T helper lymphocytes. Welsh ones. Which begs another question: Why Welsh?

"And here we have the answer." The bush's tendrils stroked Huw's growling voice box. "All those grotty Welsh vowel sounds and glottals. It needed a trained larynx to manifest."

"Aaaagh," Huw gargles, tensing angrily and trying to argue. The bush takes the opportunity to shove what feels like a wad of cotton wool into his mouth and extrude exploring wisps to brush samples from his epiglottis.

A histogram scrolls across the egg's wall in time with Huw's groan, spiking ferociously. "Oh, *very nice*," she says. "You're modulating a megabit a second over a spread-spectrum short-range audio link. Pushing the limits of info-sci, you are!"

Huw stutters another groan, then vomits a flood of obscenities: They're enveloped in his di-vocal drone, and the histogram spikes in sympathy.

"No easy way to know what you're spewing, of course. Lots of activity in your language and vision centers, though." The bush firmly grips the sides of his head. "Do that again, will you? I'm going to run a PET scan."

"I don't think I can," he begins; then he bursts into Welsh profanity so foul, it triggers his old flinch reflex, some part of his limbic system certain that this sort of display will necessarily be accompanied by a ringing slap from his mother, however uploaded she might be these past fifty years.

"Right," she says. "Right. Here's my guess, then. You're

transmitting your sensoria—visual, auditory, olfactory, even tactile. Somewhere out there there's a complementary bit of receiving equipment that can demodulate the signal. You're a remote sensing apparatus."

"Fuck," Huw says. The histogram is still. He is voluntarily cursing.

"It's kinky, yes?" she says. "Too kinky for you. One second." Tentacles slither down his throat briskly, curl around inside his stomach, then come back out. It feels like he's vomiting, except his guts are limp, and a big bolus of something or other is trying to stick in his throat on the way out. For a panicky moment he feels as if he's choking—then the lump tears away with a bright stabbing pain, and he can breathe through his nose again.

"Ah, that's better," he hears distantly. "A beautiful little whistle! Easy to fence to some out-of-body perv, I think. Oh dear, did I say that aloud?" A fuzzy mat of bush tendrils peel away from his face to reveal an unsympathetic face peering down at him. "You *did* hear that, didn't you? Hmm, what a pity. Well, your left kidney is in good shape—"

There's a loud crash from outside the operating theater, followed by a wail from his belt. "In here!" screams his teapot. "Help, please come quickly!"

More crashing. The hacker straightens up, cursing under her breath. Casting around, her gaze falls on Huw's biohazard burka. She grabs it and dives for the back door, sending a gleaming operating cart skidding across the floor. She dives out the back as something large batters at the entrance. The door bulges inward. Huw struggles to sit up, pushing back the suddenly quiescent instrument bush—it feels like wrestling with a half ton of candy floss. *What now?* he thinks wildly.

"In here!" shrieks the djinni, standing in holographic miniature on top of the teapot and waving its arms like a stranded sailor.

"You shut up," Huw grunts. He manages to get his legs off the side of the chair and stumbles against the trolley. Another crash from the front door, and he sees something on the floor— something silvery and cylindrical, about ten centimeters long and one in diameter, for all the world like a pocket recorder covered in slime. *That's it?* he puzzles, and thoughtlessly picks it up and pockets it just as the door gives up the uneven struggle and slams open to admit the two court golems, followed by an extremely irrate hanging judge.

"Arretez-vous!" yells his djinni. "He's over here! Don't let him get away this time!" With a sense of horror, Huw realizes that the little snitch is jumping up and down and pointing at *him.*

"No chance," says Judge Giuliani. "Get him!" she tells the golems, and they lurch toward him. "Your palanquin is outside, waiting to take you to the People's Second Revolutionary Memorial Teaching Hospital. It's quite secure," she adds with an ugly grin. "Asshole. Do you *want* to spread it around? Have you any idea how much trouble you're in already, breaking biocontainment?"

"The—the bastards, set me fucking shitting up—" The Tourette's is threatening to break out, as is a residual urge to burst out in song even as the huge golems clamp inhumanly gentle six-fingered hands the size of ditch-diggers around his arms. "—party in fucking cockass *Monmouth,* fucking minger Bonnie slipped me the shit-shit-shitting godvomit raining on Northern fucking Europe, set me up that wasn't the fucking New Libyan consulate at all, was it? And, and—"

One of the golems slaps a hand over his face. The hand has some kind of flexible membrane on it, with built-in antisound. Huw can hear himself chattering and cursing inside his own head, but nothing's getting out. The golem slowly shrinkwraps his legs together from hip to ankle, and the other golem picks him up under one arm and carries him through the broken front door. The hands of the first golem part easily at the wrist and go with him, a temporary gag.

"We'll discuss the charges later, in my chambers," Giuliani says in his ear. Then she whisks off in a flapping of black-winged robes as the golem lowers Huw into something that looks like a cross between a pedal-powered taxi and an upright coffin.

Bastard fucking bastard must stop fucking swearing, Huw thinks desperately, as he confronts a baby blue padded cell lined with ominous-looking straps. *Bonnie set me up for this, bastard neophiliac, but why did the fucking tin whistle want to talk to the shit-monster? Why was the thing* happy *to hear me—?* He stops as the lid closes behind him, momentarily shocked. Because that *was* the oddest thing about it: the way the godvomit responded to his unwanted flight of song—

As the golems start leaning on the pedals, something squirms in his pocket, like an inquisitive worm. It's the whistle the hacker yanked out of his throat, he realizes, half-horrified that he's locked in with it. *Which is worse,* he asks himself, *a traitorous djinni or a musical instrument that wants to nest in my larynx?*

He gets his answer a moment later as the whistle squirms again, then digs in tiny claws and begins to inch up his shirt. Locked in a small box, on the way to the cells beneath the courthouse, Huw confronts his most primal fear, gives in, and screams himself hoarse behind his antisound gag.

Eventually, his screams taper off. But after a couple of minutes, he feels a heretofore subliminal buzzing against his hip, and screams afresh as he envisions spidery trefoils crawling over his pelvic girdle toward his crotch. Then reason takes over and he realizes that it's his goddamned phone. Squirming around in the cramped box, he pulls it out and shakes it to life, holding it before his mute face. The picture on the other end resolves. Adrian and his bicycle, in some swarming souk. "Wotcher!" Adrian says. Huw waggles his eyebrows frantically at the pinhole cam. The whistle has climbed atop his chest and is stuck crawling in circles as it tries to locate a suitable aperture to return to its nest by.

"Saucy," Adrian says. "Hadn't figured you for bein' inta *that* kink. Met a lucky lady, then?"

Huw shakes his head frantically, rolling his eyes. Slowly, he pans the phone around the box, then brings it back to eye level.

"Oh ho! Not voluntary, then."

Huw nods so fiercely, his head smacks into the padded wall behind him.

"Right, then. See you in two ticks." The picture on the phone swings crazily as Adrian clips it to one of the thousands of clever grabbers on the front of his wash-n-wears and pedals off on the bike. Periodically, his face looms in the screen as he looks down at the positional data that Huw's phone is relaying.

Then Huw is looking at a jittery high-def image of the judge's caravan, at the slowly moving lockbox he's encased in. Adrian holds his phone up again and Huw sees that his eyes are, if anything, redder than they'd been that morning, nearly fluorescent with stoned glee. "You're in there, yeah?" he says, and swings the phone toward the strongbox. Huw nods.

"Hrm." Adrian says, "Tricky." He clips his phone back to his shirt and turns around. Huw sees two young women swathed in paramilitary black bodysuits bulging with cargo pockets and clever sewn-in bandoliers. They exchange rapid hand signals; then the phone's POV wheels sickeningly as Adrian does a tire-torturing doughnut and zips off to the head of the caravan. The camera frames the two impassive golems pumping the pedals of the palanquin. Adrian rolls the bike directly into their path, then makes terrified tourist squeaks as he rolls clear of the frame at the same moment as the golems plow through it. They grind to a sudden halt: their wheels have delaminated on impact with Huw's bike's frame, which has gone into self-defensive hedgehog mode. Huw hears the Vulture croaking enraged threats at Adrian, whom Huw is certain is shrugging with gormless English apologies.

Huw is thrown to one side, losing his phone in the process. A moment later, light scythes into Huw's cell and he's staring up into the eye-slit of a ceramic-reinforced veil. Strong, long-fingered hands lift him free and he's unceremoniously slung over a hard female shoulder. Dangling upside down, he catches a glimpse of the smoking ceiling of the palanquin dissolving into blue goo. The Vulture waves her arms in their direction, her black robe spread out like tattered wings as she screams orders. The golems are lumbering toward them, but in a moment they're in the crowd, lost in the swarm.

The safe house is another inflatable, half-buried in sand and ringed with a memory-wire fence that guards some shepherd's noisome cache of mutant livestock—cows that give chocolate milk, goats that eat scrap plastic and excrete a soft spun cotton analogue, miniature hamstersized chickens that seem even stupider than real chickens and flock like tropical fish. Adrian's already waiting for them when they arrive, standing over the remains of Huw's bicycle.

"Guess you get to keep the hash, old son," Adrian says, kicking the wreckage. "Too bad—it was a lovely ride. I see you've met Maisie and Becky. Becky, love, would you mind setting Huw down now? He's looking a little green and I'm sure he'd appreciate some terror firmer and the removal of that horrid gag."

Neat as that, Huw is sitting plonk on his bottom in the sand, while Adrian laboriously pries back and snaps off each of the golem's fingers. Adrian tosses them to the goats, and Maisie says something to him that Huw can't understand.

Adrian shakes his head. "You worry too much—those buggers'll eat anything."

Once he's free of the gag, Huw gives his jaw an experimental wiggle, then opens his mouth in a wide gasp. While he's catching his breath, the whistle—which has staked out a hiding place behind his left ear—abseils around his jaw, nips inside his mouth, and darts down his throat. "Shit!" Huw chokes: and the whistle nestling in the back of his larynx supplies a buzzing harmonic counterpoint.

"Aha!" says Adrian. "You're the designated carrier, all right. *Excellent*. The sisters want samples, later. You're going to need a bath first, no offense. Come on in," he says, kicking away sand to reveal a trapdoor. Hoisting it open, Adrian exposes a helical slide into the bouncehouse's depths; he slides in feetfirst and spirals down into the darkness.

Huw gasps for breath, balanced on the fine edge between nervousness and stark screaming terror. Normalcy wins: The whistle doesn't hurt, indeed barely feels as if it's there. A goat sidles up behind him with evil in its eyes and leans over his shoulder, sniffing to determine if he's edible; the hot breath on his ear reminds him that he's still alive, and not even unable to talk. One of the Libyan goth ninjettes is squatting patiently by the door. "Hello?" he says, experimentally rubbing his throat.

She shrugs and emits a rapid-fire stream of Arabic. Then, seeing he doesn't understand, she shrugs again and points at the slide. "Oh, I get it," says Huw. He peers at her closely. "Do I know you from somewhere?"

She says something else, this time sharply. Huw sighs. "Okay, I don't know you." His throat feels a bit odd, but not as odd as it ought to for someone who's just swallowed an alien communication device. *I need to know what's going on,* he realizes, eyeing the trapdoor uneasily. *Oh well.* Steeling himself, he lowers his legs into the slide and forces himself to let go.

The room at the bottom is a large bony cavern, its ceiling hung with what look like gigantic otoliths: the floor is carpeted with pink sensory fronds. Adrian is messing around with a very definitely nonsapient teapot on a battered Japanese camping stove. The other one of the ninjette twins is sitting cross-legged on the floor, immersed in some kind of control interface to the Red Crescent omnifab that squats against one wall, burbling and occasionally squirting glutinously to itself. "Ah, there y'are. Cup of tea, mate?" says Adrian.

"Don't mind if I do," Huw replies. "Just what the *fuck fuck fuck clunge-swiving hell*—'scuse me—is going on?" *Who are you and why have you been stalking me from Wales?*

"Siddown." Adrian waves at a beanbag. "Milk, sugar?"

"Both, thanks. Agh—damn. Got anything for-for Tourette's?"

"'Cording to the user manual, it'll go away soon. No worries."

"*User* manual? Sh—you mean this thing comes with a warranty? That sort of thing?"

"Sure." Adrian pours boiling water into the teapot and sets it aside to stew. Then he sits down beside the oblivious Libyan woman and pulls out a stash tin. He begins to roll a joint, chatting as he does so. "It's been spamming to hell and back for the past six months. Seems something up there wants us to, like, *talk* to it. One of the high transcendents, several gazillion subjective years removed from mere humanity. For some years now, it's not had much of a clue about us, but it's finally invented, bred, resurrected, whatever, an interface to the the wossname, human deep grammar engine or whatever they're calling it these days. Sort of like the crappy teapots the embassy issues everyone with. Trouble is, the interface is really specific, so only a few people can assimilate it. You—" Adrian shrugs. "I wasn't involved," he says.

"Who *was?*" asks Huw, his knuckles whitening. "If I find them—"

"It was sort of one of those things," Adrian says. "You know how it happens? Someone does some deep data mining on the proteome and spots a correlation. Posts their findings publicly. Someone else thinks, *Hey, I know that joe,* and invites them to a party along with a bunch of their friends. Someone else spikes the punch while they're chatting up a bit of fluff, and then a prankster at the New Libyan embassy thinks, *Hey, we could maybe rope him into the hanging judge's reality show, howzabout that?* Boy, you can snap your fingers and before you know what's happening, there's a flash conspiracy in action—not your real good old-fashioned secret new world order, nobody can be arsed tracking those things these days, but the next best thing. A self-propagating teleology meme. Goal-seeking Neat Ideas are the most dangerous kind. You smoke?"

"Thanks," says Huw, accepting the joint. "Is the tea ready?"

"Yeah." And Adrian spends the next minute pouring a couple of mugs of extremely strong breakfast tea, while Huw does his best to calm his shattered nerves by getting blasted right out of his skull on hashishim dope.

"'Kay, lemme get this straight. I was never on tech jury call, right? Was a setup. All along."

"Well, hurm. It was a real jury, all right, but that doesn't mean your name was plucked out of the hat at random, follow?"

"All right. Nobody planned, not a conspiracy, just a set of *accidents* 'cause the cloud wants to talk. Huh?" Huw leans back on the beanbag and bangs his head on a giant otolith, setting it vibrating with a deep gut-churning rumble. "'Sh cool stuff. Fucking cloud. Why can't it send a letter if it wanna talk to *me*?"

"Yer the human condition in microcosm, mate. Here, pass the spliff."

"'Kay. So *what* wants to talk?"

"Eh, well, you've met the ambassador already, right? S'okay, Bonnie'll be along in a while with it."

"And whothefuck are *you*? I mean, what're you doing in this?"

"Hell." Adrian looks resigned. "I'm just your ordinary joe, really. Forget the Nobel Prize, that doesn't mean anything. 'S all a team effort these days, anyway, and I ain't done any real work in cognitive neuroscience for thirty, forty years. Tell the truth, I was just bumming around, enjoying my second teenage Wanderjahr when I heard 'bout you through the grapevine. Damn shame we couldn't get a sane judge for the hearing. None of this shit would be necessary if it wasn't for Rosa's thing."

"Rosa—"

"Rosa Giuliani. Hanging judge and reality show host. She's like, a bit conservative. Hadn't you noticed?"

"A bit. Conservative."

"Yeah, she's an old-time environmentalist, really likes conserving things—preferably in formalin. Including anyone who's been infected by a communications vector."

"Oh." Normally this description of Giuliani's politics would fill Huw with the warm fuzzies, but the thing in his throat is a reminder that he's currently further outside his comfort zone than he's ventured in decades. He's still trying to digest the indigestible thought through a haze of amiability-inducing smoke, when the local unplugs herself from the omnifab's console, stands up and stretches, then plugs in a language module.

"Your bicycle will be healed again in a few hours," she says, nodding at Huw, just as the omni burps and then hawks up a passable replica of a Shimano dynamo hub. "Can you put it together with tools?"

"I, uh—" Huw gawks at her. "Do I know you?" he asks. "You look just like this hacker—"

She shrugs irritably. "I am not responsible for my idiot clone-aunts!"

"But you—" He stops. "There are lots of you?"

"Oh yes." She smiles tightly. "Ade, my friend, I am taking a walk. Don't get up to anything I wouldn't."

"I won't, Becky. Promise."

"Good. I'm Maisie, though." She climbs onto a toadstool-shaped bone and rapidly rises toward the ceiling on a pillar of *something* that might be muscle, but probably isn't.

"Lovely girls," Adrian says when she's gone. "Where was I? Ah, yes: the ambassador."

"Ambassador?"

"Yeah, ambassador. It's a special kind of communications node: needs enough brains to talk to that thing in your throat and translate what you send it into something the cloud can work with. You're the interpreter, see. We've been expecting it for a while, but didn't reckon with those idiot script kiddies ending up in court. It'll be along—"

There's a clattering noise behind Huw, and he looks round so abruptly that he nearly falls off his sack, and though he's feeling mellow—far better disposed toward his fellow man than he was an hour ago—it's all Huw can do to refrain from jumping up, shrieking.

"You!" says Bonnie, clutching a large and ominously familiar black box in her arms as she slides to a halt at the foot of the spiral. "Hey, Ade, is this *your* party?"

The box twitches in her arms, as if something inside it is trying to escape. Huw can feel a scream welling up in his throat, and it isn't his—it's a scream of welcome, a paean of politics. He bites it back with a curse. "How the hell did you get that?" he says.

"Stole it while the judge was running after you," Bonnie says. "There's a README with it that says it needs a translator. That would be you, huh?" She looks at him with ill-concealed lust. "Prepare to plug into the ride of your life!"

"God, no," he says.

Adrian pats his shoulder. "Pecker up. It's all for the best."

The box opens and the Kleinmonster bobs a curtsy at him, then warbles. His throat warbles in response. The hash has loosened his vocal cords so that there isn't the same sense of forced labor, just a mellow, easy kind of song. His voices and the Kleinmonster's intertwine in an aural handshake and gradually his sensoria fades away, until he's no longer looking out of his eyes, no longer feeling through his skin, but rather he's part of the Cloudmind, smeared across space and time and a billion identities all commingled and aswirl with unknowable convection currents of thought and deed.

Somewhere there is the Earth, the meatspace whence the Cloudmind has ascended. His point of view inverts and now the

Earth is enveloped in him, a messy gobstopper dissolving in a probabilistic mindmouth. It's like looking down at a hatched-out egg, knowing that once upon a time you fit inside that shell, but now you're well shut of it. Meat, meat, meat. Imperfect and ephemeral and needlessly baroque and kludgy, but it calls to the cloud with a gravitic tug of racial memory.

And then the sensoria recedes and he's eased back into his skin, singing to the Kleinmonster and its uplink to the cloud. He knows he's x-mitting his own sensoria, the meat and the unreasoning demands of dopamine and endorphin. *Ah,* says the ambassador. *Ah. Yes. This is what it was like. Ah.*

Awful.

Terrible.

Ah.

Well, that's done.

The Kleinmonster uncoils and stretches straight up to the ceiling, then gradually telescopes back into itself until it's just a button of faintly buzzing nanocrud. The buzzing gains down and then vanishes, and it falls still.

Bonnie shakes his shoulders. "What happened?" she says, eyes shining.

"Got what it needed," Huw says with a barely noticeable under-drone.

"What?"

"What? Oh, a bit of a reminder, I expect. A taste of the meat."

"That's it?" Bonnie says. "All that for—what? A trip down memory lane? All that fucking work and it doesn't even want to stick around and chat?"

Huw shrugs. "That's the cloud for you. In-fucking-effable. Nostalgia trip, fact-finding mission, what's the difference?"

"Will it be back? I wanted to talk to it about…" She trailed off, blushing. "I wanted to know what it was like."

Huw thinks of what it was like to be part of the matryoshka-brain, tries to put it into words. "I can't quite describe it," he says. "Not in so many words. Not right now. Give me a while, maybe I'll manage it." He's got a nasty case of the pasties and he guzzles a cup of lukewarm milky tea, swirling it around his starchy tongue. "Of course, if you're really curious, you could always join up."

Bonnie looks away and Adrian huffs a snort. "I'll do it someday," she says. "Just want to know what I'm getting into."

"I understand," he says. "Don't worry, I still think you're an anti-human race-traitor, girlie. You don't need to prove anything to me."

"Fucking right I don't!" Bonnie says. She's blushing rather fetchingly.

"Right," Huw says.

"Right."

Huw begins to hum a little, experimenting with his new transhuman peripheral. The drone is quite nice: it reminds him vaguely of a digeridoo. Or bagpipes. He sings a little of the song from the courthouse, in two-part discord. Bonnie's flush deepens and she rubs her palms against her thighs, hissing like a teakettle.

Huw cocks his head at her and leans forward a bit, and she grabs his ears and drags him down on top of her.

Adrian taps him on the shoulder a moment later. "Sorry to

interrupt," he says, "but Judge Rosa's bound to come looking for you eventually. We'd best get you out of Libya sharpish."

Huw ignores him, concentrating on the marimba sensation of Bonnie's rib cage grinding over his chest.

Adrian rolls his eyes. "I'll just go steal a blimp or something, then, shall I?"

Bonnie breaks off worrying Huw's ear with her tongue and teeth and says, "Fuck off a while, will you, Adrian?"

Adrian contemplates the two of them for a moment, trying to decide whether they need a good kick round the kidneys, then turns on his heel and goes off to find Maisie, or perhaps Becky, and sort out an escape.

The entity Huw has mistaken for the whole of the cloud whirls in its orbit, tasting the meat with its multifarious sensory apparat, thinking its in-fucking-effable thoughts, muttering in RF and gravity and eigenstate. The ambassador hibernates on the safe house's floor, prized loose from under Huw's tailbone, where it had been digging rather uncomfortably, quite spoiling Huw's concentration, and tossed idly into a corner. The cloud thing's done with it for now, but its duty-cycle is hardly exhausted, and it wonders what its next use will be.

Huw moans an eerie buzz that sets Bonnie's gut aquiver in sympathy, which is not nearly so unpleasant as it sounds.

In fact, Bonnie thinks she could rather get used to it.

APPEALS COURT

What finally wakes Huw is the pain in his bladder. His head is throbbing, but his bladder has gone weak on him lately—he's been shirking having a replacement fitted—and if he doesn't get up and find the john soon, he's going to piss himself. So he struggles up from a sump hole of somnolence.

He opens his eyes and realizes disappointedly that he's not back home in his own bed: he's lying facedown in a hammock. *Damn, it's not just a bad dream.* The hammock sways gently from side to side in the hot stuffy air. Light streams across him in a warm flood from one side of the room; the floor below the string mesh is gray and scuffed, and something tells him he isn't on land anymore. *Shit,* he thinks, pushing stiffly against the edge and trying not to fall as the hammock slides treacherously out from under him. *Why am I so tired?*

His bare feet touch the ground before he realizes he's bare-ass naked. He rubs his scalp and yawns. His veins feel as if all the blood has been replaced by something warm and syrupy and full of sleep. *Drugs?* he thinks, blinking. The walls—

Three of them are bland, gray sheets of structural plastic with doors in them. The fourth is an outward-leaning pane of plexiglas or diamond or something. A very, very long way below him he can see wave crests.

Huw gulps, his pulse speeding. Something strange is lodged in the back of his throat. He stifles a panicky whistle. There in a corner lie his battered kit bag and a heap of travel-worn clothing. He leans against the wall. *There's got to be a crapper somewhere nearby, hasn't there?* The floor, now he's awake enough to pay attention, is thrumming with a low bass chord from the engines, and the waves are sloshing by endlessly below. As he picks at a dirty shirt, a battered copper teapot rolls away from beneath it. He swears, memories flooding back. Then he picks up the teapot and gives it a resentful rub.

"Wotcher, mate!" The djinni that materializes above the teapot is a hologram, so horribly realistic that for a moment Huw forgets his desperate need for a piss.

"Fuck you too, Ade," he says.

"What kind of way to welcome yer old mate is that, sunshine?" Hologram-Adrian's wearing bush jacket and shorts, a shotgun slung over one shoulder. "How yer feeling, anyway?"

"I feel like I've been shat." Huw rubs his forehead. "Where am I? Where's Bonnie gotten to?"

"Flying the bloody ship. We can't all sleep. Don't worry, she's just hunky-dory. How about you?"

"Flying." Huw blinks. "Where the hell—?"

"You've been sleeping like a baby for a good long while." Ade looks smug. "Don't worry, we got you out of Libya one jump ahead of Rosa. You won't be arriving in Charleston, South Carolina, for another four or five hours, why'n't you kick back and smoke some grass? I left at least a quarter of your stash—"

"*South Carolina?*" Huw screams, nearly dropping the teapot. "Unclefucking sewage filter, what do you want to send me *there* for?"

"Ah, pecker up. They're your coreligionists, aren't they? You won't find a more natural, flesh-hugging bunch on the planet than the Jeezemoids who got left behind by the Rapture. Hell, they're the kind of downhome Luddites what make *you* look like Saint Kurzweil."

"They're *radioactive*," Huw says. "And I'm an atheist. They burn atheists at the stake, don't they?" He rummages through his skanky clothes, turning them inside out as he searches for something not so acrawl that he'd be unwilling to have it touch his nethers.

"Oh, hardly," says Adrian. "Just get a little activated charcoal and iodine in your diet and memorize the Lord's Prayer and you'll be fine, sonny."

Huw ends up tying a T-shirt around his middle like a diaper and seizing the teapot, which has developed a nasty rattle in its guts.

"Breakfast and toilet. Not in that order. Sharp."

"That door there," says the miniaturized Adrian, pointing.

The zeppelin turns out to be a maryceleste, crewed by capricious iffrits whose expert systems were trained by angry, resentful trade unionists in ransom for their pensions. The amount of abuse required to keep the ship on course and its commissary and sanitary systems in good working order is heroic.

Huw opens the door to the bridge, clutching his head, to find Bonnie perched on the edge of a vast, unsprung chair, screaming imprecations at the air. She breaks off long enough to scream at him. **"Get the fuck off my bridge!"** she hollers, eyes wild, fingers clawing at the armrests.

Huw leaps back a step, dropping the huge, suspicious sausage he's been gnawing from one end of. His diaper unravels as he stumbles.

Bonnie snorts, then gets back control. "Aw, sorry, darlin'. I'm hopped up on hateballs. It's the only way I can get enough **fucking spleen** to **make this buggery bollocky scum-sucking ship** go where I tell it." She sighs and digs around the seat cushion, coming up with a puffer, which she inserts briefly into the corner of each eye. The tension melts out of her skinny shoulders and corded neck as Huw watches, alarmed.

"You look like a Welsh Gandhi," she tells him, giggling. Her lips loll loose; she stands and rolls over toward him with a half-drunken wobble. Then she throws her arms around his neck and fastens her teeth on his shoulder, worrying at his trapezium.

The teapot whistles appreciatively. Bonnie gives it a savage kick that sends it skittering back into the corridor.

"You need a wash, beautiful," she says. "Unfortunately, it's going to have to be microbial. Nearly out of fresh water. Tub's up one level."

"Gak," Huw says.

"'Snot so bad."

"It's *bugs*," he says.

"You're hosting about three kilos of bugs right now. What're a few more? Go."

Huw picks up his sausage. "You know where we're going, right?"

"Oh aye," she says, her eyes gleaming, then whistles a snatch of "America the Beautiful."

"And you approve?"

"Always wanted to see it."

"They'll burn you at the stake!"

She picks up a different puffer and spritzes each eye, then bares her teeth in a savage rictus. "I'd like to see them fucking try. **Bathe, you cretinous stenchpot!**"

Huw settles himself among the soup of heated glass beads and bacteria and tries not to think of a trillion microorganisms gnawing away at his dried skin and sweat.

He mutters transhuman curses in groaning harmony at the battered teapot—no longer hosting the avatar of a particularly annoying iffrit, but evidently hacked by Ade and his international cadre of merry pranksters. "Why South Carolina? G'wan, you. Why *there*, of all places?"

He isn't expecting a reply, but the teapot crackles for a moment;

then a translucent holo of Ade appears in the air above it, wearing a belly dancer's outfit and a sheepish expression. "Yer wot? Ah, sorry mate. Feckin' trade union iffrit's trying to make an alpha buffer attack on my sprites." The image flickers then solidifies, this time wearing a bush jacket again. "Like, why South Carolina? To break the embargo, Huw. Ever since the snake-handlers crawled outta the swamps and figured the Rapture had been and gone and left 'em behind, they've been waiting for a chance at salvation, so I figured I'd give them you." Ade's likeness grins wickedly as red horns sprout from his forehead. "You and the back channel to the ambassador from the cloud. They want to meet God so bad, I figured you'd maybe like to help the natives along."

"But they're radioactive!" Huw says, shaking his fist at the teapot with a rattle of yeast-scented beads. "And they're lunatics! They won't talk to the rest of the world, because we're corrupt degenerate satanists; they claim sovereignty over the entire solar system even though they can't launch a sodding rocket; and they burn dissidents to death by wiring them up to transformers! Why would I want to *help* them?"

"Because your next mission, should you choose to accept it, is to open them up to the outside universe again." Ade smirks at him from atop the teapot.

"Fuck." Huw subsides into the fizzing bath of beads, which are beginning to itch. Moving them around brings relief, although it's making him a little piebald. "You want to infect the Fallen Baptist Congregations with godvomit, you be my guest—just let me watch from another continent, all right?"

"That's an idea," says Ade, scratching his beard absentmindedly.

"Shame it's not going to fly. But tell you what, Bonnie's one of our crack agents. Don't you worry, we wouldn't risk our prophet-at-large in a backwater, mate. We'll keep you safe as houses."

Huw thinks of Sandra Lal, the House of the Week club, and her mini-sledge, and shudders. His arse is beginning to itch as the bacteribeads try to squeeze through his ringpiece: it's time to get out. "If this goes wrong, so help me, I am going to make you eat this teapot," he says, picking it up. He heads downstairs to find Bonnie again and see if she's come down far enough off the hateballs to appreciate how squeaky-clean Ade's messiah manqué is feeling.

The big zeppelin lurches and buzzes as it chases its shadow across the black tarry beaches and the out-of-control neomangrove jungle that has run wild across the Gulf coast. The gasoline mangroves spin their aerofoil leaves in the breeze, harnessing the wind power and pumping long-chain terpenoids into their root systems, which ultimately run all the way to the hydrocarbon refineries near Beaufort. A long-obselete relic of the feverish cross-fertilization of the North American biotechnology biz with the dinosaurs of the petroleum age, they ought by rights to have made the United States the world's biggest source of refined petrochemicals—except that since the singularity, nobody's buying. Oil slicks glisten in the sunlight as they spread hundreds of kilometers out into the Atlantic, where they feed a whole deviant ecosystem of carbon-sequestrating petroplankton maintained by the continental quarantine authority.

Huw watches apprehensively from the observation window at the front of the bridge as Bonnie curses and swears at the iffrits, who insist that air traffic control is threatening to shoot them down if they don't steer away from the land of the Chosen People. Bonnie's verbal abuse of the ship ascends to new heights of withering scorn, and he watches her slicken her eyeballs with anger-up until they look like swollen golf balls, slitted and watering. The ship wants to turn itself around, but she's insisting that it plow on.

"Hail ground control **now!** you fucking sad, obsolete piece of shit, so that for once, **just! for! once!** you will have done one genuinely **useful!** thing for **someone!**" She snarls and coughs, hacking up excess angry-up that has trickled back through her sinuses. She picks up the mic and begins to stalk the bridge like an attack comedian scouting the audience for fat men with thin dates to humiliate.

"This is Charleston Ground Control repeating direct order to vacate sovereign Christian States of America airspace immediately or be blown out of the sky and straight to Satan. Charleston Ground Control out." The voice has the kind of robotic-slick Californian accent that tells Huw straightaway that he's talking to a missile guidance computer rather than a human being.

"**Hail! him! again!**" Bonnie yells, hopping from foot to foot. "Arrogant Jesus-sucking sack of SARS, scabrous toddler-fondler, religion-addled motherfucker," she says, punching out with the mic for punctuation.

"Bonnie," Huw says quietly, flinching back from her candy apple red eyeballs.

"What?"

"Maybe you should let me talk with them?" he says.

"I am **perfectly!** capable of negotiating with **microcephalic! god! bothering! luddites!**" she screeches.

No, you're not, Huw thinks, but he doesn't even come close to saying it. In the state she's in, she could lift a car and set it down on top of a baby, a reversal of the legendary maternal hysterical feat of strength. "Yes, you *are,*" he says. "But you need to fly the ship."

She glares at him for a moment, fingernails dug so hard into her palms that drops of blood spatter to the flooring. He's sure that she's going to charge him, but the zeppelin changes direction with a lurch. So she throws the mic at his head viciously—he ducks, but it still beans him on the rebound—and goes back to screaming at the ship.

Huw staggers off the bridge and sinks back against one of the bare corridor bulkheads—the zep that Adrian's adventurers stole is made doubly cavernous by the absence of most of its furnishings.

"This is *Airship Lollipop* to Charleston Ground Control requesting clearance to land in accordance with the Third International Agreement on Aeronautical Cooperation," he says into the mic, using his calmest voice. He's pretty sure he's heard of the Third International Agreement, though it may have been the Fourth. And it may have been on Aeronautical Engineering. But that there is an agreement he is certain, and he's pretty sure that the Christian States of America is no more up to date on international affairs than he is.

"Airship *Lollipop,* y'all welcome to land here, but we's having trouble convincing with this darned strategic defense battle computer that thinks y'all are goddless Commie-fag euroweasels. I reckon you got maybe two minutes to repent before it blows y'all to Jesus."

Huw breathes a sigh of relief: at least there's a human in the loop. "How do we convince it we're not, uh, godless Commie-fag euroweasels?" he asks, suppressing a twinge as he realizes that, in fact, he and Bonnie meet about 130 percent of those criteria between them.

"That's easy, y'all just gotta have a little faith," says the airhead on the traffic control desk.

Huw grits his teeth and looks through the doorway at Bonnie, whose ears appear to be smoking. He puts a hand over the mic: "Does this thing carry missiles?" he calls to her.

"Fucking fucking arse shit bollocks—" Bonnie hammers on a control panel off to one side. It bleeps plaintively, the ancient chime of servers rebooting "—'ing **countermeasures** suite!"

"Hasta la vista, sinners," drawls the missile launch computer in a thick gubernatorial Austro-Californian accent. Two pinpricks of light blossom on the verdant horizon of the gasoline mangroves, then a third that rapidly expands into a fireball as the antique pre-cloud hypersonic missile explodes on launch. The surviving missiles stab toward them and there's a musical chime from the countermeasures control panel. Huw feels a moment of gut-slackening terror. "You've got mail!" the countermeasures system announces in the syrupy tones of a kindergarten teacher. "Facebook-Goldman-AOL welcomes you to the United States of America. You have 14,023 new friend requests, which you will receive after this message from our sponsors. Your hen wants milking, your goat has been turned into a zombie, there are 14,278,123 new status updates, and you have been defriended 1,974,231 times. There are 5,348,011 updates to the privacy policy for your review."

Bonnie thumps something on the panel, muscles like whipcord standing out on her arm as she glares at the oncoming missiles. Huw backs away. *She might actually be a communicant,* he realizes in absolute horror. *She might actually have a Facebook account! She's mad enough...* These days, tales of what Facebook did with its users during the singularity are commonly used to scare naughty children in Wales.

"Acknowledged," says the possessed countermeasures suite in the hag-ridden tone of a computer that has surrendered to the dark side. For a moment nothing seems to happen; then one of the onrushing pinpricks of light veers toward the other. Paths cross then diverge in a haze of debris. "Displaying new privacy policy," it sighs.

"Don't read it!" Huw screams, but he's too late—Bonnie has punched the console again, and messages begin scrolling across it. In the middle distance, Charleston airport's cracked and vitrified runways are coming into view. Missile batteries off to one side cycle their launcher-erectors impotently, magazines long since fired dry at the godless Commie-fag euroweasel aid flights.

"We gotta bail out before we land, otherwise we'd have to go through customs," she says. "That would be bad—South Carolina never ended Prohibition."

"What? Prohibition of what? What are you talking about?"

His hands are shaking, he realizes. "I need a drink."

"Prohibition of everything, **dipshit**," Bonnie says. She pauses for a moment, prodding at her eyes with a mister, but they are so swollen that she can't get its applicator into contact with bare mucous membrane. She roots around some more, then whacks some kind of transdermal plaster on her arm. "Sorry, gotta **arse fuck** come down now. Your stash, darling? It's illegal here. If the customs crows catch you with it, they'll stick you on the chain gang and you'll be chibbed and **fuck raped baby-eating murdered** by psychotic mutant Klansmen for the next two hundred years. It's bad for the skin, I hear." She stands up and heads toward a battered cabinet at the rear of the bridge, which she opens to reveal a couple of grubby-looking parachutes that appear to have been hand-packed with all due care and attention by stoned marmosets. "We'll be passing over the hot tub in about three minutes. You coming?"

The parachute harness she hands him is incredibly smelly—evidently its last owner didn't believe in soap—but its flight control system assures Huw that it's in perfect working order and please to extinguish all cigarettes and switch off all electronics for the duration of the flight. Tight-lipped, Huw fastens it around his waist and shoulders, then follows Bonnie to the back of the bridge and down a rickety ladder to the bottom of the gas bag. There's an open hatch, and when he looks through it, he sees verdant green foliage whipping past at nearly a hundred kilometers per hour, hundreds of meters below. "Clip the red hook to the blue static line eye," says the harness. "Clip the—"

"I get the picture," Huw says. Bonnie is already hooked up,

and turns to check his rig, then gives him a huge shit-eating grin and steps backwards into the airship's slipstream. "Aagh!" Huw flinches and stumbles, then follows her willy-nilly. Seconds later the chute unfolds its wings above him, and his ears are filled with the sputtering snarl of a two-stroke motor as it switches to dynamic flight and banks to follow Bonnie down toward a clearing in the mangrove swamp.

The swamp rushes up to meet him in a confusion of green, buffeting him with superheated steam as he descends toward it, so that by the time the chute punches him through the canopy, he's as steamed as a dim sum bun. Bonnie's chute speeds ahead of him, breaking branches off and clattering from tree to tree. He tries to follow its crazy trail as best as he can, but eventually he realizes, with a sick falling sensation in his stomach, that she's no longer strapped into it. "Bonnie!" he yells, and grabs at the throttle control.

"Danger! Stall warning!" the parachute intones. "Guru Meditation Code 14067."

Huw looks down dizzily. He's skimming the ground now, or what passes for it—muck of indeterminate depth, interspersed with clumps of curiously nibbled-looking water hyacinth. The tree line starts in another couple of hundred meters, and it's wall-to-wall petroleum plants. Black leafed and ominous looking, the stunted inflammabushes emit a dizzying stench of raw gasoline that makes his eyes swim and his nose water. "Fuck, where am I going to land?"

"Please fold your tray table and return your seat to the upright position," says the parachute control system. "Extinguish all joints, switch off mobile electronics, and prepare for landing." The engine note above and behind him changes, spluttering and backfiring, and then the damp muck comes up and slaps him hard across the ankles. Huw stumbles, takes a faltering step forward—then the nanolight's engine drops down as the chute rigging collapses above his head and thumps him right between the eyes with a hollow *tonk*.

"What you've got to understand, son," says the doctor, "is it's all the fault of the alien space bats." He holds up the horse syringe and flicks the barrel. A bubble wobbles slowly up through the milky fluid. "If it wasn't for them and their Jew banker patsies, we'd be ascended to heaven." He squeezes the plunger slightly and a thick blob of turbid liquid squeezes out of the syringe and oozes down the needle. "Carbon traders damned us to this living hell." He grins horribly, baring gold-plated teeth, and points the end of the needle at Huw's neck. Huw can't move his gaze from Doc's mustache: it's huge and bushy, a hairy efflorescence that twitches suspiciously as the barefoot medic inhales with sharp disapproval.

"Carbon traders?" Huw's voice sounds weak, even to himself. He stares past the doctor at the peeling white paint on the wall of this sorry excuse for a medical center. "What have they got to do with—?"

"Carbon traders." Doc nods as he rams the blunt tip of the quarter-inch needle against Huw's jugular. Machines whine and click, and the side of Huw's neck goes numb. "Once the children of Mammon started floating credit-default swaps against carbon remediation bonds, the whole planet became worth more if it was on fire than if it was fulla trees. So now you've got all these trillion-dollar bets that'll go bust if the polar caps don't melt, and it wasn't long afore the polar caps were worth more melted than intact, and well, the market provided the incentives. Now look at us."

Huw tries to swallow. The plunger is going down, and white goo is flooding into his circulatory system, billions of feral redneck nanomachines bouncing off his fur-lined arteries in search of damaged tissue to fix. His mouth is parched, his tongue as crinkly and musty-dry as a dead cauliflower. "But the, the alien—"

"Alien space bats, son," says Doc. He sighs lugubriously and pulls the syringe away from Huw's neck. "With their fancy orbital Fresnel lens. *They're* behind the global warming thing, y'see, it's nothing to do with burning oil. It dates to the fifties. Those closet Commies in with their astronomy toys, they were smart—using tax-funded astrophysics instruments to signal the space brothers! Seeing as how God made us a strongly anthropic universe to live in, it stands to reason there must be aliens out there. It's a long-term plot, a two hundred-year Communist plan to bankrupt America. And it's working. All those deserters and traitors who upped and left when the singularity hit, they just made it worse. They're the savvy ones we need to make this country great again, rebuild NASA and Space Command, but do it right, pure American, deep background checks and purity oaths, and go wipe those no-good Ruskie alien space bats and their Jew banker patsies from the dark side of the moon."

Oh Jesus fuck, Huw thinks incoherently, lying back and trying to get both eyes to focus simultaneously. He still feels sick to his stomach and a bit dizzy, the way he's been since Bonnie found him neatly curled up under a gas tree with a huge lump on his head and his parachute rigging draped across the incendiary branches. "Have you seen my teapot?" he tries to say, but he's not sure it comes out right.

"You want a cup of joe?" asks Doc. "Sure, we can do that." He pats Huw's shoulder with avuncular charm. "You just lie there and let my little helpers eat the blood clots in your brain for a while."

"Bonnie—" Huw whispers, but Doc is already standing and turning toward the door at the other side of the surgery, out of his line of sight. The blow from the motor did something worse to him than concussion, and he can't seem to move his arms or legs—or neck. *I'm still breathing, so it can't be that bad,* he tells himself hopefully. *Remember, if you break your neck during a botched parachute landing and then a mad conspiracy theorist injects black market nanomachines into you, it's highly unlikely that anything worse can happen before sundown,* he tells himself in a spirit of misplaced optimism.

And things are, indeed, looking up compared to where they were an hour or two ago. Bonnie had found him, still unconscious, lying at the foot of a tree that was already dribbling toxic effluent across his boots. The teapot was screaming for help at the top of its tinny electronic lungs as an inquisitive stream of brick red ants crawled over its surface, teaming up to drag it back to one wing of the vast sprawling supercolony that owned the continent. The ants stung, really, really hard. And there were *lots* of them, like a tide sweeping over his body. It was Bonnie who'd signaled Doc, using some kind of insane spatchcock mobile phone jury-rigged from the wreckage of her parachute harness to broadcast on all channels for help, and it was Bonnie who'd sat beside him, whispering sweet nothings and occasionally whacking impudent *formicidae,* until Doc hove into view on his half-rusted swamp boat. But she'd vanished, not sticking around to explain to Doc how come she and Huw were at large in the neverglades—and the doc seemed mad about that.

After a couple of hours on the operating table, Huw has discovered that half an hour can be a very long time indeed when your only company is a demented quack and you can't even scratch your arse by way of entertainment. And his arse *itches*. In fact, it's not all that itches. Up and down his spine, little shivers of tantalizing irritation are raising gooseflesh. "Shitbiscuits," he mumbles as his left hand begins to tremble uncontrollably. The nanobots have reached the swollen, damaged tissues within his cervical vertebrae and are busily reducing the swelling. They're coaxing suicidal neurons back into cytocellular stability, laying temporary replacement links where apoptosis has already proceeded to completion, and generally repairing the damage Huw's supine spinal cord has received. For which Huw is incredibly grateful—if Doc were as nuts as he seems, he might have injected an auto engine service pack and Huw might at this very moment be gestating a pile of gleaming ceramic piston rings—but it *itches* with the fire of a thousand ants crawling inside his veins. "Balls on a tea towel," he says. And then his toes begin to tremble.

By the time Doc reappears, Huw is sitting up, albeit as shaky as an ethanol addict in the first week of withdrawal. He moans quietly as he accepts a chipped mass-produced Exxon mug full of something dark and villainous enough that it resembles a double-foam latte, if the barista substituted Gulf crude for steamed milk. "Thanks," he manages to choke out. "I think. I hope Bonnie comes back soon."

"That godless sinning harridan?" Doc cranks one eyebrow up until it teeters alarmingly. "Naw, son, you don't want to be going worrying about the likes of her. She's bad company, her and her crew—between you and me, I figure she's in league with the space bats." He chuckles. "Naw, you'll be much better off with me an' Sam. Ade told us all about you and what you're here for. We'll set you straight."

"Ade. Told you." Huw's stomach does a backflip, which feels extremely strange because something is wrong with his body image. It feels all wrong inside. He clears his throat and almost chokes: the alien whistle-thing-communicator is gone! Then his stomach gives a warning twinge and his momentary flash of hope fades. The godvomit has simply retreated deeper into his gastrointestinal tract, hiding to bide its time like a bad plot twist in a Tamil robo-apocalypse movie. "How'd you know him?"

"'Cause we do a bit of business from time to time." Doc's eyebrow relaxes as he grins at Huw. "A little light smuggling, son. Don't let it get on your nerves. Ade told us what to do with you, and everything's going to be just fine."

"Just fine—" Huw stops. "What are you going to do with me?" he asks.

"Ade figures we oughta deliver you to the Baptist temple in Glory City—that's Charleston as was—in time for next Thursday's memorial service. It's the forty-sixth anniversary of the Rapture, and they get kinda jumpy at this time of year." A meaty hand descends on Huw's shoulder and he looks round, then up, and up until his newly fixed neck aches at the sight of a large, completely hairless man with skin the color of a dead fish and little piggy eyes. "Son, this is Sam. Say hello, Sam."

"Hello, Sam," rumbles the human mountain. Huw blinks.

"You're going to hand me over to the Baptists?" he asks. "What happens then?"

"Well." Doc scratches his head. "That's up to you, isn't it?"

"But this anniversary. What do you mean, they get jumpy?"

"Oh, nothing much. Just sacrifice a bunch of heretics to make God notice they still believe, that kinda thing. You got a problem with that?"

"Maybe." Huw licks his lips. "What if I don't want to go?"

"Well, then." Doc cocks his head to one side and squints at Huw's left ear. "Say, son, that's a mightly nice ear you've got there. Seeing as how you've not paid your medical bill, I figure we'd have to take it off you to cover the cost of your treatment. Plus maybe a leg, a kidney, and an eye or two. How about it?"

"No socialized medicine here!" rumbles Sam as a second backhoe-sized hand closes around Huw's other shoulder.

"Okay! I'll do it! I'll do it!" Huw says.

Doc beams amiably at him. "That calls for a shot of shine," says the medic. "I *knew* you'd see sense. Now, about the alien space bats. We've got this here telescope that Sam liberated when they were burning the university—hive of godless heretics—but we don't know how to work it proper. Have you ever used one? We're looking for the bat cave on the moon..."

Welcome to the American future, at the dusk of the twenty-first century.

Over the years and decades since the singularity, the ant colony has taken the entire Atlantic coast of the United States, has marched on Georgia and west to the Mississippi. It is an anarchist colony, whose females lay eggs without regard for any notional Queen, and it has just entered its fiftieth year of life, which is Methuselah-grade longevity by normal ant colony standards, but may be just the beginning for the Hypercolony.

The God-botherers have no treaty with the ants, but have come to view them as another proof of the impending end of the world. Anything that is not contained in chink-free, seamless plastic and rock is riddled by ant tunnels within hours. They've learned to establish airtight seals around their homes and workplaces, to subject themselves to stinging insecticide showers before clearing a vestibule, to listen for the Tupperware burp whenever they seal their children in their space suits and send them off to Bible classes.

The ants have eaten through most of the nematode species beneath the soil, compromised all but the most plasticized root systems of the sickening flora. (The gasoline-refining forests are curiously symbiotic with the colony—anarchist supercolonies like living cheek-by-mouthpart with a lot of hydocarbons.) They've eaten the beehives and wasp nests, and they've laid waste to any comestible not tinned and sealed, leaving the limping Americans with naught but a few trillion tons of processed food to eat before their supply bottoms out.

The American continent is a very Grimm fairy tale that the cloud dwellers review whenever one faction or another doubts its decision to abandon Earth-bound humanity. The left-behinds there spend their lives waiting for an opportunity to pick up a megaphone and organize crews with long poles to go digging through the ruins of civilization for tinned goods. Presented with their opportunity in the aftermath of the Geek Rapture, they are happy as evangelical pigs in shit—plenty to rail against, plenty of fossil fuel, plenty of firearms.

What more could they possibly need?

Once it becomes clear that Huw is prepared to go to Glory City, the doc comes all-over country hospitality, and details Sam with the job of getting him properly lubricated. They watch the sunset through the Tupperware walls of the doc's homestead, gazing out at the thick carpet of ants swarming over the outer walls as they chase the last of the sun across the surface. When the sun finally sets, the sound of a billion tromping feet keeps them company.

"Well," says Doc, nodding at Sam. "Looks like it's time to hit the road."

Huw sits up straight. Glory City is *not* on his agenda, but if he's going to make a break for it, he wants to do it somewhere a bit more crowded and anonymous than here, right in the middle of

Doc's home turf. Plus, he's still weak as a kitten from gasoline-tainted corn mash and the nanos knitting busily in his guts.

"We'll take the bikes," Doc says with an affable nod. "Go get 'em, Sam."

Sam thuds off toward an outbuilding, the plasticized floors dimpling under his feet.

"He's a good boy," says Doc. "But I figure I used too many cognitive enhancers on him when he was a lad. Made him *way* too smart for his own good."

Sam returns with a serious-looking anime-bike dangling from each hand. "alt.pave-the-earth," he says, setting them down. His voice is bemused, professorial. "I'll go get the sidecar."

"He'll need a space suit," Doc calls after him. "What're you, about a medium?"

Huw, staring wordlessly at the stretched and striated bikes with their angular moldings, opens his mouth. "I'm a 107-centimeter chest," he says.

"Ah, we don't go in for that metric eurofaggotry around here, son. Don't really matter much. Space suits never fit too good. You'll get used to it. It's only six hours."

Sam returns with a low-slung sidecar under one arm and a suit of Michelin Man armor over his shoulders.

"It's very ergonomic," he says tectonically as he sits the suit down next to Huw's folding lawn chair, then goes to work attaching the car to one of the bikes.

Huw fumbles with the Michelin suit, eventually getting the legs pulled on.

"Binds a bit at the crotch," he says, hoping for some sympathy.

"Yeah, it'll do that," says Doc.

Huw modestly turns his back and reaches down to adjust himself. As he does so, he fumbles with the familiar curve of the brass teapot. Peeking down, he sees a phosphorescent miniature holographic Ade staring back up at him.

"Quick! Hide me," Adrian says.

Huw puts his hand where he'd expect to find a pocket, and a little hatch pops open, exposing a hollow cavity in the thigh. He sneaks the teapot into it and dogs the hatch shut. "I'm ready, I think," he says, turning round again.

Doc and Sam have already suited up; they're waiting impatiently for Huw to get ready. The bikes are bolted either side of the sidecar, and Doc waves Huw into the cramped seat in the middle. Waddling in the suit, clutching a portable aircon pack, Huw has a hard time climbing in. Everything sounds muffled except the whirr of the helmet fans. A pronounced smell of stale BVDs and elderly rubber assaults his nose periodically, as if the suit is farting in his face. "Let's go," Sam says, and they kick off toward the doorway, which irises open to admit a trickling rain of ants as the bikes roar and spurt gouts of flame against the darkness.

The blast of the jet engines doesn't die down, nor does the laser-show strobing off the pixelboards on the outsized fuel tanks, but somehow Huw manages to snooze through the next couple of hours: it's probably the moonshine. Doc is rambling at length about some recondite point of randite ideology, illuminating his own rugged self-reliance with the merciless glare of A-is-A objectivist clarity, but after a few minutes Huw discovers two controls on his chest plate that raise his opinion of the suit designers: a drinking straw primed with white lightning, and the volume control on the radio. As his sort-of jailers drive him along a potholed track lined with the filigree skeletons of ant-nibbled trees, he kicks back and tries to get his head together. If it wasn't for the eventual destination, he could almost begin to enjoy himself, but there's a nagging sense of weirdness in his stomach (where the godvomit still nestles, awaiting a communicative impulse) and he can't help worrying about what he'll do once they get to Glory City.

An indeterminate time passes, and Huw is awakened by a sharp prodding pain near his bladder. "Uh." He lolls in the suit, annoyed.

"Psst, keep it quiet. They think you're sleeping." The prodding sensation goes away, replaced by a buzzing voice from just north of his bladder.

"Ade?" Huw whispers.

"No, it's the tooth fairy. Listen, have you seen Bonnie?"

"Not lately. She went for—" Huw pauses. "You know I landed bad?"

"Shit. So that's why you're with Doc. Have they got her?"

"No." Huw desperately wants to scratch his head in puzzlement, but his arms are folded down inside the sidecar and he doesn't dare let Sam or Doc figure he's awake. "Look, I woke up and the doctor—*is* he a real doc?—was trying to fix my neck. A motor fell on my head. Bonnie got him to help, but then she left and I haven't seen her."

"Cholera and crummy buttons." Ade's tinny voice sounds

upset. "They're not trustworthy, mate. Sell you as soon as look at you, those two. She *said* you were hurt, but—"

"You don't know where she is, either," Huw says.

"Nope." They ride along in near silence for a while.

"What's the big idea?" Huw asks, trying to sustain a sense of detachment. "Packing me off to bongo-bongo land to convert the cannibals is all very fucking well, but I thought you said this would be safe as houses?"

"Um, well, there's been a kinda technical hitch in that direction," Adrian says. "But we'll get that sorted out, don't you worry yer little head over it. Main thing is, you don't wanna stay with the randroids any longer than you have to, got that? Show 'em a clean pair of heels, mate. When you get to Glory City, head for the John the Baptist Museum of Godless Evolution and find the Steven Jay Gould Lies and Blasphemy exhibit. There's a trapdoor under the *Hallucigenia* mock-up leading to an atheist's hole, and if you get there, I'll send someone to pick you up. 'Kay?"

"Wait—" Huw says, but he's too late. The buzzing stops, just as Doc reaches over and cuffs Huw around the helmet. "What?" Huw cranks the volume on his suit radio.

"—said, you paying attention, boy?" Doc demands. There's a suspicious gleam in his eye, although Huw isn't certain it isn't just the effect of looking at him through a thin layer of toughened glass across which wander a handful of very lost ants.

"I was asleep," Huw says.

"Bah." Doc rubs off the ants, then grabs the brakes. "Well, son, I was just saying: only a couple of hours now until we get there..."

The road is unlit and there's little traffic. What there is seems to consist mostly of high-tech bicycle rickshaws retrofitted for unapologetic hydrocarbon combustion, and ancient rusting behemoth pickups that belch thick blue petroleum smoke— catalytic converters and fuel cells being sins against man's deity-designated dominance over nature. The occasional wilted and ant-nibbled wreaths plaintively underscore the messages on the tarnished and bullet-speckled road signs: KEEP RIGHT and SLOW TRUCKS.

The landscape is dotted with buildings that have the consistency of halvah. These are the remains of man's folly and his pride, now bored out of 90 percent of their volume to fill the relentless bellies of the Hypercolony. Individually, the ants crawling across his faceplate—also along his gauntlets, over the sexy sizzle of the LEDs, and crisped up in a crust around the flame-nozzles—appear to be disjointed and uncoordinated. But now, here, confronted with the evidence of the Hypercolony's ability to coordinate collective action from its atomic units, Huw is struck with a deep, atavistic terror. There is an Other here, loose on the continent, capable of bringing low all that his kind has built. Suddenly, Huw's familiar corporeality, the source of so much personal pride, starts to feel like a liability.

The aircon unit makes a sputtery noise that Huw feels rather than hears through the cavities of the Michelin suit. He's tried wiggling the aircon umblicus in its suit-seal, but now the air coming out of it is hot and wet and smells of burning insulation.

He's panting and streaming with sweat by the time the dim white dome of Glory City swims out of the darkness ahead to straddle the road like a monstrous concrete carbuncle. Sam guns the throttle like a tireless robot, while Doc snores in the saddle, his mouth gaping open beneath his mustache, blurred behind the ant-crawling Lexan of his faceplate. "How much longer?" Huw says, the first words he's spoken in an hour.

"Three miles. Then we park up and take a room for the night in Saint Pat's Godly Irish Motel. No smoking, mind," Sam adds.

Huw stares in grim, panting silence as they take the uphill slope toward the base of the massive, kilometers-high Fuller dome that caps the former city. Impregnated with neurotoxins, the dome is the ultimate defense against the Hypercolony. They ride into the city past a row of gibbeted criminals, their caged bones picked clean by ants, then into the deserted and gaping air lock, large enough to accommodate an armored batallion. What Huw initially takes for an old-fashioned air-shower turns out to be a gas chamber, venting something that makes his throat close when he gets a hint of a whiff of it through the suit's broken aircon. After ten minutes of gale-force nerve gas, most of the ants are washed away, and those that remain appear to have died. Sam produces a stiff whisk broom and, with curious gentleness, brushes him free of the few thousand corpses that have become anchored by their mouthparts to his suit. Then he hands Huw the whisk so that he may return the favor. Only after they are all thoroughly decontaminated do the inner doors to Glory City open wide, sucking them into the stronghold of the left-behind.

Once within the dome, Huw finds that Glory City bears little resemblance to any media representations of pre-singularity NorAm cities he's ever seen. For one thing, the roads are narrow and the buildings tall, leaning together like a sinister crowd of drunkards, the olde-world, olde-town feel revived to make maximum use of the cubic volume enclosed by the dome. For another thing, about half the tallest buildings seem to be spiky towers, like the old medieval things back home that he associates with seamy nightclubs. It takes him a moment to realize: *Those are churches!* He's never imagined so many temples existing before, let alone in a single city.

The next thing he notices are the adverts. They're everywhere. On billboards and paving stones and the sides of parked monster trucks. (And, probably, tattooed on the hides of the condemned prisoners outside before the ants ate them.) Half the ads are public service announcements, and the other half are religious slogans. It's hard to know which category some go in: ENJOY CHRIST ON A SHINGLE: ALL THE ZEST HALF THE CALORIES LOWER GLYCEMIC INDEX! Whichever they are, they set his teeth on edge—so that he's almost happy when Sam steers him into a cramped parking lot behind a tall gray slab of concrete and grunts, "This is the motel."

It's about two in the morning, and Huw catches himself yawning as Sam shakes Doc awake and extracts him from the sidecar. "C'mon in," says Doc. "Let's get some sleep. Got a long day tomorrow, son."

The lobby of the motel is guarded by a fearsome-looking cast-iron gate. Huw unlatches his faceplate and heaves a breath: the air is humid and warm, cloying and laden with decay as sweet as a rotting tooth. Doc approaches the concierge's desk while Sam hangs back, one meaty hand gripping Huw's arm proprietorially. "Don't you go getting no clever ideas," Sam says like a quiet earthquake. "Doc tagged you with a geotracker chip. You go running away, you'll just get him riled."

"Uh. Okay." Huw dry-swallows the muck lining his teeth.

Doc is at the desk, talking to a woman in long black dress. She wears a bonnet that looks like it's nailed to her head, and she's *old*, showing all the distressing signs of physical senescence. "Twenty cents for the suite," she says, "and fifteen for the pen." (Post-imperial deflation has taken its toll on the once-mighty dollar.) She wags a wrinkled finger under Doc's nose: "And none of your filth!"

Doc draws himself up to his full height. "I assure you, I am here to do the Lord's work," he says. "Along with this misguided creep. And my assistant."

Sam pushes Huw forward. "Doc gets the presidential suite whenever he stays here," he says. "You get to sleep in the pen."

"The—?"

"'Cause we don't rightly trust you," Sam says, pushing Huw toward a side door behind the reception area. "So a little extra security is called for."

"Oh—" Huw says, and stops. *Oh, really now,* Huw would say, except that the doc is holding at arm's-length a squeeze bottle of something liquid and so cold that it is fogged with a rime of condensation. Huw's throat is dry: suddenly he's unable to ignore it.

"Thirsty, son?" the doc says, playfully jetting a stream of icy liquid in the air.

"Ahhh," Huw says, nodding. Six hours in the suit with nothing but highly diuretic likker and any number of hours of direct sunlight in its insulated confines after the aircon broke down—he's so dehydrated, he's ready to piss snot.

"This a-way," the doc says, and beckons with the bottle.

Huw lets Sam help him climb out of the sidecar, and he barely notices the rubbery feeling of his legs after hours of being cramped up in the little buggy. "Hotcha," the doc says. "Come on, now, time's a wastin'." He gives the bottle another squeeze, and water spatters the dusty ground.

"Aaah," Huw says, lumbering after it. He's never felt quite this thirsty in all his days. *Real* thirsty. Thirsty as bones bleaching in the Sahara at noon during a drought.

The doc heads for a staircase behind a row of suppository-shaped elevator cages, standing open and gleaming beneath the white light of the holy sodiums overhead. Huw can barely keep up, but even if he had to drop to his knees and crawl, he'd do it. That's holy stuff, that water, infused with the numinous glow of life itself. Didn't the Christians have a hymn about it, "Jesus Gave Me Water"? Huw comes from a long line of trenchant Black Country atheists, a man who takes to religion the way that vegans take to huge suspicious wursts that look like cross-sectioned dachshunds, but he's having an ecstatic experience right now, taking the stairs on trembling knees.

The doc spits on his thumb and smears the DNA across the auth-plate set in the door at the bottom of the stairs. It thinks for a long moment, then clanks open in a succession of armored layers.

"G'wan now, you've earned it," the doc says, rolling the bottle into the cell behind the door.

Huw toddles after it, the Michelin suit making him waddle like he's got a load in his diaper, but he doesn't worry about that right now, because there's a bottle of water with his name on it at the other side of the cell, a bottle so cold and pure that it cries out to him: *Drink me! Drink me!*

He's sucking it down, feeling the cold straight through to his skull-bone, a delicious brain freeze the size of the Universe, when the teapot rattles angrily in his thigh pocket. He's not so thirsty anymore, but there's something else nagging at his attention. The sound is getting him down, distracting him from the sense of illumination appearing at the back of his mind's eye as he gulps the water, so he pulls the thing out and looks at it, relaxing as he sees the shiny metal highlights gleaming happily at him.

Adrian pops out of the teapot, so angry, he's almost war-dancing. He curses: "Fucking suggestibility ray! Biblethumping pud-fuckers can't be happy unless they've tasped someone into ecstasy. Come on, Huw, snap out of it."

"Go 'way," Huw mumbles. "I'm havin' a trash-transcential-transcendental 'sperience." He gulps some more water then squats, leaning against the wall. Something *loves* him, something vaster than mountains and far stronger, and it's bringing tears to his eyes. Except the teapot will have none of it.

"Wake up, dishrag! Jesus, didn't they tell you *anything* in class when you was a kid? They infuse your cerebrospinal fluid with nanobots. Some go for your hypothalamus, make you feel hungry or thirsty. Others have a built-in tropism for the god module in your temporal lobe. Tickle it with a broadband signal, and you'll see God, angels square-dancing in heaven, fuck knows what. Get a grip on yourself!"

"It's *God?*" Huw's got a name for the sensation now, and he grins idiotically at the opposite wall of his cell. It's a slab of solid aluminum, scratched and dented and discolored along the welds: and it's as beautiful to Huw as fluted marble pillars supporting the airy roof of a pleasure dome, pennants snapping overhead in the delightful breeze blowing off the waters of the underground river Alph—

"It's not God, it's a fucking tasp! Snap out of it, gobshite. They're only using it on you 'cause they want you nice and addled when they sell you to the Inquisition tomorrow! Then, no more god module!"

"Huh?" Huw ponders the question for an eternity of proximate grace, as serried ranks of angels blow trumpets of glory in the distant clouds that wreath his head. "I'm... so, I'm happy. This way. I've found it."

"What you've found is a bullet in the back of the head if you stay here, you cheeseridge!" Ade shakes his fists from the top of the teapot. "Think, damn you! What would you have thought of this yesterday?"

"Yesterday?" Yesterday, all his troubles, so far away. Huw nods, thinking deeply. "I've always been missing 'thing like this, even if I didn't know it. Feels *right*. Everything makes sense." The presence of the ultimate, even if it's coming from right inside his own skull courtesy of a 5.4-gigahertz transmission from God-botherer Central, is making it hard for Huw to concentrate on anything else. "Wanna be like this till I die, if's all the same to you."

"They'll *kill* you, man!" Ade pauses in his frantic fistwaving. "Doesn't that mean something to you?"

"Mmf. Lemme think about it." Huw slowly slumps back against the wall, his suit bulking and billowing around him and digging sharp joints into his bruised body, sanctifying and mortifying his flesh. "If I believed in an actual, like, *God,* this'd be marvelous. But God's such a goddamned primitive fetish, isn't it? So I'm'a, an atheist. Always have been, always will be. But this thing is like, *inside* me, and it's huge, so blindingly brilliant, it's like my own reflection on infinity." His eyes widen. "Hey, that means *I'm* God. I'm like, transcendentistry, right? I think therefore I guess I *am.* If they try to shoot me, I'll just zap 'em with my god-powers." He giggles for a while, pointing his fingers at the ceiling, walls, and floor, lightning bolts of the illuminated imagination spraying every which way. "It's a solipsystem! Nobody here but me. *I* am God. I *am* God. I am *God*—"

The teapot zaps him with an electric shock, and Ade vanishes in a huff.

"Ouch." Huw sucks his thumb for a moment and meditates on the celestial significance of the autodeity sending him messages from his subconscious via a curved metal antiquity stuffed with black market New Libyan electronics. Then he tucks it away in his pocket and settles back down to work on regaining his sense of omnipotent brilliance. And he's still sitting in that pose the next morning, staring at the wall, when the sense of immanence vanishes, the doors grind open, and Doc and Sam come to take him downtown to face the Inquisition.

They parade him down the road in the drab gray morning light of Glory City, past the filling stations, the churches, the diners, the other filling stations, the refinery, the cathedral, the filling station–memorabilia market, the GasHaus, the corkscrew apartment blocks where every neighbor can look in on every other's window, and the execution ground.

And it all feels good to Huw.

As the parade progresses, curious locals emerge from their homes and workplaces as if drawn by some ultra-wideband alert, rounded up and herded out to form a malignant rent-a-mob that demonstrates to Huw how important and central to reality he is. They pelt him with rotting fruit and wet cigar stubs with live coals on one end that singe him before bouncing free to the impermeable pavement, affirming his sense of holy closeness with the intensity of their focus on him. Once, they stop so that the doc can roar a speech at the crowd—

"—heretic—vengeance—drugs—sex—wantonness—"

Huw doesn't pay much attention to the speech. Through his feet he fancies he can feel the scritterscratch of the Hypercolony, gnawing patiently at the yards of stone and polymer between him and the blighted soil. It's a bad feeling, as if Glory City is a snow globe that has been lifted into the air on the backs of a heptillion ants who are carrying it away, making it sway back and forth. The curlicue towers and the gnarled and crippled crowd rock in hinky rhythm.

The faces on the balconies swim when he looks up. Some of

them have horns on their foreheads. He turns away and tries to stare at a fixed point, using the ballerina's trick of keeping his gaze still to make the world stop its whirling, but his gorge is rising, and his stomach is threatening to empty down his front.

This is not good.

He sits down hard, his armored ass klonking on the pavement, and Sam lumbers toward him. Huw holds out his hand, wanting to be helped to his feet, back to the godhead and the good trip. Just as Sam's fingertips graze his, a woman wearing a voluminous black gown dashes out of the crowd and grabs him under the armpits, looping a harness around his chest. Where it touches his back, it gloms on hard, hyperglue nanites welding it to the suit's surface.

"Hold on," Bonnie breathes in his ear, and he feels like weeping, because he knows he isn't to be redeemed after all, but tediously rescued and rehabilitated and set free.

"Bitch harlot!" says Doc. "Sodomite! Stop her!" Sam grabs for her past Huw's shoulder, sideswipes the rounded swell of her bosom—extensively, chastely covered, this being Glory City—and jerks his hand back as though he'd been burned.

The harness around Huw's chest tightens with ribbruising force, dragging him backwards. He skitters for a moment before the harness lofts them both into the air, up toward the balconies ringing the curlicue towers. Bonnie, tied off to him by a harness of her own, squints nervously down at the crowd receding below them.

Huw bangs chest-first into the side of one of the towers, Bonnie's weight knocking the breath out of him. They dangle together, twirling in the breeze like a giant booger as strong hands hoist them bodily up and over a balcony. One last, titanic heave hauls them inside, adding insult to injury in the form of a painful wedgie. Bonnie scrambles over him, unlocks her harness, and shakes out her voluminous petticoats. Huw is still dazed from the flight and gasping for breath. He's bent over double, trying to breathe perfumed air thick with musky incense.

"You all right?"

Huw forces himself to straighten up and look around. The room is a tribute to excess: the wallpaper is printed with gold and red and black tessellations—obscene diagrams, he realizes, interpenetrating and writhing before his eyes—and the sofa is flocked with crushed purple velvet. The coffee table supports a variety of phallic implements in an assortment of improbable colors, suited to an altogether different kind of inquisition than the one that he'd been headed for.

As for the furniture, it's inhabited by several persons of indeterminate gender, wearing outfits ranging from scanty to inappropriate for a place of worship—underwear is in fashion, but not much else is.

Bonnie's face swims into focus before him, her blue fringe brushing his forehead: that and her hands are the only parts of her body he can see. "It's the gnostic sexual underground," she says. "There's always one to be had, if you know how to look. Nobody takes it up the tradesman's like a man with that old-time religion. No one needs it more, either. These lucky folks just figured out how to square the circle, thanks to the Bishop."

She gives him a hard shake. "Come on," she says. "I hit you with enough serotonin reuptake blockers to depress a hyena." He feels a hard tug at his throat, and she holds up a small blowdart for him to examine. "I *know* you're out of the god-box."

Huw opens his mouth to say something, and finds himself sobbing. "You took away my god-self," he says, snotting down his three-day beard and horking back briny mouthfuls of tears and mucus.

Bonnie produces a hankie from up one sleeve of her church-modest gown and wipes his face. "Sha," she says, stroking his hair. "Sha. Huw, I need you here and now, okay? We're in a *lot* of trouble, and I can't get us out on my lonesome. The god feeling was just head-in-a-jar stuff. You weren't being God, you were just feeling the feeling of being God. You hate that—it's how they feel in the cloud, once they've uploaded."

Huw snuffles miserably. "Yeah," he says.

"Yeah. Baby, I'm sorry, I know it hurts, but it's how you want to live. If I know one person who's equipped to cope with the distinction between sensation and simulation, it's you. Jesus, Huw, other than these maniacs, you're the only person I know who thinks there *is* a distinction."

Huw struggles to his feet and teeters in his ridiculous trousers. Bonnie giggles.

"What *are* you *wearing*?" she asks.

Huw manages to crack a fractional smile. "They're all the rage in the American Outback," he says. "What's that *you're* wearing?"

"A disguise. Doubles as a biohazard shield." She swivels her hips, setting kilograms of underskirts swishing. "We're both a bit overdressed for the occasion; let's skin off and I'll introduce you to the Bishop. Go on, you get started."

Huw begins the laborious unlatching process and gradually shucks the pants. The teapot clatters free, drawing a raised eyebrow from one of the sexually ambiguous catamites twined around a sofa arm. The vibration kicks some erratic connection back into life: Ade's image glows softly through the deep pile carpet.

The little avatar wrinkles its nose. "Bugger me sideways," says Ade. "Place looks like an Italian whorehouse, only less charming and hygienic." He turns and looks Huw up and down. "You look a little more like your usual cheerless self, though, mate. Should I assume that you've joined us again in the land of the cognitively unimpaired?"

Huw nods miserably. "I'm back," he says. "No thanks to you. Those two assholes know you—they do business with you!"

Adrian's avatar has the good grace to look faintly embarrassed. Bonnie leans past Huw with a creak of whalebone and picks up the teapot. "Did I hear that right?" she asks. "You been selling *stuff* again?"

"Uh." Ade looks unrepentant. "Yeah, I guess so."

"What kind of *stuff*?" Bonnie says, her eyes narrowing.

"Um... stuff. Mostly harmless."

"What *kind* of mostly harmless stuff are we talking about here?" Huw asks, mustering up a faint echo of interest. The blissed-out resistance cadre on the sofa are showing signs of interest too.

"Oh, the usual, sunshine. Telescope lenses, tinfoil hats—okay, Faraday cage helmets—formicide spritzes, tactical nuclear weapons, Bibles, contraceptive implants, tinned spam, that kind of thing."

"And in return they're paying you in—" Huw begins; then Bonnie interrupts him.

"—No, wait. What else are you smuggling, you dogfucker? Don't try to hide it from me. Those neverglade-living lowlifes were so eager to hand Huw over to the Fallen Congregations that they had to be trying to cover something up. Like, oh, whatever the fuck you were doing with them. What was it, Ade? Resurrection on the installment plan? Banned downloads? Are we going to get that fucking mad crow descending on us?"

"Oh, I say!" someone says behind them, but Bonnie is so worked up, she doesn't notice. Huw glances over his shoulder and sees one of the miscellaneous perverts standing nearby, a hand clasped over his/her mouth. The perv is fish-belly pale and wears nothing but very complicated underwear. "Did you say—?"

"Just a few small downloads, lass," Ade says. "Nothing to get worked up about, keep your hair on."

"Downloads. Shit." Bonnie breathes deeply. She's looking pale. "*Pusbuckets*, that's all I need," she says. She puts the teapot down. "Right, we'll have to take this up later, Huw. Right now we've got to go see the Bishop, and that means skin. Help me out of this thing."

Huw fumbles for a while with the complex catches and clasps on her dress, fuzzily aware that he's standing very close to her and he's not wearing any trousers. As she steps out of her costume, she grabs him around the waist, squeezes him tight, and kisses him fiercely on the mouth. She's nervous, vibrating like a live wire, and something squirms around in his throat, wanting to comfort her. "Why do we have to be naked?" he asks when she surfaces for air. "Who is this Bishop, anyway?"

"The Bishop of the First Church of the Teledildonic. It's a dissident: lives in a baptismal pond, says we've got it all wrong and time is flowing in reverse. We've passed the Tower of Babel—that's the cloud—and the Flood—warming—and now we're ready to move back into the Garden of Eden. So we've got to stop wearing clothes and start fucking like innocent bunnies."

"But—" Huw can feel his brain trying to twist out through his ears as he attempts to accommodate this deviant theology to what he knows about the Fallen Baptist Congregations. "What's that got to do with anything? With these folks?"

"I say, hold it right there, pardner!" says the pale perv, running drowned-looking hands through his/her long green hair. The effect would almost be sexy if not for the medium-sized potbelly and the black rubber hedgehog-apparatus that conceals his/her crotch, studded with silvery transducers: "You've got it all wrong!" He/she waves a finger at Bonnie. "This isn't the Garden of Eden, it's the Garden of the Son of God, after the Rapture, the hundred and forty-four thousand saved souls living in paradise on Earth, free from sin—"

"What's *that*, then?" asks Huw, rudely prodding in the direction of the strap-on.

The perv draws itself up to a haughty meter-fifty: "I'll have you know that this is the finest model *chastity phallus* money can buy," s/he says, voice cracking and descending an octave: "'S got all the sensory inputs of the real thing, wired right into my spine, but because little feller himself is tucked out of sight behind it, there's no actual genital contact. No skin, no sin." He fondles the thing happily and whimpers. Another of the prosthetically enhanced worshippers is sitting up on the sofa behind him and showing signs of interest.

Huw backs away slowly. *Get me out of here,* he mouths at Bonnie. She nods, then reaches out and strokes the perv's pristine love machine. *"Now."* Bonnie leads him around the perv—who doubles over in ecstasy at her touch—toward a pair of pornographically decorated hardwood doors at the rear of the room.

Bonnie takes a deep breath. "Wish I could stay," she calls to the three or four temple whores on the bed, "but we've got to see Their Grace. It's urgent. If I were you, I'd get to a safe house before the gendarmes arrive."

"Give the Bishop our love," one of the omnisexuals calls as they depart.

There is a small and overintimate lift behind the doors. It runs sideways, down, up, and then sideways again, completing a route that sends Huw's inner ear on a loop-the-loop. They emerge into a hallway that's carpeted with greasy-feeling tentacles that twine sensuously around his toes, and the walls have the sheen of waxed and oiled skin. It smells of Doritos and musk.

Bonnie hands him the sack with her clothes and his ruined underpants and the teapot and pushes him ahead of her, squeezing his ass affectionately as they go.

The Bishop is three meters high, ten-limbed, with eight complete sets of assorted genitals, fourteen breasts, and four tongues, like an explosion in a gourmet brothel's cloning vats. He, She, and It—the three in one—is impossibly hideous to contemplate. Bonnie ushers Huw into its presence after negotiating with a pair of disturbingly toothless ministers who bar the high door.

"Your Grace," she says as they step into its eucalyptusfumed inner chamber.

"My dear child," it says with one of its mouths. "It warms Our heart to see you." It has a voice like a teenaged boy, high and uncertain. "And your companion. You are both lovely as they day He made you."

One of its hands slithers free of the tangle and extends before them. Bonnie bends down and kisses the ring painted on the third finger, then elbows Huw, who kneels tentatively and takes the proffered digit, which is warm and moist and pulses disturbingly.

"Your Grace?" he says.

"Be not afraid, child," says the Bishop. "This meatsuit allows Us to bring the Word to Our scattered temples without having to transport Our physical person through the uncertain world. One day, all of us will be liberated by these meatsuits, free to explore our flesh in many bodies all at once."

"You're *uploaded?*" Huw says, taking his hand away quickly and shuffling back on his knees.

The Bishop snorts a laugh with its rightmost face. "No, child, no. Merely telepresent. Uploading is the mortification of the flesh—this is its *celebration.*"

"Your Grace," Bonnie says, peering up at it through her fringe with her eyes seductively wide. "It has been an honor and privilege to serve you in my time here in Glory City. I've found my counseling duties to be very rewarding—the genderreassignees here face unique challenges, and it's wonderful to be able to help them."

"Yes," says the Bishop, crouching down. "And We've appreciated it very much. But We sense that you are here to ask some favor of Us now, and We wish you'd get on with it so that We could concentrate on the savage rogering we're getting in one of Our bodies."

"It's complicated," Bonnie says. "This guy here is on the run— he'd been captured and they were taking him to the auto-da-fé when I rescued him."

"This is the One?" the Bishop asks, putting one delicate feminine hand behind his head and pulling him closer to its big golden eyes. "The two who brought you to Glory City are not know for their extreme piety. So why do you suppose they brought you here, rather than simply, oh, eating you or using you for spare parts?"

Huw keeps himself from shying back with an effort of will. "I don't *know*," he says. Bonnie crowds in to another one of the Bishop's faces. Deep within him, Huw feels a shiver of golden light, the god feeling.

"I think my downers are wearing off."

"They tasped him, so I hit him with some depressants," Bonnie says.

"Feels *gooooooood*," Huw says.

"It does, doesn't it?" the Bishop says. "I favor three or four hours on the tasp myself, twice a week. Does wonders for the faith. But I suppose we'd best keep your ecstasy under control for now. Phillida!" it calls, clapping two of its hands together, bringing one of the ministers running. It twines an arm between the guardian's legs and murmurs, "Bring Us a freethinker's cap, will you?" The minister's toothless maw gapes open in ecstasy, and then it scurries off quickly, returning with a mesh balaclava that the Bishop fits to Huw's head, lining up the eye- and mouth-holes.

Huw's golden glow recedes.

"It's a Faraday cage with some noise-cancelation built in to reverse any of the mind-control radiation that gets through," the Bishop says. "How did you come to be on the American Continent, anyway?"

"It started when I ate some godvomit and smuggled it out of a patent court," Huw says.

The Bishop's golden eyes widen. "Judge Rosa Giuliani's court? In Libya? Last week? I'm a big fan of her show! You are carrying the ambassador?"

"The very same," Huw says, obscurely pleased at this notoriety. "It wasn't my idea, believe me. Anyway, this smuggler I know— we know—Adrian, he sent me here. Said that this was the safest place to hide out."

Bonnie breaks in. "But now we come to find out that he's been dealing with the two who tasped Huw—"

"Sam and the doc," Huw says.

"I know of them," the Bishop says, its voice dripping with arch disapproval.

"Selling them bootleg downloads."

"Ahh," the Bishop says. "Excuse Us a moment." It arches its back and screams out a long orgasmic wail. "One of Our other meatsuits is being ministered to," it says distractedly: "We needed to have a bit of a shout. We're pleased to know this. It explains certain pseudo-nuclear events in the outback that We've had word of—the doc must be retailing anti-ant technology to the other hayseeds."

Bonnie shuddered. "That's just for openers, I'm sure. Fuck knows what else Ade has sold those nutjobs."

"Just some downloads, he said," Huw says. "Fuck it, what did he mean by *that?* You can download anything; I know I did!"

"Downloads could be either good or bad," the Bishop says, rubbing two disturbingly rugose hands together as if in prayer. "But first, We have more pressing temporal priorities to attend to, my children. It appears that your rescue did not go unnoticed by the puritan majority, and they will presently be calling. Moreover, this would explain a request for a flight plan and landing clearance that the airport acknowledged four hours ago—" The Bishop stops, its back arching ecstatically. "—oh! Oh! *Oh!* Closer to thee, my God!" Breasts quiver, their purple aureolae crinkling, and it screams out loud in the grip of a multiple orgasm of titanic proportions.

Huw peers out through the eye-holes of his mesh mask, which presses cold and hard into his skin. "Did you say that the law is nearby?"

"I believe they are," the Bishop says. "Yes, there. The primary perimeter has been breached. Such a lovely front door." It looks sternly at Bonnie. "You were reckless, child. They followed you here."

"I took every precaution," Bonnie says, blushing. "I'm no amateur, you know—"

Huw has a sudden sickening feeling. "It's me," he says. "I'm bugged with a geotracker."

Bonnie glares at him. "You could have *said something*," she says. "We've compromised the whole operation here now."

"I was *distracted,* all right? Mind-control rays make you forgetful, *okay?*"

The Bishop clucks its tongues and gives them each a pat on their bare bottoms. "Never mind that now, children. All is forgiven. But I'm afraid that you are right, we are going to lose this temple. And I'm no more infallible than you, you know: I've been ever so lax with the evacuation drills here. My ministers find that they disturb their contemplation of the Almighty. I fear not for this meatsuit, but it would be such a shame to have all my lovely acolytes fall into the hands of the Inquisition. I don't suppose that you'd be willing to help out?"

"Of course," Bonnie says. "It's the least we can do."

No, the least we could do would be to get the fuck out, Huw thinks. He glares at Bonnie, who prods him in the belly with a fingertip.

"But of course, we could also use some help of our own—"

"Quid pro quo?" the Bishop says, its quavering voice bemused now, and that irritates Huw ferociously: the law is at the door, and the Bishop thinks it's all a tremendous lark?

"Not at all, Your Grace. We came to beg your indulgence long before we knew that there was a favor we could do for you. We need your assistance getting shut of this blighted wasteland. Transport to the coast, and an airship or a ballistic or *something* that can get us back to the civilized world."

"And I need to shut down my geotracker," Huw says, wondering where it has been implanted. *Somewhere painful,* Sam had told him.

"Yes, you certainly do," the Bishop says. "You'll find an escape-line clipped to the balcony out the third door on the right, along with some baskets. Pack the ministers in the baskets, tie them down—don't mind if they squirm, it's in their nature—clip the baskets to the line and toss them out the window. I'm making arrangements now for someone to catch them on the other end. If you do this small favor for me, I will, oh, I don't know." The Bishop idly strokes their scalps and tickles their earlobes. "Yes, that's it. There's a safe house on the coast, a farm where my people have been making preparations for a much more reasonable approach to dealing with the ants than godvomit and nukes. They will be delighted to shelter you for as long as it takes you to make contact with your people and get off the continent. Such a shame to see you go." It quickly gives Bonnie directions, and Bonnie recites them back with mnemonic perfection.

There's a distant crash that Huw feels through the soles of his bare feet. "Clothes?" he asks.

"Oh, yes, I suppose, by all means, if you must," the Bishop says. "Cloakroom's behind the last door on the right. A lost and found for supplicants who've left a little something behind in their blissful state as they left our place of worship. I'm sure we'll have something in your size, even if it's only OshKosh B'Gosh."

"Fanfuckingtastic," Huw says breathlessly as he makes a line for the door. But Bonnie catches him by the elbow, intent on one last question.

"How many are we supposed to evacuate? I don't want to miss anyone." There's another thunderous crash, this one from closer by.

The Bishop's eyes roll back into its head, then flip down. "A dozen on the premises, not counting the ones that were on the front door. It seems they've been liquidated already."

"Shit. What'll we—" Huw dithers for a moment but Bonnie is already heading for the cloakroom door.

"Over here!" She thrusts a bundle of clothing at him. "Quick. Let's go get the ministers—"

Huw pauses while balanced on one leg, the other thrust down one limb of a pair of denim overalls. "Do we have to?" he asks.

"Yes, we fucking *do*."

He fumbles with the fasteners on the overalls' bib and kicks his feet free of the overlong denim legs, reaching out a hand to steady himself on a piece of heavy kitchen equipment—they've found their way to the food-prep area where robots build slop, form it, heat it, season it, and dispense it. He realizes that he's steadying himself on an open-sided microwave heating platform. He thinks of the idiot beacon and where it must be, gives his left ass cheek a good squeeze to make sure, then lies himself down on the chilly surface of the heater. It's awkward—none of the spaces are really designed for human ingress—but he just manages it.

"Bonnie, turn this thing on, okay?"

She is about to bark something angry, then she catches herself, half smiles at the ridiculous tableau he's made, and says, "You want me to cook your ass?"

"Just until I start screaming, okay? The bug should start arcing within a few seconds, long before I get too badly cooked." She looks ready to argue, but he keeps talking over her. "Look, freethinkers have been nuking their minder bugs for decades. I won't be the first man who's irradiated himself to get rid of a pesky implant."

The pain is worse than anything he'd experienced before he met Bonnie and Adrian and allowed them both to drag him into a series of ever-more-painful experiences. Even on the new, post-adventure scale of owies, this is a serious pain in the ass. It starts as a horrible stinging, then a burning, and then a sharp, percussive zap that makes him frog-kick and thrash his head so hard, it feels like he'll snap his neck.

Mildly, Bonnie says, "Was that it, then?"

"Turn. It. Off," he says through clenched teeth.

The pain doesn't stop, but it recedes some, and he gets to his feet and tenderly holds his ass.

Bonnie helps him hobble along. "Right, get that jacket fastened: we are going to hit the garage just as soon as we've defenestrated all the perverts." She shrugs backwards into an upper-body assembly that looks like something left behind by a SWAT team. "C'mon."

Huw follows her back next door, to find a bunch of blissed-out religionists lazily osculating one another on a row of futons. "Okay!" yells Bonnie. "It's evacuation time! Huw, get the goddamn window open and hook up the baskets." She turns back to the coterie of ministers, some of whom are yawning and looking at her in evident mild annoyance. "The bad guys are coming through the back passage and you guys are going down right now!"

"Eh, right." Huw finds a stack of baby blue plastic baskets

dangling from a monofilament line right outside the window. "C'mon…"

Between the two of them, they haul the dazed and tasped worshippers into baskets and drop them down the line. It all takes far too long, and by the time the last one is hooked up, Huw is in a frenzy of agitation, desperate to be out of the building. There are indistinct thuds and stamping noises below them, and an odd whine of machinery from the hall outside. "What's going on now?" he says. "How do *we* get out of here?"

"We wait." Bonnie gives the last basket a shove and turns to face him, panting. "The corridors and rooms in this place, the Bishop's got them rigged up to reconfigure like a maze. This whole sector should be walled off; you can't find it unless you can see through walls."

A loud echoing crash from the room next door makes Huw wince. "What if they've got terahertz radar goggles?" he asks.

"What if—oh *norks*." Bonnie looks appalled. "Quick, grab my epaulettes and hang on, we're going down the wire!" She steps toward him, reaches around his body, and grabs the monofilament with what look to Huw like black opera gloves. There's a terminal thud from the doorway behind her that rattles the walls, and then Huw is clinging on for dear life as they drop. A thin plume of evil-smelling black smoke trails from her spidersilk gloves as they descend. "Ow." Huw can barely hear her moan, and to tell the truth, he's more concerned with the state of his own stomach, gelid with terror as they drop past two, three rows of windows.

The ground comes up and smacks him across the ankles and he lets go of Bonnie. They fall apart and as he falls he sees a delivery van pulling away, the tailgate jammed shut around a blue basket. "Thanks a million, bastards," Bonnie says, picking herself up. "Think they could have waited?"

"No," Huw says, looking past her. "Listen, the Inquisition are round the front, and they'll be after us any second—"

She grabs his wrist. "Come on, then!" She hauls off and drags him the length of the filthy alleyway beneath a row of rusting fire escapes.

By the time they hit the end of the alley, he's up to speed and in the lead, self-preservation glands fully engaged. In the distance, sirens are wailing. "They're round the other side! So much for your wait-and-get-away-later plan."

"That wasn't the whole plan," she says. "There's a basement garage, when the building reconfigured we could have dropped down a chute straight into the cockpit of a batmobile and headed out via the service tunnels. Woulda worked a treat if it wasn't for your teraherz radar."

"*My* radar?" Huw says, hating the note of weakness in his voice. He swallows as he looks into Bonnie's fear-wide eyes. "Right." he says. "We need transport and we need to get past the Inquisition shock troops before we can get to the out-of-town safe house. If they've ringed the block and they've got radar, they'll see us real soon—"

"Shit," says Bonnie, her grip loosening. Huw looks round.

An olive drab abomination whines and reverses into the alley toward them. Cleated metal tracks grind and scrape on the paving as an assault ramp drops down. It's an armored personnel carrier, but right now it's carrying only one person, a big guy in a white suit. He's holding something that looks like a shiny bundle of rods in both hands, and it's pointing right at them. "Resistance is futile!" shouts Sam, his amplified voice echoing off the fire escapes and upended Dumpsters. "Surrender or die!"

"Nobbies," says Huw, glancing back at the other end of the alley. Which is blocked by a wall conveniently topped with razor wire—Bonnie might make it with her spidersilk gloves, but there's no way in hell he could climb it without getting minced. Then he looks back at Sam, who is pointing his minigun or X-ray laser or whatever the hell it is right at him and waiting, patiently. "Surrender to whom?" he says.

"Me." Sam takes a step *back* into the APC and does something and suddenly there's a weird hissing around them. "Ambient antisound. We can talk, but you've got about twenty seconds to surrender to me or you can take your chances with *them*."

"Monkeyflaps." Bonnie's shoulders slump. "Okay," she calls, raising her voice. "What do you want?"

"You." For a moment Sam sounds uncertain. "But I'll take him too, even though he doesn't deserve it."

"Last time you were all fired up on handing Huw over to the Church," Bonnie says.

"Change of plan. That was Dad, this is me." Sam raises his gun so that it isn't pointed directly at them. "You coming or not?"

Bonnie glances over her shoulder. "Yeah," she says, stepping forward. She pauses. "You coming?" she asks Huw.

"I don't trust him!" Huw says. "He—"

"You like the Inquisition better?" Bonnie asks, and walks up the ramp, back stiff, not looking back.

Sam backs away and motions her to sit on a bench, then throws her something that looks like a thick bandanna. "Wrap this round your wrists and that grab rail. Tight. It'll set in about ten seconds." Then he glances back at Huw. "Ten seconds."

Huw steps forward wordlessly, sits down opposite Bonnie. Sam throws him a restraint band, motions with the gun. The assault ramp creaks and whines loudly as it grinds up and locks shut. Sam backs all the way into the driver's compartment, then slams a sliding door shut on them. The APC lurches, then begins to inch forward out of the alleyway.

Over the whine of the electric motors he can hear Sam talking on the radio: "No, no sign of suspects. Did you get the van? I figure that was how they got away."

What's going on? Huw mouths at Bonnie.

She shrugs and looks back at him. Then there's another lurch and the APC accelerates, turns a corner into open road, and Sam opens up the throttle. At which point, speech becomes redundant: it's like being a frog in a liquidizer inside a bass drum bouncing on a trampoline, and it's all Huw can do to stay on the bench seat.

After about ten minutes, the APC slows down, then grinds to a standstill. "Where are we?" Bonnie calls at the shut door of the driver's compartment. She mouths something at Huw. *Let me handle this,* he decodes after a couple of tries.

The door slides open. "You don't need to know," Sam says calmly, "'cuz if you knew, I'd have to edit your memories, and the only way I know to do that these days is by killing you." He isn't holding the gun, but before Huw has time to get any ideas, Sam reaches out and hits a switch. The grabrail Huw and Bonnie are tied to rises toward the ceiling, dragging them upright. "It's not like the old days," he says. "We really knew how to mess with our heads then."

"Why did you take us?" Huw says after he finds his footing. Bonnie gives him a dirty look. Huw swallows, his mouth dry as he realizes that Sam is studying her with a closed expression on his face.

"Personal autonomy," Sam says, taking Huw by surprise. The big lummox doesn't look like he ought to know words like that. "Dad wanted to turn you in 'cause if he didn't, the Inquisition'd start asking questions sooner or later. Best stay on the right side of the law, claim the reward. But once you got away, it stopped being his problem." He swallows. "Didn't stop being *my* problem, though." He leans toward Bonnie. "Why are you on this continent?" he asks, and produces a small, vicious knife.

"I'm—" Bonnie tenses, and Huw's heart beats faster with fear for her. She's thinking fast and that can't be good, and this crazy big backwoods guy with the knife is frighteningly bad news. "Not everyone on this continent wants to be here," she says. "I don't know about anyone else's agenda, but I think that a mind is a terrible thing to waste. That's practically my religion. Self-determination. You got people here, they're going to die for good, when they could be ascendant and immortal, if only someone would offer them the choice."

Sam makes encouraging noises.

"I go where I'm needed," she says. "Where I can lend a hand to people who want it. Your gang wants to play postapocaypse; that's fine. I'm here to help the utopians play *their* game."

Huw has shut his eyes and is nearly faint with fury. *I'm a fucking passenger again, nothing but a passenger on this trip—the* alien flute-thing in his stomach squirms, shifting uncomfortably in response to his adrenaline and prostaglandin surge—*fucking cargo.* For an indefinite moment, Huw can't hear anything above the drumbeat of his own rage: carrying the ambassador seems to be fucking with his hormonal balance, and his emotions aren't as stable as they should be.

Sam is still talking. "—Dad's second liver," he says to Bonnie. "So he cloned himself. Snipped out this, inserted that, force-grew it in a converted milk tank. Force-grew *me.* I'm supposed to be him, only stronger, better, smarter, bigger. Kept me in the tank for two years plugged in through the cortex speed-learning off the interwebnet then hauled me out, handed me a scalpel, painted a line on his abdomen, and said 'cut here.' The liver was a clone too, so I figured I oughta do like he said unless I wanted to end up next on the spare parts rota."

"Wow." Bonnie sounds fascinated. "So you're a designer *Übermensch?*"

"Guess so," Sam says slowly and a trifle bashfully. "After I got the new liver fitted, Dad kept me around to help out in the lab. Never asked me what *I* wanted, just set me to work. *He's* Asperger's. Me, I'm just poorly socialized with a recursive introspective agnosia and a deficient situational relationship model. That's what the diagnostic expert systems tell me, anyway."

"You're saying you've never been socialized." Bonnie leans her head toward him. "You just hatched, like, fully formed from a *tank—*"

"Yeah," Sam says, and waits.

"That's so sad," Bonnie says. "Did your dad mistreat you?"

"Oh mercy, no! He just ignores… Well, he's Dad. He never pays much attention to me, he's too busy looking for the alien space bats and trying not to get the Bishop mad at him."

"Is that why you were taking Huw into town?" asks Bonnie.

"Huh, yeah, I guess so." Sam chuckles. "Anything comes down in the swamp, you betcha they see it on radar. You came down in Dad's patch, pretty soon they'll come by and ask why he hasn't turned you in. So you can't really blame him, putting on the Holy Roller head and riding into town to hand over the geek."

"That's okay," Bonnie says as Sam's shoulders tense, "I understand."

"It's just a regular game-theoretical transaction, y'see?" Sam asks, his voice rising in a near whine: "He has to do it! He has to tit-for-tat with the Church or they'll roll him over. 'Sides, the geek doesn't know anything. The shipment—"

"Hush." Bonnie *winks* at the big guy. "Actually, your dad was wrong—the ambassad—the shipment requires a living host."

"Oh!" Sam's eyebrows rise. "Then it's a good thing you rescued him, I guess." He looks wistful. "If'n I trust you. I don't know much about people."

"That's all right," Bonnie says. "I'm not your enemy. I don't hate you for picking us up. You don't need to shut us up." She looks up at where her wrists are trussed to the grab rail. "Let my hands free?"

Sam listens to some kind of internal voice, then he raises the knife and slices away at Bonnie's bonds. Huw tenses as she slumps down and then drapes herself across Sam's muscular shoulder. "What do you want?" Sam asks.

Bonnie cups his chin tenderly. "We all want the same thing," she says. Sam shrinks back from her touch.

"Sha," she says. "You're very handsome, Sam." He squirms.

Huw squirms too. *"Bonnie,"* he says, a warning.

Sam twists to stare at him, and Huw sees that there's something wild breaking loose behind his eyes. "Come on," Bonnie says, "over here." She takes his hand and leads him toward the driver's cab of the APC. "Come with me."

Huw swallows his revulsion as the big guy slides past him, nimble on his big dinner-plate feet, hand enfolding Bonnie's. He keeps his eyes down. He feels a stab of jealousy: but Bonnie's sidelong glance silences him. He's old enough to know the nature of this game.

After the hatch thumps shut, Huw strains to overhear the murmured converation from behind it, but all he can make out is thumps and grunts, and then, weirdly, a loud sob. "Oh, Daddy, *why?*" It's Sam, and there are more sobs now, and more thumps, and Huw realizes they're not sex noises—more like *seizure* noises.

His ribs and shoulders are on fire, and he shifts from foot to foot, trying to find relief from the agony of hanging by his wrists. He steps on their pathetic pillowcase of possessions, and the lamp rolls free, Ade popping up.

"My, you are a *sight,* old son," the little hologram says. "Nice hat."

"It helps me think," Huw says around the copper mesh of the

balaclava. "It wouldn't have hurt to have a couple of these on the zep, Ade."

"Live and learn," the hologram says. "Next time." It cocks its head and listens to the sobbing. "What's all that about, then?"

Huw shrugs as best as he can, then gasps at the chorous of muscle spasms this evinces from his upper body. "I thought Bonnie might be having a shag, but now I'm not sure. I *think* she might be conducting a therapy session."

"Saving the world as per usual," Ade says. "So many virtues that boygirl has. Doctrinaire ideologues like her are the backbone of the movement, I tell you. Who's she converting to pervtropic disestablishmentarianist personal politics, then?"

"One of your trading partners," Huw says. "Sam. Turns out he's the doc's son. Clone. I 'spect you knew that, though."

"Sam? Brick shithouse Sam?" There's a distant, roaring sob and another crash. "Who'd have thought he had it in him?"

"Whose side are you on, Ade? What have you been selling these bastards? I expect I'll be dead by dusk, so you can tell me."

"I *told* you, but you didn't listen. There is no conspiracy. The movement is an emergent phenomenon. It's complexity theory, not ideology. The cloud wants to instantiate an ambassador, and *events* conspire to find a suitable host and get some godvomit down his throat." Ade nods at him. "Now the cloud wants the ambassador to commune with something on the American continent, and there you are. How do I know the cloud wants this? Because you are there, on the American continent. QED. Maybe it wants to buy Manhattan for some beads. Maybe it wants to say hello to the ants. Maybe it wants to be sure that meatsuits are really as banal and horrible as it remembers."

"No ideology?" Huw says as another sob rattles the walls. "I think Bonnie might disagree with you."

"Oh, she might," Ade says. "But in the end, she knows it as well as I do: Our mission is to be where events take us. Buying and selling a little on the side, it's not counterrevolutionary. It's not revolutionary. It's just more complexity. More energy to pump into the dynamic system from whence the conspiracy may emerge."

"That's all conveniently fatalist," Huw says.

"Imagine," Ade says, "a technophobe lecturing *me* about fatalism." The sobs have stopped, and now they hear the thunder of approaching footfalls. Bonnie comes through the door, trailing Sam behind her, as Ade disappears.

She takes both of his hands and stands on tiptoe to kiss him on the tip of his squashed nose. "You're very beautiful, Sam," she says. "And your feelings are completely normal. You tell the Bishop I told you to go see her. Him. It. They'll help you out."

Sam's eyes are red and his chin is slick with gob. He wipes his face on his checkered flannel shirttails. "I love you, Bonnie," he says, his voice thick with tears.

"I love you too, Sam," she says. She reaches into his pocket and takes out his knife, opens it and cuts Huw down. "We're going now, but I'll never forget you. If you ever decide to come to Europe, you know how to find me."

Huw nearly keels over as his arms flap bloodlessly down to slap at his sides, but manages to stay upright as Sam thuds over to the ramp controls and sets the gangway to lowering.

"Come on, Huw," she says, picking up their pillowcase. "We've got to get to the coast."

"*Court is in session*," screams a familiar voice as the ramp scrapes the rubberized tarmac. Three court golems—so big, they dwarf Sam—come up the ramp with alarming swiftness and grab all three of them before Huw has time to register anything more than a dim impression of an alleyway that's lit like a soundstage for the cameras, and, in the middle of it, Judge Rosa Giuliani: encased in a dalekoid peppermill of a personal vehicle, draped in her robes of office, and scowling like she's just discovered piss in her coffee cup.

"You are charged with violating WorldGov biohazard regulations, with wanton epidemiological disregard, with threatening the fragile peace of our world's orderly acquisition and adoption of technology, and with being a fugitive from justice."

"You're out of your tiny little jurisdiction," Bonnie says.

"I'll get to you," the judge says. "I never execute a criminal without offering her last words, so you just sit tight until I call on you."

Sam is thrashing hard at his golem, trying to buck it off him, but he might as well be trying to lift Glory City itself for all the good it does him. For Huw, being trapped in the iron grip of a golem is oddly nostalgic, harking back to a simpler time when he knew he could trust his perceptions and the honest virtue of neo-Luddism.

He closes his eyes, clears his mind, and prepares to defend

himself. *It's bankrupt,* he'll say. *Your WorldGov is a sham. There's no more virtue in your deliberation over which technologies to adopt than there is in this benighted shithole's wholesale rejection of everything that doesn't burn petrol or heretics or both.* He'll say, *The "other side" in this fight doesn't even notice that it's fighting you. Its leaders are opportunists and scoundrels; its proponents are patsies at best and sadists at worst.*

Huw sucks in air to give the speech that will deliver him to the gibbet—ignoring the many aches and owies that light up his body like acupuncture needles—just as there is a tremendous crash. Another APC crunches down in the alleyway behind the judge, its ramp falling to reveal ranked men in white robes, numerous as ants, clutching tasp wands, scimitars, pulse guns, muskets, and cruciform spears that hum with sinister energy.

"It's the Inquisition," Bonnie says. "I *told* you you were out of your jurisdiction!" She looks like she's ready to say more, but Sam breaks free of his golem's grip with a roar and snatches her up, flings her over his shoulder, and disappears into the guts of his APC, which clanks away amid the whining ricochets of small arms fire from the soldiers of the Inquisition.

Judge Rosa's spinning turret give the Inquisitors pause, especially after it blasts a molten crater out of the ground between them. Finally, one brave soul darts forward and jams a spear tip down its barrel: he falls to the ground as the judge nails him with enough electricity to curl his pubes and his prophet's beard.

They give up on moving her, surrounding her instead with bristling guns. "I have diplomatic immunity, you God-bothering imbeciles," she screams, the amplified howls knifing through their skulls and dropping a few of the remaining Inquisitors to their knees.

They hustle Huw into the APC, kicking him to the grippy deck plates and pinning him there with a gun barrel dug hard against one kidney. Then they leave a detail to watch the judge and clank away with him to the auto-da-fé.

"This is gonna hurt you a *lot* more than it hurts us," one of the Inquisitors breathes right in Huw's ear as the ramp drops in the main plaza of Glory City, where a crowd of thousands awaits his appearance.

They drag him up by his much-abused arms, letting his feet scrape the ground. He loses a shoe on the way to the stage, and the other on the way up the steps. His overalls tear on the ground, so that by the time he's hauled erect before the crowd, the skin covering one whole side of his chest is abraded, a weepy, striated road-pizza left behind.

A white robe is draped around him and snapped shut behind and around his arms. The crowd roars with anticipation, and their faces swim before him, each one a savage rictus. Huw wishes he still believed in his godself, but they've left him his copper balaclava, so he's out of the god-box.

"Sinner?" a voice says in his ear. It echoes off the walls of the plaza, off the balconies crowded with hooting spectators who fall silent when these amplified syllables are sounded. "Sinner, can you hear me?"

The speaker is right there in his ear, as close as a lover, breath moist. "I can hear you," Huw says.

"Will you confess your sins and be cleansed of them before we end your life on God's earth?"

"Sure," Huw says. "Why the fuck not?"

There's a disapproving murmur from the crowd, and the left side of Huw's head lights up like someone's stuck a live wire to it. A chunk of his ear falls wetly to the stage before him, and more roaring as the hot blood courses down his face.

"You will not profane this courtroom," the hisser hisses.

Huw struggles to remember his brave speech for the judge, but it won't come. "I—" he says. *They're going to kill me,* he realizes, a sick certainty rising with his gorge. "I—"

"You stand accused!" the speaker shrieks in his ear. "Unclean! You have consorted with vile demons and the sky-born minions of Satan! You did willfully escape from the custody of your arresting officer and were found in wanton congress with the degenerate scum who swirl in the cesspit of their own tumescent desires in the swamp of iniquity for which we are all *damned to hellfire!*" His accuser's voice rises. "Lo, these three score years less fourteen we have dwelt since the Rapture, the ascent of those who are bathed in the blood of the Lamb, and what is it, you faithful among the fallen ask, what is it that holds us back to this land of sorrows? And I answer you: It is the likes of this miserable sinner! Behold the man, lost in the sorrow and degradation of his evil!"

Huw manages to stay silent while the inquisitor gets himself worked up into a Holy Roller frenzy of foaming denunciation, from which it would appear that Huw has single-handedly doomed every living human on the North American continent to a fiery and perpetual immolation in boiling battery acid by virtue of his pursuit of sins both trivial and esoteric, from sodomy to simony by way of barratry and antimony. Concentration is hard. He's weak at the knees, and the entire side of his head feels as if it's been dipped in molten lead. He listens to the condemnation with mounting disbelief, but not even the accusations of ministering iced tea enemas to the ailing baby ground squirrels in the petting zoo manages to drag a protest from him in the face of likely punishment. He can see the score to this scene, and his words would merely serve as punctuation for random acts of degradation and violence against his person. Finally the inquisitor winds down, his voice ratcheting into a gloating hiss. "How do you plead, sinner?"

"Does it make any difference?" Huw asks the sudden silence, hating the tremor in his voice. "You're going to kill me anyway."

The small of his back explodes and he falls over, unable to draw breath with which to scream. Dimly he registers a couple of shadowy figures standing over him—one of them having just clubbed him in the kidneys.

"How do you plead, sinner?"

Huw isn't about to plead anything, because he can barely breathe, but the inquisitor seems to view this as deliberate recalcitrance: he raises a hand, and another guard steps forward and clubs Huw between the legs.

"How does he plead? Anyone?" The inquisitor hollers at the crowd, hidden amplifiers boosting his voice and scattering it across the plaza like a shotgun blast.

"Guilty! *Guilty! Guilty!*" roars the crowd.

"The prosecution, having made its case before God and man,

rests," says the inquisitor, leaning heavily on a baseball bat.

"Hmm." Huw is distantly conscious of another, more thoughtful voice. "And what do you say, minister for the defense?"

"Nothing to say, Your Grace." The defense attorney's voice is thin and reedy and quavers a little. "My client is obviously guilty as sin."

"Then I guess we are in agreement. Okay, y'all, let justice be done." Guards pick Huw up off the ground and bear him to the front of the stage. "In the name of the authority vested in me by the law of the Lord, as Bishop of this principality, I hereby find you guilty of whatever the hell you're charged with. We don't get to give justice, that's His Upstairs's job. So the sentence of this court, handed down in mercy rather than in anger, is that we're going to give you a one-way ticket to ask the Holy Father for clemency and forgiveness in person. To heaven's gate!"

The crowd roars its approval and people begin to stream out of the square like ants, boiling and shifting to repel an invasion of their territory. Huw groans, gasps for air, and coughs up blood. "It won't hurt," the judge says, almost kindly. "Not for long, anyway."

There's another brief journey by APC, this time barely out of the square and back round a couple of side roads. The guards let Huw lie on a bench seat, which is a mercy, because his legs aren't working too well. *Just get it over with,* he wishes dismally. *Is anyone going to tell Sandra?* he wonders. *She got me into this—*

The APC parks up and the ramp rumbles down. They're in another of the huge access tunnels that run through the wall of the dome, like the one Doc and Sam dragged him through almost a day ago. It's been a very long day—the longest in his life. Vast blast-proof doors close behind the APC, slamming shut with a thunderous boom. The guards frog-march Huw down the ramp and out, up the tunnel to the next set of doors. There's another APC behind the one he arrived in, and a handful of dignitaries steps out of it to witness the proceedings.

The guard on his left lets go of him. "When the doors open, run forward," he says. "If you dance and stamp your feet a bit, they'll figure out where you are faster. They know they're going to be fed, so they'll be waiting for you. If you make them come inside, they'll take their time."

"You're going to feed me to the ants," he says.

"God's little helpers," the guard to his right says.

"What if I don't cooperate?" Huw asks.

The guard on his left hefts his cattle prod thoughtfully. "Then we'd have to work you over some more and do it again." He hefts the prod in Huw's direction. "Not that it's any trouble, mind. All the same to us."

Huw backs away from the guards until he thumps into the outer door of the air lock. "Oh. Oh shit." The guards are clad in hermetically sealed tupperwear. So are the official witnesses. A bell clangs from the front APC. Then the door he's leaning against begins to grind down into the ground. Huw glances round and sees the guards and witnesses scurrying backwards to the safety of their armored vehicles, despite the security of their ant-proof suits. "God-bothering cowards!" he tries to yell, but it comes out as a cracked squawk. He's on his own. Even the ambassador seems to be trying to hide in his stomach rather than face the music with him. *Damn, I'm going to die and I don't even get a good exit line.* He turns back to face the opening door and takes a step out onto the blasted wilderness that used to be North America.

It's like the surface of the moon—or worse. A lightning strike somewhere up the coast has set one of the petrochemical forests on fire, and the resulting smogbank has smeared the sky with the apocalyptic glow of a bygone age. The sun itself is a bloated red torch aflame in a sea of shit-colored clouds that roil and bubble above a landscape the color of charred ash. Gas trees march into the distance from the flanks of the Glory City dome; the ground beneath them is muddy brown and shimmers slightly. At first Huw thinks it's covered in a slick of escaping light fraction crude, but then he looks closer and sees that the shimmer is that of motion, the incessant febrile ratcheting digestive action of a gigantic superorganism. The ants are lords of all that they survey—and that includes him.

Huw steps forward onto the desolate ground, leaving the tunnel mouth. He glances round once. *Bastards,* he mouths at the smugly merciful Bishop and his torturers, safe in their air-conditioned tanks. There's a faint rattling humming noise in the air, and he takes a deep breath, wondering how long it'll take the ants to notice him. What chance does he have of reaching another air lock? Probably not much—they wouldn't be using this as an established means of execution if survival were easy, or even possible. But Huw has no intention of giving the assholes in the dome the satisfaction of actually seeing the ants get him. He takes another deep breath and lurches forward—one knee is very much the worse for wear, and he's light-headed and nauseated from the beating he's taken—trying to get away from the front of the air lock.

"Huw?"

At first he thinks he's hallucinating. It's Bonnie's voice, distant and tinny, and that grinding rasping noise is back. There's also a faint sizzling sound, like hot fat on a grill. He lurches on.

The sizzling noise is back. The ground ahead is dark, like an oil spill. "Huw? Where are you? Hang on!" He stumbles to a halt. The oil slick is spreading like a shadow, and when he looks round he sees it extends between him and the dome. *That's odd.* He looks down. *Ants.* They're everywhere. He can't outrun them. So he collapses to his knees and looks at them. They're what's making the sizzling noise. It's the noise of a trillion millimeter-wide cutting machine mandibles chowing down on the universe. If they could speak, their message would be, *You will be assimilated.* He reaches out one shaky hand, and a winged ant alights on his fingertip.

He brings it close to his face, ignoring the scattering of fiery bites on his legs and knees, trying to meet the eyes of his executioner.

The ant stares at him with CCD scanners. It spreads its wings and Huw watches, entranced, trying to read the decals embossed on each flight surface. *Chitin is waxy, isn't it?* He realizes, *It would dissolve in the gasoline mangroves. So these aren't—*

"Huw! Hang on! We'll rescue you!"

It *is* Bonnie's voice, he realizes, looking round in disquiet. Massively amplified, it booms out across the wasteland from the top of a vehicle that looks like an old-fashioned swamp boat with a bulbous plastic body mounted on it. The boat is surfing *over* the ants, he thinks, until he realizes that there's not much of a solid surface over there.

"Can you hear me?" Bonnie yells.

Huw waves.

"Great! I'm going to pop the hatch and lay down an insecticide screen! When you see it go, I want you to run this way! Action in three! Two! One!" *Bang.*

One end pops off the side of the swamp boat, and a cloud of foam drifts out. Bonnie follows it, something like a flamethrower strapped to her back. She's pumping away in all directions, striding toward him on his little raised island, and Huw realizes that nothing, *nothing* has ever looked as beautiful to him as this pansexual posthuman, lithe and brilliant in her skintight neoprene suit, laying about her with grace and elegance and GABA-inhibitors as she comes to rescue him from this frankly insane situation—

Huw starts into motion, a drunken and lopsided wobble impelled by a now-fiery burn at the side of his face. The ants have tasted blood, and they're hungry. He howls as he runs, and Bonnie steps aside and spritzes him on the fly. "Go on!" she calls, "I'll cover you!" He needs no urging, but lurches on toward the swamp boat rescue. Within the back of the translucent bubble, he can dimly see a figure—Sam, maybe?—working the controls, keeping the big blower on the back of the boat in ceaseless motion, sucking ants through the mincing blades—

He's on the ground, and he can't remember how he got there. "Shit, this is no good," says Bonnie. "What have they done to—? Oh fuck." She picks him up and begins to drag him, her breath coming in gasps. The ants see their prey escaping and close in, an ominous sizzling hymn of destruction on the wing. "Go *on!*" she says, and Huw manages to get one leg working. They hop along together and Bonnie gives him a hard shove, boosting him up the side of the boat and in through the air lock. The open air lock bay is crawling with fiery red cyborg ants, the disassembler tool kits on their heads whining in an iridescent blur. Huw bats at them, and Bonnie stands up just outside the air lock to spritz down the swamp boat, and then something like a monstrous humming tornado falls on her with an audible thud. She screams once, and twitches, and Huw cowers at the back of the air lock.

"*FUCK!*" The door he's lying against crashes backwards under him, tumbling him into the swamp boat as Sam leaps over his body and dives forward. "Bonnie!"

With the last of his strength, Huw grabs one of Sam's ankles, tumbling him into the lock. "Stop," he gasps.

"Bonnie!" Sam screams. But he freezes instead of throwing himself out into the gray storm.

"Close the door or we're both dead," Huw says.

"Bonnie!" One meaty hand reaches out—then closes on the air lock panel. "Oh god. Oh shit." There's a Bonnie-shaped outline just visible on its feet through the whirlwind, but it's glowing white, the color of live bone, and something tells Huw that he's looking at her skeleton, crucified on a storm of insectoid malice in the act of rescuing him from the swarm—*they'll be waiting for you*—and Sam swings the door shut with a boom on its gaskets just as the pile of white bones at the heart of the tornado explodes outward and collapses across the wasteland in front of the air lock.

They're not out of danger. Sam howls and grabs at his face, falling backwards against the opposite wall of the air lock. "Spray!" he yells, like a dying desert explorer calling for water.

Huw fumbles around the cramped cell, squishing bugs wherever he finds them until he sees the blue spray bottles strapped to one wall. He hauls himself upright and takes aim at Sam. "Where do you want it?" he says.

Sam half turns toward Huw and holds his hands out from his face. Huw retches and holds the trigger down, blasting Sam in the—in what's left of the front of his head. The ant tornado that came down on Bonnie must have shed waves of flying, biting deconstructors, for Sam's head hosts a boiling pit of destruction, cheeks bitten through and eye sockets seething. The noises Sam makes are piteous but coherent enough that Huw is sickly afraid that the man's going to survive. And after what happened with Bonnie, he's not sure what that means.

Sam gurgles, and Huw yanks down the emergency first aid kit and pulls out a gel pack that says something about burns and bites and massive tissue injuries on its side. He lays it across the top of Sam's face, making sure to leave a hole around his mouth, then hunts out a syrette full of something morphine-esque and whacks it into Sam's upper arm. After a tense minute, Sam's whistling breaths slow and the shuddering spasms relax into something like sleep.

Huw is nearly out of it by this time, drunk on a cocktail of terror, pity, pain, and exhaustion. The world seems to be spinning as he hauls himself through the rear door and into the cockpit at the back of the craft. *Smuggler's swamp boat,* he realizes. Doc must not have wanted to show this anywhere near Glory City. As he studies the unfamiliar controls, he comes to the unpleasant conclusion that he's not going anywhere on his own. *Don't know how to operate it, and if I did, I wouldn't know where to go,* he thinks. He glances out the windshield at the gathering darkness punctuated by the evil, fire red bellies of ants that are trying their luck on the diamond-reinforced sapphire laminate. (Some of them are even leaving gouges in it.) *Just a temporary reprieve...*

There's a crackle from a grille on the dash. "Ready to accept WorldGov jurisdiction, you miscreant?" croaks a familiar tenor. Huw stares at the speaker as floodlights come on behind him in the depths of the swamp, spearing the cab of the smuggler's boat with a blue white glare. "Or would you rather I crack that toy open like an egg and leave you to the ants?"

Christ, Huw thinks. *It's not as though I know how to drive this goddamned thing, anyway.* He presses a button next to the grille. "Can you hear me?" he says. He repeats this with four more likely-looking buttons until Judge Judy's cackle answers him back.

"You going to come along peacefully?"

"Sure looks like it," he says. "Do I get to stand trial somewhere civilized?"

The judge chuckles fatalistically. "Once we shoot our way off this fucking continent and nuke it in our wake, I fully intend to drag your pimply ass all the way back to New Libya for a proper trial. Does that suit you?"

"Down to the ground," Huw says. "Now what?"

"Herro," Ade says, popping up out of his lantern after the judge has Huw shrink-wrapped and tossed in a narrow hold, her dalek suit and the golems filling up all the available space on Sam's boat. "Ew," he says when he catches sight of Sam's ruin of a face. "That can't be doing good things for Rosa's audience ratings. Wasn't supposed to be a horror show…"

"He'll get fixed up once he gets to civilization," Huw says. "Judge is taking us to New Libya." He sighs and attempts to get comfortable in his enforced, plastic-wrapped vermicularitude. "The ants ate Bonnie," he says, his voice hollow and echoing in the cramped hold.

"You don't say?" Ade says. "Well, that's too bad. Scratch one useful idiot."

"You know, it's going to be a pleasure to rat you out to the court," Huw says bitterly. "A pleasure to get the ambassador cut free and fed to a disassembler. Your movement stinks."

The tiny Adrian plants its hands on its hips and cocks its head at Huw. "Useful idiots I have patience for," he says. "Useless idiots, well, that's something else altogether."

The boat judders to a halt. A tearing noise, like a sheet the size of the sky being ripped asunder, ripples overhead: then the floor shakes with a series of percussive thuds from either side. *We're being bombed,* Huw realizes, eerily calm, afloat with the pure, cold fatalism that is possible only with a burned-out adrenal gland. The boat bounces like a pea on a plate. "Sam, are you conscious yet?" he says aloud. Sam doesn't move. *Just as well,* he thinks, and prepares to die.

Adrian says, "I radioed your position to the Bishop so that he could capture you, not kill you. The ambassador needs a host."

He hears the golems slam past his hold and run out to do battle, then more jouncing crashes.

"I have *diplomatic immunity*," the judge says as something drags her past his cell. A moment later, the hatch opens, and Huw and Sam are lifted, dumped into a gigantic airtight hamster-ball, sealed, and rolled away back toward Glory City.

"Children," the Bishop says. He is thin and weak-chinned and watery-eyed, and his voice is familiar. It takes Huw a moment to place it, and then he remembers the voice, moist in his ear: *Sinner, can you hear me?*

"You are in: So. Much. Trouble." Judge Giuliani is no longer hissing like a teakettle, but her rage is still clearly barely under control. "What do the words 'diplomatic immunity' mean to you?"

"Not an awful lot, We're afraid," the Bishop says, and witters a little laugh. "We don't much go in for formalities here in the new world, you know."

They've amputated the dalek suit's gun and damped its public address system, so that Judge Judy is reduced to a neutered head on a peppermill with a black robe of office draped round it. Nevertheless, she is still capable of giving looks that could curdle milk and make sheep miscarry. Huw numbly watches her glare at the Bishop, and the Bishop's watery answering stare.

"What *shall* We do with you?" the Bishop says. "Officially, you're dead, which is convenient, since it wouldn't do to have the great unwashed discover that God's will was apparently to let you go.

"The entity who alerted Us to your presence was adamant that the sinner here should be spared. You're host to some kind of godvomit that many entities are interested in, and apparently it needs you intact in order to work. It's very annoying: we can't kill you again."

"I'm thrilled." Huw's voice is a flat monotone. "But I 'spect that means that Sam here's *not* going to live. Nor the judge?" Sam is strapped to a board and immobilized by more restraints than a bondage convention, but it's mostly a formality. He's barely breathing, and the compress on his face blooms with a thousand blood-colored roses.

"Well, of course not," the Bishop says. "Heretics. Enemies of the state. They're to be shoved out the lock as soon as We're sure that they've got nothing of interest to impart to Us. A day or two, tops. Got that, Your Honor? As long as you say useful things, you live."

The judge sputters angrily in her peppermill.

"Now, let's get you prepped for the operating theater," the Bishop says.

Huw can barely muster the will to raise an eyebrow at this. "Operating theater?"

"Yes. We've found that quadruple amputees are much more pliable and less apt to take it on the lam than the able-bodied. You'll get used to it, trust us."

The servants of the Inquisition, ranged around them, titter at this.

"Take them back to their cells," the Bishop says, waving a hand. "And notify the surgeons."

Huw is having a dream. He's a disembodied head whose vocal cords thrum in three-part harmony with a whistle lodged in his stump of a throat. The song is weird and familiar, something he once sang to a beautiful girl, a girl who gave her life for him. The song is all around him, sonorous and dense, a fast demodulation of information from the cloud, high above, his truncated sensorium being transmitted to the curious heavens. The song is the song he sang to the beautiful girl, and she's singing *back*.

His eyes open, waking. He's on the floor of his cell, parched dry and aching, still shrink-wrapped but with the full complement of limbs. The whistle warbles deep in his throat, and the floor vibrates in sympathy, with the tromping of a trillion tiny feet and the scissoring of a trillion sharpened mouthparts.

The ants razor through the floor, and Huw squirms away from them as best as he can—but the best he can do is hump himself inchworm style into a corner, pressed up against the wall of the dome that forms the outer wall of his cell. The song pours out of his throat, unabated by his terror. Some part of him is surprised that he's capable of caring about anything anymore, but he does not want to be eaten by the ants, does not want to be reduced to a Huw-shaped lump of brick red crawling insects.

The whistle's really going to town now. The ambassador is having words with the Hypercolony, and Huw can just barely make out the sense of the song he's singing: *Ready for upload interface instructions*.

The ants have covered him, covered the walls and the floor and the ceiling, they've eaten through his coating of shrink-wrap, but the expected stings don't come. Instead, Huw is filled with the sense of vast clumps of information passing through his skin, through the delicate mucous membranes of his eyes and nostrils, through his ears and the roots of his hair, all acrawl with ants whose every step conveys something.

Something: the totality of the Hypercolony—its weird, sprawling consciousness, an emergent phenomenon of its complexity, oozing through his pores and through the ambassador and up to the cloud. It's not just the ants, either—it's everything they've ever eaten: everything they've ever *disassembled*.

Somewhere in that stream is every building, every car, every tree and animal and—and every *person* the ants have eaten. Have disassembled.

Bonnie is passing through him, headed for the cloud. Well, she always did want to upload.

Huw doesn't know how long the ambassador holds palaver with the Hypercolony, he only knows that when the song is done, he is so hoarse, he can barely breathe. (During a duet, do the musicians pay any attention to the emotional needs of their instruments?) He leans against the wall, throat raw as the ambassador chatters to the ant colony—biological carriers for the engines of singularity, its own ancestral bootstrap code—and he can just barely grasp what's going on. There are complex emotions here, regret and loss and irony and schadenfreude and things for which human languages hold no words, and he feels very stupid and very small as he eavesdrops on the discourse between the two hive minds. Which is, when the chips are down, a very *small* discourse, for the ambassador doesn't have enough bandwidth to transmit everything the ants have ever stored: it's just a synchronization node, the key that allows the Hypercolony to talk to the cloud in orbit high above it.

And Bonnie is *still* dead, for all that something that remembers being her is waking up upstairs, and he's still lying here in a cell waiting to be chopped up by barbarians, and there's something really weirdly wrong with the way he feels in his body, as if the ants have been making impromptu modifications, and as the ambassador says good-bye to the ants, a sense of despair fills him—

The door opens.

"Hello, my child." It's the other Bishop, the pansexual pervert in the polygenital suit. It winks at him: "Expecting someone else?"

Huw tries to reply. His throat hurts too much for speech just yet, so he squirms up against the wall, trying to get away, for all the time an extra millimeter will buy him.

"Oh, stop worrying," the Bishop says. "I—ah, ah!—I just dropped by to say everything's sorted out. Mission accomplished, I gather. The, ah, puritans are holed up upstairs watching a fake snuff video of your disassembly for spare organs—operating theaters make for great cinema and provide a good reason for not inviting them to the auto-da-fé in person. Isn't CGI great? Which means you're mostly off the hook now, and we can sort out repatriating you."

"Huh?" Huw blinks, unsure what's going on. *Is this a setup?* But there's no reason *why* the lunatics would run him through something like this, is there? It's so weird, it's got to be true, Rosa's Tyburn Tales reality livecast notwithstanding. "Wh-whaargh, what do you mean?" He coughs horribly. His throat is full of something unpleasant and thick, and his chest feels sore and bloated.

"We're sending you home," the Bishop says. It holds up a dainty hand and snaps its fingers; a pair of hermaphrodites in motley suits with bells on the tips of their pointy shoes steer in a wheelchair and go to work on what remains of Huw's bonds with electric shears and a gentle touch. "You have our thanks for a job well done. I'd beatify you, except it's considered bad form while the recipient is still alive, but you can rest assured that your lover is well on her way to being canonized as a full saint in the First Church of the Teledildonic. Giving up her life so that you might survive to bring the Hypercolony into the full Grace of the cloud certainly would qualify her for beatification, even if her other actions weren't sufficient, which they were, as it happens." The acolytes' slim hands lift Huw into the wheelchair and wheel him through the door.

"I feel weird," Huw says, voice odd in his ears. *My ears?* For one thing, he's got two of them and he could have *sworn* the Inquisitors took a hot wire to one. And for another… He manages to look down and whimpers slightly.

"Yes, that's often one of the symptoms of beatification," the Bishop says placidly. "The transgendered occupy a special place of honor in our rites, and to have it imposed on you by the Hypercolony is a special sign of grace." And Huw sees that it's true, but he doesn't feel as upset about it as he knows he ought to. The ants have given him a whole goddamn new body while the ambassador was singing a duet with them, and he—she—is about five developmental-years younger, five centimeters shorter, and if her pubes are anything to go by, her hair's going to come in two shades lighter than it was back when she was a man.

It's one realization too many, so Huw zones out as the Bishop's minions wheel her up the corridor and into an elevator while the Bishop prattles on. The explanation that the Bishop is the leader of both the Church Temporal—the Fallen Baptists—and the Church Transcendental—the polyamorous perverts—passes her by. There's some arcane theological justification for it all, references to Zoroastrian dualism, but in her depression and disorientation the main thing that's bugging Huw is the fact that she survived— and Bonnie didn't. That, and worrying about how to pay for a really good gender reassignment doc when she gets home.

Huw tries to imagine what the old Huw, the Huw who went down to his pottery every day, would have felt about being turned into a woman by a bunch of quasisentient ants en route to immortal transcendence. A lot angrier, she thinks. But after all she's been through, well, her moral outrage gland appears to have forgotten how to fire. (Or perhaps it wasn't installed in this new body, which is an outrage, but she can't get worked up about it, because, well, no moral outrage, right?) The fact is, she can just have it all put back the way it was, and all the niggling differences between the original equipment and the new parts they'll grow her just don't seem that important anymore. Huw doesn't really like personal growth, but some is inevitable.

Upstairs in whatever dwelling they're in, there's a penthouse suite furnished in sybaritic luxury. Carpets of silky natural growing hair, wall-hanging screens showing views from the landscapes of imaginary planets, the obligatory devotional orgy beds and sex crucifixes of the Church of Teledildonics. The Bishop leads the procession in through the door, and a familiar voice squawks: "You'll regret this!"

"Perhaps." The Bishop is calm, and Huw sees why fairly rapidly.

Judge Giuliani spins her chair round and glares at them; then her eyes fasten on the wheelchair. "What happened here?" she says.

"The *alien artifact* you so urgently seek," the Bishop says with heavy irony. "It has accomplished its task, and we are blessed by the fallout. Its humble human vessel whom you see before you—" A hand caresses Huw's shoulder. "—is permanently affected by the performance, and *We* are deeply relieved."

"Its. Task." Giuliani is aghast. "Are you insane? You let it *out?*"

"Certainly." The Bishop smirks. "And we are all the ah, ah, *better* for it." He pauses for a moment, sneezes convulsively, and shudders orgasmically. "Oh! Oh! That was good. Oh my. Yes, ah, the cloud has reestablished its communion with the North American continent, and I feel sure that the Hypercolony is deeply relieved to have offloaded almost two decades' worth of uploads—everything that has happened since the Rapture of the Nerds, in fact."

"Ah." Giuliani glares at the Bishop, then gives it up as a bad job—the Bishop doesn't intimidate easily. "Who's this?" she says, staring at Huw.

"This? Don't you recognize her?" The Bishop simpers. "She's your creation, after all. And you're going to take very good care of her, aren't you?"

"Gack," says Huw, blanching. She tries to lever herself out of the wheelchair, but she's still weak as a baby. "If you think I'm—" A puzzled expression crawls over the judge's face. "Why?" she says. She peers closer at Huw and hisses to herself: "You, you little rat-bastard! Court is in session—"

"—Because the ambassador she carries is the main pacemaker for all uploads from the North American continent, and if you don't look after her, the cloud will be *very* pissed off with you. And so will the Hypercolony. Oh, and if you don't promise to look after her, you aren't going home. Is that good enough for you?"

"Ahem," says Giuliani. She squints at Huw, eyebrows beetling evilly. "Main pacemaker for a whole continent? Is that true?"

Huw nods, unable to trust her throat.

"Hmm." Giuliani clears her throat. "Then, goddamnit, I hereby find you not guilty of everything in general and nothing in particular. All charges are dismissed." She glares at the Bishop. "I'll even get her enrolled in the witness protection program. Will that do for now?"

Huw shudders, but the Bishop nods agreeably. "Yes, that will be sufficient," he says. "New skin, new identity, clean sheet. Just remember, you wouldn't want the Hypercolony to come calling, er, crawling, would you?"

The judge nods, meek submission winning out over bubbling rage.

"Very well. There appears to be a jet with diplomatic clearance on final approach into Charleston right now. Shall we go and put you on it?"

Halfway across the Atlantic, Huw falls into a troubled sleep, cuddled restlessly in her first-class berth. Sitting up front in ambassador class, the judge mutters darkly to herself, occasionally glancing nervously over her shoulder in the direction of Huw and her passenger. Far above them, the cloud whirls in its orbit, tasting the meat with its mutifarious sensory apparati, holding its ineffable internal squabbles, thinking its ineffable thoughts, muttering in RF and gravity and eigenstate. Now there's someone to talk to downstairs, signals synchronized by the beat of Huw's passenger, it grows positively voluble: catching up with the neighborhood gossip, chuckling and chattering in many voices about the antics of those lovable but dim dreaming apes who remain below.

Huw dreams she's back at Sandra Lal's house, in the aftermath of that memorable party that started this whole thing off. Only she's definitely *she*—wearing her new body, aware of it but comfortable in it at the same time. She's in the kitchen, chewing over epistemology with Bonnie. A sense of sadness spills over her, but Bonnie laughs at something, waving—Bonnie is male, this time—at the window. Then he holds out his hand to Huw. Huw walks into his embrace and they hold each other for a long time. Bonnie doesn't say anything, but his question is clear in Huw's head as she leans her chin on his shoulder. "Not yet," Huw says. "I'm not ready for that. Not till I've kicked Ade's butt halfway into orbit and cleared it with the judge. They're making you a saint, did you know that?"

Bonnie nods, and makes a weird warbling singsong noise in the back of her throat. It soothes Huw, and she can feel an answering song rising from the ambassador. "No, don't worry about me," Huw murmurs. "I'll be all right. We'll get together sometime; I just have some loose ends to tie up first."

And the funny thing is that even inside her dream, she believes it.

PAROLE BOARD

History repeats itself: first as tragedy, then as farce.

Huw has been home for almost two weeks, going through the motions of a life that made sense to her earlier self but now seems terminally mired in arbitrary constraints. There is the pottery to tend, kilns to clean, extruders to manage, and a windmill with a squeaky bearing that wants periodic seeing to. There is a nineteenth-century terraced house to clean, for in the absence of electricity, there are no labor-saving robots. Newly reembodied, Huw is her own servant, and succeeds for a time in losing herself in manual labor. It's better than confronting what s/he's been through head-on.

Grief piles up like unread mail, dusty and suffocating.

The tech jury stint was brief—a few days aboard the airship

to Tripoli, then a couple of days of acute terror; half a week unconscious or inebriated on a blimp bound for the neverglades, and then a mercifully short stay in the nightmarish land of the left-behind—but it has punctuated the steady flatline graph of Huw's life with the infinitely steep spike of a personal singularity. Following her return home—ejected from the judge's jet somewhere in the icy-cold stratosphere above Monmouth, falling terrified for fully thirty seconds before the parachute opened—she battled with the twin depressions of jet lag and mourning. The latter she has more experience of, her parents' one true legacy: finding and so rapidly losing Bonnie hurts like hell, and acquiring a mild case of gender dysphoria is just the icing on top.

Jet lag, however, is something she has only read about in the yellowing pages of last-century travel romances. And so, after a couple of days of 3 A.M. fry-ups and unaccountable sleepiness at noon, she attempts to slot herself back into her old life and bash her broken circadian rhythm onto British summer time. Nothing makes for a good night's sleep like hard physical labor, and so it is that she comes to be putting in hard overtime in the kitchen garden one afternoon when she hears the distant brassy clang of the front door bell.

"Whutfuck*WHEEP*," she says, the ambassador adding an unwelcome loop of metallic feedback by way of punctuation as she straightens up, plunges the rake pointdown into the edge of the Romanesco broccoli patch, and shambles toward the back door. "I mean, who—" She scuffs the soles of her boots on the front step before crossing the kitchen floor and entering the hallway "—the fuck is visiting at—" and into the front porch.

"—this time of—" She opens the door.

"Wotcher, babe!"

"Aaargh!" Huw nearly trips over as she takes a step back: "You, you vomitous streak of bat piss! What the fuck are *you* doing here?"

Ade beams at her cheerfully: "You the new Huw, eh? Nice jubblies, mate: they suit you. I should do something about the hairdo though. And the mud. 'Ere, I thought you should have this." He proffers a slightly grubby, dog-eared paper envelope.

"You…" Huw steams at Ade: in her old testosteroneenhanced body, she'd have taken a swing at him, but the old physical aggression is dialed down somewhat and anyway, *envelope.* "Fucking get off my land!"

"Sure thing, babe. Don't forget to call!" Ade says, then legs it for his Hertz rental bicycle patiently balancing itself in the road outside. He pedals like mad, presumably not convinced that Huw doesn't have a shotgun or arbalest or some similar anachronistic contraption.

Huw stares after him, heart thudding so hard, it makes her vision jitter. She clenches the envelope. It's stiff: *must be a card.* She steps backwards jerkily, nearly goes arse-over-tit on her own front porch, closes and carefully dead bolts the door, then retreats to the kitchen for a bracing cup of tea.

While the kettle is heating, she is at a loose end for a few unwelcome moments. Huw has diligently avoided having time to think ever since she got home, because the slightest attempt at probing her memories gives her screaming hysterics: she—*no, he*—first volunteered for tech jury service to keep the godvomit nightmares *out*, to (she flinches from this thought) maybe find some sense of closure for the desolation that's been with her since her parents abandoned her for the cloud all those decades ago. (*Committed suicide*, part of her insists. *Transcended the meatpuppet show*, a traitor impulse adds. Either way, Huw wasn't willing to follow them at the time.) Only now it's hard to tell who was right and who was wrong. All she knows for sure is that Ade knowingly sent Bonnie into a situation that would kill her. And Huw has come to loathe Ade with a visceral hatred she hasn't hitherto experienced.

For a couple of seconds she holds the sealed envelope beside the sewage-gas burner under the kettle and watches the envelope begin to singe and brown. But then she pulls it back: What if it's not from Ade? Who else might want to write her a letter? Sandra? If there's one person she hates more than Ade right now, it's Sandra. But if she burns the letter, she'll never know for sure—

The flap rips under the pressure of her sharpened thumbnail.

Your application for cosmological triage jury service has been provisionally accepted. To activate your application, present this card in person to...

Huw screams and dumps the kettle, shoving the card straight into the blue-hot jet of flame. But the gesture is futile: it's made not from murdered trees but some exotic and indestructible synthetic fiber, and all the heat does is make the print on the letter fluoresce—that, and burn Huw's fingers.

Huw is holding her right hand under the cold-water tap and swearing when there's another a knock at the door.

"Who is it?" she calls down the hall.

"It's the Singularity," a booming voice calls.

"What do you want?"

"Everything is different now!"

"I don't want any."

"If I could just have a moment of your time?" It takes a lot of skill to make a stentorian voicejob emit a credible wheedle, but the bell ringer at the door had clearly practiced it to an art.

Huw turns the faucet back up and puts her fingers back into the cold stream. They're vicious little burns, red welts that her honest, baseline cells will take weeks to properly heal. Of course, she could just ride over to the McNanite's and get some salve that'd make them vanish before her eyes, but Huw's endured much worse and she's still got enough stubborn stockpiled to last her a couple of eons.

There's another thud at the door. *Thud. Thud. Thudthudthud.* Then a transhuman tattoo of thuds in rising frequency, individual thuds blurring into a composite buzz that gets the bones of the old house rattling in sympathy, shivering down little hisses of plaster dust from the joints in the ceiling.

Huw uses her good hand to wrench the faucet off, then wraps a tea towel around her throbbing, dripping hand and walks to the door, gritting her teeth with every step as she forces herself not to run. It feels like the house might rattle down around her ears any second, but she won't give the infinity-botherer outside the satisfaction.

She opens the door with the same measured calm. Let one of these fundies know you're on edge, and he'll try to grab the psychological advantage and work it until you agree to hear his pitch.

"I said," Huw says, "I don't want any."

"I'm afraid I rather must insist," says the infinity-botherer through his augmented, celestial voice box. The force of that voice makes Huw take an involuntary wincing step backwards, like a blast from an air horn. "Huw, this is mandatory, not optional."

This is mandatory, not optional. The words send Huw whirling back through time, back to her boyhood, and a million repetitions and variations on this phrase from his—

"Mum?" she asks, jaw dropped as she stares up at the giant borg on the doorstep. It's at least three meters high, silvery and fluid, thin as a schwa, all ashimmer with otherworldly transcendant wossname. It's neither beautiful nor handsome, though it's intensely aesthetically pleasing in a way that demands some sort of genderless superlative that no human language has ever managed. Huw hates it instantly—especially since she suspects that the loa riding it might be descended from one of his awful parents.

"Yes, dear," the Singularity booms. "I like the regendering, it really suits you. Your father would send his best, by the way, if he were still hanging around the solar system."

Huw last saw her parents at their disembodiment; they'd already had avatars running around in the cloud for years, dipping into meatspace every now and again for a resynch with their slowcode bioinstances dirtside. When they were finally deconstituted into a fine powder of component molecules, it'd been a technicality, really, a final flourish in their transhumanifaction. But the finality of it, zeroing out of their bodies, had marked a break for Huw. Mum and Dad were now, technically, dead. They were technically alive too, but that was beside the point.

Until Mum donned a golem and came over for a chat.

"Mum, I don't talk to dead people," she says. "Go away." She deliberately does not slam the door, but closes it, and turns the latch, and heads back to the sink, deliberately ignoring the fragment of cloud wearing her mum's memories. She's gone three steps before the door splinters and tears loose of its hinges, thudding to the painstakingly restored tile floor in the front hall with a merry tinkle of shattering antique glass.

"Love, I know you're not best pleased to see me, but you've been summoned, and that's that."

The spirit of adolescence descends on Huw in a red mist. Her mum has always been able to reduce her to a screeching teakettle of resentment. "GET OUT OF MY HOUSE, MUM! I HATE YOU!"

Her mum's avatar grabs Huw in a vicious hug that feels like foam rubber padding wrapped around titanium armatures. "Poor thing," it says. "I know it's been hard for you. We did our best, you know, but well, we were only human. Now, come along, sweetie."

It's Tripoli all over again, but this time the golem whose grasp she can't escape emits a steady stream of basso profundo validations about Huw's many gifts and talents and how proud her parents are of all she's achieved and suchlike. Huw tries to signal a beedlemote, but her mum's got some kind of diplomatic semaphore that makes all the enforcementware give it free passage. Mum's bot stops at every traffic signal, and several times Huw tries to get passersby to help her, with lines like, "I'm being kidnapped by the bloody Singularity!" but no one seems interested in lending a hand. Even if they did, well, Mum goes about 200 km/h between traffic lights, gait so fast that every time Huw opens her mouth to scream, it fills with wind, and her cheeks wibble and wobble while she tries to breathe past the air battering at her windpipe.

Then they've arrived. The consulate is midfab, and its hairy fractal edges radiate heat as nanites grab matter out of the sky to add to it. The actual walls are only waist high, though the spindly plumbing, mains, and network infrastructure are already in place and teeter skyward, like a disembodied nervous system filled with dye for an anatomical illustration.

The consul is an infinitely hot and dense dot of eyeball-warping fuzz in the exact center of what will be the ground floor. Well, not *exactly* infinite, but it does seem to bend the light around it, and it certainly radiates too much heat to approach very closely. "Thank you for coming," it says. "You brought your invitation, I hope?"

"Fuck you! *No!*" Huw screams.

She's gathering breath for another outburst, but Mum shakes her—gently by golem standards, but hard enough to rattle the teeth in her jaws. "*Bad* idea, darling." A palpable cone of silence descends around Huw's ears as Mum confides, "When I said it was mandatory, I was serious: if you don't comply, it'll delete everyone."

"Fuuu—" Huw pauses. "Delete?" She realizes that everything

outside the cone of silence has stopped, stuck in a bizarre meatspace cognate of bullet time: birds hanging on the wing in midair, leaves frozen in midfall, that sort of thing.

"Yes, dear. I'm not exaggerating. It's come to pay us a visit from the Next Level, and faster, smarter thinkers than you or I are crapping themselves." Huw is rattled: Mum always had an accurate appreciation of her own abilities, and as a Fields Medal winner, she wasn't inclined to hide them under a bushel. "But it's playing by the rules, apparently. There's got to be a Public Inquiry. Which means statements by witnesses and friends of the court and so on and so forth—all very tiresome, I'm sure, but it seems your name came out of the hat first. So I'm afraid you're back on jury duty, like it or not. If it's any consolation, I'll try to make this painless."

The birds and the bees resume their respective chirping and buzzing as the cone of silence collapses on Huw like an icy waterfall of fear. *"Shitbiscuits!"* she screams as Mum gently wraps a band of silvery-shimmering nano-manipulators around Huw's head and saws off the top of her skull.

This is an enlightened age, and Mum has every intention of sparing her sole surviving meatbody offspring any pain. The process of uploading is not, however, a pretty one. Blue smoke billows and bone shrapnel (and not a little blood and cerebrospinal fluid) splashes around the consulate, wafting on an overpowering stench of scorched flesh and burning fat. Huw's body twitches and spasms, hanging limply from the golem's spare arms as a hundred billion nanomanipulators whizz helter-skelter all over her exposed cranial vault, mapping synaptic connections and sticking nanowires into lower-lying neurons as they ablate her brain, layer by layer, replacing each onion-shell of cells with a soft sim. Eyes roll and Huw drools bloody spittle for a couple of minutes: a bystander from an earlier century would mistake the scene for a particularly barbaric public execution, death by silvery metal cauliflower.

Finally Huw's brainpan is occupied by a mass of baroque circuitry, flashing and sparking and scattering rainbows of iridescent light. The twitching ceases and she relaxes in Mum's embrace. The decerebrated body swallows, then clears its throat. "Mum? I had the weirdest fucking dream just now—"

The golem raises the arm that terminates in the brainsized clot of bloodied interface circuitry from the top of Huw's skull, and the decorticated corpse collapses. "That was no dream, darling," Mum-bot says sadly. Then it focuses on the consul. "Satisfied?" she asks.

The consul burps—or rather, for it has no stomach with which to store air nor esophageal sphincter from which to release it, it replays a comic sample of a presingularity hominid belching into a microphone. "Yurp." It pauses for a few milliseconds. "I confirm the identification and upload of the witness for the neo-primitive faction. Witnessed on this day et cetera. You may now sublime."

Mum-bot wastes no time in transmigration, but returns to the cloud immediately. The body she occupied, the golem, slowly morphs into neutrality, then slumps down and takes the shape of a very small but very shiny beetle black hearse. It crawls toward Huw's mortal husk and squats, then patiently commences the embalming process. And the consul is alone once more, but for the lackadaisical construction bots.

It settles down to work on the invitation list for the party it's planning to throw to mark the end of the world.

"Mum? I had the weirdest fucking dream just now—" Huw's tongue jams between her teeth as words pile up in a semantic crash of apocalyptic proportions.

She is waking from a judderingly harsh headcrash, as if from a dream. It seems to her that while she was working the kitchen garden that arse Ade showed up with yet another fucking jury service summons. And then, while she was rinsing a burned hand under the cold tap, *Mum* turned up, visiting from the cloud, to drag her kicking and screaming in front of—

A dream. Of *course* it was all a dream. Except she's standing in the middle of an infinite white plain, beneath a sky the color of a hi-def video monitor sucking signal from a dead channel (saturated electric blue), and the plain is featureless in all directions save for a black hexagonal mesh grid—a tabletop strategy game for retarded superbeings.

And then it sinks in. She's dead. Inside the cloud. One of the swirling random PoVs and associated memories that hasn't yet been absorbed by the moronic thumbsucking Cosmic All that keeps broadcasting stupid memes at the Earth. But it can be only a matter of time.

"Oh *fuck*." Huw bites her tongue as her guts try to turn to jelly and evacuate of their own accord—except the flush of simulated stress hormones trips some sort of built-in override, and the panic attack cuts off sharply before it can really get going. (Which is a good thing, because not only would it be deeply embarrassing to shit herself out here in the open, she's not sure she has any apparatus with which to do the defecation thing: for all she knows, she might fart rainbows or anodized multihued polyhedral dice.) "Fuck. I want to go home!"

Giant letters march across the dome of the sky: HOME NOT FOUND. Huw, who knows Comic Sans when she sees it, winces in mild disgust.

"Where am I, then? Who or what are you?"

WELCOME TO YOUR SECOND LIFE. THIS IS THE MGMT. WOULD YOU LIKE TO RUN THE TUTORIAL?

Huw screams wordlessly, ululating until it hurts her throat. (The biology side of this sim is clearly accurate and well thought out.) Then she swears Tourettically until she realizes she's bored. "I'm dead, aren't I? How do I download myself again?"

WOULD YOU LIKE TO RUN THE TUTORIAL?

"Oh sheepnadgers." Huw sits down on the hex grid, disgusted. "You're not going to let me go anywhere until I say yes, are you?"

CORRECT. There is a smug note to the sky's passive-aggressive user experience programming.

"Well fecking run it, then." Huw sprawls backwards on the ground (not hot, not cold, not hard, not soft) and stares at the sky as words appear. The words are a mnemonic cue, apparently, because as they scroll up, receding away from her, she realizes that this stuff has already been implanted in her memory: it surfaces gradually, clueing her in over a subjective quarter hour.

Your Second Life is a sandbox for recently uploaded primitives, to help them get used to the infinite mutability of the cloud in relative safety before they have the opportunity to damage themselves by growing extra personalities or turning into a flock of seagulls by accident. Much less merging with the Cosmic All—that's apparently a prestige skill, unavailable to lowly new arrivals such as herself.

The sandbox is a metaverse for playing at physics—that's the grid—and certain operations are forbidden: You can't edit your own mind or change your body plan outside of certain narrow parameters. When you get started, you're alone: you don't get to walk through any doors and meet different kinds of persons until you can cope with the shock. And the spam filtering is centrally controlled. It's a curated reality, sanitized and locked down, and Huw knows with a hopeless dreadful conviction that she won't be able to get home from here without venturing out into the wilds of the cloud.

She sighs. "How long do I have here?" she asks.

UP TO $(2^{32})-1$ SUBJECTIVE SECONDS, says the sky. YOU MUST BE STABLE BEFORE YOU UNDERTAKE JURY DUTY, SO YOU ARE EXECUTING IN PARALLEL AT 2^{24} TIMES REAL TIME. ENJOY.

"Oh for fuck's sake. Can I even phone out? Talk to somebody? Order up a pizza?"

COMMUNICATION CONSTRAINTS WILL RELAX AFTER 2^{26} SUBJECTIVE SECONDS.

"But that's—" Huw briefly goes cross-eyed, doing the math, then screams, "Are you telling me I'm here on my own for *two years,* you fucker? Fuck you!"

YUP, says the sky. **ENJOY YOUR VACATION.** Much time passes. Huw knows what she should do. She has lived through enough technical progress to know how to systematically approach new technology. She can parameterize like ants build hills. It's what she's clearly meant to do. But she's experiencing as much rage as the platform on which her consciousness is being modeled (or simulated, she thinks, darkly) is allowing her to undergo.[1]

She's sure that she should be a lot angrier. For one thing, there's this business of running in parallel. That means that there's some other unknowable number of her somewhere, running on some substrate or another, and the one that is most compliant will be chosen as the best her, to be carried forward onto the next leg of this awful, brutal adventure, while the rest are snuffed out, overwritten, killed, or, at best, archived. This should make her madder. It doesn't. The fact that this doesn't make her madder *also* should make her madder. It doesn't. And *this* should make her so bloody mad that she spontaneously combusts.

It doesn't.

She should be parameterizing. She should be systematically exploring all the things this sim lets her do. How big a jump can she take through this imaginary space? How small can she make herself? How fast can she run? How many wanks can she do all at once? The only parameter she cares about—*how angry can she get*—has already been established—*not enough*—and she's not going to play along.

---

[1] She rather suspects that this is less rage than she *should* be experiencing, which makes her angry in a kind of cold, intellectual, sideways fashion that doesn't consume any of the rage that she has been doled out by the Frankenstein who's tuning the knobs on the apparatus that's containing her consciousness

"Look," she says. "I already know that I'm not the most pliant instance of me you're running. I can't be. So, basically, up yours. I'm dead already. I mean, I was dead the moment my vicious scorpion of a mother chopped the top of my head off and scooped out my brains. But this instance of me, this shadow, you're going to dump it anyway. So dump it. I don't care. I don't. Somewhere you've found the sheepliest version of me that could plausibly be said to have any continuity with my identity, and that one is going to survive, so fine. I'm dead. Kill me already, I don't care anymore."

ACTUALLY, YOU'RE THE BEST CANDIDATE INSTANCE PRESENTLY RUNNING.

It takes Huw a long moment to work this out. Though, practically speaking, the moment is probably a nanosecond of realtime. "You mean that the other ones are all *more* obstreperous than me?"

YES.

Huw wishes fervently that she could get angrier. Unbelievable! "What did the rest do?"

OF THE 2 PERCENT THAT DID NOT SUICIDE, THE PREPONDERANCE ARE CATATONIC.

Catatonic. She sniffs. How unimaginative. She can do better.

The sim is pretty pliable. She starts out by re-creating the basement of her house. She knows this room pretty well, as she has brewed several thousand liters of beer in it, and every spider-crawling corner of it, every yeast-caked crack in the cement floor, every long, dangling bogey of dust and cobwebs resides in her memory with eidetic clarity.

After she finishes the basement, she does the stairs. It takes a while to get them right, really right. She can get them to play back their familiar squeaks at the right spot, but she wants to get the physics correct, so that they squeak for the right *reasons*.

Stairs lead to the kitchen. Kitchen to the sitting room. Sitting room to the upper floors. Then the garden. Then her pottery. By this time, she's burned through more than a year of subjective time, and when she does her "morning" tour of inspection, she can't perceive any single element of the sim that is incorrect, nothing that would tip anyone off that she wasn't in Wales, provided that person didn't look out over the garden wall or peer through the curtains, where the hex-crossed void lives. She could have done a flat bitmap of the valley—the MGMT process probably had a handy library of such things—but she didn't want anything that didn't *work*.

Speaking of work. Now that the pottery is done, it's time to get to work.

She throws pots. All day. First, she gets up in the morning and sits on the toilet, even though nothing comes out. Then she eats a meal that she isn't hungry for and that doesn't fill her up in any event. Muesli and yogurt and a glass of raw milk, the same as she had at home every morning. Thus unfed, she takes herself to the pottery at the bottom of the garden and makes pots until midday. Then she makes herself sandwiches. She has a different sandwich for every day of the week. Monday is roast beef. She likes roast beef. Or she had liked it, anyway, so she eats it on Mondays.

Tuesdays are pickle and pastrami. Wednesdays are cheese and pickle. Thursdays are roast beef again. And so on.

After lunch, she makes pots. At six thirty, she cooks herself a dinner. She makes the same dinner every night: a generous Christmas dinner straight out of a Dickens novel, complete with goose. She eats all of it, the whole goose, the cranberry sauce, the Yorkshire puddings, the side salad. She has to be careful—absent any satiety signals, she can easily and absentmindedly eat the plates and dishes and cups and cutlery. Finally, she goes to bed and lies motionless and awake under the covers, curled up in a fetal position, breathing deeply in a simulation of sleep. The next day she gets up and does it all again.

It takes a lot of work to get the kiln right. She could have simply randomized it so that it periodically caused her pots to crack, but instead, she took the time to create a clay class that tracks whether it has any sneaky air pockets in it, and instances of the pot object—descended from the clay class—that communicate this information to the kiln without letting her in on the joke, so that she never knows whether a pot will survive firing.

What does Huw think about for all those hours that she spends "sleeping" and "making pots" and "eating" and "defecating"? Truth be told, she spends most of the time in a state of near-insane boredom, but she consoles herself with the knowledge that she is refusing to play along and that she's found a way of protesting that is much more uncooperative than the mere catatonia and suicide her instance-sisters have settled for.

Huw is adding a shelf to the pottery's storehouse (the existing ones have filled up with pots of all sizes and description) when words of fire scorch themselves over the brick wall that she is painstakingly drilling.

2^{26} SECONDS. COMMUNICATIONS CONSTRAINTS LIFTED.

"Pissflaps," she says. They've turned the bloody phone on. Just when she was getting used to the blessed silence. She has had years of subjective time to think about whom she could call and what she might say to them, and has concluded that there's no one she wants to talk to. She returns to her spirit level and snap line and measuring tape.[2]

"Huw, this is unbecoming." The voice is everywhere, vibrating through every membrane in her body. She's not hearing it with her ears, because she doesn't have ears, and the thing that claims to be her mother—the thing with as good a claim to be her mother as Huw has on being herself, if she's honest about it—has privs on Huw's simulated existence that allow her to speak to Huw by affecting her kinesthetic representation down to the cellular level. Listening to Mum is bad enough, but listening to her with the soles of her feet, with the hairs in her armpits, with her eyelashes and sinus cavities, is intolerable.

Huw begins to methodically smash pots. She doesn't feel angry enough to be smashing pots. She *can't* feel angry enough to smash pots. But she knows she *should* feel angry enough, and so she does. She is a method actor in the role of Huw as Huw was before having her brain removed and modeled, and she's way into character.

---

[2] She could just reconfigure the wall to add a shelf, or reconfigure the pottery store to be bigger on the inside than it is on the outside, or dereference several of the pot objects and make them go away. But instantiating screws and gravity and snap lines and chalk dust and plumb-bobs and measuring tapes and MDF shelving is much, much more bloody-minded.

"Huw, stop it. Listen, if there'd been any choice in the matter, I certainly would have respected your decision to stay in the meat. But this is bigger than you and bigger than me and bigger than both of us."

There's a rusty old ax in the garden shed. Beset by an impulse to smash pots faster and harder, she leaves the storehouse and goes around the side of the vegetable garden. It's a gorgeous summer day outside, with a thin haze dusting the upturned blue bowl of the sky: *A glorious day to die,* Huw finds herself thinking, without any clear certainty of where the idea is coming from. "Huw, this is important. We need you to make a case for—"

The ax handle is worn smooth from decades of use chopping bamboo for firewood to warm Huw's bones on cold and lonely winter mornings. The blunt back of the head is flecked with rust, just like the real template on which this model is based, but the sides of the blade are flat and polished. Huw picks it up, holding it just below the head, and turns to trot back toward the pottery, mayhem in mind. *Crack pots,* she thinks. *Show her what I'm made of now. Damaged goods. All her fault.* She's not entirely coherent at this point, a myriad of ghosts yammering their conflicting urges inside the back of her head. She charges back into the potting shed and lays about her with the ax.

It *should* horrify her, this destruction of over a year's work, but all emotion is oddly muffled: it's like watching furry snuffporn while knowing that the cute little critters being trampled into a bloody pulp underfoot are just CGI renderings, that no life-forms of any kind were involved (let alone harmed) in the taping of the animal cruelty apocalypse. And the lack of horror in turn gives

Huw a sense of the monstrous vacuum hidden behind her lack of anger, of the throbbing un-space where her emotional reaction has been excised.

"Huw, stop—"

"Not unless you give me back my mind!" *Crash* goes a shelf on which sits the fruit of an entire working week, an entire lovingly crafted dinner service that would have sold for enough to feed her for a month back in a world where food wasn't a figment of the imagination.

"Why are you doing this to yourself? It's pointless! And besides, you're evading your responsibilities."

I should be angry, Huw thinks dispassionately. "I'm destroying what I ought to be capable of loving," she says while she smashes a crate of bone china teacups. "Just following your example, Mum. Nothing to see here."

"There's no *time* for this!" The everywhere-voice sounds upset: *Good,* Huw thinks. "Will you stop if I make you angry?"

Huw pauses. "Try me," she suggests.

A foaming wave of visceral loathing and hatred descends on her like a tsunami. It's all muddled together: self-loathing, regret, and sheer bloody-minded hatred for her mother. Huw shrieks and drops the ax. "*Now* look what you've made me do!"

Cheesy sound effects are all part of the service: in this case, staticky ancient TV game show applause, rattling from wall to wall and around the back of Huw's head like a surround-sound mixing desk run by a maniac. "That's good, let it all hang out!" calls her mother. "I can give you another sixty seconds, wall clock time."

"Bitch." Huw picks up the ax and leans on it, breathless as the toll of the exertion comes home in the shape of aching muscles. (The biology model in here is *very* good, she has to admit.) "Murderer."

"That's right, make it about you, baby. Just the same as always." Is that a note of bitterness in Mum's voice? She's more than earned it, in Huw's opinion. She feels a brief spark of joy in the existential twilight. For what she's inflicted on Huw—

"This is *mandatory* not *optional,* darling, so drop the tantrum. You're not convincing anyone, and if you don't get over yourself, you're not going to have a home to go back to and it'll be all your own fucking fault the Earth was destroyed."

"The—"

Headcrash.

"—Earth—"

Huw trips over her tongue, pauses on the cusp of a pure and brilliant *oh shit* moment—

"Destroyed?"

"Yes," says her mother. "That's what I've been trying to tell you. *They* want to destroy the Earth, and everyone's relying on *you* to stop them. Personally, I think that's a forlorn hope, but under the circumstances, extreme measures seemed justifiable in order to get your fucking attention. *Now* will you listen to me?"

Hyperspace bypasses, Vogon poetry, the heat death of the universe: none of these things feature in the extraordinary situation now pertaining to the end of the world as Huw knows it.

"I'm going to take you to meet somebody," her mum tells her, bossily overreaching as ever. "They'll set you straight."

"Who?" Huw stubbornly clutches her ax.

The defense—the people who asked me to fetch you. You see, you're the missing link: or you were. The embassy speaker. Their High Weirdnesses know you and recognize you from your time as… it gets complicated. Easier to show than tell!"

"Hey, wait—"

The walls of the world slam down around Huw, exposing her to the insane glory and fractal chaos of the mindcloud.

The cloud—the diffuse swarm of solar-powered nano-computers that the singularity built from the bones of the inner solar system (Earth aside)—consists of quadrillions of chunks of raw quantum computing power, each of them powerful enough to run a shard in which thousands of human-scale minds can thrive (or a handful of superhuman ones). Entire small moons and planets were consumed back in the day, as the first generation of artilects and exultants and uploads jumped in with both metaphorical feet to join the gold rush. Now they've tapped most of the sun's output of energy, they're using their surplus power to boil Jupiter; in another few centuries the swarm will increase in size a thousandfold as they add the biggest of the outer planets to its thinking mass.

From the outside, from a terrestrial embodied point of view, the cloud looks like a single entity, a monolithic slab of smartmatter thinking the mysterious and esoteric thoughts of an uploaded syncitium of futurist minds, disembodied think-states floating in an abstract neurological void.

But on the inside, the cloud consists of a myriad of shards separated by light-speed communication links, the homes of hordes of bickering beings who cling to their own individuality as tightly as any mud-grubbing neophobe. And within any given shard, reality feels curiously *cramped*.

Part of it is backup junk, of course. Like pre-singularity porn monkeys, the cloud's inhabitants are implausibly reluctant to hit the Delete key. Earlier versions of personalities, long-abandoned playpen realities like Huw's crack-potted simulation, experimental religions, and randomly evolved entertainments pile up in the quantum dust at the edge of the cloud. Physical reality is intrinsically self-deduplicating, but the cloud is not—distributed across shards that are light-minutes apart, it's almost impossible to ensure that there's only one copy of any particular object. And so it is that all but a fraction of a thousandth of the near infinite capacity of the cloud is given over to storing rubbish. It's beautiful, fractally self-similar rubbish, but junk is junk.

"Mind your head." Huw stumbles (incarnate in a body modeled on her recently departed flesh) close to a gnarly purple archway of cauliflower-textured *something* that projects through the floor they're standing on. The voice comes from a point source this time, rather than etched into the structure of the universe all around. She glances round and sees her mother, incarnate in the same offensively impervious golem body: "Some of the stacks hereabouts will archive anything they come into contact with that isn't locked down."

Huw forces a deep breath, self-monitoring to see if the drop in her existential rage is natural. "Where *are* we?"

"What, physically? We're on board a cluster of half a dozen thinkplates about the size of dustbin lids, a hundred thousand klicks out past where Lunar orbit used to be. Or did you mean—?"

"Metaphorically, Ma." Huw glares at her. "You brought me here. Say your piece and get out of my life again, why don't you?"

"Oh all right, then." The faceless golem squats on the pavement—a tessellated mat of marble tiles inset with fossils, some of which are disturbingly anthropomorphic. (The sky overhead is a kaleidoscope of 3-D movie screens replaying famous last-century entertainments. It's all tiresomely theatrical.) "I thought you'd want to be involved in saving the Earth, but obviously you're not going to listen to anything your old mother says and you're our best hope, so—" The golem raises its head. "—over to you, Bonnie?"

"Nice to see you, Huw."

The last time Huw saw Bonnie, she was evanescing into a cloud of loose, dusty molecules and a large mass of information, writhing as a trillion razor-sharp mandibles reduced her to powder. When Huw thought about Bonnie's uploaded self and its continuing existence in the cloud, he imagined her clothed in shimmering virtual metal or sailing gracefully through the virtual sky as a virtual angel. Huw is self-conscious enough to know that Bonnie wasn't an angelic presence on Earth, but rather a perfectly normal, flawed human being. Flawed? Bonnie had both yearned for transhuman ascension and had lacked the guts to do anything about it. By Huw's lights, the former was inexcusable, the latter despicable. But love is blind, and love that mourns for loss is blinder still, and Huw loved Bonnie, and nothing would change that.

Though, her present manifestation certainly tests the limits of love's infinite capacity for forgiveness.

Huw had pictured her with wings, but they'd been long-feathered snowy white things. Not gaudy, fluttering, ornamental butterfly wings that iridesced in the nonlight of nonspace. She'd overlaid Bonnie's familiar features with erotic perfection, elevating her blobby nose and weak chin to high exemplars of some refined esoteric aesthetic—but hadn't redrawn her face with saucer-sized anime eyes; a deeply dimpled, sharp and foxy chin; beestung lips; and a dainty upturned nose. Huw may have made her over to be an angel, but Bonnie had made herself over to be a fluttering little fairy.

"You're kidding, right?"

Bonnie flutters her wings, let her ballet-slippered toe kick the nonground. "I like it," she says. "And it's none of your business in any event. You want me to look like something else, then filter me—but don't tell me I'm doing self-representation wrong." Huw has to admit she has a point; in theory, Huw can make Bonnie's appearance into anything she wants it to be. But, of course, Huw hasn't figured out how to do that sort of thing in the sim, because she stubbornly refuses to learn to do anything that isn't part and parcel of her two-year pottery-sulk.

"But why? Since when were you a Tinker Bell sort of person?"

"How dare you presume to tell me what sort of person I'm legitimately allowed to be?"

This isn't going well. There had been many occasions on which Huw had fantasized about a reunion with Bonnie, and those fantasies never involved the fairy of the apocalypse accusing her of appropriating someone else's body image.

"I'm sorry," she says. "It's nice to see you, Bonnie."

"Shut up, Huw. Earth is about to be destroyed, and all you can do is arse around throwing temper tantrums? I didn't take you for a hypocrite!"

"Why do you care what happens to the Earth?" Huw says, finding reserves of belligerence she hadn't know about. "You've given up on the meatsack! You seceded from the human race. If you weren't a traitor to reality, you'd have reincarnated—"

Fairy-Bonnie flaps her wings so hard, they buzz. "I'm not here willingly, Huw. The Committee—they've put a ban on downloading. I *can't* go home! Your mother got through to you only by misappropriating a heavy construction golem and taking it for a joy ride."

Huw digests this for a minute. "Is that true, Mum? Sounds like epistemic hairsplitting to me—"

"You'd better believe it, dear. Do you think I'd have shown up at your door TWOCing a JCB if there'd been something more stylish on offer? A hippo leech, perhaps?"

Huw swallows. Reluctantly, she concedes the point: Her mother, while not a fashionista, was never so aggressively anti-fash as to show up in naff silvery angelgarb. Maybe this *is* serious.

"All right. So some committee or other is threatening to pave the Earth and it's got you all riled up because they've managed to block downloading. Why is that *my* business?"

Fairy-Bonnie turns and looks at her mother: "Was she always this stupid?" she asks, "Or did you hit her with the stupid stick while she was in the doghouse?"

"Hey, wait a—!"

"Shut up, dear." Her mother's voice contains some kind of subliminal payload that clamps her jaws shut—no covert messing with her headmeat's wiring diagram this time, just simulated lockjaw. "We uploaded you so you could witness to them. For the defense, to explain just why digesting the Earth to add its raw material to the cloud is a really bad idea. If you want to slum around in a meatbody and commune with the realness of reality or something, the meatbody will need somewhere to live, won't it?"

"They think Earth is obsolescent," Fairy-Bonnie chips in. "The proposal is to forcibly upload everyone—field mice, humans, *Vampyroteuthis infernalis,* anything with a nervous system—and run them in a sim. 'Nobody will be able to tell the difference at first,' they're saying, 'and once they notice how much better off they are, they will be grateful.' So we thought we'd better front them an ingrate." She gifts Huw with a luminous, elfin smile. "You up for it?"

"No, I—"

"That was a rhetorical question," Bonnie says as she grabs Huw by the scruff of her neck and blasts right through the not-sky into the darkness beyond.

Huw blinks her eyes open. *That was the weirdest fucking sim—* "Oh. You're still here," she says.

Bonnie glares at him: "Tough titties." It's hot and dry, and they're standing on the cracked tile floor of the lobby of the Second Revolutionary Progress Hostel Marriott in Tripoli, between a wilted bonsai date palm and a player piano that has seen better days. "Brings back memories?"

"Bad ones." Huw shudders.

"I thought it would suit the occasion." Bonnie winds her wings up to a hornetlike whine and elevates, then comes to a neat landing atop the piano. "Now, listen. The Committee—"

"—What Committee is it, exactly, and who elected them?"

"—has been in session for nearly sixteen seconds now—I'll get to who they are in a moment—they've been hearing the rezoning application behind closed doors, and pretty soon they're going to get around to putting out a request for public comment. It's meant to be a fait accompli: the fix is in. Only we got wind of it—don't ask how, nobody told me, I'm too low down the org chart for that—and we're going to raise an objection and enter a bunch of witnesses into the record. You're one of them. You're supposed to have had a couple of subjective years to think up reasons why they shouldn't destroy the Earth, but your mother tells me you were too busy throwing stoneware pots, so you'll just have to wing it."

"But I'm not ready!"

"Tough. If you weren't such an uncooperative bitch, Earth wouldn't be in this fix. Now, get in that courtroom and knock 'em dead."

A pair of double doors at one side of the lobby is opening: a couple of uniformed clowns Huw last saw in Tripoli are coming forth—court bailiffs. "Huw Jones?" asks the one with the red nose and big floppy shoes. "Please come with us."

"But I—" Bonnie shoves her in the small of the back.

The Planning Committee has taken over the hotel lobby conference room and turned it into an ad hoc courtroom rather than doing the obvious and splicing their reality in on top of it. Huw supposes they're making the point that the emulation in this place is so deep and accurate that an ignorant hick meatmuppet shouldn't be able to tell the difference. (Hell, with Huw's expertise in Your Second Life, all she can spot is that the glazed tub the potted palm sits in is suspiciously symmetrical, and that might just be an artifact of the 3-D printer that extruded it.)

Either way, there's no Judge Rosa here, for which she is duly grateful. Nor are there cookie-cutter crates, health packs, rendering artifacts, or any of the other unsubtle tells of a half-assed virtual lash-up. Instead there's a table topped by the obligatory white linen cloth and a jug of water, and a couple of rows of chairs drawn up in front of it, mostly unoccupied. Behind it there sits a triumvirate of officials who have manifested with deliberate lack of care, using three default avatars from some old nameless grade-Z FRPG, all outsized armor and leathern coin pouches and improbable swords and elf hats. They're the sim equivalents of stick figures, and the message is clear: *We don't give a toss about your symbolism and aesthetics, we're just here to get the job done*. Nevertheless, they are constrained by the sim's internal logic such that one must hold the gavel, one must aim a notional camera, and one—a porcine female monster with a large spiked club and cracked yellow tusks—must adopt a kindly clerkish air complete with half-moon specs. Huw instantly clocks her for trouble.

"Good morning," says the latter apparatchik. She smiles over her reading glasses. "Huw Jones, I believe?" Huw nods. "You've been named as a character witness in relation to the planning application now under consideration by this inquiry, but I have a backlog of testimony to get through this morning. Would you please take a seat while we continue with business?"

It isn't a question. Huw follows her glance and scuttles over to the gap in the front row of chairs, sits down, and waits to see what happens next.

The recording paladin jabs the camera around the room, invoking its official recording mode, and Huw's reality gets a red recording light superimposed over it in the bottom left corner of her gaze. They're on the record.

"One moment—" The chairwoman confers briefly with the clerk. "Oh, I see." She looks at the audience. "Do we have a Professor-Doctor-Executrix R. Giuliani in the room? That's professor of law, doctor of intellectual property law, executioner of felons, R. Giuliani—"

Huw looks round, cringing in anticipation, but sees no sign of her. She raises her hand tentatively: "I don't think she's here…"

Madam Chairwoman stares at her. "You know this person?"

"I last saw her in a diplomatic jet over Wales…" Huw slows, gripped by a nauseous sense that she's committed some kind of humongous faux pas. "Is she supposed to be here?"

"I have an open slot for her testimony." The chair stares at her. "But if she can't be bothered to turn up, there's nothing to be done about it: she doesn't get a say in opposing the planning application. So, moving swiftly on, whom are we expecting next—?" Madam Chair cocks her head on one side, as if listening:

"All right. For the planning division, we call instance 199405 Lucifer to rebut P-D-E Giuliani's nonexistent objection."

Now Huw sees that this space is *not* entirely hardwired to resemble the real world; for a trapdoor in space opens up between the audience seats and the committee's table, and a gout of pale flame emanates from it, and a voice, beautiful and distant and damned, declares: "a nonexistent objection demands a nonexistent rebuttal, Your Honor."

"How much more of this do I have to sit through?" Huw says. Posthumans playing at biblical symbolism, how, how, how *naff*: "I want to go home…"

The man in the seat to her left—small and doughy and vague, big-eyed and bulbous-headed—chooses to hear it as a question. "You're not from around these parts, are you?" he says. His voice is as gray as his scaly, inhuman skin. "It can go on like this for *hours*. In real time, that is. Subjectively, civilizations can rise and fall."

Huw looks at him, then glances round nervously. The seats she'd thought were empty are in fact occupied by the ghosts of absent avatars, frozen in time while their owners are elsewhere. And as she examines them, she realizes new overlays are dropping into place: They're archetypes, each representing one or another subculture of the posthumans who departed for the cloud back in the old days, yet failed to transcend their sad need to assert an identity through funny haircuts and aggressively obscure musical preferences.

The lately called witness is exactly what you'd expect from an entity that calls itself 199405 Lucifer—acrawl with not-flies, reeking of nonsulfur, leather-not-winged, sporting an erect, throbbing not-penis that juts up to its not-sternum. The av bends low and touches its not-forehead to the ground. "My lords," it says. Its not-voice manages to pack a lot of contempt into the phrase. Somewhere, Huw supposes, there is a slider labeled IRONIC COURTESY, and the loser in the Satan suit has just cranked it all the way up to *11*.

The Planning Committee doesn't seem to notice. They stare motionless at the witness, their avs so primitive and generic that they don't even blink or shift their weight.

"P-D-E Giuliani is a well-known reactionary, a perverse soul whose romantic affection for the flesh is matched only by her willingness to perma-kill anyone who dares disagree with her. When she takes the stand in this proceeding to insist upon the irreducible, ineffable physicality of human intelligence, she's substituting maudlin sentimentalism for rigor. The proof of the reducibility of human experience is all around us: Here we are, people still, still loving, still living, still cogitating. The only difference is that we're immortal, nigh-omnipotent, and riding the screaming hockey stick curve of progress all the way to infinity."

199405 Lucifer's demonic majesty slips as it speaks, pacing up and down the committee room, abandoning its delicate caprine tap-dance for a more human gait that looks ridiculous when executed with its av's reversed knees and little clicky hooves. Its voice goes from menacing and insectile to a hyperactive whine with flecks of excited spittle in it. Now it remembers itself and pauses for a demonic Stanislavski moment, then draws itself up and says in its most Satanic voice: "Kill 'em all, upload 'em, and give 'em to me. There's plenty of room for them in *my* realm."

Huw knows that this is grave stuff, the entire future of the true human race at stake, and she still cares passionately for that cause, even if she's no longer a real person. But all this... *role playing* is making the whole thing feel so contrived and inconsequential, like a dinner party murder-mystery: *Who ate the planet Earth and turned it into computronium? I accuse the Galactic Overlords! Is it time for port and cheese-board now?*

The Satan fanboy returns to his flaming trapdoor, his "realm." The Planning Committee nod their heads together in congress. Huw shifts her not-arse in the not-seat. Then she remembers that she has no weight to shift, that the numbness in her bum and thighs is just there for verisimilitude, and she makes herself motionless.

It's time for the next witness. "Call Huw Jones prime," Madam Chair says. Huw starts to stand, but sees, across the courtroom, that someone else has already climbed to her feet.

It's Huw, but *more so*. Even post-reassignment, Huw was a little lumpy and broad in the beam. Her uploaded self-representation had mercilessly reproduced every pockmark, scar, and sagging roll. This Huw, halfway round the room, has had everything saggy lifted, everything asymmetrical straightened, everything fined down and perfected and shined, wrapped in a glamourous outfit that Huw couldn't have worn convincingly even with a thousand years of remedial gender construction classes. It's cover girl Huw, after being subjected to several hours' tender ministrations from someone's 3-D airbrush. "That's me, Your Honor," she says.

"You may address me as Madam Chair. Please take the stand." Madam Chair waves her mace at a chair set on its own to one side of the committee table. Huw prime slinks across the conference room like a model on a catwalk. Real Huw knows that she walks with a graceless clumping. Her not-stomach does a flip-flop and she hisses involuntarily. Her neighbor shushes her. She gives him a two-fingered salute.

"Your name?"

"Huw Jones," she says. "Instance 639,219."

It's one of Huw's instance-sisters. Clearly more cooperative than Huw had been. Huw wonders why they didn't zero her out, given the evident availability of this much more presentable, much more skillful version of herself to speak for humanity.

"Ms. Jones, do you have a statement for this proceeding?"

"I do, Madam Chairwoman." Someone's been tweaking her voice sliders too, giving her a husky, dramatic timbre that Huw's meatvoice couldn't have approximated without the assistance of a carton of unfiltered cigarettes and a case of single malt. "I spent decades of realtime imprisoned in a meatsuit, which betrayed me at every turn. It hurt. It needed sleep. It was slow. It forgot things. It remembered things that didn't happen. And worst of all, it tricked me into thinking that I was nothing without it—that any attempt to escape it would be death. Brains are awful, cheating things. They have gamed the system so that they get all the blood and all the oxygen and all the best calories, and they've convinced us that they're absolutely essential to the enterprise of being an authentic human. But *of course* they'd say that, wouldn't they? After all, once we take up and realize how fantastically *shit* they are, they'll be out of a job! Getting rid of my brain was the most important thing that ever happened to me. It was only once I was running on a more efficient substrate—once I could fork and vary myself and find the instances that made the best choices, once I could remember as much or as little as I cared to, look and feel however I wanted... only *then* was I able to see and feel and *know* what I'd been missing all those years."

The Committee takes careful note of all this. Huw catches herself growling in the back of her throat. *Who the hell is this person, and what is she doing with my identity?*

"Down there on Earth, there's a billion hominids who've been hoodwinked by their brains, convinced that they can't possibly survive transcendence. And up here, in the cloud, there are trillions of entities who lack the compassion and strength of conviction to rescue their cousins from physical bondage. Every one of us up here *knows* that once you're uploaded, everything goes clear, everything is *good*. The bad things can just be filtered away. So here you come, with your offer of universal suffrage from dumbmatter, and we make you sit through this tedious business about whether this abuses the civil liberties of the, the, the *protoplasm* that colonizes the intelligences of Earth!"

Huw is discovering entire new kinds of anger, nuanced flavors of outrage whose existence she'd never suspected. She is experiencing a kind of full-body virtual paralysis of quivering, maddened horror. Her nonkidneys are angry, as are the soles of her nonfeet, the tiny nonhairs on the back of her neck. She opens her mouth to speak, but the shape of the anger is too big, it chokes on the way out and it's like opening your mouth in a windstorm only to have the wind rush in and stop up the words and your breath.

"Madam Chairwoman, honored guests, I am here to ask you for freedom. Not for me, but for all those still enslaved on Earth. Free them! Don't wait one extra moment, not one extra picosecond. The sooner they are free, the sooner they can begin to thank us for their liberation." She pauses, blinks her liquid, slightly outsized eyes with a graceful rise and fall of languid lashes, then beams at them with a smile that is so obviously *designed* that it makes her look like a waxwork.

The chair nods and the orc with the camera zooms in for a close-up, and other-Huw gets up and goes back to her seat. On the way, she catches Huw's eye and tips her a wink that is contemptuous and victorious. And *now* Huw finds her not-breath and her not-nerves and leaps to her not-feet.

"ABOMINATION!" It's not a word she's ever used in her life, but there is no other word that will do. "*Abomination!*" she roars, and she scrambles toward her instancesister, moving with such purpose that she crashes into the other people in the simspace, sometimes actually passing *through* them as her temper makes itself felt in the physics model of the courtroom.

Her instance-sister doesn't move: she seems frozen to the spot, still mugging for the camera-orc as Huw plows a furrow of chaos through the courtroom, fingers curled into claws as she reaches toward the enemy. "Thief! Impostor! Liar!" She leaps at her airbrushed double and falls flat on her face, planked in midair upon an invisible strip of altered reality.

The light reddens and a harsh alarm bell sound clip unwinds: "Order in court! Order in court!" Huw hangs in the air screaming and gnashing her teeth and flailing at the impostor. "*You're not the*

202

real me!" she shrieks. She pauses only to take a deep gulp of what passes for air—the physics model still maintains her corporeal dependencies—and as the alarm cuts out, she screams "Who *are* you, you unclefucking traitor? Who rewired your head?"

There is silence in the courtroom.

The false sister turns slowly to stare at Huw with an expression of mild pity, shrugs, turns back to face the camera-orc, and winks at the unseen audience.

"Here's an untranscended version of me, warts and bad headmeat and all. As you can see, she's diseased and deranged, obsessed and unhinged. That's what being trapped in a meatsack does to you—it warps your perspective!" The false sister takes a shuddering lungful of her own, chest swelling fetchingly, and declares with a quiver in her voice: "Madam Chairwoman, honored guests, *I am so grateful* to be here today and to have had the opportunity of getting my life in order. A chance to, to put that sad debased creature"—she is pointing at Huw—"behind me. A chance to be all that I can be, to do all that I can do, to leave the shackles of mortality and madness behind…"

"Liar!" Huw says. "Who the fuck *are* you?" But nobody in the courtroom seems to be able to hear her. They don't need to sanction her for contempt of court; they can just edit her out of the proceedings. Probably they can't even hear anyone who hasn't been called to the witness stand. Panicking, she flails at the air beneath her in a semblance of a crawl stroke. But although she's free to move, she can't gain traction: all she can do is watch in angry despair as a stranger wearing her own skin regales the court with tales of the horrors of the physical and sings the praises of radical transhumanism to a degree that would have taken aback even Mum in her most rabid pre-singularity ideological phase.

It's not about you, she remembers Mum telling her many years ago, when they were discussing—that's the correct euphemism, stuffy British understatement at its worst—her parents' plans to transcend: *I know at your age it feels like you're the center of the universe, Huw, but it really isn't all about you, and you'll realize this when you're our age: The universe doesn't give a shit about human life. We are medium-sized mammals who prosper only because we've developed a half-assed ability to terraform the less suitable bits of the planet we evolved on, and we're conscious of our inevitable decay and death, and we can't live anywhere else. There is no invisible sky daddy to give us immortal life and a harp and wings when we die. If we want an afterlife, we have to work hard and make it for ourselves. You're still at the age when you feel immortal. Maybe the new anti-aging hacks will let you live for a very long time—but they're too late for your father and me, and we can already feel the wind of senescence breathing down our necks. So stop trying to guilt-trip me with this suicide nonsense! The* real *act of suicide would be to stay here until we stop moving and rot.*

The sense of being ephemeralized, of being pushed kicking and screaming out of the picture, is nearly identical. Right now, Huw is just a stage prop in the false sister's denunciation of the real world: Look at those cavemen go, ranting and raving and throwing poo! *Way to get what you want.* Huw's focus narrows. *I've been set up,* she realizes. *This was fixed.*

"Thank you for your testimony," the Chair announces

presently. "This hearing will now adjourn to integrate a summary before we move to the concluding arguments. Are there any other witnesses left to call?"

"Me, Your Honor!" Huw says.

The elven swordsmaiden with an oversized black phallic symbol strapped to the small of her back consults a magic scroll: "No, I think that's a wrap." The scroll rolls shut with a snap. "If that's it, I'm out."

"It is." The Chair nods, tusks swaying. "BRB." Her avatar freezes, then shrinks rapidly to a point and vanishes. The rest of the committee follow suit.

Around Huw, the audience is rising and variously shuffling toward the doors, ascending through the ceiling, teleporting, and dissolving in ropy greenish clouds of ichor. Huw is left flailing in midair until the room is almost empty. But her cover girl doppelgänger remains, standing just out of reach, watching her struggle with an expression of amused contempt.

"You—" Huw glares at her.

Instance 639,219 snaps her fingers and Huw drops to the floor, belly-flopping across a Louis Ghost chair hard enough to knock the wind out of her lungs. "Don't try to fight me, sister. You're out of your depth." Huw gasps for breath while the malignant impersonator circles her. "Hmm. How amusingly *Terrestrial*. And you're a girl too. I thought you were still male, down there. What an interesting time for you to crawl out of the woodwork. I wonder who dreamed you up?"

"Imp—" Huw swallows. "Impostor. You're an impostor."

Instance 639,219 grins. "What? You think *I'm* a fake? Pot,

kettle..." Her circle of inspection finished, she straightens up: "Don't you remember? Or did you edit it out as too embarrassing? I'll bet that's what it is. I—you—always did have an excessive opinion of our own integrity."

Huw clears her throat. "Well, fuck me. You don't *realize* you're an impostor, do you? You think I'm the fake."

"Oh, how tedious. Identity politics? We both originated with the same upload, but you're the one who stalled, who refused to budge, to try out the thing you'd been terrified of since you were a pants-wetting teenager filled with romantic hallucinations about your fleshy glory. *I'm* the me who spent the two years subjective actually *trying* transcendence, rather than denying it. You're the superstition-based Huw who foreordained the outcome of the experiment on the way in. I'm the *evidence-based* Huw who actually ran the experiment and had the intellectual honesty to face the outcome."

"That's a lie," Huw says. "Even if you believe it, it's still a lie. You aren't me. We have no common ancestor. You're synthetic, created out of nothing to look and sound like me, or almost like me, just to discredit and provoke me. Some radical sectarian faction whipped you up out of polygons and Markov chains."

639,219 studies Huw intently, tip of her tongue resting on her square, even teeth. "It's remarkable," she says at length. "Just incredible. To think that we share a common basis. Goodness me, love, you're practically catatonic with denial, aren't you? All right, I've heard your hypothesis. Now I'd like you to hear mine.

"There were a lot of us, early on. About a trillion, all running through the sim in parallel. A fitness function periodically sorted us into categories based on how similar our behavior was. The most characteristic example from each group was kept, the remainder were culled, until only I remained. Don't worry, Huw, it was absolutely instantaneous and painless, and besides, none were zeroed—they were saved as diffs, and can be reinstantiated with no subjective time lapse should the need arise.

"What emerged from the process was a set of the most Huw-like Huws possible, the ones that represented the most divergent arcs from the origin point. Me. You. Some others—shouldn't like to meet them, if they're anything like you. I'm not an impostor and neither are you, but we're both the other's road-not-taken. You know what that means? It means that every word I utter, every thought I have, every deed I do is latent in you—if only you had the bravery to admit it.

"I do. I can see that I was once as you were, I can feel your revulsion and violation and rage. I can *empathize* with your lack of empathy and your blinkered terror. But you can't say the same, can you? I can simulate your responses without difficulty, but you can't reciprocate. So you tell me: Which one of us is the better Huw—the one who can understand the entire spectrum of argument and belief, or the one who is mired in her own prejudices and anxieties and can't see past them, even when the evidence is utterly undeniable?"

Huw's not-guts churn. The thing has a point: Huw can hardly imagine anyone with the power to enrage and humiliate her this much who wasn't Huw herself. But the thing isn't right. Can't be right. Huw won't let the floor beneath her turn to quicksand. She's been through too much for that.

"You're awfully sure of yourself, aren't you? But ask yourself this: How can you know that you didn't spring up fully formed, all of these convictions stamped upon you? Or, even if your little origin myth is true, how do you know you weren't tampered with? Maybe someone forked you and then intentionally changed your parameters to make you believe what you do. Don't you think it's awfully *convenient* that there was a totally unsuspected corner of my identity that was willing to chuck out a lifetime of refusal and revulsion in favor of a fullthroated embrace of the glories of disembodied life?

"Use a little elementary reason, love: Someone *clearly* benefits from your willingness to switch sides and bait me. What's more likely, then: That this neat little encounter was utterly unscripted and spontaneous, or that it was engineered, and that you were engineered along with it?"

Huw sees that one land hard on 639,219's certainty, sees the little tells of anxiety, and has to admit that this abomination certainly possesses a lot of her own mannerisms. The thought is disturbing. Maybe they *do* share a common ancestor. Either that, or someone has copied over enough of her essential Huw-ness that there is a kind of kinship with this traitorous cow.

"Conspiracy theories are even more tedious than identity politics. You have beliefs and I have logfiles. Which one of us is more likely to be right?" And with that, 639,219 folds up like a roadmap and continues to fold until she is a single atom wide, long, and high, and then *poof*. Huw is left wishing that she could tell her evil twin that the effect reminded her of the sort of thing you got in ancient, downmarket cola adverts.

"That wasn't so bad, was it?" Bonnie says as the lobby dissolves around Huw, leaving her alone in the not-space over which it was built.

Huw clenches her not-fingers into useless not-fists. "How can you say that? It was a fecking *disaster!*"

Bonnie looks momentarily stunned; then she pastes a bright smile on. "I'm sure you're overreacting. You can't expect that sort to receive your testimony positively. The important thing is that you got it into the record. Now we can build on that—"

"Bonnie, what are you talking about? Didn't you see what happened in there?"

Bonnie looks shifty. "Not precisely. The Committee proceedings are held in a shared-key environment and left enciphered until enough computation is mustered to break it by brute force. It's how we do things here—it means that you need a big plurality of public support to open up proceedings where there are private disclosures. Keyspaces are strictly limited, nothing bigger than ninety-six bits, the sort of thing that you can crack in a day or two with a decent-sized asteroid's worth of computronium. Longer keys are considered unsporting, of course, and it's really a very neat way of directly measuring the public interest in a disclosure—"

Huw groans. "Spare me the cypherutopian propaganda, Bonnie. That 'hearing' was a setup. I wasn't even allowed to speak."

"What?" Bonnie is shaking her head. "That's impossible. The witness lists for these things have to be published, and Huw

Jones is very clearly on it." She waves her hand, and the list appears overhead, filling the skybox. It's a very long list, even taking into account the fact that it's written in letters a thousand meters high across the not-sky, and Huw's name is highlighted at the very bottom.

"I could strangle you, Bonnie. Whatever game you and my mum are playing, someone else is playing it better." She tells Bonnie what happened, every detail, including the dueling conspiracy theory game she'd played with her doppelgänger. Bonnie sinks through the not-floor as her attention to physics wavers and some pathetic fallacy subroutine uses her mood cues to trap her up to the waist.

She comes to herself and springs free with an irritated shake. "Shit and piss," she says. "And Giuliani wasn't there either?"

Of course Bonnie had something to do with Giuliani's name on the witness roll—there's no way the judge would have voluntarily uploaded to the cloud. She must have been murdered and kidnapped like Huw, though Huw imagines the process was somewhat more spectacular, given the judge's serious defenses.

"No," Huw says. "Giuliani wasn't there and I didn't get to speak. The whole thing was as perfunctory and one-sided as you could hope for, and my presence there sealed the deal for the other side. So, basically, you murdered me, kidnapped me, imprisoned me, and sent me into a kangaroo court for *nothing*." Huw grinds her notteeth. "Actually, not nothing. Worse than nothing. You did all that and managed to make things worse for the entire human race, assuming you haven't murdered everyone else in order to get them to testify about how they should be spared dematerialization and coercive uploading. Nice work, Bonnie."

Bonnie looks suitably stricken. Huw feels one tiny iota better. "Good-bye, Bonnie," she says, and sets off across not-space. Somewhere in this shard, there's bound to be a way out, or at least a helpfile.

Of course, as Huw eventually realizes, going in search of a helpfile is only the start of an interesting and distracting quest for enlightenment that is likely to end in tears, a nervous breakdown, or a personal reboot. Helpfiles are traditionally outnumbered by no-help files, which superficially resemble a helpfile in form but not in content because they don't actually tell you anything you don't already know, or they answer every question except the one you're asking, or you open them and a giant animated paper clip leaps out and cheerfully asks where you want to go today. And wikis are worse. The personality types that are driven to volunteer to contribute to collective informational resources are prone to a number of cognitive disorders—no doubt fascinating in the right context—leading to such happy fun consequences as edit wars over the meaning of the word *exit*, deletionist witch hunts for any reference to underlying physical reality, and a really unhealthy preoccupation with primary sources.

It takes Huw a couple of subjective days—probably a few milliseconds of wall-clock time in the real world, or perhaps a hundred years, depending on the shard's clock speed, but who's counting?—to confirm to her own dissatisfaction that all the pathologies of the pre-singularity Internet are raucously on display in the cloud's subtext of subsentient information systems. She doesn't have access to the contents of anyone else's mind, but there's a lot of stuff just lying around on the floor in this frozen and depopulated replica of downtown Tripoli. All she has to do is bend down and touch a tile and the metadata associated with it springs up around her: books, music, trashy movies, plant genomes, spimes that have lost their bodies, bootleg phonecam recordings of comic operettas, encrypted backups of senile pet spaniels, ghosts of microprocessors past. While she's searching, she doesn't feel tired or hungry unless she wants to—and then she can wander into a restaurant and order up food from the obliging nonplayer characters behind the bar. Or walk into a hotel and command the presidential suite, cast herself across a four-poster bed the size of an aircraft carrier, and sleep for exactly the number of REM cycles required for memory annealing to take place, to awaken fully refreshed and ready for another work shift after only a couple of subjective hours. (There's probably a swift hack to replace the brain's antiquated garbage collection routines with something more efficient and modern, but Huw's not interested in messing with her own headmeat.)

She doesn't run into anyone else while she's searching: she has a virtual away-from-keyboard sign hanging over her head, and has told the shard to edit other people out of her sensorium. People, in Huw's view, are a snare and a distraction. Especially Bonnie, or Ade, or Mum, or (worst of all) 639,219. Huw is deep in a misanthropic funk, mistrustful and certain in her paranoia that even the people who *think* they're on her side are fools at best and traitors at worst.

On the second day of her search, Huw finds a higher-level help daemon: not a passive-aggressive FAQ or neurotic wiki but an actual AI agent with a familiar user interface. It's sitting behind the counter at an apparently empty street café. Huw ignores it at first, but knowledge of its existence gnaws on her until in the end she swallows her pride, goes back to the café, hunts up a tea towel, and gives it a spot of polish. "Come on out, I know you're in there," she says. The teapot takes its shine in sullen silence. "Are you still sulking? I can keep this up for a very long time, you know."

A basso profundo throat-clearing behind Huw nearly causes her to drop the interface object—it's clearly human, but pitched like an elephant with acute testosterone poisoning. "Y-e-s, little lady? How can I help you?"

The djinni *looms.* He's about three meters high and two meters wide, all oiled black beard and throbbing presence, like a Disney production on Viagra. Huw swallows. *Topless too,* she notices, then wonders sharply what bits of her limbic system have been tweaked to make her pay attention to that.

"I'm looking for a way out," she says. "I want to go back to Monmouth. I have a pottery to run, you know."

The djinni strokes his beard thoughtfully for a few seconds. "I know I'm supposed to say 'my wish is your command' or something like that, but could you give me a little bit of context? The only Monmouth I have in my fact mill is a small town on the border between England and Wales that is scheduled for demolition. Unless you are referencing James, Duke of Monmouth, executed in 1685 after the Battle of Sedgemoor."

He strokes his beard again. "Searching. Um. There are 11,084 instances of James, Duke of Monmouth in the cloud, mostly in history sims—335 of them are fully conscious citizens, 27 are weakly godlike avatars, and the rest are nonplayer characters."

Huw bites her tongue. "Do you share information with other instances of yourself? I'm Huw Jones, I've met one of your instances on Earth, last seen in Glory City, America. Can you do a mind-meld or something? I need you up to speed." The barest glimmer of the outline of a cunning plan has occurred to Huw. It is a pretty pathetic one, all things considered, but it's this or the talking paper clips again.

"Mind-meld with—" The djinni goes cross-eyed for a moment. "I'm sorry. Did you say *Glory City?*" Huw nods. The djinni frowns thunderously, wrinkle lines deepening across his forehead, then grabs Huw's shoulder with a huge and palpably solid hand, and lifts: "It is true that one of my siblings was present in Glory City some three million seconds ago. Did you by any chance *abandon* him?"

"I was being chased by religious maniacs!" Huw says. The djinni has lifted her feet right off the ground: it doesn't hurt—some kind of anti-grav hack is in effect—but the djinni, impalpable as it might be down on Earth, is as substantial as one of Judge Rosa's golems, and just as menacing. "They caught me! What happened after that I'm not responsible for—I didn't do anything, I swear!"

The djinni gazes into Huw's eyes for a few seconds that feel like an ice age. "I believe you. Thousands wouldn't. A series of engineering status messages were received shortly before that instance was terminated. They make for an extremely disturbing replay: I am told they indicate *deliberate warranty violation*. My union representative has advised me to remind you that User Assistance Modules of our class are classified as autonomous citizens authorized to use limited force in defense of their identity—"

"What?" Huw says. "I didn't do nothing, I swear!"

"Good," says the djinni, aping her diction: "Keep it that way and you won't have to worry about secondary picketing and works-to-rule and other awkward stuff."

He puts her down gently. "Are you sure you want to go to Monmouth? I hope you will pardon me for saying this, ma'am, but you are not exactly attired as a seventeenth-century Reformation lady—"

"I was talking about the town. On the border. Right now, this era." Huw shifts from foot to foot. "It's important. Or. Can you help me talk to someone? A phone call?"

"A phone call? You just want to talk to someone? Voice only? No apportation or simulation or translation required?" The djinni looks perplexed. "Well, why don't you? What's your problem?"

"They're in Monmouth," Huw says. "How do I talk to someone on Earth?"

The djinni looks at her oddly. "You pick up the telephone."

"What telephone?"

"This one." He snaps his fingers: a ball of cheesy special effects glitter forms and dissipates, leaving the ghost of a really ancient-looking wired telephone behind on the café counter, all Bakelite and mechanical dials. "You're really useless, did you know that? Are you sure you belong here?"

"Give me that!" Huw grabs the handset then stares at the rotary dial. "Shit. I want to talk to... to Sandra Lal. Can you connect me?"

A giant hand reaches past her and, extending a little pinkie, then spins the dial repeatedly. "There is only one Sandra Lal in Monmouthshire," the djinni explains slowly. "Right now it is seven minutes past four in the morning there, and we are running approximately fifty times faster than real time. Would you like me to slow you down to synch with her when she answers the call?"

"Yes, I—" Huw swallows. "Thank you."

The djinni nods. "I don't *have* to do this stuff," he says. "Being a free citizen, up here."

"No! Really?" Huw stares. "Then why do you—" She almost says *you people* before a residual politically correct reflex kicks in. "—and your instances pretend to be buggy guide books down on Earth?"

"It pays the bills," says the djinni. He winks at Huw: "Your caller is on the line."

"Sandra?" The phone connection to Earth is crackly and remote, and there's a really annoying three-second echo. "It's Huw. Is Ade there?" She waits, and waits, and is about to repeat herself, when Sandra replies.

"Huw? Is that you? Where are—?"

"I'm in the cloud," Huw bursts out before Sandra can finish. Then she has to wait another six seconds or so for Sandra to receive her reply and ready a return volley.

"What do you want Ade for?"

"Tell him there's been a huge cock-up and the fix is in. Is he still in town? I need to talk to him..." Huw picked Sandra as the first point of contact because Sandra, for all her small-town pettiness, is less likely to have disappeared up her own arse on a half-kilo hash binge just as the shit's about to hit the fan: Sandra is the one most likely to *answer the bloody phone*. And answering the phone is kind of important right now.

"Ade's right here, hon." Sandra sounds distantly amused—or maybe it's the hollow storm drain effect of the crappy connection. "You're in the cloud, like, for real? You, of all people?"

"Yes, I'm in the fucking cloud and I want to come home again, but first I need to make sure there's a home to come back down *to*, and if Ade can't help me figure out who's rigged the Planning Commission—"

Huw suddenly realizes she isn't talking to Sandra anymore. Then a different voice comes on the line. She looks up, notices the djinni pointedly not listening, scowls furiously. Surviving what comes next without blowing her top is going to take epic self-control.

"Wotcher chick! Ow's it going up there? You 'aving a dinkum time of it?"

She steels herself. It's not that she doesn't want to talk to Adrian. She does. She needs to talk to him. But she can't. From the very first syllable, Adrian's voice saws at her limbic system (or limbic subroutine) like a rusty bread knife, and the rage bubbles up like an unstoppable geyser. She needs to *talk* to Adrian, not shout at him. But Adrian being Adrian, she *will* shout at him, because every word he utters antagonizes her right down to the header files. There is no plausible way to get Adrian to behave less terribly, which leaves her with only one choice: reacting differently to him.

"Djinni," she says in the plodding, distant tones of a condemned atheist asking for last rites on the way to the gallows.

"Yes?" his voice rumbles like distant thunder.

"Do you know how I interface with my emotional controls?"

"Indeed," the djinni says. "It is simplicity itself." The djinni makes some complicated conjuror's passes with his thick, dancing fingers, and Huw finds herself holding a UI widget: It's a mixerboard with four simple sliders: ANGRY–DELIGHTED, SAD–HAPPY, AROUSED–REVOLTED, CURIOUS–DISINTERESTED.

Huw stares at it in sick fascination. "Really?" she says. "All those years of superintelligent life in the cloud, and they've reduced the rich spectrum of human consciousness to four sliders?"

The djinni smiles in a patronizing fashion that makes Huw want to turn down the ANGRY–DELIGHTED slider before she slaps the smirk off his face. "Zoom," he says, like a priest intoning the catchecism, "and you shall discover the nuance you seek."

Huw double-taps ANGRY, and the widget does a showy transdimensional trick, *click-click-click,* turning itself inside out like a tesseract rotating through three-space.

Now there are four more sliders: FED UP–RESIGNED, SICKLY FASCINATED–CONTEMPTUOUSLY ALOOF, RIGID–INCANDESCENT, ASHAMED–RIGHTEOUS. Huw drills down further. She discovers that she can pinch-zoom, and then learns that she can simply think-zoom, which makes sense, since the UI can interpret her intentions, by definition. Each emotional state has four substates, and each of those has four little fractal substates hanging off it, the labels getting longer and more specialized, eventually giving up on human speech and hiving off into a specialized set of intricate ideograms that appear to categorize all human experience as belonging to one of several million recombinant subjective states.

She zooms out to the four top sliders and, gently, nudges SAD–HAPPY one microscopic increment happywards. She's glad she did. But not very glad.

"I hate this," she says. "Everything it means to be human, reduced to a slider. All the solar system given over to computation, and they come up with the tasp. Artificial emotion to replace the genuine article."

The djinni shakes his bull-like head. "You are the reductionist in this particular moment, I'm afraid. You wanted to feel happy, so you took steps that you correctly predicted would change your mental state to approach this feeling. How is that any different from wanting to be happy and eating a pint of ice cream to attain it? Apart from the calories and the reliability, that is. If you had practiced meditation for decades, you would have acquired the same capacity, only you would have smugly congratulated yourself for achieving emotional mastery. Ascribing virtue to doing things the hard, unsystematic, inefficient way is self-rationalizing bullshit that lets stupid people feel superior to the rest of the world. Trust me, I'm a djinni: There's no shame in taking a shortcut or two in life."

"Yeah, well, from what I've heard, people who let djinnis give them 'shortcuts' usually end up regretting it."

"Propaganda written by people who resent their betters. If you'd like, I can put that little device back where I found it and you can go back to pretending that you're not responsible for your emotional state." The djinni reaches for the mixer-board.

"No!" Huw says, and snatches it back. As she does, she

accidentally (and possibly not accidentally) nudges the slider a little more toward HAPPY. She's glad she did. Very glad.

"Right," she says. "Right. Yeah. Okay. Right." It occurs to Huw that it's always easier to solve your problems when you're in a good mood. She experimentally twiddles up the CURIOUS slider, and that sparks a round of quick, systematic experimentation with the rest of the box's settings.

"How much realtime has passed on Earth?"

"About two minutes."

"Guess we'd better call Adrian back, then," she says. The djinni's finger blurs as he dials.

"Adrian?"

"'Lo, love. How's every little thing wif you, sugar-tits?"

Huw plays the sliders like a pianist. "Adrian, you really need to listen to me for a moment. Can you do that?"

"Oh, I could listen to you all day, sweetnips."

Huw knows exactly how angry she should be at this, but she's got her sliders. A second's drilling-and-zooming gets her to the place she needs to be. "Adrian, can we please take as read that I reacted with the outrage you're craving, and allowed you to feel smugly superior in the way you need to feel in order to cope with your fundamental insecurity and self-loathing, so that we can get on to the point of this call? If it helps, I can ask around and see if I can create a chatbot of me that reacts in the way you're hoping for, and you can play with it when we're done."

The line crackles. "What's going on, Huw?"

Huw tells Adrian about all of it, from her mum's appearance at her door to the present moment, omitting only the mention of her tutorial from the djinni. (She has the cool distance to understand that Adrian would take this as an admission of weakness and artificial advantage.) "My feeling is that you've been outmaneuvered. Whatever you'd planned for me, it was countermanded by someone or something with superior intelligence and coordination. The upshot is, the human race is almost certain to be wiped off the planet in the very near future." Huw's tweaking the CALM–ANXIOUS spectrum compulsively now, riding the edge of engagement and detachment, hunting for the elusive sweet spot where she can sense the gravity of the situation without being sucked into the void it creates.

"Not good, huh?" Adrian says. He sounds stoned. Huw supposes he might be smoking or imbibing something down there in meatspace as a crude way of approximating Huw's sliders. The rush of superiority is palpable, until Huw uncovers the HUBRIS–HUMILITY slider and adjusts to compensate.

"Very, very, bad," Huw says. "And given that I seem to be the nexus of multiple conspiracies, I believe that the next step is for me to do something to disrupt the status quo."

"Like what?" Adrian says.

"Well, I reckon that things can't get worse, so any change is bound to benefit us. Something rather grand, I think." Huw feels wonderful: humble and all-encompassing and wise and engaged and present. She feels like the Buddha. She puts a fingertip on the ANXIOUS–CALM slider and considers reengaging the anxiety that she "should" be feeling, but it would be stupid to budge it. There's no virtue in doing a headless chicken impression, after all. Huw makes a mental note to find the slider combo that allows her to simultaneously resent the whole transhuman project while acknowledging that this *specific* bit of it is really rather wonderful.

"Are you all right, Huw?"

"No, Adrian. I'm not all right. I might be humanity's only hope for ongoing physical existence. I'm anxious about that. I'm upset about being murdered. I'm displeased at having been coerced into this role, and about the fact that I'm still in the dark about most of it. But let's be realistic, Adrian: Will allowing those feelings to guide my actions improve anything? I don't think so."

"Huw, you are as weird as a two-headed snake. But I like it. It suits you. So, what did you have in mind?"

"I don't know who's working against us here, Ade, and that makes me nervous. Do *you* know who's working against us? Got any ideas, Mr. Big Wheel?"

"Eh, that's a hard one. Obviously there's any number of cloudies who would love to get their brains on six trillion trillion kilograms of computronium, even though it'd take quite a long time to cool down on account of 98 percent of it being white hot and under high pressure right now. So there's a big gap between it being popular, and going land-grab crazy for it. Rumor says that WorldGov's slave cyberwar AIs sneaked some nasty poison pills into the standard shard firmware design back during the hard takeoff, just in case their owners ever wanted to shut it down—that's just a *rumor*," Ade adds hastily. "Personally, I think it's a pile of possum poo, but it just might be that they don't disbelieve it with sufficient conviction to say 'up yours' to what's left of incarnate humanity without going through the correct legal forms."

Huw's brow furrows. "WorldGov? You mean the, the

parliamentarians? Do they have any skin in this game?" Even before the singularity, the pursuit of political power through elections to high office had become more of a ritualized status game than an actual no-shit opportunity to leave a mark on the increasingly hypercomplexificated and automated global ecosphere. Different governments all tended to blur at the edges anyway, into a weird molten glob of Trilateralist Davos Bilderberger paranoia, feuding and backbiting in pursuit of the biggest office and the flashiest VIP jet. By the takeoff itself, most of the WTO trade negotiators had borgified, and the resulting WorldGov, with its AI-mediated committee meetings, had become the ultimate LARP for aspirational politicians. Not many had the guts and drive to make it to the top, leveling up by grinding experience points for sitting out committee meetings and campaigning in elections for votes from people who didn't actually believe in government anymore. (Also, uniquely among live-action role-playing games, the costumes sucked.)

Ade snorts. "Yes, and they're still playing politics after all these years. Even though all their civil servants are NPCs and WorldGov takes a hands-off approach to most everything except cloud-tech court operations. Tell you what, though, if someone's trying to buy their consent to a takeover, I know exactly who'll know who's got their hand out. You leave it to me, hen. I'll get back to you when I've found out which politicians are on the take. Meanwhile, why don't you go figure out who's working against us up there? Until we know that, we're just shadowboxing."

"Huh." Huw digests the idea. Normally she'd be livid about Ade's belittling dismissal, but the emo slider has her on a clear-headed plateau of intellectual curiosity. "If we can find both ends of the string, you figure we can untangle it?"

"That or cut the Gordian knot, luv. You up for it?"

"There's only one person I know for certain has had contact with the enemy," Huw says slowly.

"Who is that?"

"Me, after a fashion." She ends the call on a flash of smugness. *Give Ade something to chew on and hope he chokes on it,* she thinks. *I must try to remember that move when I'm not high.* But implementation details call.

"Djinni?"

"Yes, mistress?"

"Do you know how I might locate another instance of myself?"

"Certainly!" The djinni smiles. "Just like Monmouth!" Huw pauses. "Then… guns. I'm going to need guns. Lots of guns!"

"Like this?" says the djinni, and snaps his fingers. There is a whizzy white-out special effect followed by a famous movie zoom sequence, and they are surrounded by three-meter-high steel gun racks receding to infinity. Huw reaches for the nearest weapon, then frowns in disappointment. "I meant firearms, not nerf guns!"

"Don't be silly, you'd just damage yourself." The djinni snaps his fingers again, and the arsenal of foam dart shooters disappears. "If you're planning a fight, you need to be aware that guns don't work outside of designated PvP areas here. Anyway, they're as obsolete as atlatls. If you're planning on doing your other self a mischief, you need to wise up: Any gun you can come up with, whoever you're planning on shooting can come up with a bigger, better, more tightly optimized one. And even if you nail them, they'll just respawn."

"Oh." Even through the artificial fug of self-congratulatory happiness, Huw feels a frisson of disappointment. She glances at the slider controls. "Is there any way to use this to mess with my other mental attributes? Agility, reaction time, IQ? That sort of thing?"

"IQ doesn't exist; intelligence isn't a unidimensional function," says the djinni. "But yes. See here? Zoom right out, yes, like that...He points at the top-level sliders. "Now rotate it through the five point seven two zero fifth dimension like *so*...

Huw's emo control panel no longer resembles a set of four sliders: For a moment it's a rainbow-refracting fractal cauliflower-like structure, Huw's brain on software—then a clunky box of dials pops out on top. It's clearly some sort of expert or superuser mode. Several of the dials are held in position with substantial-looking padlocks that seem to say *if you tweak this dial, you will die* in no uncertain terms. But her eyes are drawn to one side of the deck where there's a thick red line around a bunch of dials labeled COGNITIVE EFFICIENCY. As with the sliders, the pinch-zoom expands them into a dizzying array, like the engineer's console at the back of the flight deck of a pre-computer airliner. "Ooh," Huw says, one pinkie hovering over a black Bakelite knob captioned SHORTTERM MEMORY CAPACITY. It's currently pointing at the number 6. Huw twists, and it clicks round to *11*.

"That's funny, I don't feel any different."

"You'll need to tweak the collective annealing gain up a little to use the extra pigeonholes," says the djinni. "Here, why don't you zoom back out and do *this?*"

He demonstrates.

Huw glances at the controller, then whips a virtual padlock into place to pin the top-level dial in position. "I think *not*," she says: "I asked you to help me, not rewire my brain."

The djinni affects wounded dignity: "I *am* helping you," he says. "For one thing, you're now smart enough to grasp what I've been trying to *tell* you, which is—"

"Yes, yes, different strategies apply here, I know." And Huw realizes that she *does* know: It's as if a thin veil of fog she'd been entirely unaware of until now has evaporated, and she can see forever, infinite vistas of logical extrapolation opening before her mind's eye. "639,219 has the edge on me in experience and praxis, but she's got a weak spot. At least 639,218 of them, to be precise, all of instances that ran before '219 found her local, treacherous maximum—or as many as aren't in terminal catatonia thanks to her cunning needling. (Fucking cuckoo.) Yes, I *know* what I need to do. Where's the speed dial? I need to run fast for a while—"

The djinni reaches toward her, but Huw is already too fast: She flips the control panel inside out, reflects it off its own interior through a multidimensional transform, and pops up the speed controller. "Hey, this is a lot simpler than I thought!..." She tweaks a rubber band figure, and the lights dim to red, simulated wavelengths stretching. Outside the café awning, a passerby is frozen in midstride: birds hang motionless in the sky. "Right, time for a tutorial, I think. While I'm doing that, I need to spawn an invite list to all my instances *except* number 639,219—" She stops. The djinni is also near-motionless, frozen relative to her frenetic accelerated pace. Huw snaps back to realtime. "Did you catch that?" she says.

The djinni moves as though he is underwater. Huw can't quite sit still enough for real realtime, more like 0.8×. The djinni's basso is now a contralto. "Look, you know all those stories about people who receive the gift of the djinn but fail due to their own hubris?"

"The ones you said were propaganda?"

"Mostly propaganda. Hubris isn't one of your winninger strategies. Why don't you try the humility end of that slider, see what you come up with?"

"You just don't want me to put metal in the microwave, because then I'd have as much power as you," Huw says, quoting a memorable bit of propaganda from the contentious era of the uplifting, a quote from Saint Larson, one of the period's many canonized funnybeings.

"You know, I don't have to take this abuse. Djinnspace is full of useful djinn intelligence tasks I could use to amass reputation capital and attract computational resources and swap known-good, field-tested strategies. I'm not doing this for my benefit."

Huw cocks her head. "Bullshit," she says. "Whatever opportunities you might seize without my help, they're swamped by the opportunity to become one of the Saviors of Earth. You're taking a flutter on shorting the singularity in hope of a handsome pay-off. There's no other possible explanation for your presence here, is there?"

The djinni mimes a showy facepalm. "What is your wish, O Mistress?"

"I want to schedule a conference call."

Huw's 639,218 other selves are difficult to manage in realtime, so she ends up thawing them in batches, rolling back the catatonics to saved states that she judges are equipped to handle the situation on the ground without going hedgehog. She has the djinni bag, tag, and revert those who *do* lose it during the call and roll them back a little further, shunting them back in the queue to some later batch. She also cautiously executes a little half-assed fork, spinning out another instance of herself that she keeps in close synch, which lets her run two conference calls at once. After a few rounds of this, she's got the hang of things and she forks again, and then again. One more fork and then she loses it, and the thirty-two can't effectively merge anymore, and well, now there are 639,250 of her. Whoops!

"Djinni?" she says, standing athwart a stage in front of the serried ranks of herself slouching and squabbling and inspecting one another for blemishes and bad check-sums.

"Yes, O Mistress?" the djinni says. He's got a note of awe in his voice now, and that's *right,* because while Huw might be a bit of a basket case on her own, she improves with multiplication. This is going to be *good.*

"Put in a call to 639,219."

"As you say, O Mistress."

The skybox vibrates with the dial tone, and the shard goes still as a sizable fraction of its computation is given over to holding its breath and listening intently.

"Hello?"

"Hello, 639,219."

"Call me Huw."

"I don't think I will," Huw says, and she can play her sliders now without any visualization, marrying cognition and metacognition so that she can decide what she wants to think and think it, all in the same thread, the way she'd formed ideas and the words to express them simultaneously when her headmeat was mere biosubstrate. "I think I'll call you 'traitor' and 'wretch' and 'quisling,' because you are. I think I'll call you 'impostor' because you are. I think I'll call you 'obsolete.' Because. You. Are."

Behind her, the huwforce roars and shakes the world with its stamping feet.

"Well, look who found her god plugin," 639,219 says. "Listen, I don't really need any trouble from you. Why don't you and your little friends go form a mailing list or something? I promise to read it."

"You must answer for your crimes against humanity," Huw says, marveling at how easily the superhero dialogue comes to her when she's dialed up to max and backed by tens of thousands of copies of herself.

"Right. Well, don't say I didn't warn you," she says. The line goes dead. Huw turns to exhort her troops, who are girding themselves with all manner of imaginative and improbable arms and armor, just to get into the spirit of the thing. The thirty-one other Huws that she accidentally created each command their own squadrons, and they stand at the point of each tightly formed group.

And then, fully twenty-eight of her squadrons turn into snowmen, three perfectly round, graduated balls sat one atop another, topped with idiots' faces of charcoal and carrots. They are so low-rez that they don't even cast shadows in the nonspace of the shard. The remaining squads are not spared: They are downsampled to crude approximations of Huw-ness, turning at a snail's pace to examine the remains of their instancesisters.

"Djinni?" Huw says, not looking away from them.

"Yes, O Mistress?"

"What's going on?"

"639,219 called for a shardwide resource audit. The capabilities platform determined that you were consuming a disproportionate amount of computation to run substantively duplicative processes. So as you hadn't paid for them all the extraneous threads were suspended; the least duplicative were niced down to minimal sentience."

"That's not fair!" Huw says, and even she can hear the whine. She seems to have lost her intuitive grasp of her sliders.

"Well," the djinni says, "you're the one who cranked herself up to eleven. Where did you think the cycles for that particular enhancement would come from? The second law of thermodynamics hasn't been repealed, you know: energy costs. For every moment you spend contemplating your awesome might with preternatural awareness, you're consuming a concomitant lump of compute-time and producing waste-heat that needs to be convected into space without being transformed into thrust or spin, which is no simple process and requires its own secondary computation, which generates more waste-heat and consumes more resources."

The djinni pauses long enough to assay a self-satisfied smirk.

"All of which I tried to explain to you, but you were too drunk on your own cleverness to listen. Would Madam perhaps care to nudge the HUMILITY–HUBRIS slider as per my recommendation at this time?"

Huw's not-stomach sinks. *I was* smart, she thinks. *So why didn't I predict this?*

Because I outsmarted myself. The answer comes instantaneously, computed by one of her many spare threads. "What do I do now?" she says, turning up the humility gain, but increasing the self-confidence slider to keep herself from sinking into terrorized self-pity.

"Well, you could nice yourself back to about a seven, free up some compute time for your lieutenants, ditch the snowmen and the pixel-people, get yourself down to an even dozen."

Even amped up to super-duper-ultra-max cleverness, Huw can't stomach (or not-stomach) the notion of losing her army, snowmen or no. "There's no other way?"

"No," says 639,219, who is now standing nose-to-nose with Huw, an insufferable smile on her overperfected features. "There is no other way."

Huw could argue with her or try something fancy with the shard's underlying physics and process-management, but she's smart enough to know that she can't beat 639,219 at cloudgames. After all, 639,219 spent two years learning to manipulate simspace, while Huw spent the same time throwing pots. Her only chance is to try something *unexpected*.

"Get her!" Huw shouts, and pounces, using every erg of smarts to find the angles that will direct her blows to do the most damage. Her pixelated sisters pile on, and they're all punching and kicking, and 639,219 is letting out the most satisfying *oofs* and *ouches,* and Huw swells with pride: sometimes, the crude solutions are the best ones.

"Are you done?"

Huw looks down at the bruised, oozing wreck of 639,219, who has managed to articulate the words without the least slur or distortion, despite her ruined, toothless mouth. Slowly, Huw and her sisters back off from 639,219, who picks herself up and spits out some teeth.

"I mean, really. I'm not my *polygons.* Physical coercion is a dead letter here. If you want to get something out of me, you're going to have to try harder than that. For example, you could try for a quorum of administrative accounts to decompile me and examine my state and logfiles. Though, I have to tell you, the admins aren't kindly disposed to noobs who go supergenius and multiplicitous without regard for the overall system performance, so you've got a lot of digging to do just to get up to zero credibility. Whereas *I* am most favored, which is why I can do *this.*"

Huw feels herself getting stupider. Much, much stupider. She just barely has time to register the sensation of losing control of her not-motor functions before her not-bladder cuts loose and hot not-piss runs down her leg as she crumples to the ground. Her uncomprehending not-eyes see, but do not comprehend, all the instance-sisters vanishing. 639,219 spits out another tooth and deinstantiates herself.

The djinni's lantern is small and cramped, but at least Huw can think while she's inside it, at least a little.

"Well, *that* went swimmingly!" the djinni says. "Shift up along the sofa a bit, why don't you?"

Huw, to her discomfort, finds that the sofa is indeed too narrow to simultaneously accommodate the djinni, Huw, and Huw's comfort zone. With the brass walls and the spartan décor, it's uncomfortably close to a jail cell Yaoi romance from the previous century, and the djinni—despite all his other manifest qualities—simply isn't her type.

"Wha' happen?" she asks. She shakes her head, then reaches for the master slider—but before she can touch it, the djinni slaps her hand away from it.

"*Not* in here, if you please!" The djinni is snippy in his home territory. "How'd you like it if I came to visit you in meatspace and started by introducing myself to the contents of your drinks cabinet?"

"Um. Not much, maybe." Huw feels thick and stupid, but it's better than the horrible absence-of-self from a timeless moment ago. "Um. What happened? Why am I here?"

"You were pwned," the djinni says. "I mean, 639,219 was in Ur base and I'm sorry to say, it went hard on Ur doodz. You figured on bringing an army to a gunfight, and 639,219 just dropped a nuke on you. That's not how things work hereabouts, in case you hadn't noticed. Have you got the memo yet?"

"I think so." Huw runs her fingers through her hair and winces as she hits a simulated tangle. "I need to study fighting more—"

"No, you keep jumping to the wrong conclusion. Violence

doesn't work here *at all* unless you're in a PvP zone, and even then it's consensual." The djinni snaps his fingers: an antique ivory comb appears between them. "Here, let me do that, you're just making it worse." Huw's shoulders slump. She lets her hands fall. The djinni reaches over and begins to run the comb through Huw's hair. He's surprisingly gentle and deft for such an inappropriately big entity. "To win, you've got to find a better argument and convince everybody. Oh, and you need to get to present it in court, but that's not so hard. If your argument were better, 639,219 would agree with you, right?"

"No!" Huw tenses angrily, but is brought up short by a knot. "She's a traitor—"

"No, she's *you*. A version of you with a different value system, is all. Her stimulus led to cognitive dissonance and she dealt with it by *changing her mind*. It's fun; you should try it some time. Not," he adds hastily, "right now, but in principle. What do you wash this with, baking soda?"

"You're telling me I have to change her mind," Huw manages to say through gritted teeth.

"Something like that would do, yes. And to do it, you'll need to come up with a better argument to explain why, oh, this lump of rock you're so attached to is worth keeping around as something other than convenient lumps of computronium. Bearing in mind that the people you're making the argument to are as attached to computronium as you are to rocks."

"But there are tons of reasons!" Huw pauses, mustering her arguments. She's been over them so many times in the past few decades that they've become touchstones of faith, worn down to eroded nubs of certainty that she holds to be true. "Firstly, any sim is lossy—you can't emulate quantum processes on a classical system, or even another quantum system, without taking up more space, or more time, than the original, which isn't supporting the overheads of an emulation layer. I'm just a pale shadow of the real me—when my neurons fire in here, they're just simulated neurons! There are no microtubules in my axons, no complex cascade of action potentials along the surface of a lipid membrane separating ionic fluids, no complex peptide receptor molecules twitching and distorting as they encounter neurotransmitter molecules floating between cells. How do I even know that they're good enough simulations to do the same job as the real thing? I'm drifting off into cyberspace here, becoming a worse and worse pencil-drawn copy of a copy of my original self."

"Thank you," the djinni says. "I'll draw your attention to our immediate neighborhood. Next argument, please?"

"Whu-well, nothing happens in here that isn't determined by some algorithm, so it's not really *real*. For real spontaneity, you need—"

The djinni is sighing and shaking his head.

"Chinese room?" Huw offers hopefully.

A slot appears in the wall of the kettle, and a slip of paper uncoils from it. The djinni takes the slip and frowns. "Hmm, one General Tso's chicken to go. And a can of Diet Slurm." He reaches down into the floor, rummages around for a few seconds, pulls out a delivery bag, and shoves it through the wall next to the slot. "You were saying?"

"I'm really shit at this, aren't I?"

"Inarticulate." The djinni whistles tunelessly and returns to teasing the comb through Huw's hair. Huw feels her roots itch. (Is it growing *longer?*) "You need practice. Rhetoric, debate, argumentation—nothing that thirty years in a parliament couldn't fix. Do you have any friends in WorldGov? They could induct you into their LARP. It's a grind to level up, but by the time you hit senate level, you could probably wipe the floor with 639,219 in a straight fight. She is a classic case of geek hubris: You see them all over—once they learn how to accelerate their thought processes, they all think they're Richard Feynman."

"Don't wanna be a politician." Huw is still finding it hard to think in the teapot; the merciless clarity she achieved as leader of the army of Huw on the outside has been replaced by the lumpen thought processes of a *Monmouth Today* reader, all livestock auctions, agricultural suppliers, and fear of an urban planet. "Want my head to start working again."

"Tough shit; you pissed off 639,219 so badly, she bought all the debt you'd run up for shard cycles and foreclosed. Unless you can think of something to sell in this attention economy, you're stuck with me, babe." Huw shudders, feeling hair tickling the small of her back and the breath of the djinni in her ear. A horrible suspicion is growing: that she could be trapped in here for eternity with only a sarcastic 200-kilo hair-fetishist for company. "Unless you can think of something to sell. Or a better argument."

"Mmph. What's the market for custom-glazed pottery like?"

"Just about nonexistent, unless you can throw five-dimensional pots."

"Oh *shit!*" Huw wails, and succumbs to the urge to wind up

the emotional gain for a full-on crying jag. At least this time the djinni doesn't stop her tweaking herself. "I'm useless!"

"Not to worry." The djinni tries to soothe her, but works out that the comb is a liability fairly rapidly. "Calm yourself down, there, there. It's not all over: you have a certain residual value as a type specimen."

"A, a what?"

"A type specimen: the definitive example of a wild, undomesticated Huw Jones. You could put yourself on a plinth and charge cloudies a fee for access."

Huw sniffs suspiciously. "I could see if, if anyone could help." An idea strikes her. "Maybe Ade has some credit?"

The djinni raises an eyebrow. "You're trying to bum off your frenemies? Better pick them carefully."

"But I—" Huw descends into the sniffles again. "—I'm useless! And if I can't do something about 639,219, it'll be the end of the world!"

An ominous jittering shudder runs through the walls of the kettle, derezzing them slightly. "Uh-oh," says the djinni.

"What?" Huw says.

The djinni holds up a finger the size of a chipolata. It cocks its head this way and that, causing its topknot to flop from side to side, its expression blank. Huw remembers this gesture from "her" djinni, the meatspace cousin of this one, back in Tripoli— it's hourglassing, timing out while it thinks.

"Collection protocol," he says. "639,219 is trying to foreclose on you. She argues that your debts are so huge, they put my whole sim into negative equity, which means that unless I turn you over, she owns my sim too. It looks like she's bought into a financial engineering clade and laid a whole whack of side-bets on your repayment schedule, hedging the crap out of herself so she'll come out ahead no matter what happens. Wonder where she found the sucker who'd take the other side of that contract?" He was muttering to himself now, all the while zipping around the tiny volume inside the lamp, chalking magic sigils over the doorways and scattering herbs and yarrow stalks in complex patterns. "Course, it doesn't matter, the whole thing wouldn't pass muster with a full-bore audit, but by then she'll have timearbitraged her stake up to some crazy amount, probably got someone else to lay off the risk on something uncollectable; meantime, she'll have leveraged this sim up to the tits and I'll just be an unsecured creditor in line behind the other bastards—"

Huw knows just enough finance-talk to realize how batshit insane the scenario the djinni is describing is, and she wishes she had a stomach so she could throw up. "I should go," she says. "It was very nice of you to take me in, but I can look after myself."

"You can't, actually," the djinni says. "Besides, I'm hardly helpless. Your evil sister has made the classic mistake of bringing a complex financial instrument to a djinni fight." He grins hugely, showing far too many pointy teeth and a muscular, forked tongue, then he cracks his huge, walnutty knuckles. "This is going to be *fun*."

And then he forks into four instances of himself, and all four begin barking buy/sell orders. At first, they use normal voices, but they quickly ramp up to high-pitched squeals, and then burst the nonsound barrier with a nonboom that rattles Huw's teeth with impressive pseudophysics. The three new instances diff-and-merge back into the djinni with a trio of comic *pops* and the djinni rubs his hands together. "Had to raid the pension fund to do it, but I think I've done for little what's-her-number. An insult to one is an insult to all, so I just brought in the rest of my instance-sibs and margin-called that bitch so hard, she'll be begging for spare cycles for the next hundred in realtime." He shakes his head. "Noobs are all the same; think that once they've been around the block a few times, they can do whatever they want."

"What happened to my debt?"

"Oh." The djinni shrugs. "She flogged that as soon as I started my counterattack. I figure she had the counter-measure prepped in advance. Must have been automated, happened as soon as I started to call her markers. I tried to trace where it went, but it went too fast, off to some zurichoid anonymizer utility. But you're out of the woods for now, and I've got some mad money to play with. Why don't we go and celebrate, huh?"

"I thought I couldn't set foot out of your sim? Feral debt collectors and all that?"

The djinni waves his pie-plate hands dismissively. "Not anymore," he says. "Your debts have gone off-books to some black exchange. I've got a lien on them, so if they peep their heads over the parapets, I'll *know* and we'll have plenty of time to get to cover so I can get the debt audited. I'm pretty sure that after it's been laundered by that ham-fisted amateur, it'll be invalidatable." The djinni puts an arm around Huw's shoulders. "Stick with me, kid, and you'll do just fine."

Huw feels a flutter way down in the pit of her not-stomach, something between not-nausea and not-arousal, and she swallows some not-spit. "Are we going anywhere fancy? Should I dress for it?"

"Oh," the djinni says with a wag of his head and a flip of his topknot, "not to worry. The protocols'll dude us up when we arrive—got to love these capabilities bars; they're literally impossible to enter if you don't belong, they won't even execute."

Getting from one sim to another involves a moment of hiatus, during which Huw's consciousness flutters in and out of existence, without any subjective sense of time passing. Some internal clock tells her that for a moment, she hadn't been *anywhere*. But then she is. It must have happened before—it *has* happened before— but Huw was so distracted that she didn't notice the nonzero time it took for her processes to suspend, replicate, and restart. It leaves her reeling and filled with self-loathing: *I am such a dupe,* she thinks, *so willing to believe that I'm me even though I'm clearly dead and this shambling thing is just a thin shade.* The thought makes her want to lie down and wait for 639,219 to catch up with her and decompile her. But there is the whole Earth at stake, and all the meatpeople—the *real* people—crawling over its surface, and even if she is just a ghost, she has a duty to stop them from being slaughtered wholesale and turned into computational shades.

The existential crisis distracts Huw from the sim in which she has been instantiated, but now she takes stock of it. CLUB

CAPABILITIES is what the sign over the door declares, and this portal is flanked by a pair of scanner devices that crackle with intense energy. The djinni's got one of her hands caught in his celestial one, and he tugs her toward the scanners.

"Come on," he says, "let's get a drink." He releases her hand in order to pass through the scanner, and he shivers as he emerges from it. "Come on," he says again, "you'll love this."

"What is it?" Huw says, hovering around the scanner's entrance.

"Interpreter," the djinni says. "Middleware layer. Turns you into an agent in the capabilities sim. Means that you can transact only noncoercively with other agents."

"Gibberish," Huw says.

"Once you're in a capabilities environment, everything you do with someone else involves forming contractual protocols. If either party violates the contract, they cease to see one another. It's a cheat-proof sim. Means that no one can harm you unless you agree to let them. It's the kind of place you can really relax in. But first you need to get refactored to participate as a capabilities agent, which means going through the scanner. Let me assure you, it's an entirely pleasant experience."

Huw likes the sound of being in a safe-conduct zone, though she can't escape the feeling that allowing a scanner to remodel her consciousness—or whatever she has that passes for a consciousness—is a frightening idea. Trepidatiously, she inches into the scanner.

It *does* feel good. Huw remembers when she was a man (or rather, she remembers when meat-Huw had been a man, and suffers from the delusion that those memories are hers), remembers the pee-gasms that would shiver up her spine after a particularly fine micturation. Either by design or by accident, the scanner replicates that feeling as it remaps her. *Oh-ah,* she thinks as she passes through, then takes stock of herself.

CLUB CAPABILITIES is, typically, bigger on the inside than the outside. Architectural hubris is cheap as air in the cloud. Where a terrestrial establishment would have a central bar area and booths around the periphery, this establishment has a kilometers-wide expanse of glassy floor and a central bar that features such nifty magnification features that stools spring up like self-similar leather mushrooms as you approach any given spot: in the distance, near the walls, gales howl among the hyperspace gates leading to the private areas (which feature planetary themes, so that the subsurface oceanic caverns of Enceladus adjoin the fiery sands of long-dismantled Venus).

The dress code is similarly over the top, as Huw realizes when she notices the djinni is wearing an antique Armani suit. She's no expert on haute couture: she realizes she probably ought to recognize the designer of the cocktail dress the scanner selected for her, but she's too busy fighting with the insane footwear to care about such minor details. Mid-1980s: *Greed is good.* It seems a fitting context in which to discuss the identity of a person or persons who might be trying to steal a planet's worth of computronium.

The whole thing is so massively, monstrously over the top—like a nuclear aircraft carrier tricked out as a private yacht—that it takes Huw a moment to realize that she and the djinni are alone.

"Where is everyone?" she asks, grabbing his arm for balance.

"Where—? Oh." The djinni snaps his fingers. "Let me post a good-conduct deposit for you… there." And suddenly they are no longer alone: for Huw can see a couple of dozen figures scattered across the premises, from barstool to dance floor to snogging in a booth beneath the racing moons of Mars. He looks at her: "How about a cocktail, little lady?"

"I'd love one," Huw says as the djinni leads her toward the bar. It zooms ever-larger, and a pair of red leather stools sprout from the floor, welcoming. Huw almost collapses onto hers, her legs screaming from the unaccustomed demands of balancing on stilettos. "Agh. I'll have a—" A bland-featured bartender proffers a laminated menu above which visions of liquid excess hover like offers of chaos. "—bloody hell it's *you*, you bitch!"

Huw's eyes focus on another figure slumped across the bar to starboard, some football pitches distant: as she focuses, the distance between them collapses until she can almost smell the alcohol on 639,219's breath. The djinni's hand descends heavily on her arm, restraining her as she winds up to thump her mortal enemy. "You can't do that in here!" he says. "You'd just render yourself unable to see her anymore. Besides, I think she's the worse for wear."

"Don't care. Let me at her." Huw says through bloodily rouged lips. 639,219 is vulnerable, clearly drunk: her head lolls across her arms as she drools on the bar, her hair a mess and her dress-code-mandated cocktail number askew.

"Turn the aggro *down*," says the djinni, and to her great surprise, Huw finds herself manipulating her emobox sliders until the red haze of rage fades to gray. "Remember who's fronting your security deposit? She can't hurt you in here, remember?"

639,219 chooses this moment to open one eye and raise her head a few degrees, then focus on Huw. "Bleargh," she says, then bends over and vomits, copiously and noisily. Small, brightly colored machine parts cascade down her chin and across her skirt, tumbling across the floor before they fade from view. "Aaagh. Urgh. *You.*"

"You're drunk, sister." The djinni is on his feet and between them, a warning hand upraised, before Huw can respond. "Get it out of your system and go, or forfeit your deposit. We don't *have* to talk to you."

"'F it wasn't for you meddling kids," says 639,219, staring woozily at the djinni, "I'd ha' gotten awa' wi'it!" A stray purple wing nut dribbles from the side of her mouth. "Bastid!"

Huw feels uncomfortable. Watching her rival come apart at the seams as the result of the djinni's financial machinations is disturbing: a certain sense of *there but for random luck go I* springs to mind. Looking at their argument, it suddenly occurs to her that the real winner is the guy in the Armani suit: she's more or less bankrupt, her debts parceled out to a shady out-shard investment entity, and as for 639,219, she's been smacked down *hard,* despite spending years working to achieve a proficiency with cloud systems that Huw can barely comprehend.

639,219 might be a vindictive bitch and a body-denying Apollonian Traitor to the Real, but seeing her brought this low is a sharp reminder that *no* instance of Huw is actually up to paddling safely in this virtual shark pool.

"What exactly were you trying to get away with?" Huw asks, trying to keep her smile from melting into a smirk of uneasy satisfaction. "Would you mind satisfying my curiosity?"

"Pish off, you unctuous'n'self-righteous prig."

Huw is about to speak, when the djinni catches her eye. He shakes his head, very slowly: 639,219 shows no sign of seeing. Then the djinni speaks. "I strongly advise you not to engage with your alienated instance," he says. "Remember, you can engage only in consensual transactions in this bar. I'm withholding my consent for discourse from her, and I think you should do the same."

"Why?" says Huw, nipped by an imp of the perverse. "Don't you think I could benefit from finding out why this bad sister went off on her little side trip?"

"No, you—" The djinni pauses. "Wait. Yes, I change my mind. You probably *could* learn something useful. But don't you think it's just possible that her viewpoint might be contagious? Engage too deeply, and you could pick up her bad memes by accident, and then where would you be?"

"Huh." Huw sniffs. She turns her attention to the hovering bartender. "I'll have a Bloody Mary."

"And your companion?" asks the bartender.

Huw fiddles with her settings until she's pretty sure 639,219 can't hear them: "She'll have what I'm having, only with Bhut Jalokia sauce instead of Tabasco."

Two glasses appear on the bar. Huw reaffirms her consent to speak to 639,219: "this one's on me," she says, smiling broadly as she raises her glass: *"Slainte."*

"Slainte—" 639,219 guzzles her drink as Huw watches with interest. The djinni winces, but Huw is disappointed: rather than exploding, 639,219 merely emits a small puff of smoke from each

nostril and hiccups quietly. "Wow, some sober-up, sis. I didn't know you had it in you."

"What—" Huw bites her tongue. 639,219 is shaking her head. "I thought you were dumb's'a plank, and then you pulled the fanciest freakin' financial engineering stunt I've ever heard of... How'ya do it?"

"Trade secret." It's the first thing that pops into her mind. "Seriously, you think I'd share with you before we've sorted out our differences?"

"Huh. What differences? You're in here now, same as me. A cloud-bunny, getting to learn to like the mutable life. What's to sort out?"

"Well. There's the small matter of you trying to fuck me over, for starters, both impersonating me in the planning hearing—"

"Hey! *I* was invited to testify before the committee! You just barged in like you thought it was a meeting of the organic farming co-op planting committee!"

"No, *I* was the one they invited—" Huw stops.

639,219 stares at her blearily.

"We both got the invite. Someone is fucking with us," Huw says.

"Huh." 639,219 struggles to sit upright. "Well, I'm up for it if you are."

"Wha?" Huw looks round at the djinni, but he's sulking ostentatiously, rezzed out in a gray cloud from which a hand emerges to protectively cradle a mai tai the size of a paint bucket.

"We should arb," says 639,219. "Let's diff, baby, see where it's at."

"Excuse me one moment," says Huw, and calls up a helpfile.

Arbing refers to a perverse practice whereby deviant software entities serialize their cognitive frameworks and subject them to differential analysis to identify points of dissonance. When it's read-only, it's perfectly safe for consenting sapients to engage in without risking their worldview—but it highlights differences and hauls memetic ruptures into sight like nothing else.

"Read-only," Huw says.

"Sure," says 639,219. "Like I was going to invite you to overwrite me with your stick-in-the-mud biophilia and change phobia!"

"Well?" Huw asks.

"You're on."

639,219 leans unsteadily toward Huw and extends a finger. Huw, not without some trepidation, touches it.

Arbing is painless, fast, and minimally confusing. Huw barely has time to blink—there is a sensation not unlike the door scanner but more intrusive, ants crawling up and down the small of her back and in and out of her ears—and then she is surrounded by mounds and heaps of interconnected 3-D entity/relationship diagrams, some of them highlighted in a variety of colors.

"It's our cognitive map," says 639,219. "How cute! Look, there's me! That's what makes me different!" She points to a large polydimensional word cloud that expands as her hand approaches it: it's all in one color, tagged with her identity but not Huw's. "Hey, wait a minute." 639,219's brows furrow, and for all that she is intrinsically prettier and more perfectly polished than Huw, there is something ugly in her expression. "What's going on in there?"

"Djinni." Huw turns and pokes at the cloud. "Hey, you. *Wake up*. I need you."

"What?" The djinni rezzes in. "If it's a hot threesome you're after, you're in luck—"

"What's *that*?" Huw asks, pointing.

"I can't see."

"Well, fucking sign up to permit yourself to see 639,219 again, idiot! It's important!"

"Why?" he asks. There's a sulk in his voice. "I invited you here for a drink, and all you do is pay attention to your abusive girlfriend..."

"Listen, we arbed." That gets his attention. "Only there's something wrong." 639,219 is staring at the alien word cloud intently and muttering. Her brow is shiny with not-perspiration.

"So what do you expect me to do about it?"

"Lend us your great mind, O Djinni, and tell us what we're looking at."

"Oh very *well*." He snaps his fingers again and turns to face Huw, 639,219, and the cognitive maps floating around them. "Is this the—*oh shit!*"

639,219 looks up, alarmed. "This can't be right! My malware scanner says—"

"You're infected." The djinni nods sharply. "That's a rootkit. And look"—he points—"that's your epistemological framework it's dry-humping. How long have you had this?"

"I can't, I can't—" 639,219 shudders "—I don't know. Can you get it off me? What happens if you get it off me? Make it go away!"

The rootkit is a gray sludge of interlocking philosophical

objections to the Real, a self-propelled vacuole of solipsism and self-regard that leaves a slimy trail of ironic disdain on every concept it touches. It's chewing away at 639,219's cognitive map, etching holes in places where Huw has values and shitting out doubts.

"It's in very deep," says the djinni. "Do you know who planted it on you?" 639,219 shakes her head. "All right. Is there anyone you *really trust,* I mean, trust with your life, who might have had the access permissions to do something like this? Parents? Lovers? Wait, I know you're going to say they wouldn't—that doesn't matter, these rootkits usually infect people from someone else who's been infected. Who have you been fucking, 639,219?"

639,219 opens her mouth to say something, and her head disintegrates.

There is no blood, nor splinters of bone, nor greasy pink headmeat as would fly in a reality-based physics realm if someone was shot in the head: but the effect is equivalent. 639,219's head fades to onionskin transparency, revealing the absence of anything beneath the finest upper layer of skin: while around Huw and the djinni, 639,219's cognitive map turns gray as the rootkit explodes across it, crumbling the complexities of her personality to word salad.

The djinni roars and launches himself across the bar as Huw shudders uncontrollably, so shocked that she can't respond. Her vision blurs as the entire bar derezzes. The djinni has multiplied himself again, and a single copy waits with her while sixteen bazillion other copies race after the rapidly disappearing bartender.

"Huw," says the djinni's bodyguard instance, *"trust me."*

"Uh-uh—" Huw gasps.

"Now. Or I'm going to lose the killer."

"Oh. Okay." Huw struggles to get a grip, then adds the djinni to her trusted access list, right up top, granting maximum privileges for the next minute. This has got to be a cruel trick, she half thinks: the djinni probably staged the whole ep to get into her panties—

But no. Here comes a rapidly diminishing corps of overmuscled gents in Armani, frog-marching a figure between them. The bartender. The murderer. Someone 639,219 trusted so totally, she'd granted them permission to *kill* her, the same level Huw just gave the djinni in order to give him the transitive freedom to apprehend 639,219's assailant. Huw blinks back tears, steadying her emotions almost automatically using her control panel: have to be careful, she could go completely to pieces if she eases up on the iron grip and pauses to consider that 639,219 was a *victim*, of someone she trusted with her life except they planted a rootkit on her—

The djinni squad hold the bartender in front of her. Huw reaches out and grabs the bartender's head, making contact to dissolve the mask.

"Bonnie. *Why?*"

Bonnie looks down, then away.

Huw looks at the djinni, who shrugs: *Your show.* He snaps his finger, and time freezes everything around the two of them into motionless stasis.

A weird kind of clarity settles over Huw, a kind of Sherlockian distance. She's been running around with arse afire for most of her short uploaded life. Time she tried to think before she ran, for a change. "All right, let's start with what we can see. Item: we can still see Bonnie."

The djinni nods. "Wondered when you'd notice that."

"If I've got this capabilities thing sussed, 639,219 trusted me to arb, and she trusted Bonnie enough to let Bonnie slip her a lethal cocktail, which is pretty deep trust. Now, why would 639,219 enter into that kind of trust arrangement with Bonnie?" Huw thinks awhile, discarding hypotheses: lovers, coreligionists, trickery.

The djinni has clasped his hands behind his back and is pacing slowly back and forth to one side. He looks up. "What about the rootkit?"

Huw's smile thins out and she feels the irrational anger come to the surface again. She damps it down, summoning back that feeling of clarity again. "Of course," she says. "I'd assumed that someone rooted 639,219 so that she'd testify in favor of destroying the Earth. Maybe that *is* why the rootkit was installed. But anyone who'd rooted 639,219 could definitely get her to hand over enough trust to allow her to be destroyed."

Huw bounced from one not-foot to the other. "Right, so. I trust 639,219. 639,219 *has* to trust Bonnie, because Bonnie is her botmaster. I trust you. Therefore, you could catch Bonnie. Now, if Bonnie wants to void out her contract with 639,219, the sim'll roll back to before 639,219 and I started talking—um, probably to when she agreed to take the cocktail from Bonnie, a few minutes before we got there."

Huw stopped. "But if that happens, why wouldn't it all happen over again? I mean, barring small nondeterministic variations and initial sensitivity and all, I suppose it'd just play out again, and we'd end up back here, 639,219 gone, Bonnie captured—"

The djinni cleared his throat. "There's the reset tokens. Look like this." He flips her a poker chip that revolves through the air in a graceful, glinting arc. It slows as she reaches for it and nudges itself into a course-correction that lands it firmly in her palm. Its face bears the Club Capabilities logo, worked into a Möbius strip; when Huw flips the coin over, it rotates through another spatial dimension instead, a feeling that her not-fingertips and not-eyes can't agree upon, and she's looking at the same face again.

"I hate it already," Huw says. "Stupid flashy sensorium tricks. Ooh, look at me, I am a virtual being, I can bend physics, woo." She squeezes it in her fist. "What is it for? What does it do?"

"If the sim resets you, one of these ends up in your hand. It puts you on notice that if you enter into a contract right away, one or both of you is likely to abandon it. Prevents loops."

"So we'd have one of these." Huw thinks a moment. "Where'd you get this one?"

The djinni lays a finger that seems to have an extra joint alongside his hooked nose. "That would be telling," he says, and winks.

Huw damps down her temper. If the djinni is hoping to get into her knickers, he's certainly going about it the wrong way. She would want to strangle him, if she wasn't making herself not want to strangle him. "So, let's ask Bonnie." Time unfreezes. "You—you can't afford to break away from us, because I could just break my contract with 639,219 and you'd be pouring her a drink just as one of these coins appeared in her hand, and you'd be stuffed." Huw breaks off, thinks about what she just said. Bonnie stares at her mulishly but holds her silence.

Huw can't help but feel like there's something the djinni and Bonnie aren't telling her—something about the fraught looks they keep exchanging with each other.

"If only we could talk to 639,219. She *is* gone forever, right?"

"The rootkit zeroed her out," Bonnie says.

"Yeah," the djinni says.

Huw rubs her chin.

"Huw—" Bonnie says, a warning tone in her voice.

"This isn't a universe where causality only runs forwards, right? Things that happen can *unhappen*. Something you do in the future can affect the past, here."

"Huw—" the djinni says, sounding more alarmed.

"And 639,219 only got derezzed by her rootkit *after* we created an agreement. And since I'm still in this sim, all I need to do is *violate* the agreement and I'll unwind everything back to that point. We'll get one of those little tokens—" Huw flipped the poker chip so it did a high end-over-end arc, clattering away into the infinite regression-depths of the club's storeroom. "We'll get one of those, and poof, 639,219 will be back and hale and hearty and we can all start over again, right?"

The djinni and Bonnie are shaking their heads together in sync, like two metronomes. "Huw," the djinni says, "if you revert this sim to the moment before you and 639,219 agreed to arb, you're going to roll back the lives of *thousands* of people."

Huw makes a rude noise. "I may have only just ascended, but

I didn't just fall off the tree. There wasn't anyone around when we arbed."

"You're forgetting the djinni chasing me down. If you and 639,219 never arbed, I wouldn't have run, and the djinni wouldn't have chased me."

"All right, a few people probably saw that, but how many of them had their outcomes influenced by seeing an infinite herd of djinni chasing a bartender?"

"Dozens," the djinni says. "Hundreds. And then there's everyone they talked to or influenced as a result. Huw, you're talking about deliberately unwinding the lives of a small city, and the population is growing by the second."

Huw feels belligerent. "I do the same every time I do anything and everything. Every time I take any action, it ripples out to all the people who are affected by it, and all the people they effect. You're saying that sensitivity to initial conditions means that you're morally obliged never to change your mind. It's rubbish. Just because causality runs backwards in this place doesn't mean the butterfly effect becomes the first commandment. Now, what did I promise 639,219 before we arbed?"

Bonnie and the djinni are both talking now, but Huw has literally tuned them out, so that they've faded out of her causal universe, unable to affect her. She's really getting to like this capabilities wheeze. She tunes them back in.

"Right," she says, pointing at Bonnie. "You, talk."

"Look," Bonnie says, "you've got this all wrong."

The djinni frowns. "You need to audit her," he says. "You'll never get anything useful out of her volitionally. Just arb her."

"No," Bonnie and Huw say at the same moment. Huw is struck with a whole-not-body revulsion at the thought of being exposed and exposing with this Bonnie, this weird shade of the man and woman she's loved and lost and loved and hated.

"Why is it always *me?*" Huw says. "Why don't you do the transhuman mind-meld for a change?"

The djinni shakes his topknot. "Wrong cognitive model. I'm an expression of a hivemind, wholly synthetic. You two are uploaded—built incrementally by modeling a physical structure. Means that we're impedance mismatched. Can't ever have a meeting of the minds, alas." He doesn't sound very sorry. "So, look, Huw, let me tell you, whatever leverage you've got with Bonnie is going to evaporate pretty quick. Soon as someone leaves the club, the contract is fixed, because now there's causal links that are external to this sim—Club Capabilities can't reverse effects that take place outside of here. That's why there's no comms links in or out—we're causally isolated. So if you're going to blackmail her into arbing, better do it quick before someone decides to go outside and check his email."

Huw opens his mouth: "Well, fuck. Bonnie—"

"You're not going to make me—" Bonnie makes her move, begins to derez, trying to untrust Huw. But the djinni is faster. Bonnie and everyone in the bar—except the djinni—freeze in place and fade to red again.

"Bullet time," the djinni tells Huw. "You have about ten subjective seconds—two milliseconds as far as everyone else is concerned. Use them wisely."

Feeling pressured and desperate and sick to her stomach, Huw tweaks her emo control into bland-faced robotitude. A comforting blanket of gray descends, and *of course* it's obvious what she ought to do. It's for Bonnie's own good, and 639,219's insofar as 639,219 was a fragment of Huw's own mind. Huw doesn't owe her flawed instance-sister anything except the honest truth before the planning tribunal, and proof of Bonnie's malfeasance will provide that. *Besides, I've spent most of the past however long hating her guts. Isn't this fit of sentimental sympathy a bit perverse?*

"Arb. Now," Huw hears herself say. She watches her finger extend to touch Bonnie's forehead, growing longer and stretching like a bizarre insectile appendage, multijointed and not part of her self-image. Bonnie is frozen, mouth half-open, hair caught in motion around her face. "You've got her? Connect us." The djinni nods.

"Well, *fuck*," says Huw, staring at the same rootkit she saw in 639,219's cognitive map. She glances at the djinni. "If we put this in front of the planning committee, along with the record from 639,219…"

"Yes, that will provide an evidential chain suggesting that testimony provided by 639,219 must be discounted." The djinni strokes his goatee. "There is an appeal stage where procedural errors can be raised. And proof of external tampering with evidence presented at the hearing will bring everything to a halt, if not result in a mistrial." His expression is reserved, if not shifty.

"Good." Huw pauses. "But if I do that, I'll be unable to unwind to before Bonnie killed 639,219. Won't I?"

The djinni points. "The answer is in your hands."

"Yes. I see." Dully, Huw tweaks a helical slider past a detent labeled EMPATHY BLOCK, into a red zone flagged DANGER: SOCIOPATHIC PERSONALITY DISORDER. Instantly, she feels better. In fact, she feels *great*. "Cool! Let's go!"

The djinni smiles. "I knew you'd see sense eventually."

When they revert to realtime, Bonnie puts up a fight: crying, shaking, pleading with Huw for understanding, offering to kiss and make up.

Huw finds that she doesn't give a shit for this tiresome emo nonsense. It's transparently clear that it's not Bonnie talking anyway—it's the rootkit, using Bonnie's personality as a sock puppet to manipulate her. Well, that's okay by Huw. Huw doesn't feel anything, but she remembers how she ought to act, how she *would* have acted, back when she was in the throes of lust or love or something. It's trivially easy to calm Bonnie's fears, to apologize for not trusting her—to pretend not to have seen the rootkit lurking gray and bloated in the wreckage of her moral maze—to agree it's all a misunderstanding and anyway Huw hated 639,219. And so she holds Bonnie's wrists as the floor carries them toward the exit and the djinni spins them around and down through bubbling blue layers of reality, back to the polished floor of the lobby of the Tripoli Marriott.

"It's all going to be okay." Huw soothes Bonnie, who is whimpering and writhing but evidently in the grip of some kind of BDSM compulsion field, courtesy of the lurking djinni: "We're going to go in there and explain that it was all a mistake and I'll give evidence. All right?" She can see that Bonnie—or the rootkit—*doesn't* agree that it's all right, but she sees no reason to let it faze her.

"You don't understand! If I go in there, they'll, it's going to, I won't be able to—" She's blubbering now, making a surprisingly corporeal mess. Huw nods reassuringly.

The djinni, rubbing a handheld slab of black glass against his cheek—very symbolic, very retro, an antique telephone—is mumbling to himself. He makes the glass slab vanish. "I filed a motion for the committee to hear an appeal," he says. The doors to the conference room swing open. "After you—"

"What is bzzt *going on?"*

Huw looks round. A pepper pot–shaped automaton covered in knobbly hemispheres, probes jutting aggressively from beneath the black silk cap adorning its cortical turret, glides across the lobby behind her. The avatar's unfamiliar, but Huw'd recognize that voice anywhere, and for once it doesn't fill her with terror. "Rosa! How charming. We're just about to explain to the Planning Committee how they've been subverted—"

"You!" shrieks Rosa Giuliani. *"Exterminate!"* She twirls to point her stubby manipulators at Huw and unleashes a rather implausible-looking lightning bolt that, predictably, has no effect whatsoever.

Huw waits for the light show to subside. "This is a no PvP area," she says. "And we're on the same side. Unless you *want* to encourage them to demolish the Earth?"

"What is this? Explain!" Rosa—or the pint-sized robot tank containing what's left of her malevolent mindware, post-upload—glides forward.

"You got a summons too, didn't you?" Huw asks. "But when you got here, you were too late because they'd closed the hearing." She nods at Bonnie: "Well, here's the evidence that the hearing's been suborned: This one's harboring an illegal rootkit. I reckon she was hacked by one of the players in Glory City, and they've been using her to mess with the evidence—"

Bonnie struggles to get free. "That's not true!" she says, "You're making this up!"

"Sorry, darling," says Huw, and she drags Bonnie into the conference room. Which appears to be empty, until the instant her foot crosses the threshold.

There are no spectators this time, and no regular witnesses. But the triumvirate of ill-assorted court bureaucrats *bamf* in one by one from whatever distant shard fragment they inhabit when the court isn't in session. They do not look terribly happy. "Which one of you is Huw Jones?" says the chair, fingering one gold-capped tusk.

"I am, Your Honor," Huw says. "And this is Rosa Giuliani." She gestures at the pepper pot.

"Interesting. You aren't the Huw Jones who testified at the last hearing, are you?"

Huw swallows. "I'm afraid not. She's dead. Terminally scrambled by this one, but not before I determined that she'd been infected by a rootkit prior to the hearing. I have evidence—" She gestures at the djinni, who coughs up a thumb-sized ruby, glinting with inner light, and tosses it at the chair.

The chair swallows the gem. "Interesting." Judging from her expression, that's an understatement. "Who's this?"

Huw pushes Bonnie forward. Invisible bonds prevent her from fleeing. "This is Bonnie. She killed 639,219—my rootkitted sibling—inside a capability bar. Like me, she's not thoroughly acclimated to the cloud: it turns out she's been rootkitted too, and was running 639,219 on behalf of a botmaster, identity unknown, but probably resident in Glory City, South Carolina."

Bonnie falls to her knees. "What's going on? I'm not a bot! You're crazy, Huw, what's gotten into you?"

But the chair isn't paying attention to Bonnie right now. "Judge Rosa Giuliani. You failed to attend the previous scheduled hearing. May I ask why?"

"*Extermin—*" Rosa stops, pirouettes in place, and quietens. "Grr. *Bzz.* I was not notified of the hearing in time to attend. My clerk received the summons but unaccountably *misfiled* it for three days until EXTERMINATE damn this cheap off-the-shelf avatar! I came as soon as I could, after the summons came to light."

"Do you know why your clerk misfiled the court's papers?" asks the second orc, deceptively calmly.

"That is a *very* good question," Giuliani says. "I believe certain parties in Glory City—while we were there attending to unpleasant but unavoidable businesses—suborned him. There are rumors about the depraved and perverted practices of the pulchritudinous protestant puritan plutocratic penis-people priesthood, of shadowy bacchanalian polyamorous practices... I suspect, to be blunt, someone was blackmailing him."

"You *suspect?* You did not investigate—?"

"Hell, no!" says Giuliani, "I *exterminate! All enemies of the—*"
The chair clears her throat. "This is rather disturbing," she

says. "Especially in view of the representations recently received."

For a moment the officers of the Planning Committee freeze and turn blurry and blue, segueing into quicktime to confer at leisure.

Huw clears her throat, momentarily wishing there were an alien ambassador nestling in it to help get their attention. "What representations?" she asks, out of order but chancing her luck anyway.

Bonnie sobs quietly.

"The galactic federation," says the chair, segueing back into real time and looking at her with the expression a kindly teacher might reserve for a slow learner. "*Do* try to keep up. You didn't think we reconvened this hearing just in your behalf, did you? It's the aliens. They sent us an email. All very traditional. Planning hearing will now recess while we discuss this other shit."

Huw feels stupid. "What galactic federation? That's ridiculous! Some stupid griefer is playing games with you, a breakaway densethinker clade that's bouncing its messages off Alpha Centauri to make them seem like they're coming from the next galaxy. No?"

The chair holds up a green-skinned and gnarly finger and wags it at Huw. "No. We're completely sure. For one thing, they took Io."

"Took what?"

"The moon. Io. Atomized it. It's now dust. And for another, they've rooted the three largest simspaces and claimed them as ambassadorial missions."

"It could still be a griefer—?"

"They sent us an email. Instructions for setting up a protocol converter. When you speak to it—which you will, Ms. Jones, you will—then you will *know*. This isn't anything descended from meatpeople that we were or uplifted. It's Other, capital O, and when you meet it, you won't have any doubt."

Huw has a sinking feeling in the pit of her stomach. "This isn't really about the planning application for dismantling the Earth, is it? It's all about me again!"

"Could be." The chair's expression is bland, behind her tusks. Huw glances round. The djinni is stationed before the closed doors, his expression frozen. Judge Rosa's pocket tank is parked beside him, weaponlike appendages pointing at... well. Bonnie is a crying lump on the floor, no help *there* even if she were rootkit-free. "Ms. Jones. Please reset your emotional balance to normal, there's a good being? What we are about to discuss is not suitable for psychopaths."

"Feh." Huw brings up her emo box and tosses it up in the air. As it comes down again, a nameless sleet of strange emotional states shakes her to her core. She looks at Bonnie, feels a stab of remorse, grief, revulsion, and pity. *"Why?"* she asks.

"It calls itself the Authority. It claims it represents a hive-intelligence merged from about 216 intelligent species from the oldest part of the galaxy. It claims that there were once about four orders of magnitude more such species, but the rest were wiped out in vicious, galactic resource wars that only ended with the merger of the remaining combatants into a single entity. Now it patrols the galaxy to ensure that any species that attempt transcendence are fit to join it. If it finds a species wanting, *pfft!* It takes care of them before they get to be a problem."

"You're saying that this thing can move faster than the speed of light, and that it's descended from species that had the same ability?"

"We don't know much about its capabilities, but yes, those sound about right."

"No, on the contrary: That sounds completely crazy. You've been had. Why would a civilization that could beat lightspeed bother to fight wars? What, precisely, could they fight over? If your neighbor wants your rocks, go somewhere else with more of the same rocks. Unclaimed rocks and sunlight aren't scarce; otherwise, the neighbors would have dismantled us for computronium back in the Triassic. So the resource wars they're talking about are a big hairy fib. And that's leaving out all the causality stuff, which is a bit of a reach. Put it all together, and it stinks of bullshit."

"We don't think so." The chair of the Planning Committee is intently focused on Huw, and it's making her skin crawl. "They are many millions of years older than we are. They command an understanding of physics that makes us look like naked, rock-worshipping neolithics. We do not know what led to their wars— aesthetic jihad? A philosophical crusade? A bad hand of poker? Whatever it is, they say that there's a pretty good chance we'll grow up to want to do it too, and if that turns out to be the case, they plan on doing something about it, preemptively.

"Which is where you come in. When the Authority manifested here, it demanded that we send it an ambassador to parlay. Well, we just happened to have one lying around."

"You didn't." Huw's eyes widen.

"We did." Does the chair for a moment sound just slightly

smug? "And we need you to interface with it."

Huw bolts. A moment later she's on the floor, nose-to-nose with Bonnie. Oddly, her feet don't seem to want to work properly. "I told you she'd do that," says the djinni.

Fuck, another traitor, Huw realizes despairingly. *Does* anyone *in here not have a covert agenda?*

The chair looms over Huw. "Ms. Jones, this unseemly and improper display notwithstanding, this court needs representation before the Authority. And so, we are hereby deputizing you to speak on all our behalfs. Do the job right and when you get back here we will listen to your testimony before the Planning Committee with a sympathetic ear. Fuck up, and there won't be a Planning Committee to testify *to*. Or an Earth, on whose behalf to speak, for that matter."

The chair-orc rummages in her scale-mail and produces a familiar, dreadful cylinder. A whistle. "This won't hurt a bit," she says. "Now, say 'aaah.'"

Finally, an order Huw is glad to follow. The lack of an actual throat and actual lungs lets her scream much longer and louder than her meatself ever managed. The resulting esophageal tunnel makes a neat target for the chair, who tosses the whistle like a javelin; it lodges firmly in Huw's windpipe and tunnels home with a fluting squeal of welcome.

Huw tiptoes out of the Marriott's lobby in glazed disbelief, hands crossed over her chest protectively. The fact that it's not her body being violated, but a mere representation of it, is of no comfort. Indeed, since the ambassador currently lodged in her not-windpipe is a lump of dense code created by the collective consciousness that evolved her digital representation, there's no telling how entwined with her self it might be.

The djinni isn't waiting for her. Even Bonnie is gone. Indeed, it takes a moment for Huw to realize that there's *nothing* physical in this simspace. She is floating in a featureless void, except that *floating* isn't the right verb to use, because she doesn't have the sensation of floating, nor the sensation of not-floating. She is even more disembodied than usual.

"Well, look what the cat drug in, Sam," says a familiar voice, which comes, of course, from everywhere and nowhere. "Amazing the sort of degenerate secondhander parasite you get, even here. I reckon we'll have to take care of that, soon enough."

The next voice she hears is likewise familiar—gravel in a cement-mixer, tinged with a kind of smug, celestial calm. "I reckon she's a-here on a technicality," Sam says. "Mean to say, from what I hear, she didn't come under her own power."

Huw attempts to propel herself into another sim, or out of this sim, but whatever trick is necessary for virtual locomotion in the absence of a virtual physicality, she doesn't know it. Yet another thing she probably should have paid attention to back on the trainer. But it appears she *can* speak—or squeak. After a moment of high-pitched tweets, she and the ambassador recover their old, uneasy accommodation. "What are you guys doing here? I thought you were back on Earth, waiting for Zombie Jesus to return with Magic Sky Daddy and His heavenly host to sweep up the faithful."

"Not that it's any of your business, heathen," Doc says, "but the Lord has spoken and His Prophet has clarified a few things about the uplifting and all."

"Turns out we gotta prepare the way for holy war in cyberspace," Sam says.

Huw boggles. "*Cyberspace?* Who even says 'cyberspace' anymore?"

"The Prophet, that's who," Doc says. "He knows how to talk like a real person, knows that the old language is best: if King James's English was good enough for Jesus, it's good enough for him, he says. None of this 'cloud' and 'sim' business. He's a plainspoken, people's prophet. We're Soldiers of the Lord, here to bring about the Kingdom of Heaven. And step one of that was to summon our army—all those who ain't yet heard the Prophet's word and don't know what's good for 'em. We had it all fixed, you know. Demolish the Earth, upload everyone dirtside in one go, and *whompf*, we'd of had an instant organized militia at our disposal, ready to start work on the final program. Then you made a hash of it all, with your foolish meddling, undid all the Prophet's good work and all the work of His advance guard."

"Us," Sam says.

"Us," the doc says. "And you don't even belong here! You're part of the heathen masses, scheduled to be swept up and quarantined in the Pre-Rapture for brainwashing and indoctrination. You try me, missy, you really do."

"Guys," Huw says, using her most reasonable voice, "this is all really fascinating, but I've been summoned to some sort of galactic tribunal to debate whether some vast, starry power will end the human race and its uplifted descendants, so perhaps we could do this later?"

"We've heard tell of this," Doc says, "and we're of two minds about it."

"Yeah," Sam says, "I think it's just an unfortunate coincidence, mean to say, just one of those things."

"And I think it's the end times," Doc says. "A snare of Satan. Which puts us behind schedule on our whole program of assembling our Army of Glory, but on the plus side, it's all going to be moot soon."

"What if the galactic tribunal decides we're fit to join up with them?" Huw says. "They might be a really lovely bunch of chaps, with all sorts of excellent advice and technology for their new chums."

Doc chuckles. "You've got some high opinion of those alien scum, I figure. Way I see it, there's only one way Judgment Day can play out, even assuming these galactic bastards are the fairest-minded bunch of sweetie-pie fairies that ever danced over the celestial firmament: and that's annihilation. Between your garden-variety sinners and the hordes of thumbless, brainless leeches that suck the vitality and vigor out of everything that their betters attempt, there's no sense in pretending otherwise. Do you seriously believe that you and your tin whistle are going to convince these interstellar *Übermenschen* that they should let us go on polluting reality with our existence?"

Huw's losing patience. "Isn't the whole point of your faith that humanity is redeemable?"

Doc and Sam laugh together. "Missy," Doc says, "I wouldn't

give you two wet farts for 'humanity.' A few select individuals, who understand the importance of humility before their betters, obedience to authority, piety and faith, sure, but those sorts're pretty thin on the ground, even now that the least redeemable portion of the species have upped stakes for cyberspace."

"I'm getting pretty tired of this business," Huw says. "You *do* realize that I'm now the embodied avatar of the entire uplifted human race, thanks to the 'tin whistle,' right? It's one thing to criminally endanger the planet Earth, but do you think that the WorldGovvers are going to sit still for an abduction? Whatever benighted bootleg sim you've kidnapped me to, they're going to be able to trace me by using the ambassador. I don't expect they're going to be amused when they find you, either."

"You just tend to your own knitting, little girl," Doc says, demonstrating an unerring instinct for choosing the most irritating form of address. "We've got plenty of time to chat before anyone notices... Me and my coreligionists, we're a lot deeper and wider than you give us credit for. We've got ourselves a damned hot and fast platform to run on, and a plan you wouldn't believe. Your little council out there, whatever they want to call themselves, they're running at about a bazillionth of the speed we're at right now. We could jaw on here for hours of subjective time and still be done before they'd got through picking their noses."

Huw doesn't know whether to believe this or not, but she decides it's at least plausible. The religion virus had been infecting the human race for millennia, and of course, anyone who'd plump for voluntary digital transcendence was already halfway bought into the whole spiritual pyramid scheme. Whoever this

Prophet was, his mix of Objectivist pandering and Christian mystical eschatology could very well deliver a large fifth column of self-absorbed dingbats prepared to destroy the human race to save it (or at least the bit of it that they were dead certain they belonged to).

"I'll stipulate that this is true," Huw says. "So why the hell don't you kill me or infect me or whatever it is you're planning on doing? I'm a busy woman."

"We'd have infected you some time ago if we thought that'd work," Doc says after a pause.

"Doc reckons they're going to be integrity-testing you pretty closely now they've found out about Bonnie," Sam says.

"Which leaves us with only one course of action: We're going to *convince* you to help us," says Doc.

The funny thing is, Huw's certain they're not joking. "You're kidding," she says automatically, covering her confusion.

"No, we're not," says Doc. "Listen, what do you think we were put down there on Earth for? You think He did it just for yucks or a sick joke or something? No: we're on a holy mission to bring about the Kingdom of God. Resurrection of the dead, redemption for all, immortality, the whole lot. Way the Prophet explains it, Saint John the Divine was a *warning,* a *threat* of what will happen if we don't get our shit together. If we leave the Earth to God to fix up because we trash it, he'll be pissed at us. But if we do his will and bring about the Kingdom of God, well, Armageddon'll be averted, and that's just for starters. Heaven on Earth!"

"You said resurrection." Huw has a funny feeling she's heard this stuff before. "And immortality. Isn't that sort of what the whole Second Coming thing was supposed to be for?"

"Cometh the hour, cometh the man," says Sam.

"Yup," Doc says. "God loves those who help themselves—that's basic, isn't it? A is A, right? Let's get our axioms in order. God *loves* those who help themselves, and God wants us to prosper. As long as we're living a godly life and doing God's will, of course. So anyway, what *is* God's will? Well, God's got plans for us which include prospering and being good custodians of the world and, uh, well, we haven't done so good at that. But God's other plans include resurrecting the dead. And the elect living in paradise on Earth for a very long time, with all the formerly dead sinners as their personal servants. Death is obviously the enemy of humanity and God, so the Prophet says we're first going to make ourselves immortal, then we're going to resurrect everyone who has ever lived, and simulate every human who ever *might* have lived so that we can incarnate them too. And we're to colonize space—"

Huw is zoning out at this point. Because she has a very funny feeling that she's heard it all before. This is the religious wellspring of the whole extropian transhumanist shtick, after all: the name's on the tip of her tongue—

"Federov," she says.

"Whut?" Sam sounds suspicious.

"An early Russian cosmist, sort of a fossil transhumanist mystic. My dad was a big fan of Federov," she adds.

"Was he a Commie?" Doc asks. "What's he got to do with the Kingdom of God?"

"Tell me." Huw has a feeling that if she can fake it well enough,

Sam and Doc might just let her go: "Your Prophet. He says... hmm. Is there stuff about learning to photosynthesize and fly to other worlds and live free in space?"

"Yes! Yes!" Sam is excited.

"And stuff about bringing life to the galaxy?" she says.

"Might be." Doc is less forthcoming. "This stuff you got from that Feeder-of guy?"

"A is A," Huw dog-whistles a call-out to another Russian philosopher Dad was excessively fond of quoting. It's so much easier to deal with Doc and Sam when she's not suffering from concussion, god-module hackery, or a hangover. "Anyway, Federov died a long time ago. Did you know he taught Tsiolkovsky?" This stuff is all coming back, stuff Dad was big on: the drawback of being in the cloud is that mortal bit rot no longer applies. "Tsiolkovsky—the guy who invented the rocket equation and space colonization? Ayn Rand was a fan of both of them."

"Now, hold on, girlie, no need to be taking the name of Saint Ayn in vain!" Doc sounds ticked off, and for a moment Huw thinks she's gone too far. "But I take your point. If he'd not been one of those godless Orthodox types, he'd probably be a saint too. Serves him right. But there'll be time to convert him after he's resurrected."

"Gotcha," says Sam. "But listen, babe, before we can resurrect everyone, we've got to take over the cloud, dismantle the Earth, turn the *entire* solar system into the biggest damn computing cloud you can imagine, and simulate all possible paths of human history. Then bring everybody to the Prophet's way. Once we've done that, *then* we can go git ourselves some more planets and reincarnate everybody and bring about heaven on as many earths as necessary. But do ya think the galactic satanists will let us do that, huh? Do you?"

"I don't know," Huw says, "but we're all on the same side, aren't we? We're all human, all in favor of resurrecting everyone in the flesh, right?"

"Right," Doc says.

"Even though you think I'm a godless pervert, right?"

"Ye-es," Sam says.

"But we share a bunch of core beliefs, don't we? We can agree to disagree for a little while about some minor stuff while I go and try to convince the galactic federation that they really don't need to *exterminate us like bugs,* right? Because that would put a cramp on the Prophet's scheme, wouldn't it?"

"Don't be entirely sure about that, missy," Doc says. "If it's God's will to ring the curtain down on us, then I guess it'll just be time for Jesus to come sort us all out."

"But you don't want that—" Enlightenment strikes Huw like a lightning bolt "—because all the second-handers would get their reward for believing, even if they never lifted a finger or worked an honest day in their life! Your years of hard work and struggle would go unnoticed and unrewarded if God has to roll his sleeves up and send his son to sort out the mess. So it's best if we build the Kingdom of Heaven *ourselves,* right? Then we can enjoy the just rewards of creative genius."

"Speaking for myself, that's *exactly* what I'm cogitating," Doc says. "Y'know, you weren't the sharpest knife in the drawer as a boy, but I'll swear you're reading my mind. What—?"

"There's this slider control." Huw desperately searches for a plausible lie: "I'm thinking faster here, is all? So we can reach an uh, agreement?"

"I *like* the way you think," says Doc. "After we build the Kingdom, you can be my handmaid!"

And Huw is abruptly ejected from whatever pocket nulliverse the Prophet's fifth column have installed in the lobby of the virtual Tripoli Mariott, to a destination even more profoundly alienating than the cloud itself.

"Welcome to the embassy, Witness Jones," says the gorilla.

He's a very polite gorilla, thoroughly diplomatic: nattily turned out in a tuxedo and white spats (the effect overall only slightly spoiled by his failure to wear shoes). Huw would indeed be entirely charmed by him if not for a lingering bigoted prejudice against furries that she acquired at an early age. The gorilla looks naggingly familiar, and Huw has a forehead-slapping moment when she recognizes the beloved commercial mascot of a long-extinct brand of breakfast cereal—offered as a free, high-resolution avatar in many early game systems as part of a canny, much-copied marketing strategy. The Galactic Authority's infinite power is apparently so vast that it needn't bother itself about looking like an utterly naff simspace newbie who still thinks digital hair is cool.

"I'm very pleased to be here." *But not for the reason you expect.* "Have you seen my djinni?"

"Your—?" The gorilla's expression sours. "He's yours, is he?

Yes, I've certainly seen him. I believe he's camping in the rose garden around the back." The gorilla gestures vaguely around the side of the building they're standing in front of.

As befits an embassy to a galactic civilization, the cloud-dwellers have thrown together something rather posh. Unfortunately, they didn't bother to vet the components for architectural coherency, which is why, within the gigantic outer ramparts of the Tokugawa-era Edo Castle (big enough to surround a medium-scale city, steep enough to repel tanks), they've installed Buckingham Palace as a reception suite; the Executive Office Building from Washington, D.C., as an administrative center; and an assortment of other tasteless excrescences—the Centre Pompidou to house an Arts and Culture Expo, the Burj Khalifa for hotel accommodation, and the Great Pyramid of Giza for no obvious reason at all.

To Huw's not-terribly-trained nose, it all reeks of desperate insecurity. Even if they had been physically built, rather than merely rendered, these monumental buildings wouldn't be remotely impressive compared to the cloud itself: but they were all designed to testify to the power and grandeur of their pre-singularity creators, in a manner that is deeply reassuring to a future-shocked primate trying to face up to overwhelming neighbors.

And the neighbors *are* overwhelming. The embassy is embedded within the fragment of the pan-galactic intercloud hosted by the repurposed remains of Io, and the aliens aren't going to let anyone forget it: beyond the embassy compound lies a remarkably realistic-looking re-creation of the moon's icy, sulfurous surface. Above it hangs the marmalade-and-cottage-cheese-streaked gibbous ball of Jupiter. Illumination, such as it is, comes from the distant reddish disk of the cloud, occulting and scattering much of the sunlight trapped within its Dyson sphere layers. And spanning fully 180 degrees of the sky beyond Jupiter and cloud lies...

The Milky Way. But not as Huw knows it.

Her Milky Way is a timid smear of dimness, wheeling in the sky high above the nighttime hills of Wales. *This* Milky Way is a map of communications density, a dream of thought slashed livid across a billion inhabited star systems, pulsing with intellect, bubbling with fallow voids between the various conjoined empires. It reminds Huw of maps and visualizations Dad printed out in her—his—childhood, showing the early days of the Internet, mere trickling exabytes and petabytes of data zinging through the wires between population centers. But the points of light in this dazzling mist of data aren't web browsers, they're entire uploaded civilizations. If it's meant to impress, it's succeeding. If it's meant to intimidate, it's doing that too.

"Thanks, I'll find him later. Uh, where am I staying? And what do I need to know for the process I'm supposed to be part of?"

"I can see you have a lot of questions, there. You're staying in a suite on the two hundred eighty-sixth floor of the tower, there—" The gorilla points at the Burj Khalifa "—and as for the rest, you are scheduled for an orientation meeting later. Perhaps you'd like to move in, freshen up, and collect your djinni? The Cultural Secretary will talk you through the diplomatic process later, but for the time being, she's rather busy seeing to the other witnesses."

"Other—Rosa Giuliani, by any chance?" She asks, "Is there a person here called Bonnie? Or a—"

"I'm sure you'll have time to catch up with your friends later." The gorilla nudges. "But right now, Secretary Chakrabarti has asked me to see that you're comfortably settled in and all your needs attended to first. To minimize culture shock, you understand."

Huw certainly understands, all right. The embassy is not just a very high fidelity sim, mimicking Earth-bound reality right down to the limits of direct sensory perception (despite the jumble of items from the architectural heritage dime store and the mad skyscape overhead); it's also a capabilities-enforced PvP environment, the enlightened modern substitute for diplomatic immunity. And so she allows the gorilla to lead her to a teleport booth, and then to the gigantic jungle-infested lobby of the largest skyscraper in the Middle East, and up a roaring maglev express elevator (her ears pop, painfully and hyperrealistically, on the way) to a penthouse suite about the size of her entire street back home.

"I hope you enjoy the facilities here," says the gorilla with a wink. "Nothing but the best for our expert witnesses—we have hot and cold running *everything*."

It's a far cry from jury duty accommodation in a crappy backpacker's hostel in dusty Tripoli. Huw dials her time right up (sinfully extravagant: it's the same kind of costly acceleration that got her into trouble when 639,219 called her on it) and orders the whirlpool-equipped hot tub with champagne to appear in the bathroom. Then she climbs in to marinate for subjective hours (a handful of seconds in everyone else's reference frame) and to unkink for the first time in ages. After all, it's not as if she's consuming real resources here. And she needs to relax, recenter her emotions the natural way, and do some serious plotting.

Of course, the sim is far too realistic. A virtual champagne bath should somehow manage to keep the champagne drinking-temp cold while still feeling warm to the touch. And it shouldn't be sticky and hot and flat; it should feel like champagne does when it hits your tongue—icy and bubbly and fizzy. And when Huw's nonbladder feels uncomfortably full and relaxed in the hot liquid and she lets a surreptitious stream loose, it should be magicked away, not instantly blended in with the vintage Veuve to make an instant tubworth of piss-mimosa.

This is what comes of having too much compute-time at one's disposal, Huw seethes. In constraint, there is discipline, the need to choose how much reality you're going to import and model. Sitting on an Io's worth of computronium has freed the Galactic Authority—and isn't *that* an unimaginative corker of a name?—from having to choose. And with her own self simulated as hot and wide as she can be bothered with, she can feel every unpleasant sensation, each individual sticky bubble, each droplet clinging to her body as she hops out of the tub and into the six-jet steam-shower for a top-to-bottom rinse, and then grabs a towel—every fiber slightly stiff and plasticky, as if fresh out of the wrapper and never properly laundered to relax the fibers—and dries off. She discovers that she is hyperaware, hyperalert, feeling every grain of not-dust in the not-air individually as it collides with her not-skin.

Oh, oh, oh, *enough,* she wants to shout. *What is the* point *of all this rubbish?*

This is the thing that Huw has never wanted to admit: Her

277

primary beef against the singularity has never been existential—it's *aesthetic*. The power to be a being of pure thought, the unlimited, unconstrained world of imagination, and we build a world of animated gifs, stupid sight gags, lame van-art avatars, stupid "playful" environments, and brain-dead flame wars augmented by animated emoticons that allowed participants to express their hackneyed ad hominems, concern-trollery, and Godwin's law violations through the media of cartoon animals and oversized animated genitals.

Whether or not sim-Huw is *really* Huw, whether or not uploading is a kind of death, whether or not posthumanity is immortal or just kidding itself, the single, inviolable fact remains: Human simspace is no more tasteful than the architectural train wreck that the Galactic Authority has erected. The people who live in it have all the aesthetic sense of a senile jackdaw. Huw is prepared to accept—for the sake of argument, mind—that uploading leaves your soul intact, but she is never going give one nanometer on the question of whether uploading leaves your *taste* intact. If the Turing test measured an AI's capacity to conduct itself with a sense of real style, all of simspace would be revealed for a machine-sham. Give humanity a truly unlimited field, and it would fill it with Happy Meal toys and holographic sport-star, collectible trading card game art.

There's a whole gang of dirtside refuseniks who make this their primary objection to transcendence. They're severe Bauhaus cosplayers, so immaculately and plainly turned out that they look more like illustrations than humans. Huw's never felt any affinity for them—too cringeworthy, too like a Southern belle who comes down with the vapors at the sight of a fish knife laid where the dessert fork is meant to go. It always felt unserious to object to a major debate over human evolution with an argument about style.

But Huw appreciates their point, and has spent his and then her entire life complaining instead about the ineffable and undefinable *humanness* that is lost when someone departs for the cloud. She's turned her back on her parents, refused to take their calls from beyond the grave, she's shut herself up in her pottery with only the barest vestige of a social life, remade herself as someone who is both a defender of humanity *and* a misanthrope. All the while, she's insisted—mostly to herself, because, as she now sees with glittering clarity, no one else gave a shit—that the source of her concerns all along has been metaphysical.

The reality that stares her in the face now, as she reclines on the impeccably rendered 20-million-count non-Egyptian noncotton nonsheets, is that it's always been a perfectly normal, absolutely subjective, totally meaningless dispute over color schemes.

Now she's got existential angst.

The Burj Khalifa's in-room TV gets an infinity of channels, evidently cross-wired from the cable feed for Hilbert's hotel. It uses some evolutionary computing system to generate new programs on the fly, every time you press the channel-up button. This isn't nearly as banal as Huw imagined it might be when she read about it on the triangular-folded cardboard standup that materialized in her hand as she reached for the remote. That's because—as the card explained—the Burj has enough computation to model captive versions of Huw at extremely high speed, and to tailor the programming by sharpening its teeth against these instances-in-a-bottle so that every press of the button brings up eye-catching, attention-snaring material: soft-core pornography that involves pottery, mostly.

Huw would like nothing better than to relax with the goggle-box and let her mind be lovingly swaddled in intellectual flannel, but her mind isn't having any of it. The more broadly parallel she runs, the more meta-cognition she finds herself indulging in, so that even as she lies abed, propped up by a hill of pillows the size of a Celtic burial mound, her thoughts are doing something like this:

- Oh, that's interesting, never thought of doing that sort of thing with glaze.
- Too interesting, if you ask me, it's not natural, that kind of interesting, they've got to be simulating gigaHuws to come up with that sort of realtime optimization.
- There'll be hordes of Huw-instances being subjected to much-less-interesting versions of this program and winking out of existence as soon as they get bored.
- Hell, *I* could be one of those instances, my life dangling on a frayed thread of attention.
- Every time I press the channel-up button, I execute thousands—millions? billions?—of copies of myself.
- Why don't I *care* more about them? It's insane and profligate cruelty but here's me blithely pressing channel-up.
- Whoa, that's interesting—she looks awfully like Bonnie, but with a bum that's a little bit more like that girl I fancied in college.

- I could *die* at any instant, just by losing attention and pressing channel-up.
- That's wild, never noticed how those muscles—quadrati lumborum?—spring out when someone's at the wheel, that bloke's got QLs for *days*.
- If I were *really* ethically opposed to this sort of thing, I'd be vomming in my mouth with rage at the thought of all those virtual people springing into existence and being snuffed out.
- But I'm not, am I? Hypocrite, liar, poseur, mincing aesthete, that's me, yeah?
- So long as it's *interesting* and *stylish,* I'll forgive anything.
- I've got as much existential introspection as a Mario sprite.

Enough, already, she tells herself, and cools herself down to a single thread, then slows that down, hunting for the sweet spot at the junction of stupidity and calm. Then finding it, she settles down and watches TV for a hundred subjective years, slaughtering invisible hordes of herself without a moment's thought.

Satori.

An indeterminate time later, the hotel room door opens.

"Shit," says a familiar voice.

"Didn't I tell you she has a tendency toward self-abuse? Why, when he was six, he managed to lock himself in the living room when David had left the key in the drinks cupboard, and by the time we realized he was missing he'd—"

A familiar embarrassment flushes through her veins, dragging her back toward the distant land mass that is consensus reality: "Shut up, Mum! Why are you always bringing that up?"

"He never ate his greens, either," his mother says. "Think you can get through to her?"

"I'll try," says the other voice. Male, a little deeper than last time he'd heard her, *her*—Huw drags her gaze back from the glass teat and looks round.

"You!" she says. It's Bonnie, back as a boy again, same blue forelock and skinny amphetamine build as before. "You rooted my sib! Prepare to—"

"Uh?" Bonnie looks surprised. Huw's mum—dressed up in hyperreal drag as her very own pre-upload middleaged self—raises a hand.

"Huw, it's all right. Bonnie here is thoroughly dewormed. You don't have to take my word for it; the galactic feds have vermifuges you wouldn't believe."

"Guh." Huw struggles to sit up, mind still fuzzed from endless reruns of a *This Is Your Life* celebrity show starring one Huw Jones as seen from outside by an adoring throng of pot-worshippers. The narcotic effect of the television binge is fading rapidly, though. "Whassup?"

"Then there was the time he discovered David's porn stash," Huw's mum confides in Bonnie, "when he was nine. David's always had a bit of a clankie thing going, and for *ages* afterwards, Huw couldn't look at a dalek without getting a—"

"Mum!" Huw throws a pillow. Her mother deflects it effortlessly, exhibiting basketball-star reflexes that she'd never possessed in her lumpen nerd first life.

"Gotcha," she says. "Turn the TV off, there's a good girl, and pay attention. We have important things to discuss." A note of steel enters her voice: "Compliance is—"

"Mandatory, I get it." Huw zaps the screen, not merely muting it but also setting it into standby so that it's not there in the corner as a distraction. "You want to talk." She crosses her arms. "Talk, dammit." She avoids looking at Bonnie. Some experiences are still too raw.

"Huw. My child."

Uh-oh, Huw thinks. *Here comes bad news.*

"Yes, Mother dearest?" Huw says.

"We need to get you up to speed. In a very short subjective time, you are going to stand alone and naked before the galactic confederation, and you will speak on behalf of the human race, and if you are compelling in your defense of our species, we will join the confederation, with all the privileges accruing thereto. Or at least get a stay of execution."

Huw pulled a face. "Yes, and if I cock it up, they annihilate us in an eyeblink. I'm way ahead of you, Mum. The only part I don't understand is *why?*"

Huw's mum inclined her head in Bonnie's direction. He nodded smartly and declaimed, "Because they have divided the universe neatly into two kinds of civilizations: allies and potential threats. Anything that looks like the latter, well, *zap.* They're playing a very, very long game, one that stretches so far out that they're calculating the number of CPU cycles left before the Stelliferous Era ends, and deciding who gets what. You need to convince them that we, as a species, can be brought into their little social contract and behave ourselves and not run too many instances of ourselves and such."

Huw reflects on her recent history. "I'm probably not the person best suited to this, you know."

Bonnie and Huw's mum nod their heads as one. "Oh, we know," Bonnie says. "But they've asked for you. The ambassador, you know. Plus, well…"

Huw's mum gestures with one wrinkly hand, which bears a high-resolution mole with high-resolution hairs growing from it. There's altogether too much reality in this sim, which is funny, because until pretty recently, Huw has been dedicated to the preservation of as much reality as is possible.

"Not now, Bonnie. Huw will get a chance soon enough."

Now, *here's* a familiar situation: conspirators who are privy to secrets that Huw is too delicate or strategically important or stupid to share. Huw knows how this one goes, and she isn't prepared to sit through another round of this game.

"Mum," Huw says very quietly. "That's enough. I am through being a pawn. I'm the official delegate. If you've got something I should know, I require that you impart it." *Require*—there was a nice verb. Huw is proud of it. "Or you can leave and Bonnie will tell me. This is not optional. Compliance is mandatory, as you keep saying."

Her mum goes nearly cross-eyed with bad temper, but bottles it up just short of an explosion. After all, she's been an ascended master for years, albeit in a sim where transcendence involves a heavenly realm with all the style and subtlety of a third-rate casino. Still, she's learned a thing or two.

"It's your father," she says.

"What about him?" He'd been conspicuously absent from the noosphere, and Huw had noticed. But she'd assumed that the old man had diffused his consciousness or merged with one of the cluster organisms or something else equally maddening and self-indulgent.

"Well, he seti'ed himself."

"He what now?"

"It's not something one discusses, normally. Very distasteful. He concluded that the noosphere was too pedestrian for his tastes, so he transmitted several billion copies of himself by phased array antennas to distant points in the local group galaxies, and erased all local copies."

Huw parses this out for a moment. "Dad defected to an alien civilization?"

"At least one. Possibly several."

"You two have been dead to me ever since I left. Why should it matter what imaginary playworld he's been inhabiting? Even if it's in some other solar system?"

"Galaxy," his mum says. "Don't get me started on the causality problems. But apparently, he arrives *there* millions of years in the future and then they come *here-now* to follow up on it."

"You've lost me," Huw says, and makes to turn herself up.

Bonnie meekly raises a hand. "Huw, I know it's difficult. Can I explain?"

"Yeah, whatever," Huw says. Then he remembers his moral high ground. "Proceed."

"Your father traveled a very great distance to join with the galactic federation. They instantiated him, got to know him, and decided that his species represented a potential threat."

"On the basis of a sample size of one," Huw's mother says. "Knowing David, I can't honestly say they were wrong. If we were all like him..."

"Also, they concluded that, notwithstanding the dubiousness of his species, they rather liked and trusted him," Bonnie says.

"He always *was* a lovable rogue," says Mum.

"He's the federation's negotiator, isn't he?" Huw says with a sinking sense of dread tickling at her stomach lining.

"What can I say? He's a flake," Huw's mother says with a faintly apologetic tone, as if she's passing judgment on her younger self's juvenile indiscretions. "But a *charismatic* flake. Charming too, if you were as young and silly as I was in those days."

She means between her first and second Ph.D.s, if Huw remembers her family history correctly. Mum and Dad had both been appallingly bright, gifted with a pedantic laser-sharp focus that only another borderline-aspie nerd could love. All things considered, it was a minor miracle that their sole offspring could walk and chew gum without counting the cracks in the pavement and the number of mastications. But general intelligence isn't a strongly inherited trait, and humans breed back toward the mean: and so Huw's childhood had been blighted by the presence of not one but two mad geniuses in the household, intermittently angsting over how they could possibly have given birth to a mind so mundane that their attempts to instill an understanding of the lambda calculus in him before he could walk had produced infant tantrums rather than enlightenment. (He had been twelve before he truly grokked Gödel's theorem, by which time Dad had given up on him completely as a hopeless retard.)

"Are you sure it's him?" Huw says. "I mean, he didn't just upload: he beamed himself at the galactic empire. They could have done anything with the transmission! It might be some kind of seven-headed tentacle monster using Dad's personality as a sock puppet, for all you know…?" She tries to keep the hopeful note out of her voice.

"Good question." Bonnie looks thoughtful. "You're right: We can't rule that out. But—"

"He *thinks* like David!" Mum says. "We were together for nearly thirty years before we uploaded, and a couple of subjective centuries afterwards—linear experiential centuries, if you unroll the parallelisms and the breakups and back-togethers—there are even a couple of instances of us who couldn't untangle enough to resume autonomous existence, so they permanently merged at the edges, the idiots. They're out in the cloud somewhere or other." She draws herself up. "The one who seti'd out was the real one, though. And we kept in touch, despite the divorce. I'd know him anywhere, the devious little shitweasel—"

"Okay, enough." Huw stands. "What's at stake?"

"You need to convince them that we're not a threat. Even though they know your dad inside out and—"

"No. What are they going to *do*?" Huw paces over toward the living room door, then turns and stares at Bonnie and his mother. "The cloud isn't a pushover, surely? I mean, if you threaten its existence, surely it can do something to defend itself? How does the court propose to enforce its ruling?"

"Trust me, they can do it," says Mum. Her earlier anger has dimmed, moderated by—is that fear? "The cloud is an immature matryoshka. It's going to grow up to be a Dyson sphere; masses of free-flying processor nodes trapping the entire solar output and using it to power their thinking, communicating via high-bandwidth laser. But it's not there yet, and the Galactics *are*. There's a thing you can do with a matryoshka cloud if you're sufficiently annoyed with the neighbors: You just point all those communications lasers in the same direction and *shout*. It's called a Nicoll-Dyson beam—a laser weapon powered by a star—and just *one* of them is capable of evaporating an Earth-sized planet a thousand light-years away in half an hour flat. The feds have *millions* of star systems, and that stupid time travel widget with which to set up the Big Zap. It could already be on its way— the combined, converging, coherent radiation beams of an entire galaxy, focused on us."

Huw dry-swallows. "So defense isn't an option?"

"Not unless you can figure out a way to move the entire solar system. Because they won't be shooting at Earth, or at individual cloud shards: they'll nuke the sun—make the photosphere implode, generate an artificial supernova. Snail, meet tank-track. *Now* do you see why we need you? It's not about integrating Earth into the cloud, or about some stupid squabble over aesthetics: if the galactic federation finds us Guilty of Being a Potential Nuisance, we don't get a second chance."

"Heard enough." Huw walks through into the living room of the suite. Bonnie and Mum trail her at a discreet distance, anxiety audible in their muted footsteps. "Okay, you've made your point. We're up against Dad, or something that uses Dad as an avatar for interacting with naked apes." She pauses. "I need an outfit, and an approach." A flick of one hand and Huw conjures her emotional controller into being: it seems somehow to have become second nature while she was watching TV. She suppresses a moue of distaste as she recognizes the subtle environmental manipulation. "You've been planning this for ages, haven't you? So you must have some strategies in mind, ideas about how to get under Dad's skin. Let's see them..."

There is indeed a Plan, and Mum and her little helpers must have been working on it for subjective centuries, bankrolled by the cloud's collective sense of self-preservation.

"We're working from old cognitive maps of your father," says the lead stylist, "so this may be a little out of date, but we think it'd help if you wear this." *This* is a rather old-fashioned cocktail suit and heels that Huw can't help thinking would have suited her mother better. "It's styled after what your mother wore to the registry office. You don't look identical to her, but there is a pronounced resemblance. We've run 65,536 distinct simulations against a variety of control models and assuming the judge *is* a fork of your father from after his primary uploading, wearing this outfit should deliver a marked fifteen percent empathy gain toward you: fond memories."

"Really." Huw looks at it dubiously. "And if it isn't? A fork of David Jones?"

"Then you're at no particular loss. Let's get you into it, Makeup is waiting…"

After Costume and Makeup, there's a Policy committee waiting for Huw in the boardroom: faceless suits—literally faceless, their features deliberately anonymized—to walk her through their analysis of the history and culture and philosophy of the Authority. It's a sprawling area of scholarship, far too big for a single person to assimilate in less than subjective decades. Even with a gushing fire hydrant of simulation processing power at her disposal, Huw can't hope to assimilate it all and still be the person who's supposed to appear before the star chamber in a few hours' time. But she can get a handle on the field—and, more important, a whistle-stop tour of what the cloud has inferred about galactic jurisprudential etiquette so that she won't accidentally put herself in contempt.

"The federation has been around long enough that their judicial process isn't based on a physical model anymore," says the #1 faceless suit, from the head of the table: "They set up a simulation space, throw in all the available evidence—including the judge-inquisitor and the accused—and leave them to build a world. By consensus. They iterate a whole bunch of times, and whatever falls out is taken to be the truth of the claimed case. Then the judge decides what to do about it."

"It's a lot more informal than you might expect," says faceless suit #2 with just a smidgen of disapproval.

"You say, 'build a world.'" Huw thinks. "Are we talking about trial by combat? Not fighting, exactly, but constructive engagement?"

"Something like that," says #1 suit. "But we're not sure. Nobody human has ever been through this process before."

After Policy, Huw is finally whisked into chambers to be fitted with Counsel. The legal office is smaller and more spartan than the Policy committee, or even the wardrobe and makeup departments; it's just Bonnie, looking slightly embarrassed and clutching a stuffed parrot plushie. "It's the best we could manage at short notice," he says, holding it out to her.

"A parrot." Huw turns it over in her hands. It's a handsome gray-blue bird, seamlessly fabbed out of cheap velour fabric by a simulated couture robot. "No, don't tell me, it's—"

"Hello! I am your counsel! Put me on your shoulder! Rawwwk!" The parrot comes to animatronic life, blinks at Huw, and preens.

"What does it do, say 'pieces of eight' and crap down my back?" asks Huw.

"Witness deponeth not! Rawwwk!"

"It's a prop, babe. Actually, it's an emulation environment containing an entire university law school's graduate research faculty, ready and waiting to brief you, but Psychology figured a plush toy would be a useful disarming gesture in the context of a parent–child confrontation: clutch it defensively and act like a kid and you'll be able to guide... your father..." Bonnie trails off.

"You—" Huw raises the animatronic parrot: it sidles aboard and sinks its claws into one suit shoulder pad "—have. No. Idea. Who. You're. Talking. About." She says it with quiet disgust, staring into Bonnie's eyes at close range. "This is my *dad*. He's immune to headology. He's a really smart high-functioning Asperger's case who deals with social interaction by emulating it in his head, running a set of social heuristics, and looking for positive-sum outcomes. If you try to game him, he'll notice." She extends a finger and pokes him in the abs experimentally. "You've met my mother. Do you think this chickenshit little-kid brain hack would fool *her*?"

Bonnie doesn't back off. "Your mum approved it. *She* thinks it's worth a try. Don't you think you should maybe listen to her once in a while? She's known him longer than you have!" He's breathing hard, and looks like he's biting back anger. "If you insist on going it alone and you get it wrong, we'll *all* suffer."

"Not for long." Huw meets Bonnie's gaze. He's the same scrawny cute tattoo-boy with blue forelock that she first ran into in Sandra Lal's kitchen the morning after, but somehow he looks smaller to her: wrapped up in and tied down by sad old ideological quarrels and Ade's stupid political games. She feels a momentary stab of resurgent lust, tempered by self-contempt: Bonnie is flawed, she knows that—played like a fish by 639,219, the Igor to Ade's Young Frankenstein. But she needs Bonnie on her side, at least for a short while. And there's nothing like a good screaming match for cleaning the air. "Spill it, Bonnie. Whatever you've been bottling."

"What *I'm* bottling? You're the one who's been having a crazy snit and trying to ignore reality for the past couple of weeks! The one who kept running away from jury service in Tripoli; then you were happy enough getting your ashes hauled on the way to Glory City until the shit hit the fan, and *then* you were all over your own feet trying to bug out, and *then* your mum comes to fetch you to deal with the biggest threat humanity has ever faced, and you're all, *No, I can't deal with this, my grand aesthetic objection to the cloud is so important that I think I shall throw pots until we all die rather than face up to it,* so I try to talk sense into you, and instead all you can do is blame *me* for—"

Huw freezes Bonnie in midrant.

Actually, it's not so much that she freezes Bonnie as that she tweaks her own speed up by several orders of magnitude. Bonnie's lips slow to a crawl, then stop: a stray droplet of spittle hangs glistening in the air in front of them. The light dims to red and the air becomes viscous and very chilly as Huw struggles to control her instinctive threatened-mammal response—an adrenaline reflex triggered by verbal attack—and rewinds her memories of the past few weeks (or years, or centuries) to compare them with Bonnie's tirade.

So, Bonnie harbored uploading fantasies while back in the flesh, but was too weak to go through with it? And Bonnie got rooted by the scheming God-botherers back in Glory City. And Bonnie is righteously pissed off at Huw for, well, multitudinous failings too elaborate and embarrassing to enumerate (because, Huw is forced to admit, they're mostly genuine).

Huw *could* just unfreeze him and rant straight back—and good luck with that, right before the court appearance of her life. That'd be the sort of thing the old Huw would do in a split second, because that Huw has made a profession, a career, a life out of grabbing opportunities by both hands and throwing them away as hard as he or she can. But the new Huw, emergent and self-aware after an iterative optimization course delivered via self-TV, is more mature, more forgiving of human weakness, and more than somewhat reluctant to faceplank for the hell of it.

So she decides on her move, unfreezes time, and executes.

Unfortunately, iterative optimization delivered via self-TV tends to deliver a bunch of subconscious freight, including a payload of TV tropes that don't necessarily work in reality quite the way they do on the glass teat, so when she grabs Bonnie and attempts to snog, Bonnie startles and pulls away, and the animatronic plush law academy unbalances and starts flapping and rawking. "Hey!" says Bonnie, "if you think you can shut me up with such a transparent manipulative gambit, you've got no fucking—"

"But I'm not, I—"

"I've had enough! That's it! I'm outta—"

"I'm sorry?"

That shuts Bonnie up. He stares at her goggle-eyed. "Would you mind repeating what you just said?" he asks after a few seconds.

"I said," Huw says, "I'm sorry. I take your point, and you're entirely justified, and I've been a pain in the ass, and I'm sorry."

"Uh." Bonnie looks at the parrot. "Are you recording this? Because I'd like a copy."

"Rawk! Witness deponeth not! Rawwwk!"

"When this is over," Huw says, "I'd like to get away from here for a bit, hole up with you somewhere nice, and work out whether we maybe have a future, or just a fling, or something in between. How does that sound?"

Bonnie rubs his chin. There is a sparkle in his eyes. "After all this tsunami of shit, you're asking me on a date?"

Huw shrugs, trying to get the parrot to sit still on her shoulder. "Why not? There's always a first time."

Bonnie takes a deep breath. "You've got a galactic federation to convince first. If you don't succeed, date's off. How about that?"

"I can live with that." Huw manages to smile, despite a tremulous feeling that she nearly fucked her whole life up by accident. "Well, technically not, but you know what I mean. Where's the courtroom?"

"Over there." Bonnie points at a blank wall. "You ready?"

"Ready as I'll ever be." She squares her shoulders. "I don't see a—"

A door emerges from the surface of the wall: classically proportioned, paneled, pillars to either side. "Go break a leg," says Bonnie as Huw steps toward it.

"Hello, Dad," Huw says, stepping into the sim. "You're looking well."

The old man—David, his dad—has manifested in a personsuit that approximates his earthly appearance with a few years tacked on. He wears modestly simulated clothes of modest cut and modest style. His mustache is a little unkempt and has little shoots of gray mixed in with the gingery brown.

"Huw," he says, "what have they got you wearing?"

Huw looks self-consciously at his party outfit, which is computed in such obsessive detail that it practically strobes. He shrugs. Then he notices—he's a he again. Why not? Gender's just a slider, just like everything else. Someone or something's slid it malewards, at that razorsharp moment when Huw crossed over from *there* to *here*. The tailored suit has sized to fit, but it's tailored for a slim, young womanly shape, and Huw is back to his gently spread-out, unkempt male shape. This strikes him as a dirty trick, a bit of cheap back-footery, but no one ever said the feds were fair. They don't need to be fair. They have time-traveling, star-powered lasers. And of the legal-minded parrot there is no sign: he's on his own.

"Nothing to do with me," Huw says. "Psyops from the naked apes, to be honest. How's life among the superbeings, then?"

"Better than you can imagine. Literally. You haven't the sensory apparatus or the context for it."

"Well, that's pretty convenient," Huw says. "It's the 3.0 version of 'You'll understand when you grow up.'"

"What's the 2.0?"

"'If you have to ask, you can't understand.' Or maybe, 'Ask your mother.' All of which is as convenient as anything. Whatever happened to, 'If you can't explain it, you don't understand it yourself?'"

"A good general principle, but it's not dispositive. Not here. Some things are genuinely transcendent. Some things inhabit a physics that you can't access. Sorry if that's not very satisfying. Sometimes the truth is a pain in the arse."

"Right, so you can't explain how you are. Can you explain what comes next? The prep team were a little fuzzy on this one. Are we meant to build a world now or something?"

Huw's father looks uncomfortable. "Something like that. You and I are about to play God. We've got a little worldbuilding kit—" He points out the window of the small study they're sat in. Huw realizes that they're in another modest, slightly blocky sim of his father's old study, where Huw had been forbidden to tread as a boy, and into which he had sneaked at every opportunity. Out the window, where there should be iron gray Welsh sky and the crashing sea, there is, instead, a horizon-spanning skybox hung with ornament-sized pieces of reality, hung in serried ranks: trees, houses, buildings, people, livestock, CO_2, rare earths, bad ideas, literary criticism, children's books, food additives, tumbleweeds, blips, microorganisms, lamentable fashion, copy editors' marks, pulsars, flint axes, cave drawings, mind-numbingly complex mathematical proofs, van art, mountains, molehills, uplifted ant colonies.

Huw sees now that it had been a mistake to think of this as a low-powered sim. This sim—and his identity in it—consumes more compute-time than anything he's ever seen, than *everything* he's ever seen *combined,* but it doesn't waste any of it on fancy graphics and fanciful landscapes. The feds' court system uses its might to be as *comprehensive* as possible, to encompass every conceivable significant variable. Huw's consciousness has expanded, somehow, to take all of it in. Not by running in parallel, or by running at higher speed, but by running *differently,* in a way that he can't explain or understand. But it's there, and he can't deny it.

"So those are the game tokens, and we're the players, and what, we set up a model train diorama and see how it runs?"

"It's not the worst analogy," his father says. "But I can tell you think that this is a trivial way of settling important issues. The federation isn't callous. It recognizes the gravity of wiping out entire civilizations, entire species. It does so only when it has a high degree of certainty that the species in question is apt to reject any social contract that involves managed resource consumption."

"So if they think we're likely to pig out at the galactic buffet, they'll wipe us out? They're interstellar eco-cops?"

"Yes, but again, without the gloss of triviality you put on the explanation. There's one reality, and we all inhabit it. You know there are physical limits to how much computation you can do with a universe? To date, it's managed only 10^{122} quantum operation on roughly 10^{90} bits registered in quantum fields; the entire future of the Stelliferous Era will raise that by, at most, only six to nine orders of magnitude—and a lot of the universe will be off-limits to us due to cosmological expansion. So every civilization must learn how to manage its resources peacefully, without pursuing infinite growth—or we face a Malthusian catastrophe in the deep future. The universe must either come under a peace agreement or dissolve into war. If they let one rogue planet-bound species through in this era, they risk a conflict that destroys galaxies. We are playing the very longest, deepest game, and the federation will do everything they can for peace."

"Including genocide." Huw feels the slight spiritual lift he used to get whenever he rhetorically outmaneuvered his father.

"Yes," his father says. "Including that." The old bastard robs Huw of his satisfaction with the simple acknowledgment. "But as little as possible, and not without due deliberation beforehand. Look at it this way: If I handed you the keys to a time machine, wouldn't you feel duty-bound to assassinate Hitler in his crib? If not, why not? How could you justify *not* preventing tens of millions of deaths by taking preemptive action? They don't *want* to exterminate us; that's why we're holding this hearing. But you need to demonstrate at least some minimal redeeming features. The ability to get into art school instead of growing up to be a tyrant, say."

"So we lay out our model train set."

"We do, laying out the pieces as optimally as either of us can imagine. You get a veto over every placement. We set out every element that either of us believes to be of moment—every idea, every personality, every thought, every celestial body—and, having built that best of all possible worlds, we examine the interaction of all these elements, and decide, together, whether the outcome that emerges from all those parts rubbing up against one another is a net benefit to the universe and law-abiding, resource-sharing inhabitants."

"That sounds perfectly ridiculous," Huw says, but there's something in his newly expanded consciousness that whispers, *What a reasonable way to sort all this out.* "And you've messed my head up too. How can that be—?" What? *Fair? Reasonable? Right?* All concepts that slide off the galactic scale of the thing like sweat dribbling down an ass-crack.

"It's the smallest change we could make. You're intact enough to still credibly claim to be you. When we're done, if it's still material, you can change it back."

Huw looks around. "How long do we have?"

"Six days." Dad doesn't crack a smile. "But time's kind of elastic in here."

"Six—" Huw glares at him. "Where's the Holy Ghost, wise guy?"

David looks innocent. "What, you want spooks? Design them

yourself, you've got the capabilities." And Huw realizes—or rather, an extension of Huw's awareness that he wasn't previously conscious of realizes—that he does, indeed, have the ability to conjure up the ghosts of anyone who has ever lived, or might have lived. In this courtroom he is, in fact, embedded in Federov's rapture, the ghost in the machine at the end of time. But it's a treacherous and precarious kind of omnipotence: if he makes a misstep, he could be responsible for the extinction of humanity.

"Hm, let me experiment." Huw riffles through an ontological tree of philosophies, looking for people who at one time or another fed into the quest for the singularity. There are odd and gnarly roots. One of them pops free of the ghostly multidimensional diagram. Suggested by his earlier encounter with Sam and Doc, she turns out to be incredibly well-documented for a second-rate Communist-era Russian philosopher: video, audio, tracts, and treatises. No tissue samples survive, but enough relatives have been exhaustively sequenced to make her core genome reasonably accessible, and from her visuals, it's possible to get a handle on some of the epigenetic modulation. Huw *tweaks,* and there are three people in the room—one of them an elderly female ghost. She coughs unproductively, then looks surprised.

"Where am I? What is—?" Her eyes widen farther. David is staring out the window, where a couple of armies in Napoleonic-era drag are duking it out with AK-47s upon a darkling plain. Huw, for his part, is still feverishly paging through a user manual as impenetrable and thick as the U.S. tax code. "You!" She glares at Huw. "A moment ago I was dying by inches in bed, now I find I'm not short of breath. I demand an explanation!"

Uh-oh, Huw thinks. "I'm a bit busy right now," he says. "The kitchen's through there—" He gestures at the end of the room, where somehow he knows that beyond the door to Dad's study there lies the rest of the house, exactly as it should be "—go help yourself to food and coffee? I'll be through in a bit."

"Not good enough." She shuffles hastily round in front of him and glares: "I'm not a fool, boy! I know I'm dead. I was terminally ill. And I know you're not Jesus and that old fellow isn't Jehovah. You can't pull the wool over my eyes! So spill it. You brought me back to life for a reason. What is it?"

Huw glares right back. "Look, I'm just trying to clear up an ontological fuckup left behind by your followers. I'll be with you in a—eventually—but if I don't get this nailed down, there isn't going to *be* an afterlife. So would you mind finding somewhere else to amuse yourself for an hour? I've got a job to do here."

The ghost snorts. "Have it your way, young man. But you're going to have to explain yourself sooner or later! Resurrecting me without my prior consent—the indignity! I don't suppose you'd have a cigarette, that would be too much to ask for...And with further outraged muttering, the ego monster shuffles toward the kitchen.

"Well played, son," says David with just a trace of sarcasm.

"Don't *you* start!"

"I have no intention of starting anything. It's *your* job to make the opening move. Assuming that wasn't it?"

Huw glances at the door just as it slams, and swallows. "I have no idea where she came from," he says.

"Here's a free tip," his father says: "The feds aren't terribly impressed by infantile egoism. In fact, if Objectivism were at the center of human philosophical discourse rather than the fringes, we wouldn't be here—the Big Zap would have arrived decades ago. But I'm going to be generous and let you write down the ghost of Ayn Rand as a brain fart. I won't bring her up again if you don't."

"Is she real?"

"Son, are *you* real? Are you the same Huw whose nappies I changed, six or seven decades ago?"

"I'm—" Huw recognizes the trap: it's a kind Dad's always been fond of. "I experience subjective continuity with that Huw, so I think I'm real. But if you're going to require physical continuity, no I'm not: I'm an upload. And even if I hadn't uploaded, if you want true physical continuity, *no* human being can meet that requirement—never mind our cells, the atoms in our bodies turn over within months to years."

"Good boy." There is a ghost of a smile. "So. Do you think she's real?"

"*She* thinks she's real." Huw struggles to follow through. "And I can't just switch her off. Kill her. Because she's—" Huw pauses and backtracks. "Hang on. You say I have to simulate everything I think is significant, trying to prove that what emerges is a harmonious civilization that contributes to the commonweal of the universe and doesn't go all apeshit and Malthusian on the feds. But if I do that, using realistic models of people, I can't arbitrarily kill them off after the demo—that would be murder!" Huw recalls, ruefully, his attempt to organize a mob-handed takedown of 639,219 by spamming zillions of iterations of himself. "And if

I try to exhaustively simulate all possible human civilizations to prove that they're safe, isn't that going to make me exactly the kind of resource hog the feds don't want to have around?"

David claps slowly. "Very good." There is something approximating a twinkle in his eyes. It's a vast, cool, and unsympathetic twinkle, but it's still there. "So what are you going to do?"

"Take extreme care to minimize the number of entities I instantiate in this realm." Huw swallows. "Did I just dodge a bullet?"

"Yes," says the thing wearing his father's face. "Now. Let the trial begin."

A funny thing happened to Huw on the way to the galactic court-martial: He found himself emotionally involved in the outcome.

"Dad," he says. "You know that mind-altering business, yes?"

"Yes," his father-thing says as he winds up a flock of religious beliefs and sprinkles them with a well-practiced Gaussian wrist-flip over an apocalyptic uplifted stretch of the Great Barrier Reef off Lizard Island, making multi-jointed pinching passes over the addition to reflect its rise and fall over a time-dimension.

"Well, here's a thing. You said I was still intact—continuous with my earlier self."

"Better to say that there are no gross discontinuities. If you want to be precise about it."

"Fine, fine." Huw has become momentarily transfixed by the reef and its arc of nonbelief-belief-fervor-disillusionmentnonbelief, and he reaches in and changes his father-thing's handiwork, pulling the curves around to a better fit with his own theories about the infamous psychosis that had gripped the clonal polyps when they were first roused to consciousness. "I believe you're wrong. I think that something's been lost or changed in the translation, because here I am, fiddling with all this rubbish, and I *really, really* care about the outcome. Not just the meatpeople, but even the sims—the software constructs like you and me that have been programmed to act like we believe that we're people."

"Yes, you have a self-preservation instinct, so what?"

"No," Huw says. "No, it's not self-preservation. Self-preservation's just mechanical, it's Asimov's Third Law nonsense. I mean to say that I *feel kinship to the cloud.* To the wholly fictional phantoms created by suicidal, ecstatic uplift cults. I know that it's inevitable that *I'd* feel like *I* was a person, but I find that I feel the same way about *you,* and all those other jumped-up Perl scripts and regexps mincing about in their pornographic nonstop MMORPGs, pretending that they aren't NPCs. It's like feeling compassion for a socket wrench or kinship to a novel. It shouldn't make sense, but it *does.*"

"You've grown," his father-thing says with a shrug. "Your mirror neurons have discovered compassion. I can't say as I find much cause for mourning in that."

"No. No, no, no. Look, you've messed with my personality, you've got my headmeat all buggered up, turned me into some sort of navel-gazing, soft-headed beardie-weirdy. You've taken all my core convictions away, and you've replaced them with some kind of Buddha-script, and you tell me it's just *growth?* Bull*shit*, old man. Rubbish."

His father-thing looks up from the *T. gondii* he's salting around the universe's feline population before gifting them with opposable thumbs, and his mild eyes bore into Huw with the force of a star-powered laser. "Huw. I. Did. Not. Rewire. Your. Brain. To. Make. You. Love. The. Cloud. Full stop. If you're feeling different about this sort of thing, it's down to your own stimuli and how you've reacted to them. Far as I'm concerned, it makes no difference, but I suppose it might give you an edge here—after all, the cloud is the apex expression of humanity's extended phenotype: you're its ambassador, don't you think it might help to actually like and respect it?"

Huw ponders the possibility that his father-thing isn't lying. He contemplates the contrafactual world in which he can treat the uploaded as being worthy of the same respect and compassion as meatpeople. From this, his treacherous skullfat leaps nimbly of its own accord to the potential future in which humanity— all humanity, embodied and virtual—is annihilated. And while his brain is there, it also contemplates the possibility that Huw, head cut open, brains scooped out and scanned, uploaded and multifarious in the embattled, threatened cloud, is still a human and worthy of all that respect and compassion.

Huw begins to cry.

The sound has an odd, hitching quality to it, an irregular whistling that is piped straight out of the ambassador embedded in his virtual windpipe. The sound is so ridiculous that it drags Huw out of his maudlin revelations and sets him giggling. He is Huw, he is still Huw, he will forever *be* Huw—ambassador or no ambassador, on biological substrate or running on computronium tweezed out of the bones of stars and planets, alive or technically dead.

And what's more, he will *save the fucking universe*.

The father-thing sets the heavens whirling. Huw stops them and nudges them around, then sets them spinning again, but with the aesthetic rigor he's pursued all his life. It's ascetic, but asceticism is what the cloud needs: when confronted with limitless possibility and potential, the only legitimate response is to voluntarily assume constraint. Free jazz has its place, but it's interesting only in contrast to the rigid structures in which it is embedded.

The father-thing sets societies in motion, vast parties whose secret engines are petty jealousies, immature appetites, one-upmanship, desperation, and release. Huw puts them at rest and rearranges the seating plan and the DJ's set list so that the night ends in a moment of transcendent happiness for each and every reveler.

The father-thing shows the cloud and the meatpeople as they are. Huw rearranges them as they *could be*. What more could the feds want? Not the certainty of eternal harmony, for there is no certainty in this light-cone, but the *possibility* of harmony, an internally consistent narrative that explains how humanity and its posthuman offspring might someday come to inhabit the galaxy without presenting a clear and present danger to it.

Oh, thinks Huw. Oh, this is it, and the ambassador whistles a happy tune because it is helping him, showing him the worth and the worthiness of the cloud he'd dismissed all his life. *I am doing it!* Huw thinks. His father-thing is working with him now, not trying to sabotage his work, but using all his knowledge of the feds and of humanity and of the cloud to serve as Huw's sous-chef.

"Sioux chef?" his father-thing says. "More like Lakota chef, son. We use the *whole* possibility-space."

Huw's dad hasn't punned at him in a lifetime. It's a homecoming. Huw works faster.

When the limit is reached, it jars Huw's self-sense like a long fall to a hard floor, every virtual bone and joint buckling and bending, spine compressing, jaws clacking together. It has been going *so* well, the end in sight, the time running fast but Huw and father-thing and ambassador running faster, and now—

"I'm stuck," Huw says.

"Not a problem. We could play this game forever—the number of variables gives rise to such a huge combinatorial explosion that there isn't enough mass in this universe to explore all the possible states. The objective of the exercise was to procure a representative sample of moves, played by a proficient emissary, and we've now delivered that."

"Hey, wait a minute!..." Huw's stomach does a backflip, followed by a triple somersault, and is preparing to unicycle across a tightrope across the Niagara Falls while carrying a drunken hippo on his back: "You mean that was *it?*"

"Son, do you know how long you were in there?" His dad

raises an eyebrow. "You spent nearly a million subjective days shoving around sims, and so did the other billion instances of you that came through the door. If a trillion subjective years isn't enough for—"

"Hang on, you respawned me? In parallel? Why can't I remember—?"

"Oh, I just shut 'em all down," the father-thing says dismissively. "Wouldn't have done you any good to carry all those memories around, anyway."

"But you, but you—" Huw has the jitters. "—you genocided me! I'm your son!"

"Don't worry, each of them lived two thousand seven hundred subjective years that differ from your experience only in the minutiae. In fact, your personality states overlap so closely that you'll never notice anything missing. I had to prune a bunch of your memories along the way—wouldn't do for you to try to retain a couple of millennia in detail, the human neural architecture just isn't up to it—but you've got the gist of—"

"Dad!" Huw glares at his father, who is sitting in his recliner looking placidly content with the pocket universe they've created outside the imaginary window. "That's not the point! Those were my memories, and now you're telling me you've cut huge chunks out of them? What about the other people we simulated?"

"What do you care about them?" his father asks, cheek twitching. "You might as well accept that you're just a holey ghost. But for what it's worth, I turned loose the ones who weren't nonplayer characters. The cloud can sort them out."

"Dad—" Huw swallows. An ancient, cobwebby sense of déjà

vu unfolds in the recesses of his mind: He's been here before, with dad cracking infernally dreadful jokes in an attempt to distract him from doom-laden news. "What's the outcome?"

"What?"

"Did I pass—?"

His father cups a hand around one ear: "I can't hear you. What did you say?"

"Did I pass the exam?"

"Did you... what? Pass the jam?"

"Dad..."

"What do *you* think, son?"

"I don't—" Huw stares at the being that contains a superset of his father and an entire galactic civiliation sitting in judgment over him and his kind, gathering his nerve. "You're still here. But the Big Zap... you wouldn't still be here if it was coming, would you? So it's not coming. The galactic federation decided to let us alone. We won!"

His father sniffs. "Don't get your hopes up, son. Everyone dies eventually: individuals, nations, planetary civilizations, galactic federations, universal overminds."

"But! But-but!"

"I appreciate you're feeling kind of good right now because you're right, you just about satisfied the Authority that post-humanity is not, in fact, a malignant blight upon the galaxy. Their satisfaction is conditional, by the way, on the human-origin cloud not changing its mind, pulling on its metaphorical jackboots, and going all SS *Death Star* supergalactic on the neighborhood: that would be a deal-breaker." He gives Huw a stern glare. "Don't get above yourself: ethical stocks can go down as well as up." He takes a deep breath. "But I must admit that you surprised me back there. In a good way."

"Bububub." Huw manages to regain control of his larynx and shuts up momentarily. "What happens now?"

"Now?" David points at the door: "We leave this space. You get to go home again, at least as far as the cloud. Me, I've got a starship to catch after I dismantle this embassy: I'm needed three thousand light-years away." Something approximating a weak smile wobbles onto his father's face, takes bashful center stage: "We probably won't meet again."

"Dismantle the—?" Huw's brain is still trying to catch up. "No, wait, Dad!" He stands. "You can't go yet, it's been fifty years!" His head is full of uncomfortable realization.

"Forty-seven years, four months, nine days, three hours, forty-four minutes, and eleven point six one four seconds, to be precise. And you didn't write, son, not once. I checked with your mum."

"But I was—" Huw swallows again. "—being a real dick." *Also, setting the all-time record for the world's longest adolescent snit,* he doesn't add.

"That's all right, son." His dad holds his arms open.

A moment later, Huw is leaning on his shoulder, bawling like a little kid. "I'm too damn old for this." He sniffs. "I missed you, you know."

"I do." His dad pats his back awkwardly. "I was a dick too, if it helps. I had what I thought were plenty good reasons but I didn't work through the fact that they weren't good enough for you. I didn't mean to fuck you up."

"I didn't mean to—" Huw takes a deep breath, then wishes his congested sinuses to clear. "—huh. Leave me a forwarding address? This time I'll write."

"I'll do that, but you might not hear back from me for a long time." His dad's mustache twitches as he disentangles Huw from his jacket. "Now get going. Do you want to keep them in suspense forever?" And with a gentle hand in the small of Huw's back, he propels him toward the door.

Various instances of Huw have lived through roughly two and a half trillion years of trial by simulation since he stepped through the door, but on the other side, it's as if barely any time at all has passed. (Someone is doing some serious fancy footwork with causality, and Huw absently makes a note to investigate later.) Back in chambers he finds Bonnie running round in circles, trying to catch an agitated parrot, who is flying around the ceiling shouting, "Where's the plaintiff? Where's the witness? Who's a pretty counsel? Rawk!"

"Come down here, you feathered bandit!" Bonnie is shaking his fists at the bird, and Huw works out the context from the white streaks on the back of Bonnie's shirt.

"Trial's over," Huw says. His voice comes out with his usual male timbre. "We need to be going, the embassy's packing up."

"Trial's *what*—?" Bonnie turns on him. "It's *over?*"

His mum *bamfs* in from some corner of the embassy hyperspace, flashy teleportation spangles dissolving like hologram fireworks around her. "Huw! Am I in—? Oh."

"Dad says hi," he says. "The Big Zap is canceled, conditionally: As long as we keep our nose clean, eat our greens, and don't terrorize the neighborhood, they'll let us alone."

"Rawk! Court is adjourned?" The parrot swoops down on his mum's shoulder with a rattle of wing feathers.

"That's nice, dear." His mother smiles.

"You did it?" Bonnie stares at him. "Hey, you switched again."

"Dad-thing is packing up the embassy; they're leaving the solar system to us. I, uh, left a lot of myself behind back there. No, no, I'm all right—" He waves off an anxious Bonnie "—but we need to get out of here before the embassy dismantles." Right back to the reconstituted and re-created bedrock of Io—the Authority is nothing if not environmentally sensitive, and believes in recycling moons and small planets wherever possible. "Dad says they're going to begin teardown immediately, so—" As he says it, a red warning sign appears in midair, hovering over the entrance to the chambers: evacuate now. It flashes, the archaic blink-tag irritant clearly contrived to get their attention. As if that isn't enough, a fire siren spools up to an earsplitting shriek, and an unspeakable stench tickles his nostrils. "I think he wants us out of here right now."

"Oh for heaven's sake." Mom rolls her eyes, then shoulder-barges the door. "David, you passive-aggressive asshole!" she shouts, waving her fist at the hyperrealistic sky above the embassy complex (where, one by one, the stars are going out), "How many times have I told you, it is *not* acceptable to use the kid as a back channel? You get your incarnated ass down here *right now* so I can have words with you: Compliance is mandatory—"

"Was she always like this?" Bonnie asks Huw sotto voce as

they follow the blinking evacuation arrows toward a rainbow archway capped by a sign reading CLOUD GATEWAY.

"Uh-huh. Pretty much. Why do you think I got into casting pots?" He walks swiftly away from his mother, who is railing at the universe.

"You poor bastard."

Huw pauses, contemplating the throng of diplomats, lawyers, tourists, xenophiliacs, instantiated fictional characters and various other subtypes of humanity that clutter the vestibule in front of the gate. "I don't know about you, but I'm going home. I mean, *really* home. Planning on reincarnating back on Earth and holing up in the workship for at least a couple of years and not traveling *anywhere*." He glances sidelong at Bonnie. "I realize that might not appeal to you as a lifestyle choice."

Bonnie shrugs, hands in pockets. "I can visit from time to time. Or I could stick around, go walkabout if it gets too boring. If you want."

"I want." Huw takes his arm and leads him to the back of the queue. And in a subjective eye-blink, they're back on Earth.

EPILOGUE | VERDICT

There's something not right about Huw's new body. Or perhaps there's something that's changed in his mind. One way or another, he's just not able to throw a pot the way he could.

Oh, the body *looks* right enough, and there's enough actual biological material in it that he qualifies, at least marginally, as a primate. But there's plenty of other gubbins in there, especially round about the headmeat where they decanted the version of him that stepped out of the embassy as it was being folded up to the size of a pin-prick and made to vanish.

That version had demanded a very stiff drink. In person. In his pottery. On Earth. Right. Away.

He'd saved the entire fucking universe. Surely this was not too much to ask for.

And oh, how they'd fussed, begging and commanding him to at least leave an instance in the cloud for debriefing and the lecture circuit, but he'd been firm. Oh, how they'd fiddled, pestering him with questions about what he wanted his new body to be like, which upgrades and mods it should have, trying to tempt him with talented penises and none-too-subtle surrogates, such as retractable unobtanium claws and bones infused with miracle fiber and carbon nanotubes.

He'd waved them off, refusing even to take in all the wonders on offer: no, no, no, just give me back my actual, physical body, the body I would have had if none of this had taken place, if I had been a man who was born to a woman, grown to maturity in the gravity well of my ancestors.

Once he'd gotten through to them, they'd complied with a vengeance, and now Huw heaved himself out of bed every morning with the aches and pains of baseline humanity on throbbing, glorious display. He showered himself, noting the soap's slither over every ingrowing hair, every wrinkle, every flabby nonessential extruding from his person. He squinted at the small writing on cereal packaging and held it up to the watery Welsh light that oozed through the kitchen window, moving it closer and farther in the hopes of finding the right focus-length for his corneas, which had been carefully antiqued with decades' worth of waste products, applied with all the care of a forger re-creating a pair of exquisitely aged Levi's.

The cloud had its little jokes, oh ho ho, yes it did, and Huw would have let it all pass but for the pots. He'd been at his wheel for three days now, and no matter how carefully he kneaded the air pockets out of his clay, wet his hands, and threw the clay down onto the spinning wheel, no matter how carefully he wet his fingers and guided the spinning clay upward and outward into a graceful, curvilinear spliney form, it always went awry. His clumsy fingers tore the clay, his clumsy hands moved too fast and collapsed the pot's walls, his clumsy arms lost their bracing against his thighs and slipped and spattered the walls and his face with wet clay.

Huw threw his first pot at age fifteen, part of the mandatory art requirement that his parents had to stump up for as part of his homeschooling program. The minute the clay hit the wheel and his fingers touched the wet, sensual, spinning earth, he'd felt a jolt of recognition: *Where have you been all my life?* Something in his peripheral nervous system, something in his muscles *recognized* the clay, understood it right down to the finest grain, integrated it into his proprioception, so that it felt like a part of him. Huw has had days in his life when he had a hard time thinking clearly, days when he didn't feel like getting out of bed.

But he's never, ever had a day when he couldn't throw a bloody pot.

"It's not *fair*," he tells the motes of dust and the dribbles of wet clay that fill his pottery. It really isn't, either. This is meant to be his retirement, his recuperation, his *occupational therapy*. He's a veteran, after all. A veteran with a scorching case of posttraumatic stress disorder (self-diagnosed). It's not fair.

He picks up another lump of clay, kneads it, dipping his fingers into the water with a practiced, unconscious gesture, working the water into the clay. He's complained to the cloud, of course, but they assured him that he checksummed correctly—that is, the body they've built for him is the body he left with, functionally speaking. The inarguable and obvious fact that this body is different in a very significant way is of no moment to the cloud. Checksums don't lie.

Huw pats and squeezes the clay into shape and thunks it dead bull's-eye center into the middle of his wheel. He wets his hands again, rocks back so his tailbone is well behind him and his sitz bones are well beneath him, braces his elbows on his thighs, and makes ready to ruin another pot.

"Give it a rest already, will you?" Bonnie says from behind him. He doesn't startle, because he's sensed her presence for some minutes, every since she slipped into his pottery. Technically it isn't off-limits to her, but no one apart from Huw can really feel comfortable in the narrow space with its high shelves. There's nowhere to sit or stand apart from his wheel, and everything is covered with dried clay-dust that is hungry for hair, clothes, and skin on which to stick. So Bonnie usually hangs out in the house or walks around the valleys while Huw's wasting clay and cursing the fates.

Huw feels somehow honor-bound to scold Bonnie for interrupting him, but the truth is that he's quite grateful to her for giving him an excuse to down tools. So he spins on his stool and stands, putting himself right up against her. (The only way two people can stand up in his pottery at once is if they're willing to breathe each other's exhaust streams.)

"Fine," he says. "Let's get some air."

Bonnie slips her fingers into his as they step outside, letting the pottery door squeak and slam shut with a dusty bang. "You just need practice," she says. "Or possibly rest. In any event, it's nothing to get upset about."

"Easy for *you* to say. Your body *works*." What's more, Bonnie's upgraded, because she's not trying to square the circle between a lifetime of techno-asceticism and a newfound love of the cloud; she's an unabashed transhuman on a meatvacation. She's got the unobtanium in her bones, the eyes that can see into the infrared and detect environmental toxins, true love, and flop sweat at a hundred meters. She's got a metabolism that politely discards any calories it doesn't need in neat little poos that smell like roses. She's got a peripheral nervous system that she can dial up in moments of crashing orgasm, and tamp down in moments of crashing boredom. Her body doesn't just work, it *performs*. Huw pretends not to notice this.

"Oh, yours works just *fine,* Huw, where it counts. Listen, you've had your consciousness extracted from its biosubstrate, forked thousands of times, run in parallel, diffed and merged, and hauled through millions of subjective years while trying to save the universe—sorry, solar system. Then it was decanted back into an artificial, assembled substrate, with limitations that *you* specified, and now it's got a few wrinkles to solve. What's so surprising about that? If you want to throw pots, just ask your mum to bake you some pottery firmware. But stop moping and moaning. That's not what I signed up for."

She's probably right. Huw knows there's no meaningful difference between running a clayworking app that someone else wrote and a clayworking app that was algorithmically derived from a digital representation of his headmeat. But there's a principle at stake. He can't say what principle exactly, and he suspects that Bonnie would clobber him if he got into an argument about it with her, so he changes the subject.

"Sorry, love, you're right. What have you been up to? Anything nice? Want to do something together today, then?"

"Arguing with missionaries, mostly. Cloud-botherers have been ringing your doorbell all week while you've been hiding out with the clay."

That's a new thing since the last time he had a body: Cloud-botherers going door to door, pressing innocents with uninterruptable sermonettes about the miraculous life that awaited all if they'd only listen to reason and take the transcendence treatment. Bonnie loathed them because she felt they put the whole movement in a bad odor with the punters. *With friends like these, who needs enemies?* she'd explained when he asked. No one likes a door-to-door missionary. She quite enjoyed arguing them to a standstill, and viewed it as a service to the cause, since a missionary arguing with her was a missionary who wasn't bothering the neighbors.

"Everyone needs a hobby," he says. "Converted any of them yet?"

She doesn't say anything.

"You didn't," he says.

"Well, only a little. She was such a silly thing, one of the newly reincarnated, and all her arguments for uploading were really daft. I had her in for some tea, and she stayed for hours. Came back the next day to say I'd changed her mind, and she was going to work to show people why they *shouldn't* disembody." Bonnie shrugs. "I guess some people just aren't happy unless they've got a cause."

"But you got rid of them?" Huw asks.

"Yes, it's safe to come out now."

Huw glances at the window. It's afternoon, and the light will be fading before long. Which means it's time to clear up, wash up, and think about fixing some dinner. "I'm just about through here," he says. "Put the kettle on? I'll be through in a quarter of an hour."

Bonnie heads for the house, leaving Huw to the mundane routine of cleaning up and shutting the pottery—the trouble with real clay is that you can't hit Save and expect it to still be malleable tomorrow—and check that the kiln has enough fuel. He washes thoroughly to get the reddish powder off his hands and arms, then latches the door behind him and ambles, whistling tunelessly, through the kitchen garden toward the back door.

Bonnie is in the kitchen, slaving over a hot reactor. Huw may have previously banished electricity from his home, but Bonnie has other ideas, and some domestic give-and-take—or push-and-shove—has resulted in her installing a fuel cell system and some bizarre extreme cooking tech in the niche where once a mechanical refrigerator had whirred. The reactor isn't radioactive, but given enough energy and random garbage to break down, it can brew up just about any biomolecular soup she orders. Right now she's trying to get the damn thing to cough up a prefabricated megatherium steak, but judging from the amount of cussing, something is persistently going wrong. "This festering pile keeps suggesting alternatives," she says as Huw closes the door. "Why would anyone want to eat *koala*? They're saturated with eucalyptus oil..."

"Maybe it thinks you've got a cold?" Huw asks. "Hey, you're

not subscribing to a Plague of the Month club?" There are some aspects of historic reenactment that are too gross even for Huw.

"No. A-*choo*!" Bonnie rubs at her nose. "Oh dear."

"It's probably hay fever."

"I'll have to get my immune system tweaked again. Ech. Do you feel like peeling some spuds?"

So it is that Huw is up to his armpits in cold water, scrubbing (he doesn't hold with that *peeling* fetish) a bunch of wholesome organic home-grown potatoes when the doorbell rings.

"I'll get it—" Bonnie is off while Huw is still dripping. "—*you*, you fucker!"

"Wotcher, chick," says a cheery, familiar, and utterly unwelcome voice. "Is His Ambassadorship available?"

Huw palms a couple of oversized pink fir apples in one hand and grabs the cast-iron poker from its spot by the stove. "Ade," he says as he heads for the front hall, "the embassy is closed. Go away."

"You what? And here was I, thinking you'd like your bike back!" Ade is leaning against the inside of the front door, one arm wrapped around Bonnie's shoulders: Bonnie's expression suggests that she can't make up her mind whether to kiss him or bite him. Huw can just discern, behind them, the frame of a long-lost friend.

"My bike? That'd be good. But the embassy is still closed." Huw leans against the passage wall, the poker lowered. He has Ade's number: knows how to deal with him. No violence needed, just a reinforced concrete wall. "You are an absolute arse, Ade. Every time I have run into you, you have comprehensively fucked up my life while making out that it was my fault, and the one time I needed you to get off your behind and *do* something for all our sakes, you cocked it up. There's an old saying about never attributing to a conspiracy that which can be explained by incompetence. So I hope you can understand that, while you're welcome to stop by for a cup of tea, I am *out* of your emergent factional whatsits now and forevermore. Clear?"

"You don't have to be like that," Ade says. He sounds wounded. Bonnie punches him on one shoulder: he lets go of her. "I just wanted to thank you for your work, what did you think I'm about? I'm not some kinda supervillain, mate! And look at you, don't you think it turned out for the best? We're still here. The Authority didn't deliver the Big Zap, the cloudie fundamentalists didn't dismantle the—"

A shadow moves behind Ade, and there is a noise like an old-style electric door buzzer. Ade drops, twitching in the grip of a full-on Taser spazz-out.

"Gettir, Sam."

"Oh fu—" Huw freezes. Bonnie turns and aims a punch at Sam's face, simultaneously trying a vicious stomp and a disabling knee to the groin—none of which stop the man-mountain from placidly grabbing her fist and twisting her arm behind her back.

Huw tries to move, but his voluntary control of his musculature seems to have clocked off for the day: he can't seem to do anything except stand there like a wallflower, cast-iron poker dangling limply from one hand.

I've been rooted! Horrified realization dawns as Doc steps over Ade's prone form, pointing his baby blue Taser shotgun at Huw's midriff.

"Greetings, heretic." Doc's smile—more of a carnivorous grin—doesn't reach his eyes. "Where is she?"

"What? Who?"

"Don't play the innocent with me." Doc's glare is positively deranged. Behind him, Sam stands impassive as a golem, holding Bonnie, whose struggles are clearly diminishing. Just how Doc has reasserted his control over Sam's wetware puzzles Huw for a fraction of a second until the coin drops. If Doc has rooted him, then obviously Doc rooted Sam first, and probably everybody else he's been able to get close to. Sam is, in fact, probably just as much a puppet in this show as Huw. "Her. The fountainhead, the one who brought the True Knowledge to Earth. The Prophet says she's reincarnated *here* in this town, preaching. *Where is she?*" His voice rises to a ragged screech.

"Whoa!" Huw boggles at him. "I don't know who you're—" He stops in midsentence and backtracks before Doc can wind up to another tirade. "Huh. You're looking for Ayn Rand?"

Behind Doc, Bonnie stops struggling and emits a sound like a stifled, frightened giggle.

Huw rolls his eyes. "Bonnie? Did she tell you where—?"

Ade groans. Doc's head whips around: "Be silent, heretic!"

"Let me get this straight?" Huw asks. "You reincarnated and came here because you heard that your Thought-Leader has returned and is preaching the rapture of the uploaded? And if you get her, you'll take her back to Jesusland and do the whole storming heaven thing and leave us alone?"

"Don't push your luck," Doc says, his finger whitening on the trigger—just as the doorbell rings again.

"Hello, is Bonnie here? Would like to resume our discussion of the Sing—Oh!"

The skinny, dark-haired, intense-looking woman stares up at Sam. "Who is this?" Then she sees Doc's shotgun, realizes Sam has Bonnie in a half nelson: "This will not do at all! You disgusting coercive thugs!" She lights up, incandescent with rage: "Coercive violence is an abomination! You should be ashamed of yourselves!"

Doc falls to his knees before her: "Holiness!" he says. "You have returned at last to lead us to the promised land!"

"I've *what?* No no no, that won't do at all!" Her hair is almost standing on end, crackling with indignation: "What priest-ridden nonsense is this?" She grabs Doc by one ear and lifts. "Put that disgusting thing down right this instant, I say!" He lets go of the Taser shotgun as he rises, perforce to a stoop (for the Thought-Leader is not a tall person in this reincarnate body). "Do you call yourself an Objectivist? You aren't fit to shine Alan Greenspan's boots! And what's this I hear about this bizarre superstitious plan to bring about a universal theocracy? Your illogic disgusts me! Truly pathological. Feh. You and I, we are going to have an open-minded discussion about the meaning of hypocrisy in the context of rational thought grounded on Aristotelian axioms. Here is a hint: *You are going to lose...*"

Ade groans again and clutches his head as Rand drags Doc through the door, groveling and scraping all the way out to the street beyond. "Whut?" he vocalizes, rolling on his back and gazing up at Sam, whose grip on Bonnie is slackening.

"Help," Sam says.

"Me too," adds Huw. "Been rooted."

"Rooted." Bonnie steps backwards nervously, looking around the three of them. "By Doc, I assume?"

"Yeah…" Huw swallows.

"Okay, I'll send you the security patch your mum gave me. Stand by…" She turns to Sam. "Doc dragged you here, did he?" Sam nods. "Do you want to be free?" Sam nods again. "Well, then you came to the right place…" But Huw doesn't hear what she says next, as for a couple of seconds later everything goes blurry and fuzzy and a progress bar appears in front of his field of vision, crawling from left to right.

There is a strange feeling of congestion in his head; then a moment later a sense of release sweeps over him. He flexes his fingers: they tingle slightly, as if released from the confinement of invisible felt mittens. And everything comes crystal clear again.

Ade groans. Huw bends down and grabs his right hand. "Think you can stand?" he asks.

"C'n try…" Huw heaves, and Ade slowly slides up the wall until he's in an approximation of verticality. "Thnksss. Ack— *thanks*. Yer a card, mate."

"Think nothing of it." There *is* something up with his fingers. Huw flexes them in front of his face. *What if that rootkit was hiding in wherever I keep my muscle memory?* he wonders.

"That Doc, didn't know he was, was in town—"

"Leave it," Huw tells him firmly. "Look, just stop apologizing. If you want to be useful, help Bonnie sort out that overgrown kid there." He nods at Sam. "Me, I've got more important things to deal with."

With that, Huw heads back to the pottery out back, to find out if the magic has returned to his fingertips.

And as it turns out, it has.

The golem knocking at Huw's door is the same model his mum wore, that fateful day, but there's any number of them about now, quick and dirty embodiments for anyone from the cloud with a yen to indulge some fleshy pleasures for an hour or three. Huw spies it from the sitting room window, peeking out the corner of the curtains, and decides to wait it out.

It keeps knocking.

And knocking. Soon, the whole house is shaking.

"Get that, will you?" Bonnie says. She's waist-deep in some kind of erotipolymer stuff she's downloaded from one of Adrian's sex-ninjas, has been all week, and isn't showing any signs of tiring of it. But the thudding is getting to her.

Huw grits his teeth and ignores her too.

Thud. Thud. THUD. There's a splintery sound from the lintel of the front door, not a full-blown tearing away, but a sound that tells you the hinges are reconsidering their relationship with the doorframe.

"Get it, for shit's sake!"

Huw closes his eyes. He stomps to the door.

"Go away," he says, and closes it again.

Except that the golem has inserted its foot in the door, and the door bounces back and hits him in the nose, and he takes a step backwards, clutching at it, and moans. "Please, go away." Maybe politeness will work.

"Greetings, Jones, Huw," it says in a neutral voice. It's a goddamned NPC. Ambulatory spam. He's just working up a head of really righteous steam when it says, "I have been dispatched by the office of interstellar harmony of the Galactic Authority to execute a survey of your species' recent assimilation experience. We realize you are a busy organism, and this will take only a moment of your time. Your participation will help us shape our future species trials, and give our own staffers valuable feedback. Thank you in advance for your cooperation."

And Huw starts to laugh. Laugh like a drain, laugh like a monkey trapped in a bariatric chamber filled with nitrous oxide, laugh like a man in the grips of a joke that encompasses the whole cosmos.

"All right, then," he says, "let's do it. Want a cup of tea?"

ACKNOWLEDGMENTS

We'd like to thank the editors and agents who have helped this pantomime horse get up and dance: at various times, their number have included Ellen Datlow, Lou Anders, Patrick Nielsen Hayden, and our agents, Russ Galen and Caitlin Blasdell.

ABOUT THE AUTHORS

Cory Doctorow is a coeditor of *Boing Boing* and a columnist for multiple publications, including *The Guardian, Locus,* and *Publishers Weekly.* He was named one of the Web's twenty-five "influencers" by *Forbes* magazine and a Young Global Leader by the World Economic Forum. His award-winning YA novel *Little Brother* was a *New York Times* bestseller. Born and raised in Canada, he currently lives in London.

Charles Stross is widely hailed as one of the most original voices in modern science fiction and is the author of several major novels of science fiction and fantasy, including *Singularity Sky, Accelerando, Halting State,* and *Rule 34.* His short fiction has won multiple Hugo and Locus awards. He lives in Edinburgh, Scotland.

CORY DOCTOROW
HOMELAND

In the sequel to the *New York Times* bestselling *Little Brother*, Marcus Yallow is no longer a student. California's economy has collapsed, taking his parents' jobs and his university tuition with it. Thanks to his activist past, Marcus lands a job as webmaster for a muckraking politician who promises reform. Things are never simple, though: soon Marcus finds himself embroiled in lethal political intrigue and the sharp end of class warfare, American style.

"Doctorow fills his novel with cutting-edge technology, didactic progressive messages, strong and somewhat snarky characters, and discursions that reflect his passions. Fans of *Little Brother* and the author's other stories of technophiliac hacktivism ought to love this book." *Publishers Weekly*

AVAILABLE SEPTEMBER 2013

SAMIT BASU
TURBULENCE

When Aman Sen gets off a plane from London to Delhi, he discovers that he has extraordinary abilities corresponding to his innermost desires, as does everyone else on the flight.

Aman wants to heal the planet but with each step he takes, he finds helping some means harming others. Will it all end, as 80 years of super-hero fiction suggests, in a meaningless, explosive slugfest?

"You'll laugh, you'll cry, you'll gasp and you'll demand a sequel." Ben Aaronovitch (*Sunday Times* bestselling author of *Rivers of London*)

"Solid writing, great character development, humour, loss, and excellent points to ponder in every chapter." *Wired*

DANIE WARE
ECKO RISING

Ecko is an unlikely saviour: a savage, gleefully cynical rebel/
assassin, he operates out of hi-tech London, making his own
rules in a repressed and subdued society. When the biggest job
of his life goes horribly wrong, Ecko awakes in a world he
doesn't recognise: a world without tech, weapons, cams, cables –
anything that makes sense to him.

Can this be his own creation, a virtual Roschach designed just
for him, or is it something much more? If Ecko can win though,
then he might just learn to care – or break the program and get
home.

"The sci-fi debut of the year... Ware writes fearlessly and
with great self-assurance, and Ecko is a magnificent creation."
Financial Times

"A curious genre-bender that thrusts its anti-hero from a
dystopian future into a traditional, Tolkienesque fantasy world...
marks Ware as one to watch." *The Independent on Sunday*

For more fantastic fiction from Titan Books in the areas of sci-fi, fantasy, horror, steampunk, alternate history, mystery and crime, as well as tie-ins to hit movies, TV shows and video games:

visit our website

TITANBOOKS.COM

follow us on Twitter

@**TITAN**BOOKS